THOMAS OF ULSTER

Roger Davis
1189 N Thompson Ave
Nipomo, CA 93444

D1602723

THOMAS OF ULSTER

Gayle Bookless Davis

www.bookstandpublishing.com

Published by
Bookstand Publishing
Morgan Hill, CA 95037
3951_7

Copyright © 2013 by Gayle Bookless Davis
All rights reserved. No part of this publication may be reproduced or
transmitted in any form or by any means, electronic or mechanical,
including photocopy, recording, or any information storage and
retrieval system, without permission in writing from the copyright
owner.

ISBN 978-1-61863-600-3

Printed in the United States of America

Preface

The fictional Keith family is representative of the huge numbers of Scots-Irish (a.k.a. Scotch-Irish) who immigrated to the United States of America during the eighteenth and nineteenth centuries. They were Protestants, mainly Presbyterians, who settled first in Pennsylvania. Later waves of Scots-Irish came to the States and traveled south and west, always searching for land and a better way of life. Wherever they settled these Scots-Irish immigrants lived frugally and worked diligently. They were civic minded, serving on school boards, local and county governments, and promoting the general good of the communities where they lived.

Though originally from the Lowlands of Scotland, these people lived for generations in the northern province of Ireland known as Ulster and thought of themselves as Irish rather than Scots. A great number came to Ireland during the time of Plantation in the early 1600's when the British King James1 wanted to populate Ireland with Protestants who were loyal to the Crown. Many Presbyterians were given lands that had belonged to the native Irish who were of the Roman Catholic faith, thus beginning an enmity between the Protestants and Catholics which, for countless reasons, lasts to this day in Ulster. A century later, many of these same Presbyterians were compelled to leave Ireland due to the Crown's punitive measures enforced upon all who were not members of the Church of England. Throughout the following decades there were droughts, famine, and overcrowding which forced more Scots-Irish to leave Ireland. Today hundreds of thousands of Americans, as well as several past American presidents, can trace their ancestry to this unique group.

CHAPTER ONE

Thomas decided that now was the time to say the speech he had rehearsed for days. It needed to be said while he and his father were alone. He shuffled his feet, cleared his throat, and hoped his adolescent voice would not betray him with a childish squeak.

"Dad, ah... I've been thinking..."

His father glanced up from his work to offer encouragement.

Without pausing, Thomas poured out his memorized speech. "You remember John McAllister, the fellow who went to America last year? His brother, George, is my friend. George said that John sent a letter telling him to come to America as soon as he can because there's plenty of work in America for anyone who is willing and able. George doesn't have the fare for passage yet, but I could go to over with Mr. McGowan's shipment of horses in June." Thomas swallowed and caught his breath. "Please, would you ask Mr. McGowan if I can work for him and care for the horses sailing to America?"

"If 'tis work you're looking for, you can find plenty of it right here at home." His father lifted another broken harness onto the bench, and with a puzzled frown he looked at Thomas. "Why is it you want to leave your home and family to go to the other side of world for work?"

Thomas didn't know how to respond. He groped for the right words. "It's not that I want to leave you..."

He looked down at the leather strap between his fingers and wished he could have rehearsed for this. Cold wind whistled around the large doors of the threshing barn and sent flurries of chaff across the floor. Thomas shivered and tried to concentrate.

"I want to have my own farm someday and raise my own stock. If I stay here in Ireland I will work forever on the family farm with you and my brothers." He looked up at his father and spoke with pleading in his voice, "Will you grant me permission to go to America in June?"

A child's shrill voice interrupted. "Time to come in for tea."

Agnes, who was ten years old and small for her age, was the little sister who felt it her duty to boss all her siblings. She poked her head inside the door and shouted, "Thomas, Mum said to bring in these two pails full of water and be careful not to spill."

Thomas mocked her high-pitched voice. "You know I always spill the water,"

She placed the pails inside the door, and making certain her father did not see, she crossed her eyes and stuck out her tongue at Thomas. She issued a final command to hurry in with the water, pushed the door shut, and ran to the house.

Thomas and his father cleared the workbench and hung the repaired harness on the wall. While his father blew out the candle lanterns, Thomas picked up the water pails and trudged across the snow-covered yard to the well. He would not miss that bossy little sister when he went to America.

Thomas wished he could make decisions about his life without all this need for permission. Sometimes he thought his Dad understood Thomas's point of view...Dad certainly knew the family farm would be inherited by the oldest son, James, and that Thomas would never own a farm of any size if he stayed here. But Thomas also knew that his mother would try to persuade Dad to keep their third son at home. He was angry with that pesky Agnes who had to interrupt and spoil everything!

He twisted and turned in bed that night while trying not to wake his younger brother, Willie. When the clock downstairs struck twelve, Thomas finally drifted into a fitful sleep. He woke from a bad dream where horses were lunging and screaming inside a storm-tossed ship. Thomas feared this dream might foretell the future but he reminded himself that he didn't believe in superstition.

At breakfast he was unable to look into his mother's eyes. However, nothing seemed out of the ordinary when she spoke of the day's chores in her usual calm way. He was certain that his brothers and sisters did not know of his request to leave home because their banter and antics had the same old themes. 'Mind your bony elbow, Thomas, before you put out my eye', and 'When are you going to shave that fuzz off your lip?' Maggie continued to tweak the hair that always stood up at the top of his head, and Agnes thought it was hilarious when his voice cracked and squeaked. Willie had just learned from Agnes how to cross his eyes and Thomas began to wonder if he'd ever see his little brother appearing normal again.

Only once did his father mention Thomas's request, and that was a few days after Thomas first spoke to him about it. As father and son milked cows that stood side by side in the milking barn, he simply said, "Are you still certain you want to leave Ireland, Thomas?"

Thomas replied with conviction, "I haven't changed my mind, Dad."

"Your mother and I are thinking it over," his father said without further comment.

Thomas wished he could convince his parents but he knew it didn't pay to hound Dad about anything. His father, Will Keith, was a deliberate man who did not make hasty decisions where his family was concerned. Maggie had wanted to stay overnight in town with one of her friends but she made the mistake of pleading with him too much and as a consequence Dad refused to let her go.

The first Monday in May the weather was wet and blustery. Thomas and his father were alone at the workbench repairing equipment when Thomas seized the first opportunity to ask the question that had been his only thought for months.

"Dad, have you made a decision about my leaving?"

Will cleared his throat. "Your mother and I want to know if you would be willing to wait a year or two before you make this trip. By then, you would be more than sixteen years old and others would consider you able to do a man's work."

Thomas did not want to hear this. Though he was fifteen and one-half years, it was well known he worked as hard as any man. He was able to do anything on the farm, from plowing, planting and harvesting, to milking, and helping with the births of all the farm animals. He had helped care for the horses from the time he was a small boy and now he was training the two-year-olds to the harness. Thomas tried to conceal his anger and disappointment by tightening his jaw. He looked down at his hands and shook his head slowly, indicating that he did not want to consider his father's proposal.

Will finished sharpening the crescent-shaped blade in his hand before he stated as a matter of fact, "Back in February I wrote a letter to my brother, Tom, in America. He left Ireland a few years before you were born." With practiced skill, he cut a long strip from the smooth leather that lay on the work bench. "Tom and I were close when we grew up together, so when you were born we gave you his name, Thomas Dobbin Keith. You may recall that he and his wife have written to us at Christmas time."

Thomas responded with, "Uh-hmm," and continued to remove broken and worn pieces of leather from an old halter.

His father said, "Tom and his wife live on a farm in Norwich, Ohio, and they have only one child, a girl of eight or nine years." Will reached into a small box for a brass rivet. "He has to depend on hired help and I understand he's had problems with dishonest workers. One man took off with many of Tom's smaller tools, and no one's seen him since."

Thomas stopped working and gave his complete attention to his father.

With a wooden mallet, Will set in the rivet. "In my letter I told Tom about you, that you want to go to America. I asked if he would be willing to take you under his care in exchange for your help on his farm." Will cleared his throat and looked at Thomas. "You have my permission to go as long as you agree to live with and work seven years for your uncle."

Thomas looked down at the worn halter he held between his long fingers. *Seven years? In seven years I will be twenty-two years old! I'll be giving the best years of my life as an indentured servant to this uncle.* Then it occurred to Thomas that perhaps his father expected him to give up his dream of going to America. This thought left him speechless. He smoothed out a roll of new leather on the bench before him and wondered how he should reply.

Finally, he said, "Have you heard from your brother, and has he said anything about my working seven years?"

"Yes, his letter came three days ago. He says that you may live in his house as a member of his family. In return you must agree to work seven years on his farm. He will also pay you wages of eighteen dollars a month."

Will began cutting another strip of leather with his knife. "I think your uncle is giving you a fair offer. Besides that, your mother will feel better knowing you're living with a member of the family. She doesn't want to see you leave home at all." He ended the last sentence with a coughing, choking sound.

That sound reminded Thomas of the day last fall when the family stood at Grandmother Keith's open grave for her burial. He looked away pretending not to see his father blinking moisture from his eyes. When he glanced back, his dad was deftly pushing heavy linen thread through the awl's needle eye.

"Another thing," Will said, "your uncle has a great deal of knowledge about horses, and you can learn more from him. He wrote that he recently bought a fine pair of matched Percherons. He said there's a demand for this breed in Ohio."

Thomas had seen drawings of Percherons in the *Horseman's Manual* and they were large, impressive animals. The text said they were 'intelligent, strong, and even-tempered, fit for the heaviest work, yet they step out lively when pulling the buggy to town.' He could see himself driving such a team.

Thomas was not aware he was smiling until he saw the smile on his father's face. He understood now that Dad was not really discouraging him from going to America. Living with his uncle, aunt, and one girl cousin would not be entirely bad; at least, he wouldn't have to endure the aggravation of his brothers and sisters at home. But then Thomas thought about his mother. He knew she would be filled with sorrow at the news her third son was leaving home in a few weeks.

"Dad, will you speak to Mother and the family about this? I haven't said a word to anyone except you and George McAllister."

Will nodded and said, "I'm guessing you intend to go to America and work for your uncle seven years."

"You were right, Dad. It's a fair offer." Thomas knew it would be his only offer, and the one opportunity for him to go to America.

A new thought filled him with dread. What if Mr. McGowan had already asked someone else to care for this year's shipment of horses? Thomas would be forced to wait another whole year.

CHAPTER TWO

Tom Keith headed for home in his buckboard wagon hauling some tools he had purchased in town this morning. They clanked and rattled in the box behind his seat while the dust billowed up around the wheels of his wagon. When he stopped at the Post Office to collect the mail the Post Mistress, Clara Hamilton, handed him an envelope that had foreign stamps glued to the top right corner.

"You have a letter from Ireland, Mr. Keith. I hope it's good news." Clara was always fishing for information about the mail she handed out. Tom thanked her and went back outside to climb up into the buckboard. He was eager to learn if his nephew would be coming to live with them but his disciplined habits kept him waiting until the proper time to open the envelope. He shook the reins and urged the horses toward home.

As he bounced down the dusty road, he thought about his brother Will and their relationship over the years. They had been as close as two brothers could be when they were growing up. But Will was the oldest son who had inherited the farm at Clooney, and Will also married one of the prettiest girls they knew. Anne McKinley was not only very attractive, but she was friendly, and she came from a respected family.

Tom thought back to the day he went to work for the Huntly family in Ohio and he met Margaret Huntly, the elder daughter of his benefactor and employer. He remembered how she tried to make conversation with him and how she confessed later that she wanted to hear him speak because of his Irish accent. Margaret was an intelligent, outspoken woman who had a large frame, and dark hair that she pulled straight back into a bun. Though she was 40 years old when they married, and she was less than beautiful, Margaret was a shrewd business woman, and she loved Tom with her whole being. He never regretted their marriage.

Often, Tom was tempted to write to his brother, Will, and tell him about his wife's prosperity. She had inherited many acres from her father and grandfather who had been pioneers in this region, and she leased out more than half the land which brought in a fair return each year. But Tom could make no claim to her wealth and, in fact, all the property was registered at the county courthouse under Margaret's name alone. Margaret's word was final in most decisions, so Tom's pride kept him from admitting any of this to his brother.

After Tom unhitched the horses and turned them out to pasture, he unloaded his box of tools and carried them to the machine shed. He took out his pocket watch to see that it was close to noon and decided to go on up to the house. Margaret and Sarah were not in sight so he went into the front room, sat down in a wing back chair covered by an old bed sheet to protect it from soil, and took out his pocket knife. He cut through the top of the envelope with his sharp knife edge and removed the pages filled with his brother's handwriting.

He had just begun to read when he was interrupted by Sarah who bolted through the front door and banged it closed behind her. She grabbed the wooden stair rail to propel herself upward two steps at a time.

"Sarah Hannah Keith, you go back out that door and come in like a lady." His wife's commanding voice came from upstairs.

Amused, Tom watched his daughter walk down the

stairs and out the front door. When she came in again, Sarah closed the door so softly he heard only the sound of a slight squeak in the hinges. She wore her usual white pinafore covering a faded blue cotton dress that revealed black stockings from her knees downward. Sarah deliberately and quietly placed her feet on each stair step one at a time.

But Margaret was still upset with her daughter. Her voice boomed down the stairwell, "I've been dusting and cleaning floors all morning, and when I went in your room, I seen that you have not done one thing." She thumped something hard on the floor. Tom thought it must have been the dust mop. He heard her yelling, "You get up here and make your bed *now*, and if you want to keep your dolls, you'd best put them away. They don't belong on the floor!"

"Yes'm." Sarah lowered her head. Her dark brown hair was coming loose from the blue ribbon at the back of her head. She disappeared from sight and Tom returned his attention to the letter in his hands.

Soon he looked up to see his wife's large body move back and forth as she dusted her way down each step with the long handle of the dust mop in her hands. She entered the front room and spoke in an accusing tone, "That daughter of yours is going to miss her dolls when I give them all away."

"She still sleeps with her dolls every night, doesn't she? Sarah will surely be upset if you give them all away."

"I spent many hours making those rag dolls for her and she shows her thanks by leaving them scattered across the floor."

"She's only nine years old. I think she will learn to be more responsible if we keep reminding her."

Margaret reached to push strands of graying hair

from her eyes, and wiped her sweating face with the hem of her apron. She looked at the letter in Tom's hands. "Bring the mail in the kitchen while I get your dinner ready."

Tom followed her into the kitchen and sat down at the sturdy wooden table. "This letter is from my brother, Will. His son, Thomas, who was named for me, is on his way to Ohio right now."

Margaret nodded in acknowledgement and stepped out the back door to shake the dust from her mop. After putting the dust mop away in the pantry, she went to the large cast iron cook stove where she removed the lid on the pot of mutton stew that had been simmering all morning. She gave it a stir, and added more wood to the stove before she began to make fresh coffee.

Margaret said, "We agreed to tell Sarah about her cousin after we received their letter saying he was on his way. Are you going to tell her today?"

Tom nodded, "I think she should know."

Margaret filled the dark blue enameled coffee pot with fresh water from the pail on the counter, filled the inner metal basket with ground coffee and placed the pot on the stove to heat. "It appears that Sarah will have to share her home and her parents with an older cousin. I hope the two of them will be agreeable."

"I don't see any reason why there will be a problem," Tom kept his eyes on the letter in his hands.

It wasn't long until Sarah hopped down the steps into the kitchen and came near her father's chair. She peered around his shoulder to see what he was reading. Soon she inched so close he could feel her warm breath.

He turned to look at her and broke into a smile. "Well, my curious little cat! Do you want to read it?"

Sarah backed away and giggled. "Yes, but the handwriting is not easy to read."

"This is a letter from my brother in Ireland. I'll read it to you and your mother tonight after supper." He folded the papers and tucked them into his shirt pocket because Margaret had set their bowls of hot stew on the table and lowered her ample body into her chair. They all bowed their heads while he asked the blessing over their noon day meal.

That night after supper Sarah jumped up from the table without being reminded and helped her mother clear away the dishes. She wanted to learn about the letter that came all the way across the ocean from Ireland. When Tom finished the last of his coffee, he took the folded papers from his pocket and spread them open on the table.

"This came in the mail today", he announced. "It's from my brother, Will, in Ireland. Sit down and I'll read it to you."

Margaret wiped her hands on her apron and sat at her usual place, but Sarah pushed her chair close to her father's before she sat down. Tom cleared his throat and began reading as if he had memorized every word:

18 May, 1879
Clooney, Markethill,
County Armagh, Ireland
Dear Brother Tom and Family,
This has been another wet, cool spring here in Clooney. We are hoping for some sunshine and warmer weather soon. As usual, the weather determines our prosperity or lack of it.
Your nephew and namesake made his decision to come and work for you seven years. Believe me, we are all very sad at the thought of his leaving, but it comforts us to know he will be living with you and your family.
Thomas was certain he would be working his way

over with McGowan's shipment of horses. He was most unhappy when he learned McGowan had promised his nephew he could go with the horses this year. However, when the nephew broke his leg and was forced to stay home, Thomas was near to breaking his own face with grinning. In truth, our whole family is unable to share his joy because we cannot count on ever seeing him again. How many years has it been since you left Ireland? Our mother spoke of you many times in the months before she died.

This year McGowan has agreed to buy six of our good harness-trained horses and he hopes to have as many as twenty from other local farmers before the ship sails on 2 June. Thomas will be responsible for all 26 animals as they cross the Atlantic, and they should arrive in New York near the middle of June. There he plans to work three or four weeks to earn his train fare to Norwich, Ohio. Knowing Thomas, he will arrive at your farm as soon as he is able.

We are all in good health, with the exception of our four-year-old Margery and our wee daughter, Mary. They are both ill with fevers and rash, and Doctor Pringle says it appears to be measles. We hope you and Margaret and your daughter, Sarah are in good health.
Your Loving Brother,
Will Keith

Sarah was excited. "When will he get here, Daddy?"

"He will probably be here before the end of July."

"What day is it today?"

Tom pointed to the calendar on the wall. "Today is the twelfth of July. You should know that, Sarah, because your ninth birthday was one month ago today."

Tom looked at his wife and said, "He could be here in just a few days. Is the spare bedroom ready?"

"I have some extra wool blankets and a quilt for his bed, but maybe we should ask to borrow that old chest of drawers from my sister. Your nephew will need a place to store his belongings."

"A fifteen-year-old boy is not going to be caring about furniture," Tom said. "I can build him some open shelves if he thinks he needs it."

Sarah could not keep silent any longer. "Why is he coming to live with us?"

"Thomas is your cousin from Ireland. He wants to live in America so we've asked him to come live here and help me with the farm," her father said.

"If he's my cousin will he play with me?"

Tom smiled and explained that her cousin was too old to be a playmate for her. "Besides that, he'll be too busy working."

"Do you think he might go riding with me on a Sunday afternoon? I haven't ridden Stubby in a long time, and I should ride him, don't you think so?"

Tom nodded, "Yes, maybe Thomas will ride with you on a Sunday." He was pleased to see his daughter's face beaming with a big smile.

Thomas struggled to board the train with his small trunk under one arm and the heavy leather bag swinging from the tight grip of his hand. He bumped and squeezed his way down the aisle until he found a vacant window seat. After pushing his trunk under the seat, he sat down, holding the valuable bag on his lap. It was heavy with tools from home.

"You'll be needing these tools, Thomas," his father had said as he thrust the bag toward him.

Thomas had been too excited to think much about it the morning he left home, but his father was right. He *had* needed them. Tools for the horses' grooming had already been put to use aboard ship, and Thomas was most grateful to his father for including the wool grader. With it he had found a job near the docks in New York City where he graded wool for twelve hours each day. He slept in a cheap boarding house, and though the accommodations and food were less than desirable, he was able to save most of his earnings during the four weeks he worked.

Last evening he received his pay, informed his boss he was leaving, and went back to the boarding house where he ate a tasteless supper. Thomas paid the amount he owed the landlady, an old woman who reminded him of a fairytale crone with a scrawny neck and a wart on her long nose. When he told her he was leaving very early in the morning before breakfast she merely looked at him through faded eyes and nodded her head slightly.

It took longer than he expected to board the ferry, ride across the Hudson River, and find his way to the nearest railway station, but he managed to get a seat on the train departing at five minutes after nine in the morning. He was able to buy his tickets all the way to Norwich, Ohio on the Pennsylvania Rail Road Line. As the cars began to jerk and roll down the track, Thomas felt good to be leaving the filth of coal-blackened New York City. He was eager to be back on a farm again.

The train rolled on in a monotonous bouncing and rocking motion. Thomas thought he might be able to sleep, but he could not relax in the upright seat with no place for his long legs to stretch out. He was the first one off when the train stopped to take on water and coal, and without these frequent stops he wondered how anyone could endure this mode of travel.

At mid-day the train slowed once again, screaming several blasts from its whistle. This was followed by the conductor's shout announcing a forty-minute stop for a noon meal. A man at his boarding house had told him to avoid those so-called 'dining rooms' located at some train stations for the passengers. He said the meals were overpriced and very bad, and one could always find better food at a general store.

Thomas stood on the wooden platform and surveyed the small town. He walked toward a weathered sign that read Brown's General Store. When he went inside he noticed several other passengers had also pinned their hopes on this establishment for purchasing edible food. Minutes later, Thomas was sitting in the shade of a tree devouring his first meal of the day: two hard-boiled eggs, a wedge of cheddar cheese, and some soda crackers. Washing it down with a jar of ginger beer, he brushed off the crumbs thinking how much better he felt, even if it cost more than he planned to spend. He returned the jar to the store, and stretched his legs by walking about the small town. The clanging bell and the conductor's cry, "All aboard!" sent him hurrying back to his seat.

The relentless summer sun transformed the passenger car into a furnace. Though all the windows were open, the heat was oppressive. Men mopped their faces, women fanned themselves, and small children whined and cried. Thomas removed his jacket, opened the top two buttons of his white shirt, and rolled up his long sleeves. In the late afternoon the train steamed its way into a heavily wooded area, and the welcome shade eased their misery.

After a long miserable night of slouching on the hard seat, Thomas was more than ready to leave the train car when they pulled into another small town for breakfast. He worried that his money was disappearing far faster than he had planned so he began to eat less and less. That night for supper, he bought one boiled egg and a jar of milk, which left him feeling hungry for more. He endured another long night and another hot day much the same as the ones before.

By the third evening Thomas felt nearly sick with hunger and weariness. He took all his remaining money from deep inside his pocket and found he had only two dollars and fourteen cents left. When the train came to a stop for supper, he decided to take his trunk and bag with him and look in this town for a room where he could lie down to sleep for the night.

Thomas walked along the boardwalk of the dusty street, past the brightly painted Waverly Inn to the door of the less pretentious Langmore Inn. It looked to be a small establishment with no more than six or eight rooms. The sign in the front window advertised 'Home-Cooked Meals and Comfortable Beds'. Thomas opened the door and went to the desk where he tapped the bell for service as the small hand-lettered sign directed. A short girl with a rounded, freckled face came to the desk. She looked to be no more than eighteen years old.

She looked up at Thomas. "May I help you?"

"What is the price of a small room and a meal?"

"Is that an Irish accent I hear?" She lifted her eyebrows when she questioned him.

"Yes, I'm from County Armagh in the north of Ireland."

"Ah, that explains it. My family is from County Tyrone, right near the River Blackwater, and you sound just like my dear old dad. Where are you headed?"

"I'm going to my uncle's farm in Norwich, Ohio."

"I don't believe I ever heard of Norwich. It must be a small place."

"Yes, I understand it isn't very big."

"Well now, you asked about the price of a 'small' room and a meal. Our rooms are all the same size. We charge two dollars per night for a room, and that includes a three course evening meal and a hot breakfast." Her lively brown eyes surveyed Thomas with more than a little interest.

Thomas placed his trunk and bag on the floor and reached into his pocket to remove the two dollars. That pocket held nothing but coins, so he checked the other pocket. It was empty. *What happened to the money?* Embarrassed, he looked at the young woman and stammered, "I...I think I've lost my money. I'm sorry to have bothered you." He grabbed his bags and turned to leave.

"I'm sorry you lost your money, lad. I know of an old woman in town who could use your help if you want to work for a meal and a place to sleep."

Thomas looked at her as if she threw a lifeline to save him from drowning.

"Mrs. McGinty lives four houses down on Maple Street. That's the first street to your left. She lives in the white house with the green door and green shutters. You can tell her that Pansy Langmore sent you." Her smile revealed dimples that charmed even the most aloof customers.

Thomas grinned. "I can't thank you enough." He moved toward the door to leave.

Miss Langmore said, "We Ulster folk must look out for one another. I'm sure you noticed all the signs that say, 'Help wanted. No Irish need apply'."

Thomas stopped and faced her. "Yes, I saw those signs in New York City."

Pansy came from behind the desk, leaned toward

him and spoke confidentially. "Well, the Catholic Irishmen are a lot of drunks and they give us all a bad name with their brawling and fighting. I know because we lived in New York City for six months. It was a dreadful place."

Thomas shook his head over the regretful situation. "Thank you very much, Miss Langmore, and good day to you." He went out the door and onto the street.

"Best of luck to you," she called out as he left.

Thomas rapped several times on the green door of the house with green shutters. Mrs. McGinty opened the door and peered out at him revealing a pale, wrinkled face draped on each side by long white hair that had come loose from its combs. Thomas explained that Pansy Langmore sent him. "I'd be grateful for a meal and a bed if you have any work I can do."

In a quivering voice she said, "Follow me, young man." Mrs. McGinty hobbled slowly down the front steps and along the side of the house to the back yard where she showed him his duties.

In the remaining daylight Thomas split a huge pile of wood and hauled in several armloads for the old woman's stove. Finally he brought in two buckets of water from her well, hoping for a hot meal as the hour was late and he was feeling weary.

"Take this, young man," the old woman handed him a bowl and a spoon. "You can set down on the back steps while you eat, and then leave my bowl and spoon inside the door."

Thomas looked at the bowl filled with brown, lumpy gravy.

"It's my beef stew," she said with some pride. "After you set my bowl and spoon inside the door, you can sleep in the cow shed. You'll find some clean straw behind the shed."

She showed him out the back door and left Thomas standing in the darkness. He sat on the top step and tasted the stew. With the first mouthful, he almost gagged as he retrieved some long hairs from his mouth. When he found another lengthy hair in the second spoonful he scraped the contents of the bowl into some bushes. After placing her bowl and spoon inside the door, he made his way to the well and filled his empty stomach with cool well water. He didn't remember seeing clean straw behind the cow shed, but he felt around in the darkness trying to find it. Just as he thought, the old woman's memory was failing much the same as her hair was falling into her stew.

Thomas spent the night sleeping on a bench outside the train station. He reminded himself how fortunate he was to be traveling in the summer when the nights are warm and balmy. As he thought about his lost money, he was puzzled. He always took care to know exactly where his money and valuables were and he kept a watchful eye on them. Then he remembered the fellow behind him who was shoved into Thomas as they stood in the aisle waiting to leave their train car. *That man must have been a pickpocket!* Thomas was grateful he had taken the time unbuckle the two straps at the top of his leather tool bag to deposit his train tickets deep inside with the tools.

He was the first to board the west bound train early in the morning. Trying to ignore his hungry, growling stomach he watched the passing scenery through the streaked window. Out of sheer exhaustion he fell asleep and didn't wake until the train stopped at noon. He thought of his remaining fourteen cents and went into a store hoping to find something he could afford to eat. At the sight and aroma of several loaves of brown bread, and some fresh fruit pies still steaming from the oven, Thomas nearly drooled with hunger. He decided to buy a loaf of bread and a generous wedge of yellow cheese but learned that would cost fifteen cents. Thomas asked the proprietor if he could sweep the floors to make up for the missing one cent.

"I just swept the floors, but you can stack all these tins on the shelves where they belong and line 'em up so you can read the labels."

Thomas looked at the huge box of tins and went to work, hoping he could complete the job before the train pulled away. Some needed to go on the top shelf and others went on lower shelves. He went up and down the ladder with tins tucked under his arm, working furiously until he heard the train's bell begin to ring.

"I'm sorry, sir. There are a dozen tins left but I have to catch my train."

"You earned your cheese and loaf of bread, young fella." The man handed him his bread and cheese which he had already wrapped and tied with string, and took the last of Thomas's money in return.

Thomas tucked the package inside his shirt, and called back his thanks as he hurried out the door. Across the road, the train was moving away from the station. Thomas ran alongside his car, pulled himself up the steps, and found his seat. Reaching inside his shirt, he quickly unwrapped his food and tore away a large piece of bread to stuff it into his mouth. He didn't remember eating bread that was any better than this. With his pocket knife he sliced away small pieces of cheese and savored each bite. Using all his foresight and self-control, he saved half the loaf of bread and half the wedge of cheese for later.

Along with the other passengers, he endured the bouncing and rocking motion of the overheated car until late in the day when the sun began to drop behind the trees. As they entered the shade of a green forest, Thomas ate the last of his bread and cheese. When they pulled into another small town for an evening meal, he put on his cap and walked about the streets. He drank from a ladle that hung by a leather thong at the town well, and walked across the railroad tracks where he lay down on a haystack and looked up at the darkening sky. He wondered what tomorrow would bring. Would his uncle approve of him, and what kind of person was this American aunt? He wondered if his American cousin was anything at all like his sisters. The locomotive's loud, resounding bell and whistle brought him to his senses. Thomas quickly brushed the hay from his clothes and ran to his car to spend another long night of sitting in a seat that was not made for comfort.

The first rays of morning light hit the window next to his head, and Thomas woke thinking this was the day he would meet his American relatives! He rubbed the sleep from his eyes and checked to see that his bags were close by.

Thomas called out to the conductor who was coming toward him in the aisle, "Sir, can you tell me how much longer until we arrive at Norwich?"

The man stopped and pulled his pocket watch from a small opening in his black waist coat. He studied the time piece for a moment and spoke through a thick mustache, "We'll arrive at Sundale Station in exactly thirty-two minutes."

"Thank you," he said to the conductor who had moved on down the aisle.

Thomas reached with both hands to smooth his tousled hair, tuck in his shirt and straighten his clothes. He began to observe the scenery out the window wondering if his uncle's house would be in view of the railroad tracks. He noticed several farms tucked in among the trees and rolling hills. Soon the train whistle pierced the air, and the conductor cried, "Norwich!   Sundale Station!   Fifteen minute stop!"

Thomas placed his wool cap on his head, reached for the trunk under his seat, grabbed the leather tool bag, and when the train slowed to a stop he stepped out into a bright Ohio morning.

CHAPTER THREE

Thomas had to squint to protect his eyes from the glaring sun. He looked around and took his bearings, then forced his stiff legs to walk to the ticket window where he put his bags down. The man inside did not look up when Thomas asked, "Can you tell me where Tom Keith lives?"

Thomas felt a hand on his shoulder and a voice from behind said, "I'm Tom Keith."

When Thomas turned around he looked into eyes that were astonishingly familiar; the same as his father's eyes, only a darker blue. They were set within a handsome face framed by a recently trimmed and graying beard. His mustache revealed the thin line of a mouth, and there was the same narrow, straight nose that graced the faces of so many in the Keith family. The man wore a flat-brimmed leather hat which had dark sweat stains around the base of the crown.

"You must be my nephew. I understand they call you Thomas at home." His hand reached out to Thomas and the two shook hands with a firm grasp.

"Yes, and you're my Uncle Tom?"

"You look to be as tall as any man I know. Why don't you just call me 'Tom' and leave off the 'uncle'. You must be tired from the long train ride. Are you hungry?"

Thomas nodded. "I haven't eaten since yesterday."

"We live just a short way from here. Your Aunt Margaret will have something for you to eat when we get home." Tom piled his nephew's bags into the wagon.

"We'd best be going before the day gets away from us."

Thomas climbed up onto the buckboard wagon and sat next to his uncle who, with a slight movement of the reins, directed the two matched, dappled-gray horses to pull away from the depot. They rattled down the hill on a rough road, fine dirt billowing up from the wheels and forming a continuous cloud of dust behind the wagon. Thomas was aware of the hilly terrain and the abundance of trees, but he kept his attention on the horses, admiring everything about them. He wondered if his uncle always hitched up both horses to make the trip to the train station.

As if reading his thoughts, Tom said, "These two horses were trained to work together and it's easier on them and me to continue with what they know, even if the wagon is nearly empty today."

"They're fine looking horses. How old are they?"

"Four years. I bought them last year from a farm in the next county. Mac is a gelding but Maddie is a mare I hope to use for breeding. Around here they call them French horses but the correct name is Percheron."

A change in the breeze blew dust up into their faces, making it difficult to breathe. When the wind changed direction and pushed the dust behind them again, Thomas filled his lungs with clean air. He said, "What's the condition of this road after some heavy rains?"

"It's bad enough to make me wish I were back in Ireland again," said Tom. "Here we have either dust or mud, and believe me, dust is easier to travel than mud."

The big gray horses pulled the wagon to the left and down a narrow lane. A smiling black and white collie dog, his tongue hanging out and tail fanning the air, came to greet them. He escorted the wagon past a two-story house and down to a large barn built of wood planks aged to a dark brown. Tall trees surrounded the yard and house, providing pleasant shade on this warm summer morning.

Thomas jumped down from the wagon and helped to unhitch the horses. His experienced touch sensed their strength and calm natures. Their soft warm muzzles and nostrils took in his smell as Thomas stroked them and spoke quietly to the large animals.

Tom nodded his approval. "You'll enjoy working with Mac and Maddie. They're strong and willing… worth every cent I paid for them."

Thomas saw a small brown terrier jumping and barking around a young girl who ran from the house to join them. The girl stopped in front of Thomas with her hands behind her back. She looked at him in a way that made him wonder if his face had turned green.

"Are you my cousin from Ireland?"

"Yes, I'm Thomas. Are you Sarah?"

His smile brought a shy smile and nod from Sarah, who then turned and ran back to the house yelling, "Mama, Thomas is here!"

Tom took the harness to the barn, where he hung it on the wall, and Thomas led the horses out to the pasture.

Tom removed his hat and wiped his face on his sleeve. "Let's go in and find something for you to eat."

Thomas said, "I'm ready! I think I could eat my own weight in food". He retrieved his trunk and leather bag from the wagon and followed his uncle up to the house and into the kitchen where Thomas set down his belongings and removed his cap.

Tom introduced him to the very large lady who was his Aunt Margaret. She was nearly as tall as her husband and twice his width. Her graying hair was pulled back in a bun at the back of her head. Ice blue eyes peered out of her fleshy pink face and her down-turned mouth and jowls made him think of a bulldog. When she looked at Thomas he felt those cold, blue eyes penetrating right through him. For an anxious moment Thomas wished he could run away.

Aunt Margaret spoke briefly. "Welcome, Thomas. You'll soon feel right at home here, I'm sure." Moving her considerable bulk in a swift, fluid motion, she went to the stove and grabbed the handle of a kettle. "Take this warm water up to your room, Thomas. When you've washed yourself you can come down here to eat. With that thin frame of yours, you look to be starving!" She thrust the kettle toward Thomas, then she ordered her daughter, "Sarah, you carry his bag and show Thomas to his room. Bring him some soap, wash cloth, and a clean towel, too."

Thomas followed Sarah up the stairs with his trunk under one arm and his other hand gripping the handle of the kettle, taking care not to spill a drop of water. The impressive image of his Aunt Margaret remained with him. He couldn't think of another lady who was that abrupt and forthright with her words and manners, or who had such a huge body. He wondered how he would fit into her household.

Thomas thanked Sarah for her help. Unlike his sister, Agnes, Sarah carried his heavy tool bag without complaining, and brought him the soap, wash cloth, and towel with a polite smile. Before she closed the door to his room she said, "I hope you like fried eggs 'cause Mama is cooking them for you right now."

He placed his trunk on the floor at the foot of the bed, moved his bag of tools to a corner of the room, and hung his cap on the iron bed post. The room was clean and small, containing only a bed covered with a faded quilt, and a small table which held a short candle in a tin candle holder alongside a chipped wash basin. The one new object in the room was a white embroidered cloth that covered the table. The old streaked mirror on the wall above the basin revealed a face smudged with soot and a head of light brown hair sprinkled with black cinders from the train locomotive. He poured water in the basin, and went to his trunk to look for his hairbrush. Thomas thought his appearance must have been as astonishing to his aunt as hers was to him. The smell of food assaulted his empty stomach and Thomas hurried to finish washing.

At home, Thomas usually listened to the adults at mealtime. Dad talked with his oldest brother, James, about the condition of the cows and sheep, or they discussed the farm equipment and improvements that needed to be made. Now and then, Thomas would contribute his assessment of the horses and his progress with their training. But here at the table of his uncle and aunt he found himself talking more than he had in weeks. In fact, he was so busy answering questions he barely had a chance to chew his food.

Tom wanted to know about his relatives in Ireland. Details of Grandmother Keith's death and burial services were of particular interest, and Thomas could see that his uncle held her in the same high regard as her other children did. Between bites, Thomas told his uncle everything he knew about the family at home.

Aunt Margaret began asking questions then. Struggling to remember his manners while satisfying his hunger, Thomas answered her inquiries with all the politeness he could manage. She wanted to know where he stayed in the big city, and where he took his meals.

"I stayed in a boarding house in New York City. It was near the docks where I worked grading wool. They fed us breakfast and supper...the food was not very good, and I had to share a bed with another man." He chewed and swallowed a large bite of buttered bread. "The lady who owned it was very old and she had but one woman to help her."

His aunt's lifted brows informed him she wanted an explanation.

"It was the least expensive boarding house on the street and I wanted to save money for my train fare."

Sarah leaned forward with her arms on the table. "Were you afraid, coming all that way across the sea? Was your ship very big?"

"Our ship seemed big until we came into the harbor at New York. Some of the ships there were almost twice the size of ours. But the crossing was smooth, and they said we made it in near record time."

Tom said, "How did the horses fare on board the ship?"

"They were upset and off their feed for a day or two after we left Ireland. But they settled down and started eating. I kept them brushed and groomed so they looked good when they came off the ship. I'm certain they sold for a tidy sum."

"Have some more milk, Thomas," Aunt Margaret said. "And here's another slice of bread. Put some of my apple butter on it...you need to put some flesh on those bones."

Thomas poured himself another cup of milk from the big stoneware pitcher. It was cool and fresh, reminding him of home. Aunt Margaret's fried eggs, and sliced bread with butter made a delicious meal. With his bread he wiped up the last of the egg yolk and stuffed it into his mouth. Then he piled apple butter on his last slice of bread and savored every delicious bite. Filled with good food and the satisfaction of being here in Ohio, Thomas felt he was ready for any work his uncle expected of him.

"It's almost ten o'clock and we have a day's work

ahead of us," Tom said. He stood up and put on his hat.

Thomas remembered to thank his Aunt Margaret for the meal, and followed Tom out of the kitchen. When they reached the barn, Tom began pointing out the work he wanted Thomas to do.

Thomas had imagined himself driving the Percherons, plowing large fields and harvesting crops of grain in America. He had not envisioned himself mucking out the barn and hauling manure. Nevertheless, he rolled up his sleeves and put his body to the task of shoveling out the barn. Beads of perspiration on his neck and face became streams of sweat as he hauled one cartload after another out to a pile near the fence. He could see that the overdue cleaning of this barn would take all day. Tomorrow he would have to clean out the chicken coop and then the piggery. After that the fences needed mending.

He looked out at Mac and Maddie grazing peacefully in the pasture with the other horses and cows. Thomas admired their muscled beauty as they swished their tails to chase away the flies. He swatted at the flies encircling his own perspiring body and went back to work.

Sunday was the day of rest, but the resting would have to wait until later because the necessary chores must be completed first. Thomas had been assigned to milk Daisy and Buttercup, the docile Jersey cows. He had to strain the milk through cheesecloth, and haul the pails of strained milk to a crock in the spring house where it cooled in the water. His uncle fed and groomed the horses, making sure that Mac and Maddie would look their best when they pulled the nearly new four-wheeled carriage to church later that morning. Sarah's call for them to come in for breakfast was a welcome sound.

After Tom asked the blessing, Aunt Margaret

handed out bowls of steaming hot porridge. Thomas saw that she had already poured sweet syrup over his. When he added fresh cream from the pitcher his humble bowl of porridge became a tasty treat. Of course, he helped himself to a large slice of bread and slathered it with Aunt Margaret's apple butter.

Margaret said, "You *did* bring clothes to wear to church, didn't you, Thomas?"

"Yes, I have some new church clothes but I don't have another pair of shoes. Will there be time for me to clean these?" He brought his right foot from under the table and revealed a dirty, scuffed shoe.

Aunt Margaret looked down at his foot and scowled. "I certainly hope there's time. After breakfast, you get that tin of leather soap off the shelf next to the back door, and see what you can do to make those shoes look better."

Thomas went to the enclosed back porch and worked for half an hour trying to clean his shoes. Later, he wondered why he went to all the trouble. After the ride into town, he and his relatives were covered in a fine coating of dust. But nearly everyone arriving at the church that morning wore the same layers of fine brown dirt. Families climbed down from carriages and quickly shook off their clothes before entering the big front doors of the whitewashed building. Letters painted in black above the doors let all of Norwich know that members of the First Presbyterian Church worshiped here.

Thomas had not attended church services since he left home. Suddenly he felt nostalgic for the familiar surroundings of his own church in Markethill where he had been baptized and nurtured in the faith. There was little similarity between the wooden structure of this church and the white plastered walls of his church at home. A startling contrast existed between the scholarly, quiet-mannered Reverend Mitchell in Ireland and the minister here.

Reverend Hardesty was a large man whose deep, booming voice sounded out above all the others as they sang the first hymn. His strong voice led the congregation as they stood for the Psalter reading. He roared through the Old Testament Lesson, and shouted out the New Testament Lesson, but surprisingly, his voice softened when he began the Morning Prayer. As if he and God were close personal friends, Reverend Hardesty beseeched Him for guidance and blessings of the Holy Spirit. The minister prayed God's forgiveness for 'our sins of pride and self-righteousness,' and more loudly he asked God to change the hearts of those who lead in high places of government.

Thomas dozed while the pastor prayed for widows, orphans, and heathen savages throughout the world. He nearly jumped off the pew when suddenly the preacher shouted and pounded his fist on the pulpit. Thomas looked up and realized the prayer had ended. Reverend Hardesty was well into his sermon.

When the collection plate had been passed, everyone stood to sing the Doxology. At last, the clergyman walked down the aisle to the entrance and raised his right hand above the congregation to pronounce the Benediction. He stood at the door to personally greet his congregation as they left for home.

Tom introduced his nephew from Ireland. Reverend Hardesty shook Thomas's hand with a firm grip and said, "Welcome, Thomas. I'm sure you will find that many things are different here in America."

"Yes sir, I agree," Thomas said.

Out in the churchyard Thomas found himself in the midst of people who seemed to know who he was, but their identities were unknown to him. Aunt Margaret stepped forward and introduced him to her sister and brother-in-law, Mr. and Mrs. Isaac Cole, and their three children: John, Rena, and Emma.

Rena looked to be close to Thomas's own age. She had a pretty face with deep violet-blue eyes that focused on his whenever he looked in her direction.

Mrs. Cole was speaking, "...and we'd be happy to have the four of you come to our house for dinner this afternoon. It would give us a chance to get acquainted with Thomas. Will you come?" She smiled at Thomas and looked to her older sister, Margaret, for her answer.

"Why yes, we'll be happy to come for dinner. I'll bring the berry pies I made yesterday, and a loaf of bread." Margaret nodded at Thomas with a slight smile and said for everyone to hear, "This one's partial to my apple butter so I'll bring it, too."

At that, they all looked at Thomas and smiled. He could feel his ears and his cheeks flaming with heat.

Isaac Cole patted Thomas's shoulder. "You're not the only one who's partial to Margaret's apple butter, Thomas. You may have to share some with me."

Thomas joined in their friendly laughter.

Tom began talking with Isaac about the rising cost of building materials while Margaret made plans for the afternoon meal with her sister, Hannah Cole. Sarah played a game of hopscotch with her cousin, Emma, and John wandered away to visit with his friends. That left Thomas and Rena standing together, both nervously self-conscious.

Thomas kicked at a stone and Rena curled a lock of shining, dark hair around her finger. At last, Rena asked Thomas if he knew how to play checkers because they had that game at their house. Thomas thought he had played checkers a few times. Soon they were in an animated conversation naming other games each had played. They agreed that Parcheesi was their favorite. From games they went to the subject of their favorite songs. Rena said she had a book of music called, *Best Loved Songs* and if there was time this afternoon she would play the piano while they all sang.

Rena and Thomas noticed their families were ready to leave. Before Thomas could think about it, he and Rena had said 'goodbye' and were headed for their separate homes. She waved and flashed a beautiful smile at him as they drove away. On the way home Thomas could think only of Rena and her charming voice, her pretty face, her deep violet-blue eyes, and the way she smiled at him.

Aunt Margaret's voice brought him back to reality. "Thomas, as soon as you change your clothes, you need to get out to the pasture and bring in Beauty and Stubby. You're going to brush them and get them saddled 'cause Sarah wants you to ride with her to the Cole's house."

Tom added, "Sarah knows the way, and since she doesn't have anyone to ride with her, we knew you wouldn't mind. Beauty is a good saddle horse and you won't have a problem with him, but you may have to help Sarah control Stubby. He hasn't been ridden since school let out in May." Thomas came back to his senses and looked at Sarah, who grinned up at him in eager anticipation.

CHAPTER FOUR

Sarah stood next to Thomas and waved an excited goodbye to her parents who left in the family carriage. She beamed a smile up to her cousin and said, "I'm very glad you can ride with me today."

Thomas helped his cousin into the saddle. "You're almost too big for this pony, Sarah. Here, let me lengthen those stirrups."

"I'm nine years old now and Mama says I've been growing like a weed."

Stubby was a pony with sturdy, short legs. He was unhappy to be disturbed from his grazing, and he didn't appreciate it when Thomas put the saddle on his back. To demonstrate that he didn't like Sarah's weight Stubby snorted, pulled up his head, and side-stepped away from Thomas. Adding to the pony's aggravation was the barking of Sarah's little dog, Topsy, who danced around Stubby's feet.

"Be quiet, Topsy," Sarah shouted.

The small brown terrier lost interest in the pony, and went off to lie in the shade next to Rex, the black and white collie.

When Thomas had adjusted the stirrups, he handed the reins to Sarah. "Do you want to take these or shall I lead him? He seems a bit unsettled."

Sarah took the reins and proudly lifted up her chin. "I've been riding him all my life. I know how to handle him."

As Thomas turned to walk toward Beauty, Stubby

began raring up and tossing his head about. Thomas reached him in time to grab his halter and keep the pony from bolting away.

"This little scoundrel has had his own way for such a long while, I don't think it's safe for you to take the reins, Sarah."

When the pony had calmed down, Thomas led him over to Beauty and mounted the large chestnut gelding while holding tightly to Stubby's reins. As though he were quite happy to oblige, the small brown beast trotted alongside the bigger animal. Sarah bounced up down on Stubby's back but she was not happy. Her face bore the look of one who has been proven wrong, and her lower lip protruded.

Thomas led them to an intersection in the road and stopped. "I don't know which way to go, Sarah. You'll have to tell me."

Sarah brightened at the thought of knowing something that Thomas didn't know. She pointed to the left and said, "We go that way. Thomas, don't you think Stubby has calmed down enough for me to take the reins now?"

Thomas hesitated. "See that big tree leaning out over the road up ahead?" He pointed to a tree at the top of the rise. "We'll go a little faster so Stubby has to work harder to keep up with Beauty and by the time we reach that tree he should be ready."

Sarah flashed a wide smile. "Let's go!"

Stubby was tired and Sarah was well jostled when they reached the tree and stopped. She pulled strands of hair away from her face and laughed as she leaned over to pat her pony's neck. "Stubby is your name, and today it means 'stubborn' instead of 'short legs'. But Thomas knows how to handle you."

With the reins in her hands again, Sarah sat in the saddle with a look of complete satisfaction upon her young face. Now her pony took Sarah's direction obediently. Sarah urged Stubby to run out ahead of the larger horse. When she reached the bottom of the hill she pointed to a thick growth of trees off to the right and shouted back to her cousin.

"John built a fort over in those trees. Follow me, Thomas, and I'll show you."

Thomas called out for her to stop but Sarah and Stubby were already deep into the trees. He had no choice but to try and follow her. Beauty had few problems but Thomas had to dodge branches and limbs to avoid being knocked out of the saddle. He had lost sight of his cousin and her small horse altogether.

Thomas reined in Beauty and yelled, "Sarah, where are you?" He heard a crashing sound and then a scream. Alarmed, he called again, "Sarah, where are you?" His answer was another cry of distress.

When Thomas found her, Sarah was sitting in a heap, covered with dirt, blood, and dried leaves. Her sleeve was torn and bleeding scratches covered her face and hands. She struggled to stand, wiping her tears and streaking her face with more dirt.

"What happened, Sarah?" Thomas dismounted and rushed to her.

She looked at her fallen pony and sobbed. "He stumbled and went down. I think he's hurt bad."

Thomas knelt to examine Stubby and discovered the pony had broken his front left leg. The gravity of the situation was closing in on Thomas while he stroked the quivering animal's neck and listened to Sarah's weeping. He looked at Sarah, who was streaking her face with more tears, and as gently as he could, Thomas reported Stubby's fatal condition.

"He has a broken leg, Sarah. He'll need to be put down."

Sarah sat next to Stubby's head and wept until her body was heaving with sobs. Thomas sat beside her and put his arm around her shoulders to console her while she grieved. Beauty whinnied and lowered his head, while small birds flitted through the shade of the trees, oblivious to the sorrow on the ground.

Thomas spoke gently. "Your parents will be worried about you. I think we should go and tell them what happened."

"But we can't leave Stubby here all alone."

"We have to, Sarah. Your daddy will come back and put him out of his misery. Stubby will suffer for only a little while."

Sarah leaned over and brushed her cheek against the pony's neck one last time. Thomas swallowed and held back his own tears.

He helped her up onto Beauty's saddle, cautioning her to watch for the low branches as he took the reins and led them on foot through the maze of trees and out onto the road. There he mounted Beauty and reached around Sarah to hold the reins. Feeling appreciation for the steadiness of this well trained horse, Thomas urged Beauty forward in a walk.

Seven-year-old Emma ran out to greet them when they arrived at the Cole's farm. She took one look at her cousin and cried out, "Oh my! What happened to you, Sarah?"

John rushed over to them. "Where did all that blood come from? And where's your pony, Sarah?" John was seventeen years old and considered himself a man compared to Thomas who was not yet shaving a beard. He looked at Thomas and said, "Uncle Tom and Aunt Margaret won't be happy to see this, Thomas."

By now everyone was coming out to see them. Aunt Margaret appeared on the Cole's front porch and when she saw her daughter she hurried toward her, wailing, "Oh dear God, what has happened to my baby?"

Tom strode over to Beauty and lifted Sarah down to the ground where she took off running to her mother's arms. Tom's expression was solemn. "You need to tell us what happened, Thomas."

Thomas saw Sarah go into the house with Aunt Margaret's full protective arm surrounding her daughter's body. He looked at the faces around him and suddenly felt very much alone. John was scowling at him and even Rena's lovely face was serious and questioning. Thomas continued to sit upon Beauty, not wanting to dismount and be any closer to their hostility. As he began to speak his voice betrayed him, squeaking more than it had in weeks. When at last, Thomas told them of the entire episode and answered their many questions, he realized that it was not hostility toward him they were feeling; it was concern for Sarah.

All eyes turned to look at Margaret and Sarah stepping out through the door of the Cole's home. Margaret bustled over to them with Sarah at her side. She had washed Sarah's face and hands, and brushed her dark brown hair, tying it back with a ribbon. Thomas was so relieved to see Sarah calm and clean again that he came down from the horse and took both of her hands in his.

Sarah beamed her brightest smile and said for everyone to hear, "Thomas rescued me. He's my hero!"

This brought a roar of laughter and a sense of relief to them all.

Hannah Cole announced it was time to come in and

eat. The men were fed first because they faced the unpleasant task of putting Stubby down.

After the men ate, Isaac took his rifle out and loaded it, making sure he was out of sight of the two little girls who were still at the table. Thomas left the house with John, while Tom went to get Beauty and one of Isaac's horses ready to ride. It was only a short distance to the place where Stubby went down so Thomas and John walked, shovels over their shoulders, to help with the digging and burying.

When it was finished they laid Sarah's saddle and bridle on Beauty, where they rode behind Tom in silent testimony of the little pony who served his mistress for more than half her young life. With the somber demeanor of four undertakers, they returned to the Cole's farm in dread of seeing Sarah upset again. They saw Sarah and Emma playing with dolls in the shade of a big tree, and neither girl looked up at them.

No one spoke to Sarah of Stubby again that day.

Thomas was disappointed when it came time to leave for home and he had not yet spoken to Rena. The Cole family followed them out to the carriage, all of them saying their goodbye's and thanks for good food. Sarah climbed into the carriage with her parents, and Thomas mounted Beauty. It had been quietly decided among the adults that Sarah's saddle and bridle should be left at the Cole's to be returned at a later time.

Rena walked over and stood beside Beauty, looking up at Thomas. Her voice carried to his ears alone. "I'm sorry about Sarah's pony. I think you were very good to her this afternoon." Rena smiled, revealing white, even teeth. "You're her hero, you know."

Thomas smiled back at Rena, hoping she couldn't detect the beating of his heart under his shirt. He nudged

Beauty's flanks and gave Rena a slight wave as he followed the carriage out onto the road toward home.

As soon as the horses were unhitched and unsaddled, Thomas and his uncle had evening chores to do. The milking had become a duty that Thomas regarded as easy because there were only the two calm and docile cows. At home in Ireland they always had eighteen to twenty milk cows and some of them were not cooperative. He sat on the tiny three-legged stool and aimed the teat outward to squirt the faces of two tabby cats that opened their mouths to take in the warm cow's milk. There were at least two families of cats who lived in the barn and ate the mice and rats, but so far, only a few had become brave enough to beg for milk.

Tom finished his work and went into the house, leaving to Thomas a few final tasks. Thomas made sure the gate to the pasture was latched and the barn door was closed. It was the peaceful twilight time when the chickens have gone to roost, and the farm animals are settling down for the night's rest. He stopped to look up at the sky and found the evening star. He thought of Rena, wishing she were with him at this moment.

Rex ambled over, wagging his flag of a tail and grinning up at Thomas. He bent down and scratched the dog's head and ears, speaking softly to him. "Well boy, you're a poor excuse for Rena. Did you have a quiet Sunday while we were away?"

Rex's grin grew wider with the scratching, and his tail's waving rhythm increased. Thomas crouched down to continue this pleasant exchange with the friendly dog, while he thought of Rena's parting words. He felt reassured that she didn't think less of him because of the bad things that happened today.

The back door of the house opened, and Thomas

saw Sarah's compact body framed by the light from inside. She shouted into the darkness, "Mama says to come in and eat as soon as you're done with the chores, Thomas."

They sat down to a simple meal because they had enjoyed a feast at the Cole's earlier that day. When they finished eating Margaret announced, "Thomas, tomorrow you have been here a week and I think it's time you wrote to your family in Ireland. Your parents will surely be glad to hear from you. Do you need paper, and pen and ink?"

Thomas nodded and started to speak.

Aunt Margaret went on. "We have all the paper you'll need in the bottom drawer over there." She pointed to a large cupboard that had several drawers in the lower half. "You'll see the pen and ink, and if you finish your letter tonight, Tom can take it to the post in the morning."

His first Sunday evening in Ohio ended with Thomas sitting at the kitchen table trying to organize his thoughts on paper. Tom had gone outside to see what was causing Rex to bark, while Aunt Margaret put away clean dishes and readied the kitchen for tomorrow's breakfast. As Thomas wrote the date, *24 July, 1879*, Sarah stood close to him with her elbows on the table watching his every pen stroke. This annoyed him so much that finally Thomas stopped writing and looked directly at her.

"I would like to have some privacy, please," he said with irritation in his voice.

Sarah's face expressed disbelief, followed by hurt and sadness. Her head and shoulders drooped as she turned and ran from the room.

Too late, Thomas remembered the pain and grief Sarah had experienced this day. Her words of admiration, 'Thomas rescued me...he's my hero,' returned as a sharp stab to his conscience. He wanted to tell Sarah he was sorry but she had run upstairs to her bedroom and slammed the door.

In silence, Aunt Margaret turned her ice-blue eyes upon Thomas and froze him in her gaze. He almost cringed as she tightened her mouth and frowned in disapproval. Those penetrating eyes pierced through to his soul and Thomas was certain she saw every evil thought within him. Abruptly she turned and banged a pot down onto the stove as if pronouncing judgment on him.

Thomas longed to be anywhere but here in this kitchen. His aunt had shamed him without speaking a word. The nearly blank paper on the table accused him of more callous behavior. He was filled with remorse for his neglect to write home, and he hated the way he acted toward Sarah this evening. Thomas picked up the pen and forced himself to write the letter:

Dear Mother, Father, and Family,

The trip across the big pond was smooth and everything went well. The horses looked good when they were unloaded in New York, and I'm certain they brought good prices. I worked for four weeks grading wool at the docks, and earned enough to buy my train fare to Norwich, Ohio. I've been working here for my uncle almost a week now, and today being Sunday, we went to church. Tom has only two Jersey cows and it's my job to milk them. They produce rich cream.

The country here is hilly and covered with trees. Tom and I are going to clear a field north of the barn so we can plant more wheat. Most of his land is planted in barley, oats, and some wheat. Tom and I, and Isaac Cole and his son, John, are working together in all our fields. The Cole family is related to Aunt Margaret and we went to eat dinner with them today after church. They have two daughters. Rena is about my age and Emma is a little younger than Sarah. By the way, when I first met my uncle

Thomas of Ulster

at the train station, he told me to call him Tom. That is why I do not call him Uncle Tom.

This afternoon we had to shoot Sarah's pony because he fell and broke his front left leg. Sarah was all scratched up in the fall but she was worried more about losing her pony than those scratches. She is a brave little girl.

I hope you are all well.

Your loving son and brother,
Thomas

44

CHAPTER FIVE

Thomas enjoyed the exchange of news and humor that bonded the four workers into a team. Tom, Isaac, John, and Thomas labored together for the remainder of the summer, harvesting and threshing for the Keith and Cole families. He was grateful John had become friendly and accepted him as an equal. They hauled loads of grain to the gristmill where the miller kept back a portion in payment for the sacks of flour they brought home. They sold many more loads of grain that were taken by train to the big city mills.

The contrasts between Ireland and America were many. Thomas was pleased with the efficiency of his uncle's new harvester pulled expertly by Mac and Maddie. With it, they cut the grain in long, wide rows, which were then ready to be raked and tied into shocks. At home in Ireland most farmers were still cutting their grain with hand-held scythes. Here, the fields were expansive while so many at home were divided into small plots.

At his uncle's farm, Thomas milked the two cows while they stood on a dirt floor at the end of the main barn. At home, his family milked many more cows in a large milking barn that stood just outside the house. They sold the milk, cream, and butter in town. Here, the milk was used only at the farm, and Aunt Margaret made a delicious soft cheese from some of it. Occasionally, Aunt Margaret sold butter and eggs to Walker's Store.

This year's harvest of apples from their small orchard was abundant. Sarah helped her mother wash and prepare the apples while Aunt Margaret operated the cider press. They filled several large jugs with sweet cider and placed them in the springhouse with the milk and butter. Mother and daughter preserved apples by slicing and drying them in hammocks of cheesecloth which were stretched from hook to hook near the ceiling of the large storage room behind the stairs. Apples in one form or another were eaten with every meal during this season, and Aunt Margaret's apple pies were a delicious treat at Sunday dinners. Her dark brown, richly flavored apple butter was still Thomas's favorite.

At various times throughout the summer, Thomas and his uncle had worked to cut down the trees north of the barn. Now at the beginning of September, the trees were all down, and today Thomas worked alone to strip the logs. After stripping off the small branches with his axe, he dragged the branches to a large burning pile that crackled and snapped with the fuel of sap-filled wood. When the logs were completely stripped, Thomas sawed them into firewood. He was gaining a keen appreciation for the labor necessary to clear a field.

Needing a rest, he leaned the axe against a log and stood up straight to relieve his back. The afternoon air was still and warm. Wild geese flew in a 'v' formation across the bright sky, making their constant honking noises as they headed south for the winter. Thomas caught sight of a movement at the edge of the clearing. A wide-eyed doe looked at him and saluted with a flick of one ear, but before he could take a breath she disappeared into the trees. If only Dad could see this, he thought. His father always bemoaned the scarcity of wild game in Ireland, but here the game was abundant.

Thomas recalled the day he left home three months ago. Would he go back if he could fly as those geese? He knew he would never return to stay, but a persistent longing made him think more about his home in Ireland. This is not getting the work done, he told himself. He wiped his face on his sleeve, reached for the axe and continued stripping away more branches.

That evening as they shared the day's news around the supper table, Tom made an announcement. "Friday morning we'll be taking the train to Zanesville. I have business to take care of at the county courthouse, and Sarah needs new things for school." He smiled with pride on his daughter. "School starts next Monday and it's time for Sarah to get ready."

Taking advantage of her father's smiling good humor, Sarah said, "Can I have some new hair ribbons? And I need some tablets and pencils for school, and some new nibs for my ink pen." In her excitement, she didn't realize how loudly she was talking.

Margaret could not tolerate this behavior. "Sarah, if you didn't yell all the time, we might be willing to listen to you. Sometimes I wonder if you will ever become a civilized young lady." She clamped her mouth into a thin line and frowned at Sarah. "Now, aren't you ashamed of yourself!"

Sarah glanced at Thomas, and looked down at her plate. It was apparent she did not want him to witness her chastisement.

As for Thomas, he appreciated his young cousin. At home in Ireland, no one looked up to him as Sarah did. Thomas also admired her because she was not easily discouraged. She had mourned the loss of Stubby, but she put her whole heart into working with a new horse, a small mare named Belle.

A month ago Tom traded a sturdy work horse for Belle, a six-year-old mare. Sarah was excited and a little worried about riding her first real horse. Thomas spent time with her, teaching her to groom, saddle, and care for Belle. With his encouragement and Sarah's determined efforts, girl and horse soon became partners. All through the month of August she rode her bay horse to bring cool water or apple juice to the men working in the fields. Thomas was pleased to see his efforts resulting in a responsible girl with a well-trained horse.

Wednesday morning Thomas and his uncle hitched the Percherons to the wagon and began loading it with things Aunt Margaret wanted to sell or trade at Walker's General Store. They loaded a wooden crate full of fresh eggs, a covered basket full of bricks of butter, and a large basket of choice apples. Margaret also asked them to include two jugs of apple juice.

Tom started walking to the house to see if Margaret was ready to leave when Thomas caught up with him and said, "Tom, when we go to Zanesville I'd like to buy some new trousers, and I need a new pair of shoes."

Tom slowed his stride. "You should ask your Aunt Margaret to make the trousers for you. If she doesn't have the cloth on hand you can buy it Friday. You'll need a warm coat for winter, too."

Thomas stumbled over the words, but he managed to make it clear that he had no money and his uncle had not paid him any wages since he arrived.

"Dad said you wrote that you'd be paying me eighteen dollars each month, and I've worked here for one and a half months. Do you suppose you could pay me my wages by Friday?"

Tom stopped and stood with his hands in his pockets, left side facing Thomas, and studied the soil at his feet. He coughed and spat on the ground. "Well, I'll need to hold back ten dollars a month for your room and board."

He looked away and cleared his throat. "I guess I can afford to give you a month's pay before Friday." Tom walked on toward the house, leaving his nephew speechless.

Thomas stood in place and watched his uncle's slim body lean forward as he walked toward the house, so very similar to Dad's build and stride, but the similarity ended there. Dad would never be unfair in his dealings with anyone, and he always lived up to his word. He knew his uncle received a good price for the grain crops, and he made a profit selling several hogs, some sheep, and three horses at auction recently. He saw no reason why Tom could not pay him for two months, especially since it amounted to only sixteen dollars now that Thomas was being charged for room and board. No wonder a former worker ran off with Tom's tools if the worker was not paid his due.

Thomas returned to the wagon and reminded himself that it was his own decision to come here. If his parents had their wish he would be at home in Ireland right now. Resolved to stay true to his goal, Thomas told himself he could make any sacrifice to have a farm of his own in America someday.

Thomas was surprised to see all five members of the Cole family at the train station Friday morning. It happened that Isaac also had business at the courthouse, and others in the Cole family had purchases to make. Aunt Margaret and her sister, Hannah, decided to make a family outing of this day and each woman had packed a basket of food for a picnic lunch.

Thomas was elated over this turn of events. At last, he and Rena might have some time together. The two families usually ate Sunday dinner together but it seemed

49

there were constant interruptions and circumstances that kept him and Rena from talking to one another. When they ate at the Cole's house, Rena had so many responsibilities helping to serve food and wash dishes that it seemed there was never any time to be with her. When the Keiths hosted the dinner, Rena was not quite so busy, but Thomas was called on to bring in water or firewood, and take the Cole's horses out to pasture or bring them in. Once when the Cole family was visiting, Rena played Aunt Margaret's piano while all of them gathered around to sing. But after two songs, Thomas and John were asked to bring in the horses and hitch them up because the Cole family would soon be leaving.

As the two families waited together for the train to pull in they exchanged remarks about the wonderful weather. Early morning sunlight was beginning to shine through the trees and there was not a cloud in the sky.

Rena's face was radiant. She leaned toward Thomas and whispered, "Let's stay close so we can get seats together on the train." Then she took his hand in hers and held onto it. Thomas understood now what people meant when they spoke of 'cupid's arrow piercing the heart'. He squeezed her hand gently.

At that moment the train whistle blew, and as the locomotive came into view, its clanging bell sent vibrations of expectation through their young bodies. They stole excited glances at one another while they waited for the other family members to board ahead of them. Still holding hands, Rena led the way to seats on the left side of the car.

"The views going to Zanesville are better on this side," she said to Thomas.

They took the seat directly behind Sarah and Emma. The train whistle blew again and the steaming engine pulled them away from a reality of everyday work and responsibility. At his side, Rena was sparkling and bubbling over with enthusiasm. She began pointing out the window and telling him bits of history about the area.

"Look over there. See that large tree stump in the clearing? People say a long time ago, when that was a big tree, they hanged an Indian there because he stole some horses from the white settlers." She caught her breath and went on. "Did you know my great-grandfather was one of the first settlers to come here? My mother said he and his family lived in a one-room log cabin for a time before he could build a real house. I guess they never had much trouble with Indians, but some settlers did back in those days."

Thomas was so completely absorbed with the animation of Rena's lovely mouth and eyes that he had to concentrate to hear her words. When it became apparent she expected some sort of response, he remembered she said something about her great-grandfather and the Indians.

"I've never seen a real live Indian, have you?" said Thomas.

"Once we took the train to Zanesville to see a circus, and there were some Indians that danced and performed. One of them beat on a drum and chanted while the others danced around in a circle. Their faces were painted and they wore feathers on their heads. It was quite strange, but interesting, too. I can't remember what tribe those Indians came from, but they hardly wore any clothes at all."

Almost before she ended the last sentence, Rena's face began to turn red and she bit down on her lower lip while looking away from Thomas. Proper young ladies were not supposed to speak of unclothed bodies.

To save her from further embarrassment Thomas

quickly changed the subject. "I heard that Zanesville is your county seat. Is it a very large town?"

Regaining her composure, she looked back at Thomas with wide eyes that were the deep color of violets. "It's much bigger than Norwich. I guess you could say it's a fairly good-sized town. I prefer to shop there because the stores sell things you don't see in Norwich."

They became engrossed in more conversation as Thomas told Rena about Ireland and his family there. Her interest in him was removing his former shyness, and he began to feel he had known her all his life. He learned that Rena was just one year younger than him, and each had completed eight years of school. She looked at him with admiring eyes when he confided his desire to have a farm of his own here in Ohio someday.

Rena said, "I think you are very courageous to leave your home and family, and come across the ocean to a place you've never seen. I'm certain I could never do that."

She asked if he had been named for his uncle.

"Yes, Dad said they gave me my uncle's name because my dad and his brother were close. So we both have the name, Thomas Dobbin Keith, but my parents insisted that everyone call me Thomas instead of Tom. It sounds too formal to some people, but I'm used to it."

Thomas learned that 'Rena' was the shortened name for Lorena, the name she was given at birth. She explained, "Before I was born there was a famous song about a young woman named Lorena. My mother thought it was such a pretty song that she named me Lorena." Then she pleased him by singing the first verse of 'Lorena' in a soft voice that was true and clear. Thomas was entranced.

Neither of them was aware that members of their families took turns glancing back at the two young people, and then smiled or winked at one another. When Emma and Sarah both turned around to stare and grin at them, Thomas and Rena were forced to notice.

They wagged their fingers at the little girls who giggled with pleasure. For several minutes they kept the girls entertained with periodic hand waving that progressed to the making of silly faces. The more unusual the grimaces, the more the two girls laughed, until Aunt Margaret turned and gave them her icy blue stare and scowl. Feeling reprimanded, Thomas and Rena assumed adult behavior again.

Almost with regret, they saw the train was pulling into the station at Zanesville. Now they would have to part and go their separate ways. But the two families had agreed to meet on the grassy banks of the river for their picnic lunch.

Rena spoke to Thomas as she walked out of the train station with her mother and sister. "I hope you're successful with your shopping, Thomas." Then she disappeared into the crowd leaving the station.

CHAPTER SIX

Thomas and John found themselves standing in the shade of an awning at the front of a jewelry store. They had been appointed to watch the picnic baskets while Tom and Isaac went to the courthouse. John whittled a stick of wood with his knife while Thomas leaned against a post and watched the parade of carriages and wagons rumble past. Zanesville was a busy and prosperous-looking town.

"Are you going to buy anything today?" John said.

Thomas said, "I need some new shoes, and I should buy a heavy coat, but I don't know the cost of things here in Ohio. Do you have any idea what I'll have to pay?"

John looked up from his whittling. "Well, you might be able to buy some plow shoes for a dollar, but if you want some good, sturdy boots you'll have to pay three dollars. My heavy winter coat cost about four dollars last year."

Thomas chewed his lower lip. His serious expression changed to a frown that didn't escape John's notice.

"About how much did you plan to spend?" John said.

Thomas admitted that his uncle had given him only eight dollars for one month's pay. "I've worked for more than a month and I don't know when he plans to pay me again."

"Just between the two of us, Thomas, Uncle Tom is awful tight with his money. I think you'll have to keep reminding him that he owes you." John lowered his voice and leaned close to Thomas. "Dad found out that his last hired helper left because he wasn't paid the agreed amount. I don't know how Uncle Tom can expect people to work for next to nothing." John appeased his conscience for saying these derogatory remarks by adding, "But he runs his farm well and he's a good husband to Aunt Margaret."

Clouds covered the sun and a cool breeze caused them to button their jackets. When the wind blew dust in their faces, they picked up the baskets and moved close to the building.

John said, "I don't like the looks of this. We may get a rain storm before the day is over."

Thomas said, "What will we do about the picnic?"

We've eaten our lunch inside the train depot before, and we may have to again today." John pushed his elbow into Thomas's arm and gave him a playful shove. "You and Rena won't have such a romantic setting as the river bank, but you can snuggle up to her on the hard wooden bench at the depot."

Thomas laughed in his embarrassment, then countered with, "It's a shame you can't meet my sister, Maggie. She would knock you off your feet with her good looks. She has all the fellows mooning over her when we go to church on Sunday."

"Tell me more. Is she coming to Ohio?"

Tom and Isaac came around the corner at that moment and greeted the two young men who were more than ready to have some freedom. Isaac stopped them, pulled out his pocket watch and looked at the time.

"It's a few minutes past eleven. You two meet us at the train depot in one hour if it's raining. If we don't get rain, then meet us down on the riverbank."

The boys nodded and left in a hurry. John said, "Follow me, Thomas. We both need shoes and I can show you the best place to buy them."

An hour later, relentless rain was pounding down on the town of Zanesville. Thomas and John ran down Market Street and across the tracks to the train depot. They tried to protect their purchases, which were wrapped in paper and bound with string, but the wind-driven rain soaked everything. When they pushed their way inside they met a crowd of people who were escaping the rain as they were. Thomas, who was taller than John, looked over the tops of many heads and saw his uncle's old hat.

"I see them over there in the far corner." Thomas nodded in that direction as he led the way.

Aunt Margaret and her sister were handing out food to Sarah, Emma, and Rena. The women found just enough bench space for themselves and the girls, but the men and boys had to stand while they ate boiled eggs, and buttered slices of bread filled with generous pieces of ham.

When they were through eating, Aunt Margaret informed them all, "Our train for home won't be pulling in until half-past three. It's miserable out there in that pouring rain, so we'll have to stay here and wait."

Hannah politely contradicted her sister. "There are a few things we still need to buy, so the girls and I will have to go out and finish our shopping, I'm afraid."

Margaret said, "Well, you can suit yourself. Sarah and I are staying right here."

As it turned out, the rain stopped completely before two o'clock. Most of the family members left the depot and scattered to various parts of town leaving Margaret and the forlorn Sarah sitting inside the empty depot to watch over all the packages.

The train ride home was not nearly as interesting as the ride to Zanesville. Aunt Margaret told Thomas to sit with Sarah and keep her from acting silly, but what she really meant was that she disapproved of his and Rena's behavior which caused the uncontrolled laughter of the two small girls.

Rena had to sit next to Emma, and soon the young child's body was draped across her big sister's in deep slumber so that Rena couldn't turn and glance back at Thomas.

Thomas half-listened to Sarah's chatter about her new school supplies, new shoes, and all the other things she wished she could have but didn't. To himself, he wondered when they would be making the next trip to Zanesville. This had been the best day of his life.

Saturday evening after supper Tom sat at the kitchen table making entries in his ledger while his wife finished sweeping the floor. Thomas was outside making a final check on the animals, and Sarah was upstairs in her bedroom. Margaret hung her apron on the hook in the pantry and sat at the table across from her husband. It was obvious she wanted to talk because she cleared her throat and patted the well-worn table top with her hand. Tom looked up from his large book, ready to listen.

Margaret said, "I haven't heard you say anything about Thomas lately. Are you pleased with your nephew's work?"

Tom scratched his graying beard. "Well, I have to admit, he's a hard-working boy. He nearly has that five acres cleared and he's done most of it by himself. I'll need to get Isaac and John over here so they can take home a load of firewood; that should pay Isaac for the use of his mules when we go to pull out those stumps."

Margaret pursued the topic of his nephew. "If you ask me, Thomas has some growing up to do."

Tom nodded. "He's still a boy in a man's frame."

Margaret complained, "He and Rena acted like a couple of fools on the train when they got Sarah and Emma to laughing and giggling the way they did. They set a bad example for those girls."

"You did the right thing by separating them on the way home."

Margaret's accusing tone softened. "But you know, Sarah thinks the world of Thomas, and in many ways, he's helped her become more responsible. Since he came, Sarah hardly ever complains about her chores. She works with me in the kitchen and helps with work around the house. I almost hate to see her go off to school on Monday."

As an afterthought, Margaret added, "You know Tom, that boy looks enough like you to be your own son."

Caught off guard, Tom admitted, "Sometimes I get to thinking of him as my son and then he asks for his pay and I'm brought back to my senses."

Tom signaled that the conversation was over by looking back down at the ledger on the table before him. He began writing in the amounts paid out in the past week for sugar, kerosene, and a length of hemp rope.

Monday morning arrived in a burst of golden sunshine. Unlike the calm weather, Sarah's excitement kept the household in a whirlwind of activity. Thomas thought his cousin was being too dramatic about such an ordinary event as going back to school. She changed her mind three times over the color of ribbons to wear in her hair, and then she couldn't decide whether she should take an extra apple to school for her teacher. When she finally mounted Belle, with her dinner pail and books strapped onto the front of the saddle, Sarah's face was a pink glow.

Thomas had been asked to escort Sarah to school on this, her first day in the fourth grade. He sat on Beauty's back and waited for an end to Aunt Margaret's final admonishing words to her daughter. At last, he and Sarah rode out onto the lane, headed for Wilderness School. It was only a mile to the school and Sarah could have walked, but most of the other children rode horses and Sarah insisted on riding, too.

Soon they caught up with a group of children on horseback. The older ones were laughing and exchanging comments about school and the new teacher.

"Hey mister. Are you goin' t'school and learn how t'read 'n write, too?"

Thomas realized the small, freckle-faced boy was speaking to him. "No, I've already completed my schooling. I'm riding along with my cousin, Sarah, here. She's in the fourth grade."

The young boy grinned, revealing the lack of two front teeth. He rode behind an older girl, the two of them on a broken down, old horse. He said of the girl who was obviously his sister, "Ellie's goin' t'be all finished with school next year, but I'm in the first grade."

Ellie tried to look grown up as she smiled at Thomas. Her freckles were fewer than her brother's and her teeth were complete.

A boy of ten or eleven years called out to the first-grader. "My brother, here, is in first grade, too." He pointed with his thumb to the very small child riding behind him. "His name is Nathaniel. What's yours?"

"My name's George. Hullo 'Thaniel." He shined his jack-o-lantern grin at Nathaniel who waved back and shyly ducked his head.

Thomas felt very mature as he listened to the children who were attempting to hide their apprehensions and fears at the start of a new school year.

When they arrived at the schoolhouse and dismounted, Sarah was greeted with an enthusiastic hug from Emma. Some other children ran over to her with the news that their new teacher was not old and bald as Master Green had been. The oldest boy reported the new teacher was very tall with a full head of black hair.

Immediately the schoolhouse door opened. A gaunt young man stood in the doorway and began ringing a large hand bell. He was dressed in black formal clothes and his pale face was frozen in a sour expression of distaste, as if he had eaten something that disagreed with him. His pained expression and distant gaze filled the students with dread as they lined up at the door and watched him shake the bell.

At last, he became aware that all sixteen children were in front of him, waiting expectantly. He silenced the bell and barked, "Two straight lines. Boys on this side." He sliced the air with a long finger that could have been a knife. "Girls over here." The knife sliced through the air again and a strange grimace of his face displayed crooked, decaying teeth.

Thomas imagined the youngest children would see themselves as victims to be clutched by the bony hands and devoured by the dangerous teeth of this ogre.

Thomas staked out Sarah's horse for her and walked over to the two lines of children at the schoolhouse steps. He leaned over to Sarah and said a soft 'goodbye'. Sarah looked at him with tears glistening in her eyes. "'Bye, Thomas," she said. Her lower lip quivered and a tear escaped to roll down her cheek, but Sarah quickly wiped it away.

The new teacher cleared his throat and glared at Thomas with black, malevolent eyes. Thomas understood that it was not the time to make things worse for his small cousin by lingering to incur the wrath of her teacher. He mounted Beauty and waved to Sarah as he left the schoolyard. Sarah, Emma, Nathaniel, and George all sent him subdued little waves with their hands, as if silently pleading with Thomas to take them with him.

Out on the road toward home, Thomas wondered what might be in store for Sarah and her classmates this day. He also wondered what he should tell Sarah's mother or if he should say anything at all.

CHAPTER SEVEN

At last, the wood was cut, and stacked. Thomas looked on the rows and felt a certain amount of pride for his accomplishment. In spite of the big load Isaac and John took home with them, Tom said this was enough wood to last for a year or more. But first they needed to use up the seasoned wood in the shed.

At home in Ireland they never used wood for heating. They bought coal from England and turf from the ancient Irish bogs. His mother preferred to use coal in the kitchen for cooking and heating water. It was his father who enjoyed the glow of the turf fire in the front room. Long winter evenings he would often sit in his high–back chair before the fire. The family could be busy all around him, but Dad would gaze quietly at the fire as if looking back to a time that Thomas would never know. Those brief evening hours were the only moments Thomas could recall when his father was idle.

The new field was cleared, except for the stumps, and Thomas was working on those now. Before attempting to pull them out with Isaac's team of mules, Thomas needed to dig a trench around each of the largest stumps and cut away the big roots. He hacked at them with his axe, thinking how much stronger he felt compared to those first days back in July when he began clearing this field.

Not long ago Aunt Margaret had exclaimed, "My, but you have filled out, Thomas! Why, just look how your shirt fits so tight around you. I think it's time for me to make you a couple of new shirts."

It was true, his chest, arms and shoulders had expanded. Thomas admired his larger muscles when he undressed for bed, wondering if Lorena had noticed them, too. The reflection in his streaked mirror revealed a more manly face. Perhaps he should buy a razor and begin shaving.

Sarah had returned to school three weeks ago and her absence throughout the day was forcing them to adjust. Formerly, she had done all the fetching, and delivering. Now when Aunt Margaret wanted Thomas to come into the house for the noon meal she opened the kitchen door and sent Topsy out to fetch him.

Thomas looked up from his chopping to see the brown bundle of fur bouncing toward him. Topsy jumped around Thomas's legs barking out his message. Thomas reached for the small terrier and picked him up,

"We all miss Sarah, don't we Topsy?"

Topsy applied his wet tongue to Thomas's fingers.

He put the little dog down and headed for the house while Topsy danced around him all the way. Thomas stopped at the hand pump. He pulled up and down on the handle a few times to clean his face and hands in the stream of cool water that gushed forth. Topsy's pink tongue lapped from the pool at the base of the pump.

Conversation at the dinner table that day concerned the new schoolmaster. Since hearing Sarah's sinister description of him, her parents were eager to learn some facts.

Tom swallowed the last bite of his boiled turnips and said, "When I was in town today, C.J. Miller told me that the new school master is old Reverend Ferguson's grandson. In fact, he lives alone in his grandfather's house and keeps a horse and a few chickens." He reached for another slice of bread and began spreading butter on it.

"He's not twenty years old yet but he can't do any hard labor due to the fact he's been sickly all his life."

"I hope he doesn't have a disease that will make the children sick," Margaret said.

"No, Miller said the boy was born with a bad heart." Tom spread dark brown apple butter over his bread and butter. "You remember, Miller and Atkins are on the school board. They talked with young Ferguson before they hired him. He has a good education, and they thought he could do the job as well as old Master Green."

Tom took a large bite of the bread and savored it as he chewed. Between bites, he explained to his nephew, "Master Green was so deaf he most likely never heard a thing that went on in the classroom. But he was a kindly old gentleman, and the children loved him." Tom added with a hint of a smile, "Whether they learned much is doubtful."

Thomas said, "Master Ferguson didn't warm our hearts with his cordial ways but I think he was uncertain about proper proceedings on the first day of school. And the bad heart explains why he looked so thin and pale. He must be a scholarly chap if he's spent most of his life reading and studying." Thomas impressed himself with his own thoughtful remarks.

Tom said, "According to Miller, young Ferguson studied for two terms at the college in New Concord. He was advised by his doctor to give up the idea of going into the ministry. Told him it could shorten his life even more. Said teaching school might be easier on him."

Margaret brought hot coffee for her husband and herself.

Tom raised his cup to drink and stopped. He said to Margaret, "Thomas might want a cup of coffee, too." He turned to Thomas. "Aren't you about sixteen years old now? Time you tried it. You'll like the flavor better than any tea you ever drank in Ireland. They say it isn't good for young children, but you're not a child now."

"I'll be sixteen on the second of December. Yes, I'd be pleased to have some coffee." Thomas beamed with pleasure.

"I'll put some milk in your cup," said Aunt Margaret. "If you're not used to coffee, it'll taste too strong without the milk."

Thomas sipped the richly flavored warm drink, enjoying it as Tom had promised. Their acceptance of him as a young adult was an agreeable experience. When Sarah was here, they regarded him as an older child, expecting him to set an example for her just as his own parents expected their older children to exemplify proper behavior to the younger members of the family. In Sarah's absence, he was being allowed into the adult world of this very practical couple. His parents had never discussed controversial issues or encouraged disagreeable topics at the table. But with only the three of them at this table, things were different. Conversations at the noonday meals provided Thomas with insights into the opinions and prejudices of his uncle and aunt.

Thomas was not surprised to learn his relatives held little regard for several other churches in the area, each of which proclaimed to possess the 'true faith'. Though he had never given much thought to theological differences, he was well aware of the strong disagreements between the 1st and 2nd Presbyterian churches at home in Markethill.

Tom explained, "I suppose they are all Christians but the different churches around here can't agree on much of anything. During the war-between-the-states they spent all their efforts tearing one another apart over the question of slavery. It was a sad time." Tom looked as sad as he sounded.

Margaret added her thoughts. "Worst of all, good men like our former minister, Reverend Wilkins, who didn't want to take sides, became the target for rumors and slander."

"Yes, that's true," Tom said. It's a good thing you weren't old enough to come over here during that time, Thomas. Many boys from Union Township lost their lives in the bloody war. Andy Lorimer lost his son, Harold. He was a fine young man, and I know they miss him."

Attempting to change the subject, Margaret said to Thomas, "In the letter you received yesterday from your mother, did she say anything about your brother, the one who's going to be a doctor?"

"Mother wrote that Gilbert will be completing his studies at Edinburgh University next May. He's studying hard to pass all his exams."

Tom said, "Gilbert should be a good doctor. Any town he goes to will be fortunate to have him." He made a sour expression with his mouth and slowly shook his head. "I haven't seen a doctor worth his salt since I came over here."

Tom gazed absently into his cup and complained, "Ol' Doc MacKenna came to Norwich about fifteen years ago thinking he needed to run everybody's business. He attended church only now and then, but he managed to stir up enough trouble that he caused a split in the church and we lost half our members. That's when they started up the *United* Presbyterian Church." Tom sat back in the kitchen chair and crossed his arms over his chest. "Then just a few years ago, Doc Given tried to tell me how to run my own farm. I had to tell him it wasn't any of his business."

"Now, Tom, you know it won't do you any good to talk about that," Margaret said. "It's all water under the bridge."

"You're right." Tom sighed and raised his cup toward her for more coffee.

Margaret filled all three cups again, remembering to add milk to Thomas's. "Did your mother say anything else about your brother, the one who's studying to be a doctor?"

Thomas said, "Mum wrote that Gilbert hopes to be the new doctor in Markethill. She said there is talk of Doctor Pringle retiring in a few years and Gilbert may be able to take his place."

"It's been a long time since I thought about old Doctor Pringle...he was the father of the present Doctor Pringle." Smiling, Tom said, "I'll never forget the time Dad's shoulder came out of its socket, and Doc Pringle came out to the farm. He pulled on my father's arm until we thought it would come off. Dad was grittin' his teeth and sweatin', Will and I were tryin' to hold him still, and Doc Pringle was turnin' red in the face. He finally got it back in place, but he earned his pay that day."

Margaret interjected, "I should think your parents will be very happy to have Gilbert as their doctor in the nearest town."

Tom raised his graying brows and looked at his nephew. "I've wondered how my brother could afford to send one of his sons off to Edinburgh University to study medicine. It must cost a dear price for such an education."

A note of pride crept into his voice as Thomas explained. "If you remember, my mother's family, the McKinleys are from Scotland. She has an uncle and some cousins who studied at Edinburgh University and one is a doctor over there now." Thomas drank the last of his coffee and set his cup down. "I was not told this, but I believe my Grandfather McKinley has paid much of the cost for Gilbert's education."

Margaret stood and began stacking the dirty dishes on the wooden counter top where the wash basin sat in readiness. She turned and said to Thomas, "You should sit down tonight and answer that letter. Tom will add a few lines and we can all send our regards to your family for Christmas."

Tom stood up and put on his hat. "Speaking of Christmas, it will be here before we know it. Let's get Beauty and those two mares ready, Thomas. Jenkins said he'd shoe them today if we got them there before two o'clock."

Thomas whistled a jaunty tune as he strode out to the pasture to bring in the horses.

On a Saturday morning in late November they woke to see a layer of glistening snow on the ground and roof tops. The snow melted quickly but Sarah's enthusiasm for the arrival of winter's joys had remained.

Thomas thought he could live without snow for a while longer, but he kept silent throughout the discussion at their noonday meal. He put some potatoes on his plate and passed the bowl to his cousin.

Sarah put a potato on her plate and said, "Daddy, can we go to town and buy some colored paper and special things to decorate our house for Christmas?"

"There's no hurry, Sarah. Christmas won't be here for a few weeks." Tom smiled at his daughter's eagerness.

Margaret spoke up, siding with Sarah. "It may be too early to decorate for Christmas but it's not too early to think about gifts. I'll be needing more yarn, and fabrics and threads for sewing. We always exchange gifts with Hannah's family and there are five of them. We need to plan a trip to town right away."

"If you think it's necessary," Tom agreed

Roger Davis
174 ?

reluctantly.

Margaret emphasized her point. "I hear they have some new wool cloth at Walker's store. I think we should all go to town this afternoon."

Thomas listened and wondered if he would be able to buy any gifts to give this Christmas. He dreaded asking his uncle for money again, but he remembered what John Cole had said: 'Don't let him forget that he owes you.'

After dinner, as the two worked together to repair the barnyard gate, Thomas spoke to his uncle. "With Christmas coming, I'd be glad to have my back pay so I can buy some gifts." Thomas felt as though he were five years old, and was afraid he sounded that age as well.

An evasive look came over Tom's face and he became very intent on his work. At last he said, "Well now, didn't I pay you just a while back?"

Thomas tried to sound confident. "You've paid me only eight dollars since I've been here. The agreement was eighteen dollars a month, minus ten for my room and board, and I've been working here almost four months."

Tom was silent. He went to get another tool from the machine shed and when he returned he did not look at his nephew.

Determined, Thomas pressed on. "I have tried to give you my best work. I think I deserve to be paid."

Tom said, "We'll see."

When it came time to leave for town Thomas received ten dollars in gold coin, which his uncle handed to him in front of Aunt Margaret and Sarah as if it were a generous gift. His uncle still owed him several dollars. The whole day was ruined for Thomas, and he wondered how he could be related to such a stingy man. He came home from town with the same ten dollars in his pocket and a heart full of loathing for his uncle.

Tom frowned and tightened his mouth. "These sows are all sick with cholera." He stood up after his close inspection and looked at his nephew. "Didn't you notice the discharge from their snouts?"

Thomas nodded. "I think I told you about it two days ago. Some had loose bowels yesterday."

"The boar isn't sick yet but his eyes aren't right." Tom shook his head in resignation. "Well, from the looks of things they are the same as dead right now. I've never known any hogs to recover from it." Tom wiped his face with his sleeve. "Thank God we butchered two healthy hogs before this happened."

Three days later they dragged the dead hogs behind Mac and Maddie to a far edge of the field where they poured kerosene over the carcasses and burned them. Thomas worked to clean out the piggery and nearly became sick himself. The stench left by the sick and dying hogs was close to unbearable.

His uncle was downcast and filled with gloom, but Aunt Margaret looked on the bright side. "We have our hams and pork for the months to come and you won't have to feed and care for hogs over the winter. You can buy a few pigs in the spring."

Thomas thought his Aunt Margaret had more common sense than the ordinary farmer's wife. Secretly, he wondered if she was in agreement with her husband over the wages Thomas hardly ever received. As he mulled it over in his mind he decided that she probably knew nothing of the situation. Thomas almost wished there were some honorable way to inform her, but his better judgment told him this was not a possibility.

CHAPTER EIGHT

"Thomas, it's the most beautiful doll I've ever seen!"

Sarah held the doll up for all to see, and then she twirled around the room with her doll lifted high. She was excited and animated, speaking in a loud voice.

"Look at her golden hair and blue eyes. And her long white dress is so pretty with the ribbons down the front. She is perfect!"

Margaret admonished her daughter with a rare gentleness. "Sarah, you need to lower your voice, and tell Thomas, 'thank you'"

"Yes, thank you, Thomas. Thank you very much." Sarah's face glowed with pleasure. "This is the best Christmas gift I ever had."

Her parents gave her a lovely dark-green coat with a white fur collar but she was enthralled with her new doll.

Margaret said, "Thomas, that is a very nice doll, but you didn't need to buy such a costly gift."

Thomas tried to explain. "If I were at home I would give only small gifts to my sisters and brothers because there are so many of them. But Sarah is the only child here, and I thought... well, I thought she might like this doll."

"I've never had such a beautiful doll." Sarah kissed its porcelain face. The doll's glass eyes reflected the blue in Sarah's eyes, and its hair was the color of wheat fields at harvest time. A perfect small mouth smiled between rose-colored cheeks. The head, arms and hands, and legs and feet were made of porcelain, but the doll's cloth body was stuffed with sawdust.

Thomas had seen the doll in town a few days before Christmas. Though he had but ten dollars, he decided to spend four of them on this gift to Sarah. He knew Sarah would be pleased with it.

Thinking back to that same day, Thomas remembered the gold locket hanging from a delicate gold chain in Meyer's window. It was elegant with a green gemstone mounted in the middle of the oval shape. He went inside, thinking he would buy the locket for Rena, but was disappointed to learn it was too costly. Mr. Meyer showed him another gold locket with a floral design engraved on its surface. Thomas had just enough to pay for this one so he handed over the remainder of his money to Mr. Meyer. The locket came in a blue, silk-covered box that helped to make it look special. Thomas hid the box in the top branches of the Christmas tree. Rena would be arriving with her family later on this Christmas Day.

Thomas noticed that Sarah went to her mother and whispered in her ear. Margaret nodded in agreement and Sarah skipped to the decorated tree where she reached inside the branches to retrieve a box tied with red ribbon. She handed it to Thomas.

"Mama and I chose this for you." Sarah stood next to Thomas' chair to watch him open the gift.

Inside, he found a white china mug, which held a cake of soap. Next to the mug lay a brush, and another compartment held a shiny metal razor, its sharp, straight blade folded into the handle. Thomas didn't know what to say. He looked up to see his cousin and his aunt smiling at him. Even his uncle looked pleased.

"Thank you." Thomas stammered, "It's a very…useful gift."

Aunt Margaret spoke with her usual voice of authority. "You have time to try it out before the Coles come. Come in the kitchen and I'll get the basin ready for you."

She ushered him into the kitchen, took the basin from a hook on the wall, and filled it with warm water from the kettle on the stove. As she left, she said to Sarah, who had followed them, "We'll wait in the front room while Thomas shaves his face."

Thomas stepped into the pantry room just off the kitchen, and placed the basin on top of a waist-high storage cupboard. He lit the lantern that hung from a hook on the wall, just as his uncle always did when he shaved. Thomas removed his shirt and looked into the mirror on the wall, hoping he could do this without slicing himself open. Lathering his face with soap, he tried to remember exactly how his own father held the blade. He turned his face as far as he could, making sure he could still see himself in the mirror, then made the first long swipe across his jaw. Thomas looked closely and saw his skin was perfectly smooth and bare. Another swipe and Thomas was beginning to feel confident. He attempted to clean off his upper lip with short quick strokes of the blade and that's when the blood began to flow. Thomas leaned over the basin and washed away blood until he had a basin full of red water. With his thumb he pressed the bleeding cut while he counted silently to one hundred. When he released the pressure, the cut had stopped bleeding. Very carefully he shaved the rest of his face, drawing blood only one more time. Finally, his face and neck were clean and smooth. The cuts were evident, but Thomas felt pride in the fact that now he was a man who shaved.

Tom came in to check on his nephew's progress. He saw the basin full of red water, looked at Thomas's face, and tried to suppress a smile.

"Sometimes shaving can be a risky business," Tom said. He reached for the towel that hung near the mirror and handed it to Thomas. "Don't forget to dry your blade on this, and then it would be a good idea to sharpen it on the strop a few times before you put it away."

Thomas did as his uncle advised. When his new shaving articles were put away, he put on his shirt and stepped outside with the basin to dump the water. His feet crunched through a thin layer of old snow that remained on the shady side of the house. There was no need to advertise he was a novice at shaving, so instead of dumping the red water on the snow, he threw it into some bushes that resembled upright sticks in the winter. He scooped up a handful of snow to clean out the basin, and then because he was reluctant to meet the stares and grins waiting for him inside, he placed the basin by the back door and made a visit to the privy.

He was chilled and shivering when he came back into the kitchen. His senses were overwhelmed with the warmth and delicious aromas of baking ham, roasting turkey, and boiled potatoes. His aunt and cousin were too busy to notice him. Sarah stood on a stool in front of the big black cook stove helping her mother by stirring a sauce in a small pot. Aunt Margaret was in charge, giving out orders and warnings to be careful. Thomas saw that Topsy stayed in the corner where his basket was a refuge from Aunt Margaret's hurrying feet.

Aunt Margaret called out orders for Thomas. "Go put on your heavy coat, Thomas, and bring in wood for the stove. You can stack a large pile here behind the stove and then make sure we have a good supply right outside the door. But first, look and see if we need more wood for the heat stove in the front room."

Her full face was pink and moist with perspiration. She bent down and opened the oven to check on its contents, releasing more mouth-watering smells into the room.

Thomas put on his coat and went about his task. As he brought load after load of wood to the house, he remembered all the pleasurable times of the past few days and felt guilty that he didn't miss his own family in Ireland.

Last Friday there was a program at Sarah's school, and the little schoolhouse was packed with families who came to see the performance. Saturday, Tom took Sarah and Thomas with him to find a tree. They inspected many fine trees and finally found the perfect one to cut down. Saturday night, the young people in the church went caroling around the town. Thomas and Rena sang with the group but stayed close together, often holding hands. Afterward, they were invited into the pastor's manse to warm up with hot tea and cakes.

Last night, which was Christmas Eve, Tom and Thomas hauled in the sweet-smelling evergreen tree and set it up in the front room. All four of them helped to decorate the tree with ribbons and an assortment of ornaments from a big box. Aunt Margaret attached many small candles to the branches and when they were lit, the little family was enthralled by the beauty of the tree.

"Oooh, it's perfectly amazing and wonderful!" Sarah said in a near whisper.

They all had to admit it was one of the prettiest Christmas trees they had ever seen. Tom passed around the colorful hard candies he had purchased in town, and Aunt Margaret served them cups of hot chocolate, which was a rare treat.

Late last night as he was dropping off to sleep, Thomas remembered his family in Ireland and wondered if they were thinking of him. It was already Christmas Day there and they would be up and busy getting ready for a feast.

Thomas placed the last load of wood on the huge stack outside the kitchen door and covered it with burlap in case it began to snow again. Rex barked and Thomas looked out to the lane to see the Cole family arriving in their wagon. John followed his family on horseback. Thomas hurried to the wagon, and Tom came from the barn to greet them.

"Merry Christmas! Merry Christmas!" they shouted to one another.

Isaac jumped down from the wagon. "I'm telling you, this is a biting cold Christmas Day! Most of the animals are inside at our place, and I hope there's room for our horses in your barn."

"We'll make room for them," Tom said. "John can help us get them unhitched and in the barn while Thomas unloads your wagon."

Thomas helped Hannah down from the wagon, and then reached to help Rena. She studied his face for a moment, noticing his smooth skin.

"Thomas, you look... you look good." Rena smiled.

"You look good, too," Thomas replied.

"Isn't anybody going to help me get down?" Emma's voice informed them she was growing impatient.

Thomas teased, "We thought you might want to stay out here and guard the wagon, Emma." He swung her down to the ground.

"Don't be silly, Thomas. It's too cold out here." Emma stuffed her hands inside her coat pockets and scurried off to greet her cousin, Sarah. Her mother and sister smiled at Thomas and followed Emma to the house.

Thomas brought in armloads of things from the

Cole family's wagon. There were covered baskets filled with food, gifts tied with ribbons, and blankets that had been wrapped around the family members as they traveled.

When everyone was inside, the excitement increased. They all exclaimed over the good smells of hot food. Sarah had to show off her new doll, and Emma displayed a small garnet ring on her finger, which everyone admired. Rena showed them her new hair combs and described the new dresser set she had received. John had a new pocket watch, which he pulled out and exhibited with pride.

Emma looked up at Thomas. "What did you get for Christmas?"

Thomas didn't know what to say. He felt his face growing hot.

Margaret spoke for him to explain the gift of shaving articles they had given him. "He already used his new razor and he only cut his face twice. Doesn't he look handsome?"

Thomas wished he could sink out of sight as all eyes surveyed his face to locate the cuts.

Margaret began giving orders. "You men move out of the kitchen now while we get this dinner ready to serve."

In half an hour the ladies began bringing bowls and platters of food to the table. With the table loaded and the sideboard groaning, all nine of them stood together and bowed their heads for the blessing. All eyes were closed except for Sarah's and Emma's. The girls stole glances at one another and stifled giggles.

Tom spoke reverently. "Heavenly Father, we thank Thee for the many blessings Thou hast bestowed upon us. On this Christmas Day we remember Thy Son who came into this world as a babe. We are grateful for Thy loving kindness, and ask for Thy continued guidance. In the name of Jesus Christ, our Lord and Savior, we pray."

All voices joined together to say, "Amen."

They sat down to a feast. Thomas had never seen such a large variety of foods. Some of the dishes were not familiar to him but he tried them all. Most of all, he enjoyed the special dessert, which Aunt Margaret made. It was plum pudding with a flavorful sauce poured over the top. His aunt had some qualities he would change if he could, but her cooking was not one of them.

When dinner was over the women and girls removed all the dishes and remaining food to the kitchen while the two young men moved the table back against the wall. Everyone found a place to sit and the little girls handed out the gifts. Each person had at least one gift to open and Thomas was surprised to see he had two. They took turns opening them so that the contents could be seen and appreciated by all.

Emma, who was the youngest, opened her package first. She untied the red ribbon, pulled the white paper away, and held up a full skirt which was made of navy blue wool and trimmed with a brighter blue band near the bottom. Her Aunt Margaret had taken much care in its construction. Hannah prompted her little daughter to remember her manners and say, 'thank you'.

Sarah opened her present and found a lovely hand mirror with matching brush and comb from the Cole family. This was the sort of gift given to an older girl and Sarah wore a proud look on her face as she thanked everyone in the Cole family.

Rena was next to open a gift. She also had two gifts, one from the Keith family, and a small blue box from Thomas. They all urged her to open the small box first.

'Ooohs' and 'aaahs' filled the room when Rena held

up her gold locket suspended from its gold chain. Her mother helped Rena put the locket on, and more words of admiration and praise followed.

Rena looked at Thomas and, all at once, she became very shy and lowered her voice as she spoke. "It's a beautiful locket, Thomas. Thank you."

"Now open your other gift, Rena." Emma was anxious to get on with the opening of gifts.

Rena's gift from the Keith family was a skirt identical to Emma's except it was made from gray wool and trimmed with a band of black. Rena looked at it with the eyes of one who understands all the work involved in its creation. "Thank you, Aunt Margaret; it's a lovely skirt."

Emma continued to hurry things along. "Open the flat package, Thomas. It's from Rena."

When Thomas opened Rena's gift to him, he found a white shirt with a small pleated trim down the front to hide the buttons.

"This is the nicest dress shirt I've ever owned. Did you make it yourself?" he said.

"Yes, I hope it will fit you. Aunt Margaret helped with the measurements."

Soon all the presents were opened. Hannah and Margaret made shawls for one another. Tom, Isaac, John, and Thomas found hand knitted wool socks and gloves in their packages. Exclamations and words of thanks rang out around the room.

Margaret stood. "Sarah, you and Emma gather up all the wrapping papers and ribbons," she said. "Be careful to fold the paper and wind up the ribbons so we can use them next year, then pile it all right here on my chair."

Eager to please, the two little girls began their task. Margaret went to the large upright piano, pulled out the bench and opened up the keyboard. She motioned to Rena. "Do you want to play the piano so we can sing?"

Hannah spoke up. "Margaret, don't you think we should start washing up in the kitchen? We can sing later."

Magnanimously, Margaret agreed with her sister. "You're right. The longer we put it off the worse it will be." She gathered the papers and ribbons the small girls had placed on her chair and opened a closet door under the stairway. Margaret reached to the top shelf to put them away. She backed her ample figure out of the closet, straightened her dress and said, "But this would be a good time for Sarah to show you something she has learned." Margaret beckoned to Sarah and pointed to the piano. "Come and show them, Sarah."

Sarah very carefully placed her hands in the correct position. Hesitantly, she played a simple version of the Christmas hymn, 'Away in a Manger'. When Sarah finished everyone exclaimed over her accomplishment.

Her Aunt Hannah said. "Sarah, that was lovely. When did you begin learning to play?"

"Mama started teaching me right after school began this year, and I practice almost every day." Sarah looked at her older cousin and announced, "I want to learn how to play as well as Rena."

Rena smiled at Sarah in appreciation.

Margaret stood. "Let's start to work in the kitchen."

Hannah and the girls followed her to clean up after the large meal.

At Tom's suggestion, Thomas and John went out to feed and water the animals, leaving Tom and Isaac alone to enjoy a quiet conversation in the front room. Tom settled back in his chair to relax after the sumptuous meal. He watched as his brother-in-law tamped down the tobacco in his pipe and lit it with a thin stick of kindling. Margaret didn't like to be in the same room with pipe smoke and Isaac had waited for this moment when the ladies were out of the room. He found a chair across from Tom and sat down with a satisfied smile.

Isaac exhaled a cloud of smoke. "Another Christmas has come and nearly gone. Our farms have prospered this year, and we've just completed a meal fit for a king." A look of pleasure spread across his face as he inhaled and released another plume of smoke from his lips. "I'd say we should consider ourselves well blessed, don't you agree?"

Tom crossed his arms over his chest. "Well, I guess this year would have been better if all my hogs hadn't died of cholera. It's a good thing we butchered two before the sickness came."

They sat in silence for a while and at last Tom said, "I almost never think of the old home country except at Christmas. I wouldn't go back there to stay, but I remember my brothers and sisters, and old friends in Ireland. It's been so many years, I wonder if we would know one another."

Isaac smiled around his pipe stem as the smoke curled above his head. He removed the pipe from his mouth and said, "I think you are more homesick than your nephew is. Thomas seems perfectly happy here." He put the pipe back to his mouth briefly, then withdrew it. "That nephew of yours has been a good addition to our combined families." Isaac looked at Tom. "You know, he looks enough like you to be your own son."

This was the second time a member of the family had mentioned the resemblance between Tom and his nephew. "I sometimes get to feeling that he *is* my own son, then he asks for his payment and that spoils the illusion."

Isaac said, "Well, your nephew seems to be smitten with my daughter. That was not a cheap locket he gave her."

Tom retorted, "That locket must have cost him most of a month's pay. The boy has no idea of the value of money. It's for his own good that I don't give him all his pay at once." Tom made no mention of the fact that he was behind in paying Thomas what he owed.

Isaac merely smoked his pipe in calm silence.

Sarah and Emma came in and sat down on the carpet in front of the Christmas tree. Sarah wanted to show her cousin the new doll, including every small detail of its clothing and hair. Isaac and Tom looked on in amusement.

"Can I hold her, Sarah?" Emma was almost pleading.

Reluctantly, Sarah handed over her precious doll. "Be very careful. Her head will break if you drop her."

"She is so beautiful. I wish I had a doll like her." Emma touched the doll's golden hair and fingered the white satin ribbons on its dress. "What did you name her?"

"Her name is Rena," Sarah said.

"But you can't call her Rena. That's my sister's name." Emma was indignant.

"I can call her any name I want," Sarah said. "Besides, Thomas gave her to me and he is in love with Rena."

Tom decided this was enough. "Sarah, take the doll up to your room now. We don't need any disagreements on Christmas Day."

Sarah snatched her doll away from Emma and left.

Thomas and John burst into the room, their arms filled with firewood, and faces reddened by the cold. They announced that the animals were fed and watered and everything was secure. Thomas stoked up the fire in the big pot-bellied stove and the two young men warmed themselves over the radiating heat.

Rubbing his hands together, John said, "It's almost dark and the snow is coming down thick and fast. If it keeps snowing like this we may have to stay here 'til morning."

Emma heard this and looked at her father. "Daddy, can we stay overnight?"

Isaac stood and knocked the ashes from his pipe into the stove. He sat down again and smiled at Emma. "That would please you, wouldn't it?"

"Oh yes, it would be the best kind of Christmas if we could stay here." Emma was so happy and excited she forgot her conflict with Sarah. When Sarah came down the stairs, Emma ran to her and said, "It's snowing, and we might stay the night." The two cousins embraced while they hopped about the room, laughing.

The women came in from the kitchen. Margaret said, "What's all this commotion in here?"

They all laughed because it truly was a commotion.

Tom explained. "John said the snow is coming down thick and fast. That means we need to think about where we'll all sleep tonight." He was grinning along with everyone else.

Margaret ended any discussion with her final words on the matter. "Of course, the women and girls will sleep upstairs, the men and boys downstairs. Now, let's gather around the piano. I want to sing, don't you all?"

Isaac interrupted and said in a worried voice, "Our animals at home need to be fed and watered." He looked at his son, and said, "The only way we can stay overnight is if you are willing to ride home and take care of those chores."

Tom said, "Thomas will help him and they should be back in a couple of hours."

After John and Thomas left, Rena played the piano and they sang many songs of the season. Hannah's and Isaac's voices joined together weaving perfect harmony to the melody carried by the others. Tom passed around the last of the candies, saving two pieces for John and Thomas.

When the two young men returned chilled from the cold, Margaret made a pot of hot chocolate and gave John and Thomas large portions in two big mugs. Everyone drank hot chocolate while Tom lit the candles on the tree. The whole room was hushed as they admired the tree's beauty. More songs and laughter followed, warming the house with joy while the cold, silent snow continued to fall outside. Tom looked about the room at all these happy faces and suddenly he felt very blessed indeed.

CHAPTER NINE

The men and boys woke with the first light. Their beds were uncomfortable pallets laid out on the front room floor and they were eager to be up, moving about. Thomas and John built roaring fires in the stoves to warm the house and heat water while Tom walked up to the top stair and called out to the women, "We're up and have the fires going."

Margaret opened the bedroom door just a crack and said, "We'll be down in a few minutes. Tell Thomas and John to clear a path to the privy. The chamber pots are full."

"The first thing we have to do is shovel a path to the privy," Tom said when he returned to the front room. "Thomas, you and John go to the barn and get the shovels."

Dressed in warm coats, gloves and hats, the young men opened the door and encountered a bank of snow that came up above their knees. It was a world of white broken only by the black outline of leafless trees and dark walls of the barn and outbuildings. Thomas and John trudged through drifts of snow while cold air filled their lungs and returned as white puffs of vapor.

Tom and Isaac also went out to the barn and met the young men headed back with shovels over their shoulders. Without stopping, Tom said, "We'll take care of the stock while you boys shovel."

Chores completed, they sat down to a hurried breakfast of warmed leftover ham and potatoes. Isaac was concerned about his animals at home; they would have no water until he and John cleared away the ice.

Tom chewed and swallowed a mouthful of ham. "You won't be goin' anywhere in your wagon while the snow is this deep. I think we'd best move the sleigh out of the shed and hitch your horses to it."

Isaac nodded in agreement. "Wagon wheels won't move in those snowdrifts."

As soon as they had eaten, Tom, Isaac and the boys went out to the machinery shed to wrestle with equipment, clearing a path for the sleigh to be moved outside. They hitched up Isaac's horses, wiped most of the accumulated dirt from the seats in the sleigh, and began loading the Cole family's belongings into it.

Isaac, Hannah, Rena, and Emma rode in the sleigh while John, on horseback, led them out to the road. The four Keiths stood together in the snow, waving and calling out their farewells while the Coles returned their good-byes from the sleigh.

"It was a very good Christmas, and thank you for everything!" Isaac shouted. "John will return your sleigh tomorrow."

The last they heard from the sleigh as it carried the Cole family away was Emma's high-pitched voice. "Bye, Sarah. Take care of your new doll."

Margaret's sleeves were rolled up above her elbows, and her large arms and hands were white with flour as she worked the bread dough. Sarah was off to school, and Tom had gone to town. Thomas was working with a young colt in the fenced training area. From outside, she heard a voice that sounded like Sarah's.

Soon Sarah burst through the back door. The child was breathless and her hair was coming loose, straggling across her face.

"Sarah! What are doing home at this hour? It isn't

even ten o'clock."

"Oh, Mama…." Sarah's face was contorted. "It's terrible." She dropped her books and lunch pail on the nearest kitchen chair and ran to her mother.

Margaret hurriedly wiped her hands on the big white apron and leaned down to hold Sarah close to her bosom.

"Are you hurt, Sarah? What happened?"

Hearing only weeping, Margaret removed Sarah's coat and gloves, draping them over a chair. Her patience was growing thin because Sarah continued to cry uncontrollably. She placed her hands on either side of Sarah's face and looked directly at her.

"Tell me what's wrong, Sarah," she demanded.

Sarah spoke between sobs. "It's Master Ferguson, Mama."

"Did he hurt you, Sarah?" What did he do?" Margaret used the hem of her apron to wipe Sarah's nose. "You must stop crying and tell me."

Sarah took a deep breath and said in halting words, "We waited and waited but Master Ferguson never opened the door, not even after we pounded on it." She shuddered and expelled a trembling breath. "The big boys were able to look through the window and saw him on the floor. They said Master Ferguson was all sprawled out and he looked terrible." Sarah wailed the words, "Mama, they said he was dead."

Margaret hugged Sarah. "Oh, dear child, surely they are wrong." She gently directed her daughter to a chair. "Here, sit down and I'll have some hot tea ready for you in a few minutes."

Margaret stoked up the fire under the teakettle. "Sarah, you didn't have time to take care of Belle. You need to put on your coat and do that now while I make tea."

"Thomas saw me coming, and he took Belle into the barn. He said he'd take care of her."

Margaret consoled her daughter with hot sweet tea and a biscuit piled with apple butter. She gave Sarah a pat on the back and returned to her bread dough.

Sarah was distracted by this rare indulgence from her mother. She sat at the table, swinging her black-stockinged legs while she nibbled her treat.

Margaret punched the dough with her fist and rolled the white mound on the flat wooden surface of her flour box. She did this again and again, and as she worked she wondered what had really happened this morning. Everyone knew that Master Ferguson had a bad heart. Could he be dead at the age of twenty? The Mallory family lived closest to the school and they had surely gone to see about him by now. If he had died, where on earth would they find a new teacher at this time of year? Sarah's handwriting and arithmetic would suffer even more if she missed a half-year of school.

Dividing the dough into two mounds, she placed the rounded mounds into pans blackened from years of use. She set the pans on a long shelf above the stove for the dough to rise again, covered the pans with a clean cloth, and reached to gather some firewood. A few small logs tossed into the burning cavity now would bring the big oven to just the right heat for a perfect browning of the loaves.

Sarah spoke in a trembling voice. "Do you think someone has gone to see if Master Ferguson is really dead, Mama?"

"You don't need to worry yourself over it, Sarah. I'm sure Mr. Mallory has gone to the school by now." Margaret cleaned the surface lid of the flour box with a damp, sturdy cloth. "Besides, it could be that Master

Ferguson only stumbled and fell, and he'll be fine in two or three days." Margaret hoped this was true, but she knew it was unlikely.

From Mr. Mallory they learned that Doctor Givens came and examined Master Ferguson, pronouncing his death due to heart failure. Two days later on a cold, gray afternoon all the students of Wilderness School attended the funeral service with their families. Tears were wiped from faces of children who had grown to appreciate their school master. His sense of fairness and his love for sharing his knowledge made a lasting impression on the pupils. After the service inside the church, everyone filed out into the cemetery. Four gravesites in a row had been dug before the freezing weather arrived, and Master Ferguson's remains were to be buried in the first grave of the winter at Norwich Presbyterian Church Cemetery. Reverend Hardesty stood next to the wooden coffin to read the appropriate scriptures and say prayers.

As the weeks passed and no one came forward to teach at the Wilderness School, many parents became resigned to teaching their children at home for the remainder of the school year. Some families enrolled their children in the Norwich School but it was already overcrowded. The Cole family placed Emma in Norwich School and she had to share a bench and table designed for two small students, with three others. Margaret had mixed feelings about teaching Sarah at home but she and Tom finally decided it was the best course for their daughter.

Margaret had no problems teaching history, spelling, reading, or handwriting but she told her husband one night after they had gone to bed, "Sarah is like a stubborn mule when it comes to working the problems in her arithmetic book. She wastes my time while she stares at the walls." Margaret complained, "I don't know how she will ever complete that book."

Thomas was recruited to work with Sarah each evening but as much as Sarah adored her cousin, she hated arithmetic more, and the evening study sessions became a waste of time.

Thomas enjoyed the foaling season because horses were his first love and each new colt or filly brought more wealth to the farm. Before the end of January, Belle had given birth to a beautiful little filly. His cousin, Sarah was delighted but when her father said they would be selling Belle's filly soon after she was trained to the saddle Sarah lost all interest in naming her. Three other mares on the farm had given birth, and Maddie was due to foal anytime now.

Thomas spoke softly to Maddie as he entered her stall. With deliberate but careful movements, he slid his hands across her neck, down to her rounded body. The big horse was heavy and burdened with the new life growing inside. As Maddie stepped to move away from his touch, Thomas noticed milk dripping from a teat. He left her stall and walked to the opposite end of the cavernous barn to speak with his uncle.

"Maddie's almost stopped eating, and she's overflowing with milk. I think she'll foal tonight or tomorrow, don't you?"

Tom was pushing the nose of Daisy's young calf into a pail half full of milk. He looked toward the other end of the barn where his Percheron mare stood in her stall.

"She's been restless and jittery lately. I think we'd best keep an eye on her tonight."

That meant Thomas would sleep another night in the barn, his bed a heap of straw. Rex was always eager and willing to share it with him, and the dog provided warmth, even if he woke up several times each night to scratch his fleas. Saturday night, when Thomas would be able to bathe his whole body, could not arrive soon enough. But this was Thursday and perhaps Maddie would foal before morning. His thoughts were interrupted by Sarah's call to come in for supper.

After supper Thomas sat at the kitchen table with Sarah, coaching and prodding her to concentrate and complete her assignment in the arithmetic book. She would slowly figure the answer to one problem and then find any diversion before beginning the next problem. Thomas was grateful when his uncle came inside and spoke to him.

"It's time to go out to the barn, Thomas. Keep a close watch on Maddie and you come wake me if there's any sort of trouble." Tom handed over the lantern to his nephew and said, "I'm goin' to bed."

As Thomas said goodnight to his uncle's retreating back, he pulled his coat on, gathered up the faded quilt and two wool blankets, which lay folded on a stool near the door, and with the bail of the lantern hooked over two fingers he went out to make up his bed in the barn.

He had just drifted off to sleep when he woke with a start. Maddie's breathing informed him she had begun the hard labor of birth. He reached for the tin of lucifers and soon had a bright flame burning in the lantern. Thomas held the lantern high and went to have a look at Maddie. She was lying down on the straw in her stall but she raised her head to give Thomas a wild-eyed look.

"It's going to be alright, Maddie." Thomas knelt next to her, talking softly.

Maddie's trust in him seemed to ease her fears. Her contractions forced the air out of her lungs with sounds of grunting pain that continued on and on. Her body revealed the strength of those contractions with a regular downward rippling. As the minutes went by, Thomas watched for a protruding front hoof of the new foal.

Several minutes later Thomas wondered if he should wake his uncle. But this was a first birth and perhaps he should give Maddie a little more time. Finally, he decided it was time to reach inside to make sure the foal was still alive and in the proper position. He removed his clothes to his waist and lay down on the straw at the rear of the expectant mother. With his right arm extended inside the birth canal he found a front hoof that immediately withdrew from his grasp.

Thomas smiled. "You've a lively one in there, Maddie."

A strong contraction gripped his arm and Thomas waited, hoping Maddie would continue to lie in the same position. When he was able, Thomas reached again to find the other hoof and discovered it was trapped behind the pelvic bone. Pushing his arm in as far as possible, Thomas gained a hold on the hoof and released it. He removed his arm and stood out of the way to monitor the imminent birth.

In the next minute the foal was being pushed out into the world. Thomas tore the membrane away from its nose and face, and gently held the front legs to help bring the rest of the foal's body out. He inspected the mouth, removing a plug of mucous, and checked to see the cord had broken away a few inches from the filly's body. He tied the afterbirth to Maddie's tail so that she would not stand up and step on it before it was completely expelled.

The new mother rose up onto her chest and saw her baby. Standing now, she began sniffing at the wet creature with her nose. Maddie made a soft nickering sound, which was answered in the darkness by corresponding calls from other horses in the barn. They seemed to be calling out their congratulations. Maddie's maternal instincts were expressed by a complete inspection and cleansing of her infant with a rough tongue.

Thomas washed himself quickly in a bucket of ice-cold water and donned his clothes. He continued to admire the mare and her newborn, taking in the wonder of this moment. Such a perfect young creature! Her coat was black but Tom said all Percherons are black when they're born. Thomas wondered if this one eventually would have the lovely gray and white coloring of her mother. He hoped his uncle planned to keep this filly and breed more Percherons out of her. One thing was certain; Thomas would not soon forget this night, his first time to help with the birth of a Percheron.

Maddie drank from her water pail as though her thirst would never be quenched. Thomas brought her some oats and she ate it all. The foal attempted to stand up but her long legs were wobbly and she went down. When at last she stood and took some steps without falling, Thomas directed her to her mother's udder. The foal knew exactly what to do. Thomas looked on with warmth of feeling for the new life before him. Then rubbing his hands together, he realized how cold it was, and how tired he felt.

Instead of going into the house to sleep, Thomas decided to stay in the barn to continue his watch over Maddie and her foal. He scattered fresh straw on the floor of her stall, then went to his own straw bed. Thomas extinguished the lantern light, wrapped himself in the blankets and quilt, and with Rex settled next to him, was sleeping soundly almost at once. The dark, silent barn enveloped all its creatures in peace.

CHAPTER TEN

Maddie's foal was the topic of conversation at breakfast. Sarah wanted to know why the foal was black and not gray like her mother.

"She's a Percheron, Sarah, and all Percherons are born black," her father explained, trying to be patient. "Her sire was black, and her mother gray, so she could be either black or gray when she's fully grown."

"Well, I hope she grows up to look like Maddie, don't you Thomas?" Sarah had definite opinions about many things.

Thomas shrugged his shoulders and gave her a look that meant, 'I don't know'. Though he agreed with Sarah, he thought it wise to keep silent about the new foal. Tom was the expert on horses and he repeatedly reminded Thomas of that fact. He lectured his nephew upon learning Thomas had reached inside his valuable mare to release the foal's hoof. Thomas tried to explain that he helped with the births of many foals at home in Ireland and he had done this very same procedure before, but Tom would not listen.

Later that morning, after a thorough inspection of the mare and her new foal, Tom had to admit that all was well. He stood at Maddie's stall admiring her offspring.

"Yes, this filly is a fine looking animal," he said. "She and her mother will make good breeding stock." His hands stroked the dark coat of the foal. "I think she'll be every bit as big as her mother, too."

Thomas was cleaning stalls and pens, a job that would keep him busy much of the day. Placing his shovel on top of another cartload of manure, he wheeled it outside to dump it in a clearing he'd made in the snow.

When Thomas returned to the barn Sarah came running from the house to see Maddie's foal. Her father motioned with his hand, reminding Sarah to slow down and talk softly.

"She is so big!" Sarah was wide-eyed but she remembered to speak in a subdued voice. "Belle's foal is not that big!"

Her father smiled and said, "Belle is a small horse, and it's only right that her foal is small."

Sarah stroked the young animal's neck. The newborn was so large Sarah had to stand on tip-toe to scratch around her ears. Admiration and approval were audible in Sarah's voice. "She has such bright eyes, and she already seems to know us. Are we going to keep her, Daddy?"

"Yes, she'll be a fine worker, the same as her mother." Tom reached over and patted Maddie's rump. Then he went to pick up a pail half filled with milk, which he handed to Sarah. "Do you want to take this and give it to one of the calves?"

Sarah's face was long with a 'woe is me' expression. "Mother said I should only look at the new foal, and I have to come right back to the house to work on my lessons." She stroked Maddie's foal one more time and reluctantly turned to leave the barn.

"You work hard on those lessons, Sarah. It would be a shame if you had to repeat the fourth grade next year," her father said.

Later, when the four of them sat down to their noon meal, Sarah waited impatiently for the 'Amen' at the end of the blessing. Sarah said, "Daddy, what will you name Maddie's new foal?"

Tom stopped before placing a large portion of mutton stew in his mouth. "She doesn't have a name yet. Do you have any ideas?"

Sarah was always full of ideas. She began to make suggestions.

Margaret interrupted, "Now, Sarah, stop and think how this young filly will look when she's grown. Do you think 'Sparkles' or 'Bright Eyes' will fit a large work horse?"

"But I was thinking how her eyes are so bright and sparkling," Sarah said in defense of her names.

Tom said, "Your mother is right. This filly will grow up to be a big, powerful horse and she needs a name that fits." He ate another bite of buttered bread and added, "You're right about those eyes, though. That young animal has eyes and ears that make her look very intelligent."

Sarah said, "I've heard Queen Victoria of England is a wise and powerful queen. Can we name her 'Victoria'?"

Thomas said, "Mightn't the Queen be offended having a *horse* named for her?"

"How will the Queen ever know?" Sarah said. "I wouldn't be bothered if someone gave a fine horse my name."

Sarah's mother said, "Those who admire Queen Victoria might think we were being disrespectful."

Her father said, "No, we shouldn't use Queen Victoria's name. But if you like the names of nobility perhaps you could call her 'Duchess' or 'Lady'."

"Lady! That's her name!" Sarah's face was beaming. "Remember, Mama, when we were reading the story of King Arthur, and the Lady of the Lake granted him the wonderful sword?"

Margaret bobbed her head up and down while her

whole face appeared to be involved in chewing a large mouthful of mutton. After she swallowed, Margaret said, "Yes, Sarah. Now eat your dinner before it's cold."

Sarah spooned up a small piece of meat but before she reached her mouth with it, she said to her father, "'Lady' is a good name, isn't it Daddy?"

"'Lady' is a fine name and it will be her name from now on. Mind your mother now and eat."

Winter did not release its icy grip on the land until late March when the continuing storms began to wane and sunshine waxed warmly upon the receding snow. Thomas grew to understand his uncle's comments about the mud, and how it was easier to suffer the dust of summer. The oozing mud kept them from working in the fields and it nearly stranded them on the farm. The one way to get into town was on horseback, and even then, horse and rider were exhausted after the five-mile round trip. Only those who lived in town were able to attend church.

White Eyes Run overflowed its banks and flooded the lower pasture. They tried to keep the stock close to the barn but a ewe and two lambs were lost when they wandered too far and drowned in the raging water. Rex, with his inherent ability to herd, was on duty around the clock, while uncle and nephew seemed to be running from one emergency to the next. Endurance and patience were stretched to maximum limits.

Topsy scratched at the back door, and out of habit, Margaret got up from her chair at the table and opened the door to let him in. Mouth open and stub of a tail wagging, the small dog pranced into the kitchen, leaving tracks of mud across the recently scrubbed wooden planked floor. Margaret's short supply of patience escaped as steam from the kettle. Her words exploded into the room. "Sarah!

From now on that dog of yours lives in the barn with Rex. Every time he comes in that door he brings in all the mud he can find." Then she turned her rage on the family seated at the dinner table. Margaret's jowls trembled in anger, and her wide arms flailed as she yelled, "And if *any* of you cannot wipe your feet on that pile of gunnysacks by the back door, then you can live with Topsy in the barn."

While Margaret mopped the tracks from the floor, the other family members sat in injured silence; not one word was spoken throughout the remainder of the meal. Margaret's anger was too formidable to risk another of her eruptions, so they ate quickly and prepared to leave.

Sarah put on her coat, pulled her mother's old boots on over her own shoes and gathered up Topsy's basket. Trusting his mistress, Topsy came when Sarah called and followed her outside. Thomas had chores to do in the barn so he walked out with Sarah. Inside, she found a place for Topsy's basket and set it down not far from the main entrance to the barn. When Topsy hopped inside and looked up for her approval, Sarah's eyes filled with tears.

"I'm sorry, Topsy." She knelt down, rubbing and scratching his rough coat, and wiping away her tears. She felt Rex's cold nose, and turned to see the bigger dog inspecting this new development.

"You're a good dog, Rex. Watch after Topsy, will you?"

Rex sat down and gave her his most intelligent expression, as if he understood. Thomas looked on and felt great sympathy for his little cousin.

One night in early April the temperature dropped well below freezing. The memory of previous late spring freezes ensured that Tom was prepared; he and Thomas brought most of the animals into the barn the night before. Tom and his nephew put on their warm coats and hats before they left the house. On this pre-dawn morning they had to make their way carefully to the barn over the uneven frozen mud. They held their lanterns high to see where it was safe to step.

"These spring freezes feel colder than any day in the dead of winter," Tom said as they entered the barn. "I guess our blood is thinning out and we notice it more, but most everyone says spring freezes are coldest."

"For sure, this cold goes to the bones," Thomas said. He turned and headed for Daisy and Buttercup at the far end of the barn. He hung his lantern from a hook and placed the milking pail beneath Buttercup's udder. Thomas blew on his hands and rubbed them together as he sat on the small stool. "Easy now, girl. These cold hands of mine will warm up soon."

Thomas was aware of the early morning sounds: the swish of Buttercup's warm milk streaming into the pail, and all the distinctive sounds coming from individual animals in the barn. His uncle made the usual clattering noises that came with the task of filling water pails and feed boxes.

Alarmed by the sudden sound of a thud and a groan, Thomas left his milking and hurried to find his uncle lying unconscious on the barn floor. He knelt down next to Tom. "What happened? Can you hear me, Tom?"

Tom did not move nor did he give any indication he heard Thomas. Thomas lifted him to a sitting position, holding him in a tight grip to keep Tom from slumping over. He asked again, "Tom, can you hear me?"

His uncle remained silent and limp in Thomas's arms.

Feeling helpless and wondering what had happened, Thomas looked around the immediate area. When he focused on the stallion directly across from them, it became apparent that Tom had been kicked. Ransom was a large warm blood, the only stallion on the farm, and the sire of some fine horses which had sold for equally fine sums. Normally, he was an even-tempered animal, but today he was stomping his feet and tossing his head, straining the chain that was attached to his halter.

At that moment, Tom moved. He opened his eyes and gasped for air. Rubbing his hand over his chest, he looked up at Ransom.

"That damned horse tried to kill me," Tom whispered. Seeing it was his nephew who held him, he said in a rasping voice, "Help me up, Thomas."

With his uncle's arm draped over his shoulders, Thomas gripped his own arm about Tom's waist. The two struggled to stand, and together they staggered toward the barn door. The light of early dawn revealed how treacherous it would be to maneuver over the uneven, frozen surface to reach the warmth and safety of the house.

Thomas said, "We'll take small steps, just one at a time." He could see that his uncle was hurting, and he hoped Tom would not lose consciousness again. Without speaking they made slow progress toward the house.

As they approached the back door, Thomas yelled, "Aunt Margaret. Can you open the door?"

A moment later, the door opened. When Margaret saw her injured husband draped over Thomas's shoulders she gasped and her hand flew to her throat.

"What happened?" Margaret backed away allowing them to enter.

"Ransom kicked him. He was unconscious when I found him,"

Thomas struggled through the door trying not to cause any further injury to his uncle. Once inside the kitchen, he sat Tom down on a straight-backed kitchen chair, where he immediately slumped over. Margaret and Thomas managed to catch him before he fell to the floor. "Hold him, Thomas, while I go find the smelling salts."

Tom breathed in the sharp odor of the salts and opened his eyes. He looked at his wife and wheezed out the words, "I feel sick. Get me a basin."

With amazing speed, Margaret placed a basin in front of her husband. He lost the contents of his stomach, and whispered that he needed to lie down.

Margaret looked at Thomas and said, "We'll never get him up those stairs to the bedroom. Wait here, and I'll cover the sofa in the front room."

When she returned, Margaret and Thomas each took one of his arms and helped Tom up the two steps from the kitchen into the front room. They eased him onto the sofa she had covered with an old quilt. Tom sat and trembled as his wife and nephew removed his coat. His face was colorless. Margaret placed a pillow over the rolled arm of the sofa and told her husband to lie back and rest. She and Thomas removed Tom's boots and lifted his feet up to drape them over the other end of the sofa.

Sarah came into the room and stood staring at her father. "What happened to Daddy?"

"Ransom kicked him. He'll be better soon," Margaret said. "Sarah I need for you to go upstairs and bring down the good quilt off our bed."

After she covered her husband, who was already asleep, Margaret spoke to Thomas in her usual commanding manner, "I'm sure you have many unfinished chores outside. I'll keep an eye on Tom."

Thomas remembered poor Buttercup and left the house to resume his milking. He worked furiously all day trying to do his own work as well as his uncle's. When

Sarah came out to tell him it was time for dinner, Thomas said he could not stop to eat. However, he was grateful for the generous slice of cheese between two thick slices of buttered bread which she brought out a little later. He thanked her and ate in large bites, barely stopping to wash it down with the mug of hot tea she handed him.

After supper he helped Tom up the stairs and into bed. It seemed his uncle was heavier than he had been this morning. Thomas left Aunt Margaret hovering over her husband, and went outside again. It could be another freezing night and the youngest animals needed to be inside. He completed his chores, lifted the lantern from its hook, and closed the barn door. As Thomas headed for his bed that night he returned to the thought that ran through his mind all day long: would his uncle fully recover from this injury or would Thomas need to run the farm all alone? A farm this size and with this many animals needed more than one man to keep it going.

CHAPTER ELEVEN

Tom attempted to get up the next morning and fell back on the bed with a groan. Dizziness and nausea forced him to lean over and heave into the chamber pot. He tried to sit up again, this time much more slowly.

Margaret was already out of bed. She pulled her dress down over the bulges of her body and buttoned it as she watched her husband.

"As soon as Thomas is done with the milking, I'm sending him to fetch Dr. Givens," Margaret said. When Tom objected she thrust her round chin forward and spoke firmly. "You are not getting any better, Tom. The doctor is going to see you *today*."

Dr. Givens came in the early afternoon and Margaret led him upstairs to the bedroom. The doctor questioned his patient, poked and prodded, and finally said, "You may have fractured your skull and you didn't do your heart any good when you got yourself kicked in the chest." Dr. Givens always made it seem that it was the patient's own fault for being sick or injured. He gave Tom orders to stay in bed for a week, handed him a paper envelope filled with pills for pain, then he accepted his payment and left, seeing himself out of the house.

"That man causes me more trouble than any horse ever did," Tom complained to his wife. He sat on the edge of the bed holding his head in his hands. The pain was not letting up.

She said, "I don't care what you think of Dr. Givens, he knows more about medicine than we do."

When Tom began to argue against her reasoning, Margaret shook her finger and glared in defiance at her husband. "Tom Keith, I want to see you lying flat on that bed, and you will stay there for seven days."

Tom had managed to get dressed before the doctor came, and now Margaret helped him remove his clothes. She gave him one of the pain pills to swallow, pulled back the covers to help him into bed, and tucked him in as if he were a child. Laying his sore head upon the pillow, Tom sighed in resignation and closed his eyes.

As the days went by, Thomas found he could not keep up with everything that needed to be done. At supper he was almost too tired to eat but he still needed to go out and make a final round of the pens and the barn. His working hours had increased from the usual eleven or twelve to sixteen hours each day, and the work left undone constantly nagged at him.

Thomas put on his coat, preparing to go out to the barn when Margaret returned to the kitchen with the tray full of dirty dishes and the remains of Tom's evening meal.

"Thomas, tomorrow morning I'll do the milking while you feed and water the stock. The warmer weather is drying up the mud, and it will soon be time to start shearing the sheep." Margaret set the tray on the kitchen countertop.

Too tired to speak, Thomas responded with a nod.

While Margaret and Thomas worked outside, Sarah was pressed into duty taking care of her father. She had orders to check on him several times a day, and bring him food and drink. She also had to wash the dishes, scrub the kitchen table, and sweep the floors. No one had time for school lessons and Sarah never mentioned her studies.

At the end of his long week of enforced bed rest,

Tom came down the stairs very slowly, and made his way into the kitchen for breakfast. He fell into a chair, glancing bleary-eyed about the room.

Tom's hair was uncombed and his beard was shaggy. Thomas thought his uncle looked sick and confused.

Tom blinked and looked through squinted eyes at his nephew. "Don't we need to get Maddie over to Moore's farm today?" he said.

Thomas said, "Why do we want to do that?"

Exasperated, Tom said, "She won't have a foal next year unless we get her bred."

Margaret gave her husband a scrutinizing look. "Why Tom, you know that horse was bred shortly after Lady was born."

"Who is Lady?" Tom asked.

Margaret and Thomas both looked at Tom to see if he might be making some kind of joke.

Sarah was the only one who wasn't upset by this turn of events. "Daddy, you remember Maddie's foal. You let me name her Lady."

Tom mumbled something unintelligible, looked down at his bowl, and began spooning hot porridge into his mouth.

After breakfast Tom followed his nephew out to the barn where Thomas began his milking chores. Tom stood and watched for a minute and said, "What do you think I should do first?"

A sense of alarm swept over Thomas. He wondered if Tom remembered anything at all about this farm. Tom had always shown disregard for any advice his nephew offered, but now he was asking Thomas what he should do first.

Thomas attempted to speak to his uncle in a 'matter

of fact' tone of voice. "You always check on the animals and see they are fed and watered while I milk the cows," Thomas said.

The whole day continued in the same way it had started. Thomas told his uncle *what* to do, and often *how* to do the ordinary routine chores. Their work was accomplished at a frustrating and slow pace.

After a few days, Tom's memory returned but he still suffered from weakness and headaches. He had to stop work often and find a place to sit while he rested.

Margaret said to Thomas, "Tomorrow morning after the usual chores, I'll help you shear the sheep. I can see that it won't get done this year without my help."

Margaret wore her oldest dress, rolled up the sleeves, and for three long days she and Thomas worked together. Perspiration dripped from the folds in her neck and arms as she held each sheep and Thomas sheared off its thick wool. With Rex's help, Tom brought in each one for shearing and then ushered the animal out to pasture.

Sheep shearing completed, Margaret returned to her many household chores. Two days later at breakfast Margaret spoke to her nephew, "Thomas, I need you to get out the cultivator and prepare the garden for planting."

As soon as Thomas had worked manure into the soil with the horse drawn cultivator, they began planting the vegetables that would see them through another winter. Wearing sunbonnets, mother and daughter toiled to plant potatoes, carrots, turnips, cabbage, onions, and peas in long rows. Thomas helped them as they made many trips to the water pump to fill the large watering cans so the new plants would survive.

Thomas continued to feel weighed down with his responsibilities. At least, he was able to use the best horse power on the farm because Tom had given him the use of

Mac and Maddie. Plowing and planting all the fields was the most immediate task right now. He was more than grateful for Isaac's and John's help.

Sunday was the one day of the week that brought some relief from the constant work, and the Keiths began to spend Sunday afternoons with the Cole family again. The two families were unable to see much of each other during those weeks of muddy roads.

Morning worship service had ended and the congregation stood outside the church visiting in the warm sunshine. When Rena came out the big door and walked down the stairs, Thomas stood waiting for her. Her long dark curls gleamed in the sunlight, and her face shone with youthful radiance. Together they walked to her family's new carriage. Many friends had gathered round to admire it, and Isaac was explaining all the features of his shiny black carriage with its oiled canvas top.

Knowing Rena would appreciate his humor Thomas bowed in mock sincerity. "Lady Lorena, may I say that's a very fine carriage. Now you will ride in the style most fitting to one of such beauty." His face betrayed his merriment.

Rena laughed and said, "Well, if we had a team such as Mac and Maddie to pull our new carriage, we would be as stylish as the Keiths."

The young couple moved to the shade of a tree and stood together holding hands, enjoying a rare moment alone. Their families were occupied with visiting and catching up on the news of the neighbors.

Rena said, "Will you be going to the church picnic next Sunday?"

Distracted by her deep violet eyes and the pleasing sound of her voice Thomas responded, "What's that?"

Rena repeated her question. "''Do you know if

you'll be going to the church picnic next Sunday?"

"I haven't heard anything about it at our house."

"Well, I can guess that you'll be there because Aunt Margaret always brings her famous chocolate and vanilla layered cake to the annual picnic. Everyone raves about it so she has a reputation to uphold."

Thomas marveled to himself that Rena's smile continued to affect him the same way it did when he first met her almost a year ago.

She grew more serious. "Do you think Uncle Tom will ever be as strong as he used to be? Daddy says that horse kicked the strength right out of him."

"I wish I knew." Thomas glanced over at his uncle who stood with the other men around the Cole's carriage. "He grows tired and has to sit down to rest often. He still has headaches. Aunt Margaret worries about him all the time."

"How do you manage if he can't do his share of the work?"

"We are behind with everything. If Aunt Margaret hadn't helped me I'd still be shearing the sheep."

"Isn't that just like her? She appears to be so prickly and sharp but she is truly a helpful, caring lady. How many sheep did you shear this year?"

"Fifty-five head, and that's twice as many as we should have. I've told Tom we should sell off some of the stock. The price of wool is low and there's no market for mutton."

Rena looked at him with concern. "What did he say to that?"

"He said something about how he remembers the days in Ireland when they would have faced starvation without their flocks of sheep. But this isn't Ireland and times have changed."

Thomas was filled with youthful indignation, and when he saw the sympathetic interest in Rena's face, it seemed he couldn't stop talking.

"Since we lost nine of our hogs last winter to the cholera, I thought we ought to buy only two or three weanlings and raise them 'til they're ready to butcher. Or we could always trade with another family when we need a hog for butchering, and then we wouldn't have to raise hogs at all. But Tom wouldn't have it. He thinks every farmer should raise hogs. I think it's not wise to raise more than you can care for or sell at a profit."

Rena's nod of agreement prompted him to go on.

"We need to do something to keep the farm manageable, but the more I talk about selling off stock, the more stubborn he is and he won't consider any of it. Of all the animals we raise, the horses have brought us the most profit, but it takes time to train them."

Rena said, "I'll talk to my father about this. Uncle Tom respects Daddy and if these ideas come from him it might be more convincing."

The Cole family sat in their carriage beckoning to Rena, indicating it was time to leave.

"I have to go now," Rena said when she saw John walking toward them to fetch her, his face betraying his impatience. Rena leaned in close and whispered to Thomas, "I'll see you this afternoon at dinner." Her hand left Thomas's and she hurried off with her skirts swinging and dark curls flying.

Thomas stood watching, returning her wave as the new carriage pulled away from the churchyard.

Sarah ran to him and grabbed his hand, pulling him toward the Keith family carriage.

"Come on, Thomas; it's time to go home. You can swoon over Rena later. They're coming for dinner today, you know."

Thomas climbed into the carriage, sat down next to Sarah, and remained silent all the way home. Did he speak his mind too freely? Perhaps he shouldn't talk about his uncle the way he did with Rena. But the more he thought about it the more he was certain Rena could be trusted to do the right thing. Besides, he knew there was an understanding and a trust between Rena and himself.

Isaac must have talked some sense into Tom that Sunday afternoon because the following Saturday Tom told his nephew to bring in the lambs. He planned to take many of them and several older ewes to the auction in Norwich. While Tom sat on his horse directing the procession, Rex herded twenty-six sheep out the lane and onto the dust-filled road into town. When dog, horse, and rider returned, not a word was mentioned about the transaction at the auction. However, Thomas noticed two brown sacks, one hanging from either side of Tom's saddle, and it was obvious they contained something alive.

At his uncle's bidding, Thomas untied the squirming sacks from Tom's saddle and carried them down to the piggery. With a satisfied smile he opened them to see a weanling pig in each sack. He turned the pigs loose inside the low-ceilinged structure where they ran to explore their new home. This year the farm would be spared from dealing with a mean-tempered boar and sows that rolled over onto their piglets and crushed them. God willing, these two would become healthy hogs ready for butchering next autumn.

By late afternoon dark clouds rolled in and violent winds began to howl. Thomas had to forcibly close the back door against the wind and rain when he came inside that evening. He wiped his feet on gunnysacks and removed his hat to shake off the rainwater before hanging it next to Tom's hat on the wall. Lightning struck nearby and thunder boomed.

Margaret stood at the big stove preparing supper. In a lull between claps of thunder she asked Thomas if he had finished the milking and all his outside chores.

"The milking's done, but I'll need to go out and see to the horses after supper. This weather has them upset."

"If it rains like this all night we'll have nothing but mud by tomorrow morning and that means the church picnic will be called off", Margaret said.

Tom was sitting in his chair reading the newspaper he had purchased today in town. "Says here, there will be a special train going into Zanesville for the Fourth of July." He waited until another loud roll of thunder ceased and read aloud, "*'Thousands are expected to be in Zanesville for the big Fourth of July celebration this year. Included in the day's festivities will be a parade through town with marching bands, followed by foot races and games, and a picnic at McIntire Park. All are encouraged to bring their families and picnic baskets for a day of enjoyment. Well known state and county officials have been invited to speak on the issues facing our country. This newspaper will print the names of the officials speaking at the momentous occasion when those men have declared their acceptances.'*"

Margaret said, "I think we should plan to go. This weather is going to cancel the church picnic tomorrow, and it doesn't seem right to have a spring and summer without a big picnic."

Sarah was setting the table for supper. When she heard her mother's announcement she immediately chimed in. "Oh, yes! Can we go, Daddy? Won't it be splendid if we can ride the train to Zanesville and watch the parade?"

Tom looked over the top of his paper at his wife and daughter. He smiled and said, "You may be right, Sarah. If the weather cooperates, we'll take the train to Zanesville on the Fourth."

In exclamation of this statement a booming roar of thunder shook the house. Speaking louder than the sound of the beating rain, Sarah said, "I hope the weather cooperates on the Fourth of July."

Thomas sat at the table Sunday night after everyone else had gone to bed. He dipped the pen in the inkwell and wrote today's date, *14 June, 1880.*

...I am sorry this letter is coming to you much later than I wanted. Uncle Tom was hurt badly about 10 weeks ago. Ransom, the farm's stallion, kicked Tom in the chest, and he hit his head so hard when he fell that he was unconscious for a while.

Thomas continued to write until he had filled three pages. He looked up at the kitchen clock and saw that it was almost eleven o'clock. He set the pen down and rubbed his eyes, then read his letter, trying to imagine his family reading it a few weeks from now. Thomas dipped the pen into the inkwell once more and wrote:

Your loving son and brother,
Thomas

He blotted these last few words, folded the papers and pushed them into an envelope that bore his family's name and address. He found the small pot of glue and sealed the envelope, wishing he could somehow seal himself inside with his letter.

CHAPTER TWELVE

Thomas was amazed at the number of people crowded together at the Sundale Station. He heard there would be an extra passenger car added to this train bound for the Fourth of July celebration at Zanesville, but he began to wonder if everyone would find a seat. He craned his neck searching for the Cole family, who was surely somewhere in this crowd. Thomas heard his name called and turned to see John pushing his way toward him.

"Over this way, Thomas." John pointed to a place near the road where the Cole family had their wagon and team in the shade of some trees.

Thomas grabbed Sarah's hand. "Come on, Sarah. The Coles are over here."

"Where's Margaret and Tom?" Hannah asked as soon as she caught sight of Thomas and Sarah.

"Daddy had a bad headache and he didn't want to come," Sarah said.

Thomas added, "Aunt Margaret wouldn't leave him, but she said that Sarah could come with me if we both stayed with you and your family. She packed us a picnic lunch, and I've already purchased our tickets."

Hannah was upset over this news about Tom. "Those headaches seem to be bothering him more and more. I hope he feels better tomorrow."

Sarah spoke with confidence, "Mama said he just needs to get more rest."

Isaac said, "Did you ride or walk?"

"We rode together on Beauty. I left him staked out

in Mr. Mason's yard. He told me it was alright," Thomas said.

Isaac said he was leaving their wagon and unhitched team where they were. His horses were staked and Isaac had left them a bucket of water. "There are wagons and horses staked out under every tree around here."

Because Thomas was committed to his responsibility for Sarah, he would not let her out of his sight. He sat next to Sarah on the train while Rena and her little sister sat several rows away.

Most everyone on the train was in a holiday mood and they talked and laughed loudly. This was a very special day and they were proud that so many from Norwich were going to the big celebration in Zanesville. Thomas and Sarah were amused at all the antics going on around them. A group of boys were playing kazoos and one was even dancing in the aisle. People began clapping in time to the music.

Sarah said, "I'm glad Mama isn't here because she wouldn't approve of this rowdy behavior." She grinned up at Thomas.

Thomas grinned back at her and nodded his head. He thought Sarah's remark was very insightful.

When the train finally reached Zanesville Thomas took Sarah by the hand. They were jostled and pushed until they stepped down from the train and out onto the crowded street. Thomas was glad for his height that allowed him to look over many heads and find a way to reach John. John had spoken to a man who told them the parade was supposed to come down Seventh Street and make a turn on Main Street, to march past the new courthouse.

John leaned close to Thomas in order to be heard over the noise of the crowd. "We should all try to be near the courthouse because the bands will make their best performances in front of the Mayor and other dignitaries." He beckoned and said, "Follow me."

Thomas held Sarah's hand tightly as they pushed through the crowd. At last they found the place John thought was best, about halfway between the courthouse and Seventh Street where they could see the parade coming around the corner. John told them to stay there while he went to find the rest of his family. Rena was breathless when she and Emma caught up with them. The little girls were so excited they hugged one another, glad to be together again. At last, Hannah and Isaac arrived and they all stood waiting in eager anticipation for the parade to begin.

The trumpets and drums were heard before they could be seen. When the marching band rounded the corner the crowd greeted them with applause. Their black uniforms were draped with sashes of red, white and blue, and they stepped in precision as their shining horns flashed in the warm summer sun. The big bass drums boomed, while the trombones and trumpets sent the majestic music echoing down the street.

Flags waved from poles carried by proud men in military uniforms. A group of military cavalrymen rode by on fine mounts festooned with ribbons of red, white and blue.

A band of local musicians marched past wearing white shirts, black pants, and red, white and blue stovepipe hats made of stiff paper. A group of children dressed in red, white and blue waved flags as they trooped past, and then a clown in the same patriotic colors turned cartwheels down the street. Another band followed the clown, and their instruments included bells, piccolos, and tin whistles. Over the sounds of spirited marching music, the crowd cheered and applauded.

More parade entries followed: some were horse drawn wagons decorated with flowers and banners; there were fraternal organizations whose members waved flags. Another clown came down the street seated on a donkey with a small dog that did tricks. The crowd laughed in appreciation when the dog appeared to unseat the clown, who fell sprawled on the street while the dog rode off on the donkey's back.

The bands and parade participants filed past the courthouse, and as John predicted, they all did their best to perform for the celebrities. Then they marched on down to Front Street where they turned to bring the parade to an end.

The town mayor gave a little speech and invited everyone to come to McIntire Park for speeches, games, and a picnic. The masses made their way down Main Street to cross the 'Y' Bridge on foot.

Rena and Emma walked in front of Thomas and Sarah and as they crossed the Muskingum River, Rena turned and shouted back to Thomas, "I've never seen so many people on one bridge, have you?"

"I hope it's a sturdy bridge," Thomas answered, smiling.

When they reached the park they found many blankets spread across the grass and some people were already seated to begin eating from their picnic baskets. Hannah quickly found a place to spread their blanket. Sarah opened the small basket that Thomas had carried, and they sat down to eat the boiled eggs, buttered bread slices, and thick slices of soft cheese. Their jug of water was poured into a tin cup from which Thomas and Sarah drank in turns. Hannah had prepared chicken for her family and she offered some pieces to Sarah and Thomas. Thomas politely refused, but Sarah took a piece of chicken and soon had grease on her face and fingers. Neither Thomas nor Sarah refused a piece of Hannah's spice cake.

A man stood at the edge of the picnic area and shouted into a bullhorn, "It's time now for the three-legged races." He repeated himself to make sure everyone heard. "All the young people are invited to enter the three-legged races." With one arm raised high in the air, he announced, "First we'll have the boys and girls six to twelve years run the race. Ages thirteen to seventeen will run in the next race." He pointed with his free arm. "Here is the starting line. Contestants must run up and touch the row of hedges at the far end of the field," the man flung his arm toward the tall shrubbery, "turn around and come back." Again he pointed at the starting line. "Everyone six to twelve years should line up now and our assistants will tie partners' legs together."

Sarah wiped her face on her sleeve and jumped up. "Come on, Emma. Let's run the race together."

Hannah spoke up. "Sarah, do you think your mother would want you running in a three-legged race? You could fall and get hurt."

"I'll be very careful, Aunt Hannah. Emma can't run as fast as I can so she will keep me from going too fast."

Isaac said, "Let the girls have a chance to run, Hannah. They might as well have a good time with all the other children."

At those words both girls were up and running toward the starting line. Sarah and Emma stood with sides touching while a young man tied their nearest ankles together with a torn strip of cotton sheeting. By the time each child was tied to his or her partner, some of the contestants had already fallen from the mere effort to get in place at the starting line.

The man with the bullhorn shouted, "On your mark. Get set. Go!"

Because Sarah and Emma were unmatched in height, they began slowly, trying to keep from falling. At last, they each placed one arm around the other and found a rhythm that slowly moved them ahead of the others. Sarah could hear the crowd cheering behind them.

Now they were almost to the hedge. Only two couples were ahead of them, and they were older boys. When the boys looked back to see Sarah and Emma coming up behind them they hurried even more. The oldest and biggest team of boys touched the hedge first, and then turned around for the last half of the race. That's when they collided with Sarah and Emma who were looking down at their own feet.

The crowd screamed, "Watch out!" and "Look where you're going!"

But they all crashed down in a pile of arms and legs. On the bottom of the heap was Emma, the smallest child. The boys managed to pull themselves up and continue on with the race.

Sarah tried to stand but Emma continued to lay there. Her face was contorted and she cried out in pain, "Don't move! My leg hurts."

Sarah sat next to Emma and worked to untie the knot that bound them together. She had to be very careful or Emma would scream in pain. After what seemed to be an eternity, she freed herself from Emma and ran toward Isaac who was standing right on the starting line with a worried look on his face.

By now, the man with the bullhorn was shouting, "All race contestants return to the starting line. It appears we have an injury on the field."

Isaac said to his niece, "Is Emma hurt?"

"Yes! She's crying and she says she can't stand up."

Isaac ran to his daughter, scooped her up, and hurried back to the blanket where his family sat. Carefully, he placed Emma on the blanket next to her mother. Emma began to cry and sob when her mother caressed and kissed her.

Sarah sat on the blanket and started to shed her own tears. "Oh, Emma, I'm sorry I asked you to race with me. If we'd stayed here you wouldn't be hurt now."

Thomas patted Sarah's back while Rena and John patted their little sister's arm and shoulder. People gathered round asking if they could help.

Isaac said, "I think my daughter's leg is broken. Does anyone know of a doctor in town?"

"Doctor Young lives across the street from the park." A burly man with a dark mustache pointed. "See that big, white house with the wide front porch? That's where Doctor Young lives. If you wish, my son can run over there to see if he's at home." The man gestured toward his son, a strapping boy of about fourteen years.

"That would be appreciated. Thank you," Isaac said.

The boy returned to say that Dr. Young was not at home. The burly man and his son left to speak with the man holding the bullhorn. Soon he began shouting through his speaker, "We need a doctor. Is there a doctor in the crowd? A child has been injured."

After a few minutes, a man wearing spectacles approached them. He saw Emma lying down with her head on her mother's lap.

"I'm Doctor Young. Is this the injured child?"

Isaac introduced himself and his wife to the doctor, who immediately began to examine Emma's leg. Emma cried in pain at his probing touch.

"Mr. Cole, her leg is broken. Can you carry her very carefully across the street to my house? I have everything in my dispensary for setting the bone."

Hannah gave instructions to her older children. "I want you to stay right here while I go with your father and Emma."

She looked at Thomas and said, "I know your Aunt Margaret would want you to stay with Sarah and watch over her every moment. We don't need anyone else hurt today."

And then to Sarah she said, "You do whatever Thomas says. Do you understand?"

Sarah nodded with a sober and solemn expression. "Yes, Aunt Hannah."

They all sat in stunned silence and watched them carry away Emma, who sobbed in pain and fear. Sarah began weeping for her little cousin again. Rena sat close, placing her arms around Sarah, smoothing her hair and wiping the tears from her face. The four of them waited throughout the agonizing afternoon, while the games and political speeches continued.

Emma returned to them in her father's arms. Her right leg had a heavy plaster cast that extended from above her knee almost to her toes. Everyone asked if she was alright. Emma looked exhausted and disheveled but she gave them a weak smile. Sarah kissed her cousin on the cheek saying, "I'm sorry you got hurt, Emma."

Many people were aware of the accident that broke the leg of the little Cole girl. When it came time to board the train for Norwich, they stepped aside telling Isaac to proceed ahead of them with Emma in his arms.

The train ride home was much different than the morning's ride. Children slept and many adults dozed, nodding weary heads to the rocking rhythm of the train.

Sarah leaned against Thomas and slept, while several rows away Emma sat in her mother's lap with her plaster-covered leg across her father's knees. Rena and John sat together in the seat ahead of Thomas. He looked at the back of Rena's head, admiring her glossy dark hair, and regretting that he had not one moment alone with her today.

The sun had dropped below the tree tops when the train steamed into Sundale Station. They all rose to their feet, collected belongings, and slowly made their way out onto the large platform. Thomas held the basket in one hand and guided Sarah with his other hand to Mr. Mason's yard. After he untied the horse, Thomas helped Sarah mount Beauty and then he sat behind his cousin with the reins in his hands.

"Hold on tight to that basket, Sarah," Thomas said. He headed the horse toward the Cole family wagon where he reined in Beauty and stopped. "Is there anything we can do to help?"

Isaac said, "Thanks, Thomas. No, we're headed home to get this girl into bed."

Sarah said, "I hope you feel better soon, Emma. I'll let you have my new doll to play with while your leg heals up."

Emma smiled weakly. "Thank you, Sarah."

Hannah said, "It's getting late and we all need to go home. Tell your folks we missed them, and we hope your daddy is feeling better."

"I will," Sarah said.

Everyone said 'goodbye' and waved. Beauty carried Thomas and Sarah down the road toward home while the Cole wagon rattled over the rough, dusty road behind them. The bouncing wagon caused Emma to cry out in pain. Thomas and Sarah turned to see Hannah holding her daughter in her arms as the Cole wagon swung to the right toward their home.

Throughout the summer the three able bodied men worked harder than usual to make up for Tom's weakened condition. They still had two fields to rake before the threshing could begin. Most days Tom was able to drive the team but often he needed to sit in the shade of a tree while one of the others took his job and allowed him to rest for half an hour or so.

Isaac brought the team to a halt near the tree where Tom rested. He and John and Thomas sat down under the tree with Tom while they passed around a jug of water.

Isaac took a long drink, wiped his face with his sleeve and said to Tom, "Are you thinking you might be able to take the team now?"

"It must be warmer than usual. The headache and dizziness are comin' back on me."

"Do you want us to take you home?"

"No. Just leave me here to rest in the shade. I feel better when I don't move. When you get this field done you can take me home."

"If this dry weather holds, I think we'll finish soon and be done with the threshing in another week or ten days." Isaac stood up, removed his hat and wiped his brow. He looked at Tom and said, "You wave and shout at us if you need to go home before we're done here."

Tom frowned and looked out across the field. "I can't tell you how helpless I feel." He looked up at his brother-in-law and spoke with conviction. "I'd give anything to work alongside all of you again."

Isaac reached down and patted Tom's shoulder. "Don't you worry. You'll be fit as a fiddle soon."

CHAPTER THIRTEEN

As the Keith family sat around the kitchen table for their noon day meal, it was obvious to Margaret that Tom had something to say because he laid down his knife and fork and cleared his throat.

"C. J. Miller told me this morning the school board has hired a new teacher. Her name is Miss Maysell and she comes from New Concord."

Sarah squealed, "Oooh, a lady teacher?"

Tom scowled at her. "Don't interrupt again, Sarah."

He looked at his wife and continued. "School will begin a week from last Monday. Miller said all the families are supposed to come next Saturday to clean up the yard and the schoolhouse. The school hasn't been used for several months so we'll have a great deal of work. I told him to count on all of us."

Margaret said, "I hadn't planned for it but I guess it's something we can't avoid. I wonder if Hannah will be able to come with Emma."

"I thought Emma would be healed up and walking by now," Tom said. "They pulled her around for weeks in that little wagon Isaac made, but didn't the doctor tell them to have Doc Givens remove the cast by the first week in September?"

"I think you're right." Margaret began clearing dishes from the table. "What about those plans you had for the Fair at Stoner's field? Are you going to have time to organize it and help get the schoolyard ready, too?"

"When we're all working together at the schoolhouse I'll talk to the men and find out who will be showing livestock at the Fair. I can judge the horses, but I'm looking for someone to judge hogs, sheep, and cattle. I was hoping to hold a horse race, and if anyone's interested we could have a pulling contest; one with horses, and one with mules. After church Sunday I'll ask around and see who will help out. Several men have promised to give their support already."

Saturday morning the Keith family arrived at the schoolhouse before nine o'clock. The Mallorys were there already as were the Miller and the Atkins families. They left their wagons out by the roadside and brought hand scythes and rakes for clearing the yard; brooms, rags and pails for cleaning inside. Women and girls were hard at work knocking down cobwebs, sweeping floors, cleaning windows, and washing the slate chalk board. Men and boys were cutting overgrown grass and weeds, dragging downed tree branches to a burning pile of debris, and generally cleaning up the yard. Margaret noticed that Thomas already had been put to work digging a hole for the new privy along with one of the older Mallory boys.

Margaret covered her hair with a dust bonnet and picked up her broom. She saw Sarah standing in the doorway of the schoolhouse and was about to tell her to get to work when Sarah called out, "Look at Emma, everyone. She's walking!" Sarah ran down the stairs and went to her cousin to embrace her.

Hannah put out her hand and said, "Don't run into your cousin, Sarah. She had the cast removed yesterday and she's learning to walk again."

Emma informed her cousin, "My leg is sore, but the doctor told me to keep walking on it. He said it would get strong again." She let go of her mother's skirt and with a look of determination, she grabbed the stair rail.

Margaret reached out to help her niece but Hannah stopped her with a shake of her head. Hoisting herself up one step and then another until she stood on the landing, Emma limped into the schoolroom and sat down on the nearest bench.

Sarah sat next to her. "Does it hurt very much?"

Emma nodded, "Uh huh."

Margaret said, "Sarah, you don't have a sore leg. Take this rag and start cleaning the tables."

Sarah made a sour face. She took the damp, soapy rag and began scrubbing the nearest table. She and all the other girls listened to the women's conversation as they worked.

"We haven't had a woman teacher here in a long time. Does anyone know where she'll be living?" Hannah spoke as she pushed at a pile of dust with her broom.

Mrs. Atkins adjusted her old dust bonnet. "Mr. Atkins is probably speaking to the men about this right now. She'll have to live with the families of the students. We'll take her for the first six weeks but other families need to volunteer for the rest of the school year."

"We don't have a spare room at our house," said Mrs. Mallory, the mother of six children. "If she stays with us, she'll have to share a bed with the two girls."

"But the schoolteacher must have a room of her own. It's been a rule for years, and one that we can't break now. We were fortunate in recent years that Master Green and Master Ferguson had their own living arrangements, but Miss Maysell's family lives in Zanesville." Mrs. Atkins lowered her voice as if sharing a secret. "Miss Maysell has been offered a position at the Salt Creek School, and we can't take a chance on losing her. She's one of the most qualified teachers we've had because she studied for two years at the college in New Concord.

"Do you know if she's taught school before, or is this her first year?" Mrs. Miller was rinsing a rag in her metal pail. "It would be nice if we had an experienced teacher for a change."

All eyes were on Mrs. Atkins, the only one in the room who had met the new teacher.

"She looks very young so I would guess this might be her first year."

Emma spoke to Sarah, "I hope our new teacher is pretty, don't you?"

Sarah sighed, "I just hope she's nice and she doesn't die right after Christmas."

Margaret noticed the other mothers hiding their smiles as they overheard Sarah's remark.

Margaret and Hannah washed and dried the dishes after Sunday's meal at the Keith home. Rena swept the floors, and with Sarah's help, removed the extension boards from the dining table. Tom, Isaac, and the boys had eaten and left for Stoner's field right after dinner.

Margaret scrubbed vigorously at the large roasting pan. Wet lines of perspiration ran down each side of her face and she knew her face must be beet red from the heat. She also knew the cloth shields underneath her arms were soaked, and her dark brown Sunday dress was stained. Summer's heat made Margaret's life miserable, and today was as warm as any day in August.

She stopped scrubbing for a moment to tell her sister, "Tom's headaches and dizzy spells seem to be going away, and he has grown stronger lately in spite of all his responsibilities organizing this Fair."

"That is such good news. Everyone admires Tom

for heading up Norwich's first Fair. It's high time we had a Fair of our own." Hannah carefully placed her sister's best dishes on the cupboard shelves. "We heard that yesterday's events were well attended, and I'm looking forward to the mule team competition this afternoon."

Margaret looked at the kitchen clock and said, "The men and boys left an hour ago and we need to get into town right away or we'll miss it. We're almost done here. Let's leave everything and I'll finish when we get home." Margaret was quick to remove her apron and prepare to leave.

"Sarah, are you and Emma ready? It's time to go." Margaret rolled down the sleeves of her dress.

The women and three girls hurried down to the shady part of the yard where the horses stood switching their tails at flies. Isaac left the horses hitched to the Cole's carriage so the women would have ready transportation. Hannah held the reins and before long they were pulling next to many other wagons and carriages lined up around the boundaries of Stoner's field.

They could see Isaac's mules were harnessed together and ready to compete against two other mule teams. The field was being leveled by a horse drawn road scraper, which made the dust fly everywhere. All the ladies held handkerchiefs to their faces until the area was smooth and the dust had settled.

As each team competed at pulling a sled loaded with heavy stones, the crowd cheered them on. The first team dragged the load a total of twenty-five and a half feet, the second team pulled the same load only twenty-four feet, and Isaac's team of mules pulled twenty-six feet in the time limit, winning by six inches. Isaac unhitched and led his team off the field to loud cheering and applause. He grinned as he walked up to a table set on a platform where he claimed his blue ribbon award.

A man in the crowd called out, "How much you want for them mules?"

Isaac shouted, "They're not for sale."

Good-humored laughter from the people followed this exchange.

Hannah beamed and said to Margaret, "This fair was the best idea! Be sure to tell Tom how much we all appreciate his hard work."

Next there was a greased pig race. The pigs were so fast and slippery that none of the boys could hold onto one. Not only were the pigs slippery, but the boys were covered in grease and dirt from wrestling with the pigs and falling on the ground.

Hannah said, "Aren't we glad that John and Thomas didn't want to enter this contest?!"

Margaret laughed. "Maybe they're smarter than we thought."

The final event of the day was the sheep herding competition and a man from Rich Hill entered a dog that made the others look like amateurs. This black and white collie was trained to obey a myriad of whistle and hand commands, and he herded the sheep to the proper pens in record time. The crowd applauded loudly when the announcer awarded the winning prize to the dog and his owner from Rich Hill.

"I wonder how much it would cost to get a pup sired by that dog," Hannah mused.

"I hear he's won every competition for many miles around. I'm sure we couldn't afford one of his pups." Margaret spoke with authority.

A man in a straw hat stood up on the seat of a nearby wagon and shouted through a bull horn. "Ladies and Gentlemen, thank you for coming to the first annual

Fair at Norwich. We want to thank Mister Tom Keith and his committee for all their work to make this event successful. Climb up here, Tom, so we can thank you properly."

Tom looked flustered and somewhat embarrassed, but he climbed up to stand next to the man in the wagon.

"Let's hear a round of applause for Tom Keith."

As soon as the cheering and hand-clapping subsided, Tom said something to the man holding the bull horn.

"Ladies and Gentlemen, Mister Keith wants you to know that three other men worked as hard as he. Come on up here Andy Lorimer, Jack Hadden, and C.J. Miller."

Tom jumped down to make room for the other three men who stood up on the wagon and accepted their applause.

The man with the bull horn announced, "We hope you all come back again next September for the second annual Norwich Fair." He removed his straw hat and waved while the people applauded and began to leave Stoner's field in clouds of rising dust.

Margaret, Hannah and the three girls headed toward the Cole family carriage. Margaret climbed up with much effort and sat down to fan herself with her handkerchief. "Take us home, Hannah. We all need a cool drink of water fresh from the pump."

After the first week of school, Sarah reported at the supper table that Miss Maysell was beautiful, and she smiled at her students when they gave correct answers. "Miss Maysell smiled at me when we had our first spelling test because I got one hundred percent correct."

"But what about arithmetic, Sarah? Did Miss Maysell put you back in the fourth grade book?" Margaret gave her daughter a scrutinizing look.

Sarah's self-satisfied smile disappeared and she spoke bitterly. "Yes, and I don't think it's fair!" There are only one hundred sixty-five pages in the book and I remember that I worked up to page one hundred last year. I almost finished the book, and she's making me start at the beginning again!"

Her mother swallowed the large bite of mutton she had been chewing. "You have no one to blame but yourself."

Sarah looked at Thomas, but he put another forkful of food in his mouth and said nothing.

Her father said, "Life doesn't always seem fair, Sarah, but we all need to keep trying to do our best."

Sarah's lower lip protruded from a sullen face. Soon she left the table and ran upstairs to her room to weep and feel sorry for herself.

She worked herself into such a fit of self-pity they could hear Sarah's wailing all the way down to the kitchen where they ate the last of their meal. Margaret poured another cup of coffee for her husband and nephew and said, "I'll be right back. I'm going up to talk to her."

She stood in the doorway and saw her ten-year-old daughter sprawled face down on her bed. Margaret walked to the bed and sat on the edge causing it to squeak as it sloped to one side under her weight. Though she was very much against bribery, Margaret was ready to resort to it this one time because Sarah needed to complete all her school assignments and catch up with her fifth grade classmates. Aware of her mother's presence, Sarah stopped crying.

Margaret placed a heavy hand on her daughter's back. "Sarah, your father and I are worried about you and your failure to complete the fourth grade arithmetic book. We know you can do those problems even though you might not like it."

Sarah continued to keep her face buried in her pillow.

"Your father tells me that the circus is coming to Zanesville. He says we might take you to the circus if you make a solemn promise to finish your fourth grade arithmetic book by Christmas."

Sarah sat up in the middle of the bed and wiped her face on her sleeve. She saw a slight smile on her mother's face and all at once, Sarah's mood changed from gloom to elation. She hopped down off the bed, and went downstairs into the kitchen while Margaret followed behind.

"Is it true we might go to the circus in Zanesville, Daddy?"

Tom placed his coffee cup in its saucer and looked at his daughter who had a red face and puffy eyes from all the crying. "Can you promise to work hard and finish the fourth grade arithmetic book by Christmas? We want you to start working in the fifth grade book when the New Year comes."

Sarah said, "Oh yes, Daddy, I'll work very hard to finish it by Christmas."

The next Saturday Thomas took them to the train early in the morning. Margaret climbed up the steps to enter their train car and sat next to Sarah who had the window seat while Tom sat behind them.

As the train blew its whistle and pulled away from the station, Sarah looked up at her mother and said, "Why couldn't Thomas come with us today?"

"We talked about this before. Your father has work for him to do at home."

"But that doesn't seem fair. We're going to have a good time at the circus and he has to stay home by himself and work."

"That's just way things are sometimes. Life is not always fair."

"Well, it seems to me that Daddy could make it fair for Thomas if he wanted to."

"Sarah, I'm sure your father has good reasons for everything he does. Now let's talk about something else." Margaret opened her bag, and took out her tatting thread and needle. "This circus is supposed to have some elephants and tigers. I think it's going to be a very good show."

"I still wish Thomas could be with us," Sarah said.

Sarah sat in silence for much of the trip into Zanesville. When they took their seats inside the big tent and the circus began, Sarah laughed at the clowns and enjoyed watching the animals perform, but when they boarded the train for home she became quiet again.

As soon as they pulled into Sundale Station and stepped down from the train, Sarah caught sight of Thomas and ran to him, throwing her arms around his waist. Margaret followed close behind Sarah and heard her daughter say, "Thomas, I wish you could have come with us!"

Thomas looked surprised. He pulled his cousin's arms away from his waist and held her hands out in front of him. "Was it a good circus?"

"Oh yes! You would have loved it!"

At Sarah's request, she sat next to Thomas in the carriage while her parents sat behind. All the way home she told him about the circus and patted his back as if she needed to touch him to make sure he was right beside her.

"I wish you could have seen the circus, Thomas. They had some beautiful horses that carried a boy and girl on their backs while the children did flips and handstands. And the elephants were so big I could hardly believe they were real!"

Sarah continued to regale him with the amazing things she saw, and she said it again and again, "I wish you could have been there with us." She talked to Thomas all the way home and through the evening until she went upstairs to bed.

Later that night Margaret lay in the bed next to Tom. "We should have invited Thomas to come with us today. Sarah was right. He would have enjoyed the circus as much as we did."

"You're sounding just like your daughter now. By the time we paid for his train fare, and fare to the circus, plus the food, it would have cost another six dollars. We have to remember that Thomas is working for us the same as an indentured servant."

"Tom, I'm surprised at you! He's your nephew and Sarah's cousin and he's an honest, hard-working boy. He's nearly always kind and helpful to Sarah and it's no wonder she idolizes him."

Tom was finished with the talking. He reached to extinguish the candle and said, "Goodnight."

Margaret lay in the darkness and wondered where her husband got his streak of stinginess. He was a good husband and father, and she never regretted marrying him. Except for this one bad flaw, he was almost perfect. She recalled he had reacted in the same manner when she had gone to the courthouse and deeded seven acres of land to their minister, Reverend William Hardesty.

Tom had protested, "The Session makes sure he is paid fairly and I don't see why you think it's necessary to deed a parcel of land to him."

Margaret had replied, "Tom, you *know* that when the Reverend is too old to preach, he will have no income other than a small pension, and no house to live in. On this piece of land he can build a home and keep a cow and some chickens. Besides that, he's a Godly man and one who deserves our help where we can give it."

Margaret rolled away from her husband and settled onto her left side. Her last thought before dropping off to sleep was a hope that Sarah would not take after her father in this one aspect of his character. She was pleased that her daughter had inherited many of her father's physical features and his dark blue eyes; she hoped Sarah would be as industrious and hard-working as her father. Margaret remembered the words from the Bible that said we must 'give thanks in everything' so she silently said a prayer of thanks for her husband. Without him she would be a lonely spinster, and she would never have known her beloved daughter, Sarah.

CHAPTER FOURTEEN

Miss Maysell stood erect as she inspected the bedroom that had been Thomas's. She looked at Margaret and said, "This will do just fine, but do you not have a chest of drawers where I can store my things? And I'll need a table and chair where I can plan lessons."

Margaret had grown used to Thomas's acceptance of the sparsely furnished room, and had not given much thought to the needs of the young school teacher. Irritated with herself for not thinking of these things before, Margaret considered a solution.

"My sister may have a chest of drawers that we can use, and I'll look for a table."

Turning to her daughter she said, "Sarah, go downstairs and bring up the kettle. Miss Maysell will want to wash before supper."

Sarah closed her mouth, blinked once, and quickly nodded to her mother. Then without a word, she turned and ran down the stairs.

Margaret wondered about her daughter's good sense because Sarah was obviously over-awed by this demanding young woman. This wisp of a girl with her long yellow hair and turned- up nose was already turning their household upside down.

Thomas was not exactly pleased that he would have to sleep in the barn for the next six weeks, but at least it was not yet freezing at night. He wondered how many more inconveniences would come about while Miss Maysell boarded at their house.

His first meeting with her had left him with the impression that Miss Maysell thought very highly of herself. She was pretty in a washed-out sort of way. Her pale yellow hair and eye lashes contrasted with blue eyes, soft pink skin, and white even teeth. But her long neck and slightly turned-up nose made her appear even more pleased with herself than a young person had the right to be.

Sarah ran to him in the barn. She was out of breath and more excited than usual. In a shrill voice she commanded, "Thomas, Mama says that Miss Maysell needs the chest of drawers that Aunt Hannah has, and she wants you to hitch up the wagon right away to go over there and bring it back."

"It's almost time for supper. Can't it wait until tomorrow?"

"No! Mama says you can eat with the Cole's before you come home."

Sarah departed in a hurry, leaving Thomas to finish his milking chores. He was on his way to the spring house with the strained milk so he moved faster.

The sun was below the horizon by the time he had hitched Mac to the wagon. In a few minutes it would be dark so he pulled a lantern away from its hook on the barn wall. He left in a cloud of dust, rattling up the road toward the Cole family farm.

John saw him first and ambled out to greet Thomas with a grin.

"What brings you here at this time of night? Is everything alright?"

"Everything's fine. It's the new school teacher. She's moved into the house and she needs the chest of drawers that your mother offered to Aunt Margaret."

"Come in the house. Mom will know more about it than I do."

Thomas explained Aunt Margaret's request to Hannah and learned that John would help him load the chest after they all ate supper.

Thomas's eyes brightened at the sight of Rena who entered the dining room carrying a platter of roast pork. When Rena looked up and saw Thomas she nearly dropped the platter. Emma's laughter shrilled out while Rena placed the meat on the table and beamed at Thomas.

Then Isaac walked in and his face broke into a big smile. "What is this? Our favorite nephew has come to join us for supper?"

The inconvenient visit had turned into a party and Thomas was finding himself grateful to Miss Maysell.

At the end of the pleasant evening, with the chest tied securely into the wagon, 'good-byes' and 'thanks' were called out into the darkness. The light of the lantern spied out the shadows as Thomas drove Mac out of the yard and onto the lane toward home.

Another Christmas had come and gone. Thomas sat at the kitchen table on a Sunday evening and tried to finish a letter to his family in Ireland.

...and because Miss Maysell required her own room with a bed, chest of drawers, and a study table, I had to sleep in the barn until she left right before Christmas. I have never been around such a bossy young woman in my life. She corrected me and Sarah all the time and she even corrected Aunt Margaret's speech. Sarah loved her teacher until she moved in with us and now I think Miss Maysell is no longer on the favored list.

January weather has arrived and with it some heavy

snow. In fact, the snow is piled to the eaves on the north side of the buildings. I am very glad to be sleeping in the house again. Tom's headaches have gone away and he seems to be back to normal. Everyone else is fine here. I hope you are all well, and that the farm is prospering. I thought of you all at Christmas and wondered if everything was the same as when I was there. I hope Gilbert was able to be with you this Christmas. We went to eat Christmas dinner with the Cole family this year, and after dinner, Rena played the piano and we all sang Carols.

Foaling season is upon us here, and lambing will follow soon. I am very glad that Tom sold off half of the sheep and he is no longer breeding his own hogs. We have only three milk cows, but the horses keep on multiplying and they have been profitable for us.

The hour is late and I must close this letter with my love and greetings to all.

Your loving son and brother,
Thomas

"Sarah, I know you have something to say, but first your father will ask the blessing." Margaret reminded her daughter once again about the rules of the house.

Sarah gave a quick glance toward Thomas and bowed her head while her father prayed over their evening meal.

As soon as she heard her father say, "Amen", Sarah said, "Mama, can I talk now?"

Margaret nodded, "Yes, Sarah." She handed the platter of chicken to her husband.

With much excitement in her voice, Sarah reported, "Miss Maysell is going to get married and she has invited the whole class and our all our families to her wedding in Zanesville."

Her father cut thigh meat away from its bone and said, "Do you want to go to her wedding after all the grief she gave us when she boarded at our house?"

Sarah said, "That was a long time ago, Daddy." Clearly, Sarah had forgiven Miss Maysell over the past five months.

"Do you know the date for wedding?" Margaret asked as she took a helping of potatoes and onions.

"Miss Maysell said it will be the eighteenth of June and she will be sending us written invitations in the mail. Please, can we go?"

Margaret said, "Let's wait until the invitation comes and then we'll decide."

Two days later Tom came home from town with the mail and there among some other letters was the invitation. When he handed it to Sarah that evening after supper, she tore into the envelope and pulled out the fine stationery which bore the formal invitation in fancy script. She studied it and then showed it first to her mother, then to her father, and last of all, to her cousin.

Sarah proudly told them what they had read, "It says there will be a carriage to take people from the train station to the church and back. And then there are the letters, R.S.V.P. What does that mean, Mama?"

Margaret explained, "It means we need to reply and let them know if we are coming."

Sarah said, "I really think we should go to Miss Maysell's wedding. After all, she lived with us for six weeks and she was a member of our family."

Her father almost choked over Sarah's words and looked at his wife who had to cover her mouth with her hand while she tried to stop laughing. Thomas grinned as he looked down at his plate.

Sarah said, "What is so funny?"

"Never mind, Sarah. Your mother and I will talk it over in private and we'll decide this matter later." Her father buttered another slice of bread.

"Why can't we decide right now?"

Margaret said, "Enough of this talk. Let's start clearing the table so you can go to work on your arithmetic."

Finally, it was decided that the girls and women in the Keith and Cole families would make the train trip to Zanesville to attend Miss Maysell's wedding the morning of June eighteenth. She had arranged for two carriages to meet the people from Norwich at the Zanesville train station to take them to the church and return them later in the day.

Sarah and Emma were excited because they each had new taffeta dresses to wear. Sarah's dress was a soft yellow and Emma's was pale green. The girls loved the swishing sound of the taffeta when they walked. Margaret had washed Sarah's hair and twisted rags into it the night before, and Sarah delighted in turning her head from side to side to see her long dark curls swirl. Rena and Hannah wore their best church clothes, and Margaret had made herself a new dress of soft, lightweight gray wool. To make it look more like a summer dress, she added a lovely tatted collar of white that came down the front of the dress in a V shape.

The wedding, attended by many of Zanesville's elite, was very elegant. The bride wore a long white gown of brocade satin which included a long train made of lace. On her head she wore a white lace veil trimmed with seed pearls. The groom was handsome in his black tails and bow tie. After the wedding everyone gathered out on the large grassy area behind the church where many tables and chairs were set up with bouquets of flowers on each table.

Small fancy sandwiches and sweet fruit punch were served, and then the bride and groom cut a large, decorated wedding cake. Everyone was served a piece of the white confection on a china plate. This was the most beautiful and impressive occasion that many from Norwich had ever witnessed. Almost everyone saved their delicate paper napkin with the wedding date stamped in the corner.

Sarah spoke quietly to her mother, "Can we save our piece of cake and take it home with us?"

"Now tell me, Sarah, how would we get home with the cake and keep it from crumbling all over our new clothes?"

In reply, Sarah merely grimaced and looked down at her cake. She and Emma took tiny bites to make it last as long as possible.

The bride had removed the long, detachable train so that she and the groom could walk hand-in-hand from table to table thanking the guests for attending the wedding. When they came to the table where the Keith and Cole families were sitting, Sarah and Emma beamed.

"Thank you for inviting us," Sarah said, "and I hope you and your new husband will like the milk pitcher we gave you for your present."

No to be outdone, Emma chimed in, "I'm glad we came to see you in your beautiful wedding gown, and I hope you like the dish towels because I embroidered them."

Graciously, the bride said, "I'm sure we'll enjoy both of your gifts and we'll think of you when we use them."

Hannah and Margaret cringed at their daughters' forthright, but innocent remarks, and simply said, "Thank you for inviting us."

The train ride home was warm, long, and tiring. Sarah and Emma looked forward to taking off their fancy new dresses and putting on some old, comfortable clothes as soon as they returned at home. Margaret and Hannah talked only of the chores they had left undone because of this extravagant wedding. They surmised the new bride would have a cook and a housekeeper when she moved into her big house in the city.

"I wonder how it would be to have servants do most of the work at home," Hannah said.

Margaret sighed, "I'm sure we'll never know."

CHAPTER FIFTEEN

As the seasons passed and the Christmas of 1883 drew near, Thomas looked forward to another festive time with the Cole family, and especially with Rena. He recently passed his 20th birthday and Rena was almost 19 years old. Their relationship had grown closer and warmer over the passing months; she was not only his best friend, but now Thomas thought of her as his future wife.

He still had two and a half more years to work for his uncle, and he had managed to save very little money. Tom's miserly ways had not changed over time, and Thomas no longer kept a record of all he was owed. This would be another Christmas when he would be forced to give very inexpensive presents to family members. This thought made him sad because he didn't want Rena to think of him as tightfisted. But when he remembered their many shared confidences, he knew she understood his situation. If only he could find a way to save more money and be able to buy even a few acres of land at the end of two and a half years! Then he could ask Rena to marry him and his life would begin.

A heavy snowfall made it necessary to travel by sleigh, and Tom had given his permission for Thomas to use the sleigh to take Rena caroling with the young people at church. Thomas hitched up Mac and Maddie, and went into the house where he quickly washed and shaved, put on a clean shirt and his warm coat.

As he donned his hat and walked out the door, Aunt Margaret stopped him. "Thomas! Take this." She extended her hand and gave him two pieces of buttered bread wrapped around sliced and salted boiled eggs.

"Thank you, Aunt Margaret." The eggs were still warm and Thomas ate with enthusiasm as he climbed into the sleigh and urged the horses on.

He exchanged friendly greetings with everyone in the Cole family before he and Rena left for the evening. The young couple sat close together, warm wool blankets wrapped around them. He slowed Mac and Maddie to a walk so they would have more time alone in the early darkness of the winter evening. He leaned over and kissed her gently and she kissed him back with passion.

"Thomas, I have to tell you something and I don't even want to think about it."

Thomas heard the distress in her voice. "What's wrong?"

"It's my father's mother, Grandmother Cole. She's not well, and her son, my Uncle David took a bad fall and broke his leg in several places. Doctors are telling him he may lose his leg because of infections. He was the one who watched over Grandmother and took her to church and to shop in town. He arranged all her affairs and helped her in many ways. Now he is almost helpless and his wife is not strong."

"How are they going to manage?" Thomas said.

"They have asked me to come and live with Grandmother and take care of her." Rena began sobbing, and in between sobs, she managed to tell Thomas that she was to leave right after Christmas on the train for Pennsylvania.

The rest of the evening was a painful charade. Thomas and Rena went through the motions of having a good time; they joined in the caroling with little enthusiasm. They clung to one another grieving over the thought of being separated by such a distance.

When he took her home that night, she put her arms around him and said, "I wish we could run away together and not be separated like this."

It took all his strength to remain calm and not agree to such actions.

He kissed her and said, "We'll write to one another as often as we can. I promise you that in two and a half more years, I will ask you to marry me. My service to Tom will be ended then. Pray that we can endure this time apart."

They embraced, feeling they belonged right here in one another's arms.

At last, Thomas said, "I need to walk you to the door or your father will be coming out here to fetch you. Besides that, you're shivering with the cold."

Christmas Day was less than joyful because by now they all knew that Rena was leaving in two days and they would not see her for many months, perhaps a year. Tactfully, the family gave Thomas and Rena time to be together, to hold hands as they looked longingly at one another. Even Sarah and Emma were subdued because they were beginning to realize how much they would miss Rena.

When the day came for her departure, they were all gathered at the Sundale Station, waiting for the eastbound train. Her big trunk stood in the baggage area ready to be loaded in the baggage car. Rena wore her best Sunday dress, new warm coat, and a new hat which helped her to appear as an adult instead of a frightened girl. A few others, also waiting for the train, stood nearby. She and Thomas said their good-byes on Christmas Day and agreed they would make the parting as calm as possible; there would be no tears.

Both families tried very hard to keep this time light-hearted and to make jokes about any little thing. But too soon the train came clanging and steaming into the station. Rena quickly gave them each a hug, climbed onboard and found a seat where she waved through the window to her family, trying to smile at them. When she looked at Thomas her eyes filled with tears. The two families stood on the platform waving and watching as the train went around the bend and through the trees to Pennsylvania.

Thomas was in a bad mood most of the time these days. He worked hard and long to keep up with everything on the farm, but his patience was thin, and he didn't want to talk unless it was necessary. He wrote to Rena at least once every week, and she wrote often to him. In his letters, he poured out his heart to her, telling her how much he missed her. He complained about his uncle, who remained as stingy as ever, and now there was an added problem. Tom was growing more forgetful each day. Thomas found fault with his over-indulged cousin, and he criticized Aunt Margaret's bossy ways. He was not proud of the content of those letters but he felt better knowing that Rena understood.

In turn, Rena bared her soul to Thomas, writing about how much she missed him, and how the memory of his kisses were her last thought at night. Her Grandmother was not as helpless as Rena had been led to believe. In fact, she was quite spry, but often forgetful. Because her grandmother never put away anything and could never remember where her things were, Rena had to follow her around like a shadow.

Thomas and Rena agreed they would not save one another's letters because of all the personal and incriminating things they had written, so they promised to burn them soon after they had been read.

Sarah was disappointed to learn that the letters Thomas received from Rena were burned. If he had saved the letters she would have found them because she very much wanted to know what they said. Now that she was almost fourteen years old she was curious about many things that never concerned her before. Her body was changing into the shape of a young woman's, and adult male and female relationships suddenly became paramount in her thoughts. She was impatient with Emma and made fun of her because she was still playing with dolls. Sarah had put away her dolls only recently, but that was different.

Sarah became fast friends with Mercy Mallory who was a few months older than Sarah. The two girls went through all the grades at Wilderness School together and just recently they graduated from the eighth grade. They both felt very grown up because the days of being school children were past. Neither girl ever wanted to attend school again.

But the lessons were not over. Mercy took Sarah under her wing and taught her many things that opened up a whole new world to Sarah.

Mercy, whose real name was Mercedes, explained to Sarah, "I started having my monthly flow last March, and now if I slept with a boy I could have a baby."

Sarah, protected as she was, didn't know what Mercy was talking about so Mercy proceeded to explain all she knew. Having grown up in a large family, Mercy was well acquainted with the anatomy of the opposite sex and she made it her goal to inform Sarah. Precocious in many ways, Mercy could extrapolate all she knew about animal behavior and apply it to humans.

Throughout the summer months the two friends spent a great deal of time together and often they went swimming in the creek by Mallory's farm. They had to wear old clothes when they swam in the big swimming hole with the other children, but further down the creek the girls discovered, hidden among the shade of many trees, a smaller swimming area. Here, the two girls took off all their clothes and while they were in the water laughing and splashing, they openly observed one another's bodies. In contrast to Sarah's curvaceous body with rounded breasts, Mercy was tall and slender with almost no waist and tiny breasts. After their play in the water, the two girls found a sunny spot on the bank where they could lie in the grass to dry off in the warmth of the sun. Many secret things went on between them, and it was here, with the help of Mercy's knowledgeable touch, that Sarah became sexually awakened.

Sarah was so intoxicated with all her new knowledge that she began spying on Thomas as he wrote letters to Rena. She asked Mercy one day, "Do you suppose Thomas has ever lain with Rena and made love to her?"

"I doubt it. He knows if he did that, he would be forced to marry her because she could be carrying his child."

Sarah thought about Mercy's wise comments for a long time after that.

Three weeks later, Sarah informed Mercy that she was a woman now, too. She was wearing a rag that very day, in fact. Sarah told her, "My mother said I must be very careful around boys now, and never allow any boy or man to touch my private parts."

Sarah and Mercy laughed together because they believed they were so worldly.

As the summer wore on, Sarah became aware that her father no longer acted like himself. He couldn't remember the names of people he had known for years, or the words for many things, and he seemed to be lost much of the time.

After their noonday meal, Sarah helped her mother with the dishes, wiping them dry with a large towel and placing them on the shelf in the dish cupboard. Finally, Sarah spoke the question that had been bothering her.

"What's wrong with Daddy? He can't remember anything at all these days."

"I know, Sarah, it's something that happens to people sometimes." Margaret's face was creased with worry. She squeezed out the rag and began wiping the kitchen table. "I give him notes to help him remember but he forgets to look at the notes or he loses them. He went to town last week and forgot what he meant to do there so he had to come back home." Margaret picked up the cooking pot from the stove, lowered it into the basin of warm water and began scrubbing it. "I think we must be as patient with him as we can."

But Sarah knew her mother was not a patient woman. She felt anxious and fearful when she heard her mother shouting at her father, "Tom, you left the gate open again and the animals have trampled my garden!" or "Tom! You forgot to button your shirt." or "Where did you leave your hat this time?" The most upsetting of all was, "Tom! You must not relieve yourself in the yard, and in plain sight of Sarah! Go to the privy and close the door!"

The next Sunday afternoon the women and girls were cleaning up after dinner when Sarah overheard Aunt Hannah say to her mother, "I hate to tell you this, but Isaac and John do not want to work the fields with Tom anymore because he can't be trusted. He forgets the ordinary things that he's done all his life, like oiling the machinery, or setting the brake when they work on a hillside. One of them could be hurt very seriously."

All of this alarmed and threatened Sarah so much that she didn't want to be near her father anymore. She was grateful that her mother did not object when Sarah hurried through her chores each day, then saddled Belle and rode to the Mallory's farm where she helped Mercy with her chores. More and more frequently, Sarah stayed to eat dinner with the Mallory's and often she was given permission to stay overnight.

A born actress, Mercy entertained and delighted Sarah by quoting passages of poetry or long recitations about lovers who were parted. Mercy could transform herself into another person altogether, at times frightening Sarah, and at other times, thrilling her to the point of swooning. She had such a memory that by reading over the lines once or twice, Mercy knew the poem or prose by heart. In Sarah, she had an appreciative audience and a friend who applauded her acting skill. Mercy became Sarah's relief and shelter from all the worries at home.

Thomas came through the back door into the kitchen to see his Aunt Margaret sitting at the table with pencil in hand, working at the ledger book. He extinguished the lantern and hung it from its hook on the wall. The hour was late and Thomas wanted to hurry up to his bedroom and go to bed.

"Thomas, will you sit down here and give me some help with these entries and amounts?"

Thomas removed his hat and jacket, hanging them on a hook near the back door. He pulled out a chair and sat next to his aunt. "Has Tom gone to bed already?"

"Yes, I put him to bed an hour ago. Sarah is staying at the Mallory farm tonight." She moved the ledger book closer to Thomas and pointed with her finger to places that were causing a problem. "See here…last month Tom wrote in these figures for sugar, molasses, nails, brass rivets, and leather. I can't understand how he arrived at this amount."

Thomas studied the entries for a few minutes. "Maybe he added them up and forgot to subtract the total."

Margaret looked and nodded. "You're right. I can't trust him to enter anything into the ledger these days…his mind is not working anymore. He hasn't entered kerosene in weeks, and that is something we use all the time." She looked at Thomas. "When was the last time he paid you? I can't find a record of it in any of the books?"

Thomas wondered what he should say to his aunt. He felt very uncomfortable and wished for a way out of this situation. His silence lasted longer than he wanted and confusion must have been evident on his face.

"Why don't you begin at the beginning and tell me how much he agreed to pay when you first came?"

"Before I left Ireland, he wrote to my dad and said he would be paying me eighteen dollars per month." Thomas swallowed and proceeded to tell the whole story. "When I had been here for a couple of months, I asked for my pay, and Tom told me he would have to take out ten dollars each month for my room and board, and he would pay me eight dollars every month."

"I've looked back at ledger books from two years ago and I haven't found a record of your payment." Margaret's questioning look caused more discomfort for Thomas.

"I finally gave up reminding him. Months would go by and when I needed money I would tell him my needs, such as work boots, or a new warm jacket, and he would give me just enough to pay for them."

Margaret held her head in her hands and moaned. "Oh, Thomas, I wish you had told me." She rubbed her face with rough red hands. "I could never understand Tom's tight-fisted ways. He is such a good husband and caring father... I always found it hard to believe he could be so stingy." She closed the large book with a resigned sigh. "I'll make sure you receive some of your back pay. I have some money here at the house, and I'll give you one hundred dollars tomorrow." She stood upright and moved her chair out of the way. "It's late, and we need some sleep."

The first day of November Thomas was in the training ring working with a colt. The young horse was learning quickly how to respond to Thomas's commands.

He heard someone call his name and he looked to see his Aunt Margaret standing at the fence. She had a worried look on her face.

"Where is your uncle? I can't find him anywhere," she said.

"I thought he was in the house with you."

"He was, but now he's gone."

Thomas opened the gate and walked over to his aunt. "I'll start looking out here and inside the barn if you'll look in the privy and the spring house. Maybe you should look in the root cellar, too."

Fifteen minutes later, Thomas saw his aunt again and her face told him she had not found her husband. He said, "I'll saddle Beauty and go out on the roads to look for him."

It was late in the day when Thomas found his uncle walking on the road with Rex beside him. Tom was not wearing a hat or a coat and he was in a precarious state, shaking violently from the cold. Thomas called to him, "Tom, where are you going?"

Tom turned to look at his nephew and said, "I'm goin' home."

"I'm here to give you a ride home. Stop walking and I'll help you get on Beauty." Thomas dismounted, took off his coat and put it on his uncle's shivering body. Then he helped Tom into the saddle.

When they got back to the house Aunt Margaret was waiting, her fleshy pink face looking grim with worry. "Where did you find him, Thomas?"

"He was walking down the road, more than a mile past the lane into the Cole's farm."

Thomas and his aunt quickly escorted Tom into the kitchen where Margaret removed Tom's boots and socks and put his feet into a basin of warm water. Thomas added more wood to the stove and put fresh water in the coffee pot.

Aunt Margaret said, "Thomas, would you run upstairs and pull all the blankets off our bed and bring them down here?"

Soon Tom sat wrapped in blankets while his feet soaked in warm water and he drank hot coffee diluted with rich milk. Margaret scolded her husband all the while, and finally his color returned and he stopped shivering.

These days someone needed to help Tom dress, wash, shave, and comb his hair because he no longer knew how to do those ordinary tasks. Thomas could see what a burden it was for Margaret and he tried to help her as much as he could. It was as if they had a giant-sized toddler living in the house who needed constant supervision.

The next morning Margaret was working alone in the kitchen. She had left Tom in the front room seated near the black, cast-iron heat stove while he read the newspaper. Margaret measured out the flour into her big mixing bowl, preparing to make bread when she heard a commotion in the front room.

She called out, "What's going on in there?"

When she heard no answer she dropped what she was doing and went to look. There in the front room she saw Tom waving his arms and jumping around. He had added so much wood to the stove and created such a blaze that the fire escaped and the carpet was in flames.

Margaret screamed at him to move away; she raised her skirts and began to stamp the carpet with her feet to put out the fire. This was not helping so she pulled the quilt off the back of the sofa and threw it down on the burning carpet. Then she hurried into the kitchen and grabbed the teakettle. As she poured water over the quilt, smoke and steam billowed out and the flames died down. She fell to the floor, and at the same time she heard the teakettle clatter when it landed on the quilt, but she heard or saw nothing else.

CHAPTER SIXTEEN

Thomas saw his uncle running crazily around the yard like a chicken whose head has been decapitated. He yelled, "Tom, what's the matter?"

"Margaret...Margaret..." He seemed unable to say anything else.

Thomas said, "Where is Margaret?"

His uncle's eyes were wild as he pointed to the house.

Thomas ran to the house and through the back door. In the front room he found Margaret lying on the floor with a wet but scorched quilt next to her. The teakettle was on its side in a puddle of water. He could only exclaim, "Oh, no!"

Thomas called her name and shook her but there was no response. He felt her neck for a pulse and detected nothing. He checked her wrist for a pulse but she remained lifeless.

"God, help us." He spoke in a whisper. Thomas sat on the sofa staring at Aunt Margaret's body. He could smell the burnt odor and thought what a shame it was that her new quilt had been sacrificed to halt the fire. He waited a few minutes in hopes she would take a breath and wake up. But after checking for her pulse again, he realized Margaret was gone and he must do something. Before he left the house, he grabbed coats and hats for himself and Tom. He made sure Tom had his coat buttoned up before Thomas saddled and mounted Beauty.

"Tom, stay right here at the house," he shouted.

"I'm going to get Isaac."

He galloped Beauty all the way to the Cole's house. Thomas ran to the front porch, banged on the door and yelled, "Is anybody here?"

Hannah came out and saw his distress. "Are you alright, Thomas?"

"Yes...I mean no. There was a fire in the house and I think Aunt Margaret must have put it out. Tom came running out to find me and when I got there Margaret was lying on the floor in the front room. She had no pulse and she wasn't breathing."

"Thomas, are you certain? Sometimes people faint and when they begin to wake up they take a breath."

"I stayed with her for several minutes and checked for her pulse and breath. There was nothing."

Hannah put her hand to her mouth. She closed her eyes and stood weaving back and forth for a few seconds. Thomas reached for her and caught her before she fell. He held her tight to himself and wished this were only a bad dream which would end soon. He eased her to a sitting position on the steps of the porch.

Hannah gasped for breath and put her hand at her throat. A few seconds later she said in a whisper, "I think I'm alright now, Thomas."

"Hannah, I'm so sorry."

Hannah broke into tears. She pulled an old handkerchief from her apron pocket and wiped her nose. Hannah's gray eyes were brimming over and her smooth cheeks were shining from the flow of tears.

"Where is your Uncle Tom?" she said, wiping her face with her apron.

"I left him standing in the yard and I told him to stay at the house."

"I think you'd better go home to see about him. I'll

make sure that Isaac comes over there as soon as possible. Is Sarah at home?"

"No, she stayed last night at the Mallory's house and she hasn't come home yet."

"Go home right now before Sarah comes in and finds her mother's body."

"Do you know where Isaac is now?"

Hannah heaved a sigh of impatience. "Yes, Thomas. He and John are out in the machine shed repairing the runners on our old sleigh. I'll go and tell him what happened. You hurry home now."

"Would you ask him to bring Dr. Givens when he comes? Won't he need to sign a certificate of death?"

"Isaac will take care of it. Leave now." Hannah patted him on his back and stood to see him off.

Thomas did not want to return to the nightmare he left at the house. Nevertheless, he urged Beauty into a gallop. When he arrived, his uncle was still wandering about the yard in circles. Thomas grabbed him by the arm, guided him into the house and helped him out of his coat. He told Tom to sit down at the kitchen table while he went to retrieve the teakettle from the floor in the front room, stepping around Aunt Margaret's lifeless body. He stoked up the fire in the kitchen stove and soon the water was boiling. He made two cups of hot, strong tea, and placed one in front of Tom.

Thomas said to his uncle, "Drink all of this. Isaac will be here shortly and he will take care of everything."

Tom picked up the cup and blew into his tea. He looked with frightened eyes at his nephew, saying nothing. He blew and sipped, again and again, as if the tea would make everything right.

Thomas blew into his own cup of tea to cool it and wondered how much Tom understood or if he comprehended anything at all. He heard hoof beats in the yard and hoped it was Isaac. When he went outside, Thomas felt sick to his heart. Sarah was dismounting Belle and smiling at him.

"Beauty is all saddled up. Have you been to town already?"

"No, I had to go over to the Cole's with some urgent news. While you unsaddle Belle, I'll take care of Beauty, and then I'll tell you about it."

Dear God, help me tell her this news as gently as possible, Thomas prayed silently.

"Why the long face, Thomas? Has Rena written that she's found somebody else?"

"No Sarah. Let's give the horses some feed and water and then I'll tell you. First, I need to go inside and bring your father out here with us."

Tom was still sitting at the kitchen table sipping his tea. Thomas said, "Here, Tom. Let me help you into your coat and we'll take the tea outside to the barn. You can drink the rest of it out there." Thomas helped his uncle with his coat and then pulled on his own warm jacket before leading Tom out the kitchen door.

Sarah had already unsaddled Belle and was watering and feeding her horse. Thomas quickly removed the saddle from Beauty and made sure the big gelding was fed and watered. He had put off the dreaded task as long as he could.

"Sit here in the hay next to me and your Daddy, Sarah. I have to tell you something you won't want to hear."

Sarah eyes widened and she turned pale. She sank down beside Thomas. "What is it?"

Thomas couldn't look at her; he leaned his arms on his knees and spoke to his hands instead.

"It's your mother. She died this morning right after she put out a fire in the front room. Her heart must have given out or maybe she had a stroke. When I found her she was lying on the floor next to her burnt quilt. She had used her new quilt to put out the fire, and then poured water over it." Thomas swallowed back his tears and said in a raspy voice, "Her last act on earth was to save the house from burning down."

When he looked over at Sarah, her face was hidden behind her hands. She began to moan while she rocked back and forth. Then she began sobbing. Thomas held her to himself and rocked her in his arms as if she were a small child.

With the teacup in his hand, Tom sat on the other side of Thomas and wept also.

Isaac and John walked into the barn and found them grieving. Isaac came over to Sarah, bent down and smoothed her dark hair with his rough hand. He took hold of her hands to pull her up very gently.

Isaac said, "Let's go inside. God will give us the strength to do what needs to be done now."

It was a cold, but clear November day when the funeral service was held in the First Presbyterian Church at Norwich. After the solemn service, Mrs. Hardesty and the ladies in the church hosted tea and refreshments at the Manse. Then the Keith and Cole families followed the horse-drawn hearse to Pleasant Hill Cemetery where Margaret's body was buried. Throughout the morning, Tom was silent and pale as an alabaster statue, almost as if he had left his body and gone somewhere else. However, when they arrived at the cemetery and Margaret's coffin was lowered into the grave, Tom began choking and sobbing. Isaac put his arm around Tom's shoulders to steady him. Sarah became inconsolable, weeping into the shoulder of her Aunt Hannah. The frigid wind blew dry brown leaves across the dead grass of the cemetery, and the two families huddled together in the bone-chilling cold and the aching sorrow.

It was dark when they returned home late that afternoon, but Thomas was almost glad for the usual chores that helped to take his mind off the recent tragic events. He milked the cows, strained the milk, and poured it into one of the large crocks in the spring house. He wondered what would be done with all the surplus milk now that Aunt Margaret was not here to make butter and cheese. He hoped Sarah would churn butter for them, but he didn't think she had learned to make cheese yet. He fed and watered the horses, stroking and patting each one as he spoke softly to them.

Aunt Hannah had insisted that Sarah come and stay with their family for a while. He was glad for Sarah that she could be somewhat removed from her overwhelming sadness. She was all but an orphan now that her mother was gone and her father's mind had left him. But what would the coming days and weeks bring? Thomas was the only one capable of working the farm or making the decisions, and the thought of that responsibility felt like a heavy weight.

CHAPTER SEVENTEEN

After explaining his intentions to his uncle, Thomas hitched Mac and Maddie to the wagon and helped Tom climb up and sit next to him. Once in town, they left the horses and wagon on a side street and walked to Walker's General Store. Everyone they met expressed his or her sympathy. Thomas thanked them kindly, but Tom gave them a blank look and said nothing.

After the proprietor had given his condolences, Thomas said to Mr. Walker, "We're looking for a carpet to replace the one we had. It was a Persian style with a red background and blue and yellow flowers."

"Come this way." Mr. Walker was a wiry man who moved at top speed. When they caught up with him, he was standing next to a pile of carpets stacked nearly to his waist.

"These are all sized nine feet by twelve feet as that is the most popular size these days. You can look through the pile until you find something you like."

Thomas wrestled with the carpets for several minutes but the only carpet close to the colors of the old one had a red background with geometric figures in purple, green, and gold. He said to Tom, "What do you think? Will this one do?"

Tom looked at it but gave no indication of his opinion. Thomas doubted that his uncle even had an opinion.

He asked Mr. Walker, "How much for this one?"

"That is an authentic Persian rug. Its price is

sixteen dollars."

Thomas spoke quietly into his uncle's ear. "Do you have sixteen dollars in your wallet, Tom? That's how much we have to pay for this new rug."

Tom moved away from his nephew and started walking toward the door.

"Wait a minute, Tom!" He turned to Mr. Walker and said, "I'll be back later. Will you save that rug for us?"

Thomas caught up with his uncle and directed him toward the wagon. He helped him climb up and sit on the seat.

"Tom, will you let me see your wallet? I need to know if you have any money."

Tom surprised him by taking out his wallet, opening it up and showing several paper bills to his nephew. Attached to the side of the wallet was a small purse that contained coins of copper, silver, and gold. Thomas could not believe his uncle was carrying around that much money!

"Tom, you have much more than sixteen dollars in your wallet. Will you give me twenty dollars and we'll go back and get the carpet? When Sarah comes home to stay, we want the house to look like it did before her mother died."

At those words Tom began to weep.

Thomas sat next to his uncle feeling sorry for him. It seemed that Tom was weeping several times a day and it made Thomas feel helpless. He patted his uncle on his back and said, "Do you want to give me the money and we'll go and get the carpet?"

Tom handed over his wallet and Thomas took it saying, "Thank you. Let's go back to Walker's now. I'll need your help to carry the carpet to the wagon."

When they pulled into the yard at home, they

carried the new carpet into the front room and placed it where the old one had been. Quickly, before Tom could begin weeping again, Thomas guided his uncle back out to the wagon to make the trip to the Cole's house. Since the funeral, Hannah had insisted they join the Cole family for noonday dinners.

It was a good feeling to walk into Hannah's house where everything was clean and tidy just as it had been at home when Aunt Margaret was alive. And the food was so much better than anything Thomas could put together. In fact, he was getting tired of eating his own porridge every morning and night. Tom never said anything these days, so there was no complaining from him.

Sarah greeted Thomas and her father with a smile. "Everything you are eating today is food I have prepared. Aunt Hannah is teaching me to cook enough different dishes that I can come home and cook for you."

She set down a platter of roast pork in the center of the table. Next to the pork she placed a bowl of cooked sliced carrots and another large bowl of boiled potatoes. Gravy was served from yet another bowl.

Thomas said, "We've missed you at home, Sarah. Are you coming home with us today?"

"Aunt Hannah says I should stay here until Rena comes home to visit. By then I should know how to cook more things." Sarah was obviously proud of her accomplishments.

Loyal Emma said, "Sarah even knows how to make gravy now, and that is hard to do. Mine is always lumpy."

Christmas Day was just about as sad as the day of Margaret's funeral the month before. They gathered at the Cole family home for dinner. Hannah, Sarah, and Emma had worked hard to make a fine meal and Hannah even served a tasty Christmas pudding with hard sauce for dessert. After dinner they gathered in the Cole's front room and went through the motions of singing the few songs Sarah knew how to play. Then Emma played a few pieces on the piano. But two of their favorite people were missing. Rena would be home in a few days but Margaret would never celebrate Christmas with them again. Tom sat by himself in a straight back chair and wept quietly most of the day. At last, Thomas said he needed to take Tom home and get the chores done before dark. They all sighed with relief and said their farewells to one another to end this miserable day.

Rena was to arrive at the station shortly before noon three days after Christmas. Isaac and Hannah graciously allowed Thomas to go by himself to fetch Rena home while Tom stayed with the Coles to be looked after by the family. Fortunately, there had been no snowfall in a week or more so that Mac and Maddie had an easy pull to Sundale Station.

Thomas saw Rena before she saw him. She was so lovely his heart began to leap inside his chest. She caught sight of Thomas, smiled, and ran to him. It was a warm embrace, but because they were in a public place, they did not kiss. Thomas directed her to the wagon and helped her climb into it. She carried only a small bag and Thomas placed it in the wagon before hoisting himself up to the seat for the drive to the Cole family farm.

As the wagon rolled down the hill away from Sundale Station, they both began speaking at once. Then they both laughed while Thomas held her close to him with one arm, his other hand holding the reins. Out of sight of the station now, he leaned over and kissed her with all the longing he had felt over the past year, and she kissed him back.

"It's been a very long time…I thought this day would never come." Rena said.

"I know. All I want to do is hold you close to me and never let you go. I hope you don't have to return. Is your grandmother able to do without your help, or will she still need you?"

"Oh, it looks hopeless. She has a daughter who lives less than two hours away by train, but she doesn't want to bother to help her mother. Uncle David wrote to his sister and I think he shamed her into coming for a week to stay with Grandma while I came home to see my family. Besides that, Grandma is becoming even more forgetful and we are afraid she will burn the house down. I wrote to you that Uncle David lost his leg a few months ago, and he has his hands full taking care of himself and his own sick wife."

"Don't speak to me about houses burning down. I'm almost certain that Tom started the fire in our front room. Aunt Margaret died directly after she put out the fire with her quilt."

"It's so sad. How is Sarah taking this?"

"She's been staying at your house ever since the funeral. She's sleeping with Emma and seems to be happy that your mother is teaching her how to cook. I don't know how she will act when she has to come home and be reminded every day that her mother is gone. She has been protected all her life… I worry about her."

"What about Uncle Tom?"

"His situation is the saddest of all. He can't be trusted alone because he wanders away. Ever since Margaret died, he weeps several times a day, and he has stopped speaking altogether."

Thomas's need to talk about these worries, and Rena's concerned listening spurred him on to further revelations.

"These past few months I've had to sell off all the sheep and some of our valuable horses, including Lady, our Percheron out of Maddie. If your father had not been so generous to share half the proceeds from the harvests this year, we might be in financial trouble. Tom had to stay at home with Aunt Margaret while the three of us did all the work in the fields."

Thomas held Rena and kissed her before he went on with his narrative. "When Aunt Margaret was alive she could advise me about the farm, and she was the one who told me to sell off the animals at auction. She also told me about the many acres of land that she owns here and over near Rich Hill. I understand she has a reliable, steady tenant farming the cleared property at Rich Hill and he pays her forty percent of the profits. Now that Aunt Margaret is gone I'm expected to make all the decisions but I have no authority."

"Let me talk to Daddy about this. Maybe you will need legal help. If, by law, the farm goes to Uncle Tom, it will be disastrous."

"Sometimes I think I should walk away from here and wash my hands of it. But what would happen to Sarah and Tom? They are so helpless."

All too soon, they pulled into the drive at the Cole's house. Everyone came out of the house and headed for Rena. She was greeted by many exclamations, warm embraces, and smiling faces.

"Let's go inside where it's warm." Isaac put an arm around his oldest daughter. "Your mother and Sarah and Emma have prepared all your favorite food, and it's smelling good in there."

Dinner around the Cole's table that afternoon was more festive than any meal they could remember in recent

months. Even Tom endured the afternoon without
weeping. Everyone commented that Rena looked prettier
than ever, and she blushed when Thomas's voice joined in
agreement. Then Rena, who had been away for a whole
year, said that Emma and Sarah both looked much older
and Sarah did not even look like her little cousin anymore,
but rather, a grown woman. It was Sarah's turn to blush.

Hannah cleared her throat and said, "Sarah has
asked if she can stay here to be with Rena this week.
Emma and Sarah have enjoyed one another's company, and
Rena can have John's bed. He said he doesn't mind
sleeping on a pallet in the kitchen where it's warm."

"Anything for my pretty sister," John teased her
with pride in his voice.

Secretly, Thomas wished Rena could sleep at their
house in his bed, but he knew that would never happen
until they were married. He was happy for Sarah that she
could postpone her return to the harsh reality of home
without her mother.

That whole week the noonday meals were enjoyed
much more than usual. With winter in full force there was
not a lot for the men to do around the farm until the animals
began giving birth. The cows had stopped giving milk until
their new calves were born sometime within the next week
or two. Thomas hitched the Percherons to the sleigh and he
and Tom made frequent trips back and forth between the
Keith and Cole houses.

After dinner one afternoon, Isaac asked Thomas to
accompany him to the barn. It was cold so they both wore
their coats and hats. In the dim light of the barn, Isaac lit
up his pipe and looked Thomas square in the face. "Rena
tells me you're worried about what will happen to the farm.
I can tell you that by law, it will go to Tom, but it rightfully
belongs to Sarah. Since she is a minor she has no claim

until she reaches the age of 21, or her father dies."

Thomas nodded thoughtfully. "How can I continue to make decisions and work there if I have no authority? You know and I know that Tom is not able to handle this responsibility."

Isaac said, "I think we need a lawyer to appoint power of attorney to one of us. Are you twenty-one years old yet, Thomas?"

"I had my twenty-first birthday just a few weeks ago."

"You are qualified to run this farm on behalf of your uncle and your cousin. I will testify to that. Do you mind if I make an appointment for us to talk with a lawyer right away?"

"Do you know of an honest lawyer?"

"You remember the man Miss Maysell married? His father, Harold Stanley is an attorney with an honest reputation. I'll write him a letter tonight and ask if we can see him soon. In my letter, I'll give him some background information and ask about his fee for such a transaction. It will mean a trip into Zanesville but it will be worthwhile to get this settled."

"Thank you. I appreciate your help." Thomas offered his hand to Isaac and they shook hands on the matter.

Hannah and the girls were just finishing their clean-up of the kitchen. Rena looked up from her sweeping to see her father coming inside. He removed his coat and hat and placed them on a hook by the back door.

He spoke into Rena's ear. "Thomas is hitching up the horses to their sleigh. Would you like to have a few minutes alone with him before he leaves?

Rena pulled on her coat and mittens, and went out the back door. She hurried to Thomas' side. Darkness was creeping upon them bringing the close of another day; in fact, her whole week at home was nearly over and she would have to return to her grandmother tomorrow.

"I can't wait another whole year to see you. I'm going to insist that I get time off to come home next summer." Rena spoke in a determined voice.

Thomas embraced her and said, "I hope you can come home sooner than that."

She threw her arms around his neck and kissed him again and again. "In a year and one-half, are you still planning to propose to me?"

"I would propose to you right now if I were free from my obligation. In my mind, we are already husband and wife." He kissed her tenderly.

Thomas released her and said, "I must go in and get Tom and take him home. I'll see you tomorrow at the train station, dearest Rena." He reached for her and kissed her one last time before he went inside with his arm around his future wife.

CHAPTER EIGHTEEN

The two families stood close together on the platform at the Sundale Station watching the train leave around the bend. Overcast skies and the biting cold weather magnified their feelings of loss. Margaret was gone from them forever, and now the train was taking Rena's sweet smile and cheerfulness away.

When the train was out of sight, Hannah spoke first. "Sarah, are you going home with your father and Thomas today?"

"Oh, I wish I could stay with Emma a little longer. Would you mind, Aunt Hannah?" Sarah looked with pleading eyes at her aunt.

"You're welcome to stay with us as long as you like, but don't you think Thomas might need your help?"

Sarah looked forlorn.

Hannah took pity on her and said, "You come home with us today, and Emma and I will take you to your home tomorrow morning. We'll spend the whole day cleaning your house, and baking bread."

Sarah nodded her head in half-hearted agreement. She was dreading the thought of going home and walking through the room where her mother had died. And Sarah knew she would have to take responsibility for her father's welfare. It almost made her sick to think about it.

As Hannah had promised, she and Emma went home with Sarah and they all worked hard to sweep, dust, scrub, and mop throughout the house. Hannah also gave one more lesson on bread-making to Sarah, and by the time her aunt and cousin left, the bread smelled delicious. Hannah also brought left-over ham and potatoes with gravy that were now warming in the oven for supper.

Sarah called Thomas and her father in for supper. Thomas said a brief prayer before they began to eat their evening meal in silence. Finally, Thomas looked at his cousin and said, "It's good to have you home again."

"Thank you, Thomas." She moved some food around on her plate, and remembered the new carpet in the front room. "Did you choose the carpet?"

"Yes, I hope you like it."

"I do. It's very nice."

"It cost more than I expected, but I thought it was one of the best-looking carpets at Walker's Store."

Her father began weeping, and Sarah, who felt like joining him, choked back her tears.

Thomas got up from the table and said, "I'll take him upstairs and get him ready for bed. He worked hard stacking wood with me today and he must be tired."

Sarah was still cleaning up in the kitchen when Thomas returned.

"Would you like some help?" Thomas said.

"No, thank you. I'm almost done." She leaned over and put some scraps of meat in Tospy's bowl. He was older now so Sarah pushed the bowl close to her little terrier.

"Topsy may be getting old but he's still the best little ratter I've ever seen," Thomas said. "Last week he killed two big rats in the root cellar."

Topsy knew they were talking about him so he perked up his ears and opened his mouth to reveal his pink tongue, all the while wagging his stump of a tail.

Thomas leaned over to pet him, and then he said to Sarah, "I'm going out for one last check on the animals, and then I'll be going to bed. You can go on to bed and I'll see you in the morning."

Sarah tapped softly on the door of Thomas' bedroom.

He called out, "Who's there?" His voice was hoarse from sleep.

"It's me. Can I come in?" Sarah's voice was muffled.

"What's wrong, Sarah?"

"Let me in and I'll tell you."

"Alright, come in."

Sarah was holding a candle in a tin holder, and she shook so violently that it appeared the candle might fall to the floor.

He whispered, "Close the door behind you and put the candle on the chest over there."

Sarah did as she was told, then she approached Thomas who was sitting on the edge of his bed. "Thomas, I can't stop shaking. This has been happening to me every night since Mama died, and it could only be stopped when Emma laid herself down across my back. Her weight stopped my shaking so I could get to sleep."

"Emma isn't here, Sarah. Why don't you try to go to sleep without her?"

"I've been trying all night. The clock struck three a while ago and I have not slept at all."

Remembering to keep his voice quiet, Thomas said, "I don't know how to help you, Sarah."

"Please let me get in bed with you, and maybe you could press down on my back with your hands."

Thomas pulled back the blankets and motioned for her to get under them while he stood up wearing only his long johns. "Roll onto your stomach and I'll press down on your back."

Thomas pressed his hands on the blankets covering Sarah's back.

"Push harder, Thomas."

He pushed so hard they could hear the bedsprings complaining. Several minutes passed and Sarah still shook the whole bed with her trembling.

"Sarah, move over against the wall so there will be room for me to lie down. I'm freezing to death."

First he blew out the candle and then Thomas lay down and pulled the blankets over himself. He continued pressing against her back with his hand. After a long time, Sarah's shaking ceased and she was breathing deeply. Thomas fell asleep beside her.

The next night Sarah came to his room much earlier. She lay down under the covers and shook the bed with her trembling. Again, Thomas used his hands to press hard on her back until she quieted and fell into a deep sleep. Night after night, Sarah crept into Thomas's bed and it became so commonplace that neither of them spoke of it.

Sunday morning the three remaining members of the Keith family went to church. Afterward, they went to the Cole home for dinner where Isaac told Thomas and Sarah to be ready to board the 8:30 train to Zanesville Monday morning because they had an appointment with the attorney, Harold Stanley. Mr. Stanley wanted to meet Sarah and her father.

That night Thomas sat at the kitchen table with paper and pen poised to begin a letter to Rena while Sarah finished sweeping the floor. He had already received a letter from Rena but he had not written since she left nine days ago.

Thomas looked up at his cousin. "I've already put your father to bed. I need to write a letter to Rena so you can go on up to bed now, Sarah. I'll come to bed soon." Thomas looked at the blank page and wrote the date at the top.

He did not see the look Sarah gave him nor did he pay attention when she dropped the broom and hurried out of the kitchen. Later, when Thomas crawled into bed, he began to think that Sarah had overcome her problem with trembling because she did not come to join him. He rolled over and went to sleep to dream of Rena's deep violet eyes and her full, soft mouth. Sometime later he woke to the sound of his bedroom door opening. He felt dismay knowing that Sarah continued to shake with fear, and he wondered when it would ever stop.

She lifted the blankets and lay down beside him. Thomas, half asleep, reached over to press on her back, and instead, his hand came down on her bare breast.

Wide awake now, he said, "Sarah! Where is your nightgown?"

She answered by turning toward him. Her fingers began

to unbutton his long johns from his neck downward.

"What are you doing?" There was near panic in his voice.

As she unbuttoned each button, Sarah said, "I think... I will feel better... if I can be... as close to you... as I can." She unbuttoned the last button.

Thomas could only groan. He began to object, telling her she must leave, but Sarah was busy defeating his objections by all that she was doing to arouse him. Thomas groaned again, submitting himself to this force of nature.

Afterward, Thomas could not believe he was lying in bed with his young cousin naked in his arms. Where did she learn all this? How did he succumb so easily? He was still reeling from the sheer pleasure of the act, but at same time he was disgusted with himself for letting it happen.

"Do you understand what has just happened?" Thomas asked.

"I only understand that I love you and I have always loved you."

"Sarah, I love you as my cousin but I'm in love with Rena."

"Oh, how can you mention her name at a time like this!?"

"Because I've loved her ever since I first met her, and now I've betrayed that love."

For once, Sarah remained still and silent. A few minutes later she began kissing him on his lips, ears, eyelids, and neck. She caressed him as one would caress a lover. Before the night was over they joined their bodies together again in passionate love and lust.

Thomas was up and out of bed long before the sun came up. He hurried through the morning chores, hitched Mac and Maddie to the sleigh, and came inside to help his uncle get washed, shaved, and dressed. They sat down to a light breakfast of porridge and coffee. Sarah left the dirty dishes soaking in the basin filled with water while the three of them donned their coats, hats, and gloves. They left the house to climb into the sleigh and the big gray Percherons pulled them through the heavy snow to the Sundale Station where Isaac was already waiting.

While Isaac unhitched the horses, Thomas purchased their tickets. Thomas led Mac, Maddie, and Isaac's horse to the livery stables a short distance away where he paid a fee to have the horses watered, fed, and sheltered for the day. Thomas had to run back to the station because he could hear the train coming. When he climbed on board and found his family members, he sat next to Isaac while Sarah and her father sat across the aisle from them. As the conductor approached, Thomas handed him the tickets to be punched.

The small amount of sunlight coming through the gray clouds provided no heat and only bleak light in the passenger car. Wrapped in their heavy coats, the four family members said very little throughout the journey, and Thomas avoided looking at Sarah. After the train pulled into the Zanesville Station, they trudged through dirty snow to Mr. Stanley's office three blocks away.

"Come in and sit down. I'm Harold Stanley, and you must be Isaac Cole." The well-tailored attorney held out his hand to Isaac, and then shook hands with each of the others. His conservative, short, gray beard and, his firm handshake confirmed his reliability. He spoke in a quiet, but authoritative voice and wasted no time in conversation but proceeded directly to the business at hand. Since they were paying him by the hour, this pleased Thomas.

"Now, am I correct in saying that you want to obtain power of attorney for Thomas Keith, the nephew of the elder Mr. Thomas Keith...or perhaps you will want joint power of attorney given to both the nephew and the brother-in-law, Mr. Isaac Cole?"

Thomas said, "Which would be in the best interest of my uncle and his daughter?"

"Mr. Cole has informed me that you are 21 years of age and legally responsible. However, because of your youth, it might be preferable for both you and Mr. Cole to have joint

175

power of attorney over the farm house, animals, buildings, and lands which will rightfully belong to Sarah Keith in time."

Thomas said, "Joint power of attorney sounds good to me. What do you think, Isaac?"

Isaac nodded thoughtfully and said, "I think it's a good idea. Sarah, would you have any objections?"

"I agree with anything you two decide, but what does it mean, 'joint power of attorney'?"

Mr. Stanley explained it to them in terms they could understand. They were very impressed with his knowledge, and felt that his fee of $20 was not unreasonable. Thomas and Isaac signed the legal forms and Tom scribbled his name on the line pointed out by Mr. Stanley. Thomas pulled some paper bills from his uncle's wallet and handed the attorney's fee over to the male clerk in the front office before they left.

It was close to noon and they were feeling hungry. Isaac said, "Let's walk over to the hotel and eat in the dining room. We have plenty of time before the 2:30 train leaves for home."

Thomas pulled the chair out for Sarah to sit down at the table. She looked at him and glowed with pleasure as she sat like a lady to enjoy a meal she did not have to prepare. They had completed the necessary and unpleasant task with the attorney, and now they could relax over a hot meal served on fine china at a table covered with a white linen cloth. Soon they were talking and smiling, feeling hopeful again, all except for Tom who spooned his soup noisily and never looked up from his food.

It was almost dark when they finally arrived home, and Thomas had to hurry to complete the evening chores. When he came back inside the house, Sarah had the fire going in the kitchen stove, and she was warming up some left-over stew for supper. Thomas brought in firewood for the next morning, and after they ate supper, he took his uncle upstairs and put him to bed. Sarah washed all the dishes from breakfast and supper, fed Topsy, and swept the floor.

Thomas came back down to the kitchen to ask if Sarah needed any help before they retired for the night.

"Thank you for asking, Thomas. I think I've taken care

of most everything here."

As Sarah looked on, Thomas took the letter he had written, but never mailed to Rena, and dropped it into the stove where it was immediately consumed by fire. His heart was wrenched by profound sorrow as he watched the flames obliterate his words of love for Rena.

Without speaking they went upstairs to Thomas's room and quietly closed the door. Thomas turned toward his cousin and said, "Sarah, I want you to know that tonight we will sleep with our night clothes on and we will each stay on our own sides of the bed. I will push on your back if you start shaking, but that is all the contact we will have."

Sarah looked sad, but she said only, "I'll do whatever you say, Thomas."

When they were both ready for bed Thomas lifted the blankets for Sarah to climb into bed, and he blew out the candle. Soon Sarah's shaking started again, and she rolled onto her stomach for Thomas to push on her back. As he pushed, Thomas heard her quietly sobbing.

"Why are you crying, Sarah?"

"Oh, Thomas," Sarah said between sobs, "I love you so much. I wish you loved me."

"I'm here to take care of you and your father. I don't plan to leave you. Isn't that enough?"

Her continued weeping broke Thomas's heart. His thoughts convicted him. *I always disappoint and hurt other people. Rena will be hurt when she learns how I betrayed her, and Sarah is heart-broken because her mother is dead, and I can't love her.*

Gently, he encouraged Sarah to face him, and with his hands framing her face, he kissed her forehead to let her know that he cared. The shaking and sobbing were beyond her control now and Sarah reached to hold Thomas close to her. His arms went around her trembling body and the two clung together in their combined sorrow. Soon their sorrow became passion that erased all of Thomas's earlier resolve.

CHAPTER NINETEEN

Saturday night was the time for bathing in the big metal tub. Topsy took one look at the dreaded tub Thomas had placed on the kitchen floor and the small animal hid out of sight. He remembered many times before when he had been dunked in the tub after his people finished bathing, and Topsy hated baths!

First, Thomas helped his uncle wash, and then dried him off before he helped him into his clean long johns. While Thomas went upstairs with Tom and put him to bed, Sarah climbed into the tub and began washing her body. Thomas came downstairs in time to pour clean vinegar water over Sarah's freshly washed hair. While Sarah dried herself, Thomas quickly climbed into the tub and began to wash.

"Sarah, will you pour some of the hot water from the kettle into the tub? This water is not warm at all."

"Spread your legs apart so the hot water doesn't hit your skin." Sarah poured all the contents of the kettle into the tub, filling it nearly to the brim.

"Ahhh…that is much better. It's too bad this tub isn't bigger. I would pull you in here with me." Thomas grinned up at Sarah.

Sarah reached down and caressed his chest. "You and I are thinking the same thing."

She washed his back for him and helped him dry off after he was clean. Her touch was a strong aphrodisiac that tempted him to make love to her right there in the kitchen. Reluctantly, he pulled on his clean long johns.

Sarah wore a nightgown that buttoned at her neck and covered her all the way down to her toes. As she stood there in the glow of the soft candle light brushing her dark brown hair, the intimacy of the moment touched him, and he was aware that he was feeling more than affection for his cousin. Thomas wondered if he might actually love Sarah.

"Thomas, I don't want to go to church tomorrow. I'll stay home with Daddy if you want to go by yourself." Sarah continued to brush her hair as she spoke.

"Doesn't it help you to hear the Scripture readings and hear Reverend Hardesty's sermon?"

"I always liked to go to church before Mama died, but now I only think of how much I miss her. Daddy sits there and cries, and it's all I can do to keep from crying myself. You remember how my mother loved to sing the hymns, and how she always made sure I was paying attention. That's all I can think about when I sit in church now."

Thomas thought about Sarah's words. Finally, after they had gone to bed he said, "I'll stay at home with you tomorrow. We'll read some Scripture verses, and say a prayer. If you feel like singing a hymn, we'll do that, too."

"Thank you, dear Thomas. I love you very much."

When they went to the Cole family home for dinner that Sunday, Thomas explained why they did not attend church. They all expressed their sympathy to Sarah, but encouraged her to begin going to church again as soon as she felt she was able.

Gradually, the Keith family stopped going to eat Sunday dinners with the Cole family. Sarah didn't seem to care that she never ventured away from home. Her love for Thomas and his increasing desire for her filled her with a sense of well-being. Sarah was grateful that her night shakes had ceased, and she was more amazed at her own patience with her father's condition. She began to care for him as one would care for a small child.

It was a clear, cold day in late February when a lone rider came into the yard. Sarah was at home alone because Thomas and her father had ridden into town. She opened the back door and saw her old friend, Mercy, who grabbed hold of Sarah and lifted her off her feet.

"Look at you! You are the picture of health and here I

thought you must be withering away because we never see you at church or anywhere else."

"It's good to see you, Mercy. Come in the kitchen where it's warm. I'm in the middle of my bread making." Sarah motioned for Mercy to sit down at the kitchen table, while she continued working the bread dough.

Mercy removed her hat, coat, and mittens, draping them over the back of a kitchen chair. She was full of news and began telling Sarah all about her brother, James.

"Sometime before Christmas, James found a stray horse wandering around behind our barn. He didn't know who owned him but he kept the horse in one of our sheds. The bad part was that James never told Dad or anyone else about the horse and he kept it a secret for a long while. He made the mistake of riding the horse into town one day and the horse's owner saw him. Now, James is in the county jail at Zanesville."

"Oh, no! Your mother must be very upset over this. Will she or any of the family be able to go and visit him in the jail?"

"Mother went to see him once, but my father is so angry with James that he hasn't gone to see him at all. Who would ever guess that someone in our family would be in jail!"

Mercy watched as Sarah deftly turned and pushed the dough, placed it in a large greased bowl, covered it with a dish towel and set it on the shelf above the stove where the dough would rise.

"I'll make us some tea, and we'll be able to have a proper visit." Sarah got two cups and saucers from the cupboard, and set the kettle of water on the hot stove. Soon they were sitting at the table sipping tea like two grown ladies.

"Tell me truthfully, Sarah, how are you feeling these days? You must miss your mother very much."

"I do miss Mama every day. I couldn't even come home and live in this house for several weeks after she died. I stayed with my Uncle Isaac and Aunt Hannah. When I did come home to stay, I felt bad for a while. I had night shakes and I couldn't sleep at all." Sarah looked into her tea cup remembering those days.

Mercy reached for Sarah's hand and said, "I'm so sorry you have to suffer through this. Are you still shaking at night?"

"No, Thomas has helped me, and now I'm able to sleep."

"What do you mean, 'Thomas has helped'? How did he help?"

Sarah needed to tell someone so she made Mercy promise to keep her secret. Then Sarah told her friend how it happened that she was able to go to sleep without shaking.

Mercy's eyes grew wide with understanding. "You are sleeping with Thomas!"

Sarah felt her face becoming very warm and she knew it was a bright red. She got up from the table and refilled their tea cups.

"Sarah! You're sleeping with Thomas, aren't you?"

Sarah managed to say, "Yes," and nothing more.

"Are you carrying his child?"

"Not yet. I had my monthly flow last week, but I hope I will have his baby."

"Sarah, you can't mean that. You are only fourteen! Thomas is your first cousin and you two are not married to each other. Has he broken off his courtship with Rena?"

"Thomas wrote her a letter and said that he was sorry but their plans to be married are ended. He didn't tell Rena why or give her any reasons, but he wrote it twice in the letter saying he and Rena would never be able to marry. He showed it to me before he mailed it."

"What a disappointment for Rena!"

"I know she feels bad about it, but she is so pretty and everyone loves Rena. She will find someone else." Sarah spoke philosophically, as if she were an old woman.

Mercy stood up to leave, pulling on her coat and saying, "Am I really talking to my old friend, the one who shared so much with me?"

Sarah smiled and stood next to Mercy. "You were a good friend when I needed a friend. Now Thomas is my best friend and he's the one I love more than anyone."

Once more Mercy became the actress, and with dramatic style she said, "Farewell then, my princess. Parting is such sweet sorrow." She kissed Sarah lightly on her lips and left as abruptly as she had come.

Sarah never spoke to Thomas of Mercy's visit.

The very next day a visitor appeared at the back door just as they were sitting down for dinner. Sarah opened the door and said, "Hello Reverend. We're just sitting down for dinner. Would you care to join us?"

Thomas heard the anxiety in Sarah's voice and he knew this would not be a pleasant visit.

Their pastor said, "If it won't be too much trouble, Sarah, I'd be happy to join you."

Sarah took his coat and hat and hung them on a hook. The tall, broad-shouldered man entered their warm kitchen, shook hands with Thomas, and asked about his health.

"I'm fine, thank you." Thomas pulled out a chair for the minister and asked him to sit at the table. Reverend Hardesty nodded toward Tom and said, "Good day to you, Mr. Keith."

Tom remained silent and merely stared at the pastor.

Sarah placed a dinner plate in front of their guest and gave him a knife and fork. Then she took the stewing hen from the pot and set it on a platter before she carved it into serving sized pieces and placed it in the center of the table. She put the plate of sliced bread and butter alongside the bowl of boiled turnips.

"Reverend Hardesty, would you like a cup of coffee to go with your meal?"

"Yes, thank you, Sarah."

Sarah's anxiety became apparent as the cup rattled in its saucer. She carefully set it down in front of the Reverend.

Thomas asked him to say the blessing over their meal. At the sound of Reverend Hardesty's 'Amen', Thomas passed the platter of chicken to their guest so he could choose his favorite part. When all the food was passed around the table they began to eat. The discussion topics remained on neutral ground: the weather, the minister's three children, and people in the church who were seriously ill this winter.

Sarah got up and removed their plates when they had finished eating. Thomas noticed that Sarah's plate was still filled with food. She poured more coffee in their cups and served them the last of her bread pudding.

Reverend Hardesty said, "We have not seen you in church in many Sundays. I wanted to come and see if you were sick or if you needed any help."

Thomas cleared his throat and tried to tell their minister how Sarah felt when she attended church these days. He related how it made her sad and she missed her mother so much that it was easier on her if she stayed home.

The minister turned to her and said, "Sarah, I know our Lord understands how you feel. When you pray to Him, will you ask Him to give you the strength you need to come to church?" Reverend Hardesty looked deep into her eyes.

Sarah nodded, and said, "Yes, sir" as if she were five years old.

Their pastor said, "Would you pray with me right now?"

Thomas and Sarah nodded in agreement.

"Our Gracious Father, bless Sarah and this family with thy love and peace today. Comfort them in their sorrow and heal Sarah's broken heart over the loss of her mother. Give them all the strength they need to obey thy will, and to worship thee in thy house. We thank thee for blessing them today and in the days to come. We pray in the name of our Savior, Jesus Christ who died for our sins. Amen."

The pastor stood and pushed in his chair. "Thank you, for the good meal."

Thomas quickly stood to shake the hand of their minister and thank him for his visit while Sarah went to get his coat and hat. As he pulled on his coat, Reverend Hardesty thanked them again for the dinner.

"Remember, Sarah, your mother was a woman of faith. She would want you to be in church on Sundays to keep your own faith alive."

Silence reigned after Reverend Hardesty's departure. Thomas was overwhelmed with thoughts he did not want to share. Sarah was busying herself with the dishes. Tom merely sat at the table and wept quietly.

Thomas felt a tremendous sense of guilt and shame. He had betrayed his beloved Rena who was loyal and faithful in her love for him. He was well aware that he and Sarah were committing the sin of fornication. At the same time he justified his actions because of Sarah's great need to be loved and comforted, and Thomas cared about her very much. He also recognized his desire for her body was very powerful.

The weeks passed and winter turned to spring. The roads were mired in mud and they were forced to stay at home. It had been many weeks since they had seen the Cole family.

It was a day in early April when Thomas rode into town on Beauty to buy a few needed items. He was surprised when he met Isaac in Walker's General Store. The two went outside on the boardwalk to talk and Isaac began by telling Thomas that Rena had written to them. She was heart- broken because she had not received any letters from Thomas except for one letter which informed her that her future with Thomas was ended.

"Tell me, Thomas. What is going on that you no longer want to be with Rena? You had us all believing that you two would be married one of these days."

Thomas swallowed back tears of regret and sorrow. He looked down at his hands and said, "I'm sorry, Isaac. I never meant to hurt Rena. But it's something I can't talk about now."

"Well, you sure had me fooled! I thought you were an honorable young man, but I can see now that I was very mistaken." Isaac turned on his heel and left Thomas standing there alone.

That night Thomas told Sarah about Isaac's remarks. She tried to console him but he was so deeply hurt that he would not be comforted. Thomas had always admired Isaac and thought he would be fortunate to have Isaac for a father-in-law someday. Hannah must be angry at him, too, and this thought hurt Thomas even more because she was a kind and gentle woman.

Not even Sarah's kisses could distract Thomas, so they lay side by side in a miserable state throughout the long night.

Sarah woke Thomas the next morning by telling him to move out of the way.

"Hurry, I feel sick!"

As soon as her feet hit the floor she reached for the big chamber pot under the bed and heaved into it. Her stomach was almost empty so very little came up. She wiped her mouth on the long sleeve of her nightgown, lay back down and pulled the blankets over her.

"Maybe this sick feeling will go away if I lie still for a while."

Thomas placed his hand on her forehead. "You don't have a fever. When did you last have your monthly?"

Sarah hesitated while she thought about his question. "It was in February."

"I think you're going to have a baby." Thomas looked worried.

Sarah smiled and said, "That would make me very happy. Aren't you happy, too?"

Thomas held her in his arms and did not reply.

Throughout each day Sarah looked radiant and extremely happy, humming and singing as she went about her household chores. Thomas felt he was carrying a heavy weight upon his shoulders.

Tom had been put to bed, and the two cousins were in the kitchen finishing the last of their chores for the day. Thomas wound the old kitchen clock while Sarah prepared the oats for tomorrow's breakfast.

Thomas placed the brass key behind the clock and sat down at the table. "We need to talk with Reverend Hardesty because he's the only one who can help us now."

Sarah turned from the stove to look at Thomas. "He won't want to marry us. He practically accused us of living in sin when he came to eat dinner here." Sarah did not have warm feelings toward their pastor.

"I think you did not understand his reason for coming. He was concerned about us, and I think he cares about us."

"I think he only wants us to come to church so his congregation will not get smaller."

"I'm going to find out because I'll be going into town to talk with him soon. Do you want to come with me?"

"What are you going to say to him?"

"I'm going to tell him that you are expecting my baby and we want to get married."

"In those very words?! You might as well say, 'Sarah and I have been fornicating'."

"The whole world is going to know in a few months. Your shape is going to change and it will be obvious that you are with child."

The difficult truth hit Sarah like a blow. She sank down on a kitchen chair and put her face in her hands to conceal her tears.

Thomas sat beside her and gently rubbed her arm and shoulder while he waited for the weeping to end.

Sarah wiped her eyes and nose. "Let's go away from here. We can get married in another town somewhere, and find another place to live."

"We need to be married before we can travel any distance together. But I've been thinking. How would you like to sail to Ireland and meet my family?"

"Oh Thomas, we could go to Ireland for our honeymoon!" Soon her expression changed from elation to apprehension. "But we wouldn't stay there, would we?"

"I think we might stay there for you to have the baby and when the baby is old enough to travel we would come back to the States. I haven't planned it all out yet."

"I'll go with you to talk to Reverend Hardesty. Do you think we could go tomorrow?"

CHAPTER TWENTY

The pastor's wife met them at the front door of the Manse holding her eighteen-month-old baby boy on her hip. Her voice was soft and refined. "Why, hello Mr. Keith, and Sarah and Thomas. Are you looking for my husband?"

Thomas said, "Yes, we'd like to speak to him in private if he's available."

"Do come in and sit down here in the parlor. I'll go and find him."

Shortly, the doorway to the parlor was filled by the impressive frame of the smiling minister. He was dressed in plain trousers with a shirt open at the neck, and he looked like an ordinary person instead of a pastor. He greeted them with handshakes, and asked how he could be of help.

Thomas didn't quite know how to begin. He said, "We'd like to talk to you in private. That is, Sarah and I would like to talk to you in private. Is there another room where we could speak, just the three of us?"

"My study is right across the hall. But first, I'll ask my wife to bring Mr. Keith a cup of tea, and sit with him in the parlor."

The minister left the room and was gone for several minutes before he returned. He spoke to Tom in slow, distinct words, "Mr. Keith if you will sit right here, my wife will bring you a cup of tea. Sarah and Thomas will be with me across the hall."

Reverend Hardesty closed the door to his study, and after he pointed to chairs for them, the pastor sat down at his desk. "Now, how can I help you?"

Thomas said exactly the words he had said to Sarah the night before. "Sarah is expecting my baby and we want to get married."

The pastor looked down at his desk for a few seconds, and when he looked up at them his expression was warm and caring. "A baby is a gift from God. I know this child will be a blessing to you both."

This response caught Sarah off guard and she began weeping.

"Are you unhappy about this, Sarah?" the pastor said.

Sarah wiped her eyes and nose with a small handkerchief. "Oh no, I thought you would be lecturing and shaming us. Instead, you're saying this baby will bless us."

Thomas said, "You see, we realize that we've broken God's commandment and that everyone will accuse us of being sinful. And besides that, I have offended the Cole family a great deal because I promised their daughter, Lorena, I would ask her to marry me in a years' time."

Thomas cleared his throat and gathered his thoughts. "Sarah's father is not right in his mind and we don't think he would understand. You are the only one who can help us."

"Do you want me to perform a quiet little marriage ceremony for you?"

Sarah said, "I wish we could go away somewhere to get married."

"That might be arranged," said the minister. "I have a good friend who went to college and seminary with me. He has a church in Jamestown, New York. With your permission, I'll write to him and ask if he will perform your wedding ceremony. The train will get you to Jamestown in one long day of travel."

Thomas said, "I don't know what we'll do with Sarah's father while we go to Jamestown. I can't ask Isaac and Hannah to take care of him."

Reverend Hardesty said, "Leave that to me. I'll speak with Mr. and Mrs. Cole about it. Now, I want you to return home with God's peace in your hearts, and I want to see you in church next Sunday. In the meantime, I'll write to my friend, the Reverend Richard Fulton in Jamestown, and I'll speak with the Coles."

Sarah began crying again as she grasped the minister's hand in both of hers and said, "Oh thank you, thank you!"

Equally grateful, Thomas shook the minister's hand in a warm, strong grip and said, "Thank you, Reverend."

As they stood ready to leave his study, the pastor said, "Will you stay on at the farm and continue to run things by yourselves?"

Thomas said, "We have plans to go to Ireland so my family can meet Sarah. We'll be taking Tom with us. I think it will be good for him to see his brother again, who is also my father."

"That's an excellent idea. It should be a joyful family reunion." He ushered them out of the study and back to the parlor where Tom was enjoying his second piece of cake while the pastor's wife and their toddler entertained him.

In gratitude to their minister, Thomas and Sarah brought Tom with them to church on Sunday. Tom wept through much of the service while Sarah sat very close to Thomas.

After the pastor pronounced the benediction, they all came out into the sunshine of a glorious day in early May. As the Keith family hurried to their carriage, Sarah felt someone pulling her arm. She turned to see her Aunt Hannah who caught up with Sarah and grabbed her in a warm embrace.

Hannah said, "The pastor told us everything, Sarah. How are you feeling?"

Sarah, who was overcome with emotion, wiped tears from her eyes and said, "Oh, Aunt Hannah, it's good to see you. I'm feeling fine." She spoke into her aunt's ear, "I still have morning sickness but it lasts only a short while."

As Hannah and Sarah embraced once more, Isaac approached Thomas. All eyes watched as Isaac stiffly extended his hand to Thomas and said, "We hope you will take good care of Sarah. She's a special member of our family." He released Thomas's hand and looked more relaxed as he said, "The pastor tells us you are going to Ireland. That will be good for all of you to be with your family over there."

Emma came running and she, too, embraced her cousin and said, "It's been a long time since we've seen you. Are you coming home to eat with us today?"

"I think that would be a fine idea," Hannah said with a nod toward her husband.

"Yes, of course, please come and eat dinner with us." Isaac echoed his wife.

Dinner that day with the Cole family was stressful. John never spoke much at meal times, but today he looked down at his plate and ate in total silence, a silence that was condemning. It was obvious that twelve-year-old Emma was the only one who did not understand the situation between Sarah and Thomas. She began talking about all the things that concerned them last November and December when Sarah had lived with the Cole family.

"Sarah, are you still shaking at night?" Emma said.

"No, not anymore." Sarah's voice was barely audible.

Emma announced, "Sarah used to shake so much that I had to lay my whole body on top of hers before she could stop shaking and go to sleep."

The look of surprise was evident on the faces of Isaac and Hannah. All conversation stopped briefly while they thought about the implications of Emma's innocent remark.

Thomas was quick to change the subject. "We are looking forward to our trip to Ireland. Tom hasn't seen his brother, my dad, in many years. And one of my sisters has married since I left home."

Everyone agreed that their upcoming trip to Ireland would be a good thing.

As they prepared to leave that afternoon, Sarah was warmly hugged by her aunt and cousin. She saw her Uncle Isaac take Thomas aside for a moment to speak into his ear before the three Keith family members climbed into the carriage and headed for home. It was a relief to leave, but Sarah was glad her aunt and uncle had not rejected her.

That night as Thomas climbed into bed next to Sarah, she said, "What did Uncle Isaac say to you right before we left?"

"He said they will look after your father while we go to Jamestown, New York to get married."

"Oh, that was kind of him. Now we can go ahead with our plans."

"We haven't heard from Reverend Fulton yet. Maybe he will refuse to marry us."

Sarah said, "Why would he do that after his good friend, Reverend Hardesty has asked him to help us?"

Thomas said, "We need to consider all the possibilities, but you're right. I would be surprised if Reverend Hardesty's friend refused us."

Thomas came home from town with the mail which he carried into the house by way of the back door into the kitchen. Sarah was making bread and her hands were covered with flour. Her father sat at the table drinking coffee.

Thomas held up the letters and said, "Which one shall I read first, the one from Reverend Fulton in Jamestown, the one from Wynne and Davidson, Memorial Stone Cutters, or the one from the New York Maritime Shipping and Transportation?"

Sarah looked up and said, "Read the one from Reverend Fulton first."

Thomas opened the envelope and unfolded the paper. He began reading to Sarah,

"Dear Mr. Keith,

Congratulations on your forthcoming marriage. If you and your bride can arrive here in Jamestown on June 11, I will meet you at the train depot. Since it will be late in the day when you arrive, I will perform a simple wedding ceremony here at the manse. Afterward, my wife has planned a small wedding supper for you, and you are invited to stay here in our guest room for the night if you wish.

Please respond as soon as possible. We are looking forward to meeting you.

Sincerely yours,

Reverend Richard Fulton"

Sarah said, "He sounds like a very nice man. I think we should tell him we'd like to stay our wedding night in their guest room at the manse. Will you write to him tonight, Thomas?"

"Yes, I'll do that."

Thomas held up the other two pieces of mail. "Which one do you want me to open next?"

"The one from New York."

Thomas opened it and pulled out two pages of shipping schedules and fares from New York harbor to harbors across the Atlantic. "This looks rather complicated. I think I'll have to spend some time studying it."

He folded it up, put it in his pocket, and opened the last envelope.

Thomas read out loud:

"To the family of Margaret L. Keith: this is to inform you that the memorial stone you ordered has been installed at the Pleasant Hill Cemetery over Mrs. Keith's grave site. Your bill of $150.00 is paid in full. We thank you for calling upon us to create a memorial stone that will honor your loved one forever.

Always at your service,

Wynne and Davidson, Memorial Stone Cutters"

At the sound of Margaret's name, Tom began weeping. He continued to weep and wipe his eyes until Sarah put her arms around his neck and kissed his forehead.

"Daddy, we'll ride over to see this lovely gravestone that will honor Mama forever, won't we, Thomas?

"I think we should visit the cemetery this coming Saturday. You can pack us a picnic lunch, and we'll make a day of it."

Pleasant Hill Cemetery was about five miles away and it took them a while to get there. When they came for Margaret's burial in November, it had been cold, gray, and bleak. Today was a beautiful, warm day and everything was green.

Sarah looked around the cemetery and exclaimed, "Oh look, there is the stone! It's bigger than I thought it would be."

Thomas stopped the carriage in front of the grassy plot and they all climbed down to inspect Margaret's memorial stone which stood over six feet in height.

Tom walked over and looked at it through his tears. His hand reached up to touch the smooth polished stone of dark gray and rose colored granite. The obelisk-shaped stone widened at the base where these words were written:

Margaret L. Keith
Beloved Wife and Mother

Tom knelt down and traced the letters with his fingers. He bowed his head and sobbed with body-shaking grief.

Sarah also knelt and touched the letters as her father had done. She looked up at Thomas, and with tears streaming down her face, she said, "Mama will never know her grandchild."

She stood and wept into Thomas's chest as he tried to comfort her. For a long while they grieved, each one lost in memories and feelings of tremendous loss. At last, there were no more tears; only numbness and weariness remained.

Thomas said, "Why don't we walk over there and sit down on that grassy knoll?"

"Isn't it close to noon? You could get our picnic basket and take it over there, Thomas."

"Let me unhitch the horses and tie them in the shade first."

Thomas brought the basket and a jug of cold tea that Sarah had put in at the last moment. They sat down on the blanket that Sarah spread out on the grass, and she poured each one of them a cup of sweetened tea. Thirst slackened, they began to feel better. She passed around a bowl of boiled eggs, and handed out slices of buttered bread with sliced ham on each one.

Fortified with good food, Sarah began speaking about others they knew who had been buried here at Pleasant Hill.

"Mama told me her father was buried here with his three wives. His second wife was Mama's mother. Her name was Hannah and she died not long after Mama was born. When Mama's father married a woman named Mary, they had three more children and Aunt Hannah was the oldest of those three. Mama always liked Aunt Hannah the best."

"Why don't we see if we can find the graves of your grandparents?" Thomas said.

"Alright, let's look over in that corner near Mama's grave."

It didn't take long to find the plot where her grandfather's headstone was surrounded by those of his three wives.

Sarah said, "The light colored stones look so old."

"That's because they are a soft limestone. Your mother's granite stone should look just the same a hundred years from now."

"I wonder if we can find the place where the old Pleasant Hill Academy stood. Mama said it burned down years ago, but her father was one who helped build it and he even taught math in the Academy part of the time. It's a shame I didn't take after my grandfather when it comes to math."

At that comment, she and Thomas shared a grin.

"Look, Sarah. Doesn't that look like a rectangular depression in the grass below? I think that may have been the site for the old Academy."

"I think you're right. It was quite big for a log building. When it burned down all the Presbyterians around here decided it was time to build a bigger and better school. That's when they started building the college in New Concord."

When they walked back to their blanket, they found Tom lying there sound asleep.

Thomas said, "Let's leave him here to sleep while we walk to the other side of the cemetery."

They walked arm-in-arm around the cemetery reading names on the stones and thinking of their own mortality. Once in a while they would stop to read out the name of someone whose moniker sounded ridiculously strange.

Laughing, Sarah said, "They must have had a bad dream when they named him that!"

Thomas looked over at the blanket and saw that Tom

was sitting up. "Your father is awake now. We should gather up our things and head for home."

On the way home Sarah sat close to Thomas and said, "Thank you for taking us to see Mama's gravestone. It has made me feel at peace, and I think it has helped Daddy, too."

CHAPTER TWENTY-ONE

"This is the only dress that fits well these days, and it hardly looks like a wedding dress!" Sarah was holding up a navy blue dress with white lace trim at the collar and cuffs.

Thomas said, "Do you want to go into town tomorrow and see if we can find something better?"

"No, it would start all kinds of gossip if people learned I was looking for a dress to wear at my wedding. This navy blue dress will have to do. But, if I see a nice traveling suit I would like to buy it for our trip to Ireland."

Sarah looked at Thomas's tall frame and said, "I think we should look for something you can wear. The one jacket you've worn to church every summer is too short. Let's go to town and see if we can find a dark colored suit with matching trousers, waist-coat, and jacket. If people are curious we'll tell them it's for our trip to Ireland."

The next day Thomas, Sarah, and Tom went to town to shop for new clothes. Stores in Norwich offered few choices, and Sarah was not happy with anything they were shown. Finally, they agreed that the black suit would have to do for Thomas even though Sarah thought it made him look like an undertaker. For Tom they bought black and gray pin striped trousers and a dark gray jacket.

At a dress and milliners shop, Sarah found a lightweight wool traveling suit in burgundy red. The skirt had a small bustle which pleased Sarah, but the matching jacket seemed way too short. The lady-proprietor assured her that was the latest style. Sarah liked the way the collar framed her face and the deep red color flattered her fair skin. They even bought a stylish woman's hat that added years to her youthfulness.

Sunday they went to church and then to the Cole's home

for dinner. After the meal, Thomas asked to speak to Isaac alone. The two walked outside and stood under some shade trees while Isaac smoked his pipe.

Thomas stuffed both hands in his pockets and said, "Sarah and I are leaving at quarter past four on the train to Jamestown, Thursday morning, the eleventh of June, and I need to ask some favors of you."

Isaac said, "I'll try to help if I can."

"Would you mind if we brought Tom over on Wednesday afternoon before we leave the next morning? Sarah and I have been invited to stay with the Reverend Fulton and his wife on Thursday night, but we can't ask them to take us to the train station before dawn the next morning. I thought it would be better for them if we left Jamestown at half past seven Friday morning. But that will bring us into Sundale Station at close to midnight.

Isaac said, "It appears you'll need for us to keep Tom here Wednesday, Thursday, and Friday nights. I see no problem with that, but what about the animals at your place?"

"Next Saturday at auction I'm going to sell all the animals on the farm except for Mac as we need him to pull the carriage and the wagon. I hope you agree to this because we need the money to pay for our train fares, and for the ship crossing, going to and returning from Ireland. We're leaving Mac at the livery stable so by the time we leave for Jamestown there will be just the two dogs at our place. Perhaps you could send John over to feed them a couple of times."

"I agree to whatever you decide, Thomas. These past few months have not been easy on any of us, and I want to help make the future better. But tell me, how long do you plan to stay in Ireland and when do you think you'll be coming back?"

Thomas looked away and cleared his throat. "We'll stay in Ireland until the baby is old enough to make the trip across the Atlantic." He paused and studied his hands. "I think we've caused enough shame to the family that we should not return here but head out west." He looked at Isaac and said, "I've been reading that it's still possible to get free land by homesteading out in Kansas. Most likely we'll go to Kansas and settle there."

Isaac nodded but a look of doubt clouded his face. "That will not be an easy life for Sarah and the baby. Are you sure you want to put her through that?"

"We talked it over last night and Sarah said she does not want to return here. She's willing to try homesteading out west."

"I'm guessing you will want me to lease out the farm along with the house and buildings."

"Yes. I know it will be a burden for you, but I'm hoping you will work out a deal with the tenant whereby half the proceeds of all the crops will go to you and your family. Out of that half, would you be willing to send money to my father in Ireland to help pay for Tom's upkeep? He won't be returning with us to the States. I was thinking you could send one hundred twenty to one hundred fifty dollars each year."

"That is only fair. I'd be glad to send them the money for Tom. You be sure to write down their address and give it to me before you leave."

Thomas flicked his hand at a fly buzzing near his head. "The tenant who farms the land over near Rich Hill will need to know that he must pay forty percent of his profits to you, or if you agree, I can arrange it with Mr. Stanley to receive the funds and invest them in an account in Sarah's name."

Isaac drew in on his pipe and exhaled a cloud of smoke. "By all means, Mr. Stanley should invest those funds into Sarah's account. You'll have to write to Mr. Stanley and let him know of all this right away."

Thomas shifted his weight to the other leg and crossed his arms over his chest, "We will leave Mac hitched to the wagon near the depot the morning we leave here for Ireland, June 20th. I want you to come and take Mac home with you and keep him. You can have the wagon, too, if you want it. And before you lease the place you can take anything in the house, barn, or machine shed that you can use. We can't take anything with us except for a few clothes. I know Sarah is hoping you will keep her little terrier, Topsy. He's getting old but he's still a good ratter. And I'm hoping you can use Rex... he's a reliable herding dog and a good watch dog, too."

Isaac nodded. "Be sure to send a letter to Mr. Stanley right away to let him know your plans and that you will no longer be named as power of attorney. It will be very inconvenient for me to make any decisions about the Keith property if I have to wait several weeks for you to receive my mail and then more weeks for your answer."

"You're right. I will do that tonight."

Thomas sat at the kitchen table until midnight. He wrote a letter to his parents explaining that on the twentieth of June he would be leaving the farm in Ohio and travel to Ireland with his wife, Sarah, and his father-in-law, Tom. He went on to explain that Sarah was expecting his baby next January, and they were planning a wedding the eleventh of June. He also wrote that he and Sarah planned to stay with them until the baby was old enough to travel and then they would return to the States. It was awkward to convey all this to his family but Thomas persevered until he had written the whole story, right down to the amount that Isaac would be sending them each year for Tom's keep.

Then Thomas wrote a letter to the attorney, Mr. Stanley. In as few words as possible he explained the situation and directed the attorney to act upon all those things he and Isaac had discussed earlier in the day. Then he wrote another brief letter to Mr. McGregor, the man who leased the property near Rich Hill. With all letters sealed in envelopes and addressed, he wondered what his family at home would think when they read his news. He hoped they would not judge him too harshly.

Thomas chewed on the pencil he used for figuring the train and ship fares. It was going to cost a small fortune for the three of them to make this train trip and ship crossing. He needed to lay his hands on a lot of cash and he hoped the horses and other animals he sold at auction this Saturday would bring enough to pay for all of it.

Monday morning Sarah decided to wash all the bed linens and bath towels, along with a lot of dirty clothing. She asked Thomas to help her build a fire in the yard to heat the wash water in the large metal tub. She shaved a bar of lye soap into the hot water and carried huge armloads of dirty laundry downstairs and out to the yard. She boiled the sheets, and pillow cases while stirring them with a stick to release the soil.

Thomas pointed and said, "I strung lines between these trees where you can hang the laundry to dry."

"Thank you. I hope you didn't string them so high they're out of my reach."

"No, I think you'll be able to reach them without any problem this time."

It was a monumental task that took most of the day, but when everything was dry she gathered the clean laundry in her arms and carried it into the house. Her mother would have ironed the sheets and pillow cases but Sarah took the time to iron only the pillow cases and the shirts that belonged to her father and Thomas. She sprinkled all her own cotton and linen clothing with water, wadding them up and stuffing each article into a basket to stay damp until she could do the rest of the ironing the next day.

As she placed the clean bottom sheet on her father's bed, she lifted up the feather-filled mattress to tuck the sheet under it and her hand touched a pile of papers. She lifted the mattress higher and discovered the papers were money. She pulled them out and counted all of it, learning her parents had stashed away a tidy sum. It amounted to five hundred fifty dollars!

Sarah couldn't wait to tell Thomas. She ran downstairs and out to the barn to find him.

"Thomas! You'll never guess what I found!"

Thomas looked up from shoveling manure.

She reached into her apron pocket and pulled out the wad of money. "Look! I found five hundred fifty dollars under Daddy's mattress!"

Thomas dropped the shovel. With a huge grin on his face, he grabbed hold of Sarah and lifted her high in the air, then lowered her face to his and kissed her again and again.

Tom had been shoveling manure with his nephew but now he put down his shovel. He looked at the happy couple for a few seconds and the hint of a smile appeared on his face.

Sarah went to her father and hugged him. "Thank you, Daddy, for saving this money for us. It will help pay our way to Ireland and you can see your brother, Will, again."

Thomas had attended the Saturday auctions for years and many of those who bought and sold animals and equipment knew him. They also knew that he and his uncle had a reputation for selling only sound, quality horses.

When the bidding started high and went even higher for Maddie, Thomas was excited. As the afternoon went on and the prices remained strong for most of the horses, he began to feel that they would have no worries about financing this trip to Ireland and the return trip to the States. He was disappointed the cows and their calves brought only average prices but Jersey cows were not everyone's favorite.

That evening at the supper table he told Sarah about the good results of the auction. Tom seemed to be paying more attention than usual, and they wondered if he understood any of their conversation. But then he began weeping and they both encouraged him to finish his supper.

Sarah said, "With the five hundred fifty dollars from under Daddy's mattress, and the six hundred twenty dollars from the auction, we'll not have any worries."

"We should have enough to pay for all our train fares and sailing passages and still have money to tide us over for a while." Thomas smiled.

They went to church Sunday morning but they begged off the invitation to dinner with the Cole family. Thomas said, "Sarah has been working so hard all week trying to get our things ready that I'm worried about her. I want her to stay home and rest this afternoon."

Sarah said, "We'll see you Wednesday when we bring Daddy to your house."

Her Aunt Hannah hugged her, and whispered into her ear, "We don't want to take a chance on losing the baby. You stay at home and get some rest.

Reverend Fulton and his wife, Jane, had returned them to the station in their carriage, and now Mr. and Mrs. Thomas Keith sat side by side waving to their hosts from the train window. Before the newlyweds boarded the train, Jane hugged Sarah and told her to keep in touch with them, and be sure to let them know if the baby was a boy or a girl. Pastor Fulton had gripped Thomas' hand and said, "God bless you both."

The train built up more speed as they left Jamestown and rolled into the countryside. Sarah took out the pin to remove her hat from her head. She leaned against Thomas' shoulder sighing, "They were so nice to us. Our little wedding ceremony was perfect, and they even had fresh flowers and new candles on the table. I can't believe Jane made that beautiful wedding cake for us. It was a brilliant idea to decorate the white frosted cake with those rose buds! And she sent the rest of the cake with us in this box." Sarah held up a box that had the lid tied on with string, and looked at her husband. "When we get hungry we'll have to eat some more of our wedding cake."

Thomas chimed in with his own praises of the evening, "The pastor said a very good prayer over us during the ceremony. I wish I had a copy of that prayer."

Sarah sighed again. "I'm glad we went to Jamestown to get married. It was a beautiful wedding and I've never been so happy. And today is my birthday...everything is perfect!"

Thomas leaned over to kiss her. "Happy birthday, Mrs. Keith."

It was almost midnight when they arrived at Sundale Station. Mr. Jackson, who owned the livery stables, had left their horse staked out in the field behind the livery, and the wagon was nearby so Thomas wouldn't have to wake the proprietor from his sleep. Though it was dark, there were many stars and half a moon was still shining in the sky. Mac knew the way home and he took them there in a brisk trot.

CHAPTER TWENTY-TWO

The next morning Sarah busied herself with mending clothes and darning socks. Thomas left to fetch her father home from the Cole's house, while she worked as fast as she could to finish repairing the clothes spread out on her bed. She heard footsteps coming up the stairs and looked to see her husband and father enter the bedroom.

She said, "Do you realize we leave this place forever next Saturday? That is only one week away!" Sarah's voice was filled with panic. "There is so much to do and so many things I wish we could take with us."

"We'll take only what fits in each of our trunks. You have a small bag you are carrying with you, and that will hold your own personal things." Thomas surveyed the pile of clothing on the bed.

"I'm still mending our clothes. I don't want to pack anything that isn't clean and mended."

"Remember, you can always shop for anything you need in Markethill. I'm sure we'll need to buy a few things for the baby." He smiled and looked at Sarah's belly which had not yet begun to expand.

He said to Tom, "Let's go outside and see what we can do. There are still a few chickens left and we can get one ready for the pot."

The next morning they sat in church together. Sarah hid the small wedding band Thomas had given her because she did not want to make any explanations. When her father began to weep, she felt the tears streaming from her own eyes. She would never sit in this church again, nor would they ever again hear Reverend Hardesty preach. Suddenly she knew how much she would miss the church, and all the people in it. She kept dabbing the handkerchief at her eyes and nose throughout the remainder of the service.

Before they left through the large wooden doors, Pastor Hardesty greeted them with a warm hand shake. "Is this the last Sunday with us before you leave for Ireland?"

Thomas said, "Yes, we leave early next Saturday morning. We can't thank you enough for everything you've done."

Sarah added, "We won't ever forget you, Pastor. Thank you."

"May our heavenly Father be your Guide." He looked warmly at them before they stepped down the stairs.

Sarah stopped at the carriage and said, "Give me a few minutes. I want to see if I can find my friend, Mercy, so I can tell her good-bye." She wandered about among the many people standing in the church yard, and finally found Mercy's mother.

"Mrs. Mallory, I'm looking for Mercy. Did she come to church with you?"

"Why, hello, Sarah. We've missed you at the farm." She patted Sarah's shoulder, and said, "Mercy and her sister, Edna, left on the train yesterday to go and spend part of the summer helping their Grandmother Mallory. She lives alone in Zanesville and she needs more help as her rheumatism grows worse."

"I wanted to say good-bye to Mercy because we're leaving next Saturday for Ireland."

"Clear across the ocean to Ireland? But I recall now that your father is from Ireland, and your cousin is, too."

"Yes, we thought it would be a good idea for Daddy and Thomas to see family there again."

Mrs. Mallory embraced Sarah. "You have a safe journey and enjoy your time in Ireland. When do you think you will return?"

Avoiding the truth, Sarah said, "We don't know for sure. Be sure to tell Mercy I said good-bye to her. I must go now as they're in the carriage waiting for me."

As the Keith's carriage pulled away from the church, Sarah could see Mrs. Mallory speaking to a group of ladies, no doubt spreading the news of the Keith family's trip to Ireland. Sarah smiled, thinking of the celebrity status this brought them. Only the very wealthy traveled across the ocean.

Later, the three of them went to the Cole family home for their last Sunday meal with them. Sarah looked around the table and wished that Rena could be there. But then she thought how painful this would be for Thomas, and decided it was best that Rena wasn't there. She listened to members of the Cole family talking, and tried to memorize how they each sounded and how they looked. She was going to miss her Aunt Hannah and Uncle Isaac. She would miss Emma, too.

Sarah and Emma helped Hannah clear the table, and wash and dry the dishes after dinner. Emma dried a plate and said, "Well, Mrs. Keith, aren't you lucky that you didn't have to change your name when you got married?"

Sarah thought for a minute. "You're right. I won't need to learn to write a different name behind 'Sarah'. When Thomas took us out to Pleasant Hill Cemetery a while back we saw some strange names on some of those stones."

Hannah said, "You didn't tell us you went out to the cemetery. Did you see your mother's stone?"

"Yes, you must go and see it sometime. It's tall and beautiful. Thomas says the polished granite will look the same in one hundred years as it does right now."

Emma said. "What color is the stone?"

"The granite is mostly dark gray with some rose colors mixed in it. At the widest part near the bottom are these words carved into the stone: 'Margaret L. Keith, Beloved wife and mother'." Sarah had to swallow back tears after saying her mother's name.

Hannah scrubbed at a large pot. "Tell us more about your wedding, Sarah. Did the pastor perform the ceremony in the Manse?"

"Yes, it was a simple but beautiful wedding and Thomas wished we had a copy of the prayer that Reverend Fulton said over us. Not only did they have fresh flowers on the table but the pastor's wife made a small bouquet of flowers for me to hold. And besides that, she prepared a nice supper for us and afterwards she brought out a wedding cake. She made a white cake with white frosting and she decorated it with real rose buds of pink and white. I wish you could have seen it."

"What dress did you wear and what kind of flowers were in your bouquet?" Emma wanted to know."

"I didn't want to spend money on a new dress so I wore my navy blue one with the lace trim at the neck and cuffs. There were pink and white roses in the bouquet I held. I wish I had a photograph to show you, but hiring a photographer would have cost a great deal of money.

Enthralled with the description of Sarah's wedding, Emma said, "Oh, it sounds like a wonderful wedding! I wish I could have been there to see it."

Isaac wanted to smoke his pipe away from the ladies so the three men went outside to enjoy the nice day. They stood together in the shade of a large tree.

John asked Thomas, "How did the auction go? Did you get some decent prices for your livestock?"

"Maddie brought a very good price, and Ransom, too. Some of our other mares sold for good prices, and the three cows and calves made about what you'd expect. I hated to break up Mac and Maddie but at least Mac will be staying with you, members of the family."

"And a fine addition to our work force. Thank you, Thomas." Isaac patted Thomas' back. "Emma's looking forward to having Sarah's little dog for a pet, and if we can get Rex to stay with us, I'd like to use him. Will you bring them over here or do you want us to come and get them after you've gone?"

"It would be best if we brought them here and left them. It might help them understand this is where they belong. Do you mind if we show up here on Friday with the dogs?"

"That will be just fine. I'll tell Hannah and she'll have supper ready for all of us."

"Thank you. I know Sarah will be happy to see you all

one more time." Thomas had begun to grow a mustache and he reached to smooth it with his finger. "After we've gone I hope you will be able to come and get all the food and supplies in the storage room behind the stairs. There are a couple of large hams hanging from the ceiling and some sacks of flour and oats in the corner of the room. Besides a sack of coffee beans and two tins of tea, you'll find a pail of lard and some other tins of food sitting on the shelves, and I think there are two or three cones of white sugar. The root cellar is almost empty of anything edible, but you can look to make sure. If you want to take home any of the fire wood, please help yourself."

Isaac said, "It appears we'll be driving your wagon over to your place Saturday morning to load all that food and bring it home. I'm sure it will be used to make some good meals for us." Isaac patted Tom's back and spoke as if he expected Tom to understand. "We've had many good meals together over the years. I hate to see our family gatherings come to an end."

"Our trunks are upstairs and they're packed but I can't get them closed without your help," Sarah said to her husband. She felt tired and worn out. Her hair hung limply around her face which was wet with perspiration. She stood at the kitchen stove and continued to stir a sauce pot.

Thomas said, "I'll help you close the trunks before we go to bed tonight." He pulled out a chair for Tom and motioned for him to sit.

The meal they ate that Friday at noon was a strange mix of canned meat and vegetables that Sarah had opened from tins. She made a white sauce to pour over the mixture and stirred it together. She had cooked the last of the rice and served each of them a bowl of rice.

Sarah explained, "I read that it's fashionable to cover the rice with the meat and vegetables mixed in white sauce. I think they usually use pieces of chicken instead of beef, but it will probably taste alright." She tasted the mix and immediately she grabbed the salt shaker. "Let me add some salt before you spoon it over your rice."

They bowed their heads while Thomas said a brief prayer of thanks, and then they began to eat Sarah's concoction. Thomas said, "This is not bad, and it's a good way to use some of the many tins of food we have left."

When they finished eating, Sarah poured some of the leftovers into Topsy's small bowl and placed it on the floor in front of him. She emptied the rest into a larger bowl for Rex and handed it to Thomas. "Would you take this out to Rex?"

Thomas took the bowl and opened the back door to whistle for Rex. He and Tom left to make a final check on the buildings and the whole area around the house. Thomas wanted to be certain they left everything in order.

Sarah bent down and gently scratched Topsy's head. "You're a good little dog, and I'm going to miss you." Topsy licked the bowl clean, then looked up at his mistress and wiggled with expectation. She smiled at his hopeful expression and said, "You are not getting anymore, you little beggar." She filled his empty bowl with water and set it down in front of him before she went back to cleaning the kitchen.

Sarah looked around the kitchen and in the pantry. *Some of these dishes are gifts that Mama and Daddy received at their wedding. How I would love to take them with me. Mama's knives, her butter churn, and coffee grinder have been carefully used and cleaned over the years. They would be familiar and useful when Thomas and I begin setting up our own home in Kansas.* Sarah sighed, knowing all her mother's belongings would stay right here to be used by complete strangers. She swept the floor and placed the broom and dust pan in the pantry where they had been stored as long as she could remember. Everything here was very dear and precious to her. Mama's presence lingered in this kitchen and she felt her mother was watching over her. *Mama, I don't want to leave you.* She turned her face to the wall and wept.

Sarah was mending clothing when the clock chimed six times. She felt it was tolling the end of everything she had known and loved. She put away her needle and thread, and folded up the last item, a mended camisole. All was ready for their departure early tomorrow morning. Thomas came in and said Mac was hitched to the wagon and they should be going to supper at the Cole's house.

Thomas helped her up into the wagon. She held Topsy in her lap while Rex was tied into the wagon where he sat behind them. Her father sat beside her, his body rigidly upright and his face forward, like a man waiting for the firing squad. She looked at him and knew that he must understand something about their situation. Her emotions were making it difficult to think straight, and Thomas had to repeat himself when he spoke to her.

Thomas said it again. "Sarah will you take the lantern and stow it under the seat?"

They pulled into the yard at the Cole's home and came to a stop in front of Emma, who ran out to greet them. With great excitement she announced, "Guess who came home on the train last night! Rena's here and she's going to stay for two whole weeks!"

Sarah looked over at Thomas and saw him turn pale. She felt sick to her stomach and wished they could turn around and go home. Instead, they climbed down from the wagon and headed for the back door of the house. Sarah walked into the kitchen with Topsy in her arms and put him down on the floor. He danced around the room with his pink tongue showing while he looked up at all the people.

Emma picked him up and held him close to her face. "You are going to be my little puppy from now on." She looked at Sarah. "Thank you for letting me keep Topsy. I'll take very good care of him."

Sarah said, "He's not a puppy anymore. He's almost ten years old, but if you take good care of him he should live for five or six more years."

Thomas came into the kitchen with the little dog's basket. "Where do you want Topsy to sleep?"

Hannah said, "I think you should place his basket in that far corner so it's out of the way." She adjusted her apron. "If you'll all go in the dining room and take your seats, Emma and Sarah and I will bring in the food."

When the men had cleared out of the kitchen, Sarah said to her Aunt Hannah, "Emma told us that Rena came home last night."

"Yes, she's not feeling very well and she doesn't want to eat so she's resting in the bedroom upstairs," Hannah said.

"Can I go upstairs and say goodbye to her before we leave?"

"I think she plans to come down before you leave and say goodbye to all of you."

Sarah dreaded that future moment and hoped it would pass quickly. All through the meal she put food in her mouth and chewed and swallowed, but she tasted nothing. She kept stealing glances at Thomas wondering what he was thinking.

Everyone seemed to be preoccupied throughout the meal. Sarah knew their thoughts were elsewhere as they talked about the many things that were left for the Cole family to take from the Keith home. Thomas urged John and Isaac to take anything they could use from the barn and sheds.

Sarah pleaded with her aunt to come and take any of her mother's things from the kitchen, or any of her linens. "I would love to take Mama's wedding dishes with us, and her good knives, and her coffee grinder… I wish you would take them, Aunt Hannah."

"Thank you, Sarah. I would love to have some of my sister's things. I'm only sorry that you won't be able to take them yourself."

"The ship's fare includes only one trunk per passenger. When we start adding more, the price rises tremendously," Thomas said.

Isaac and Hannah did not want Emma to know about Sarah's pregnancy so Sarah and all the others refrained from making any references to the forthcoming addition to their family. Sarah was aware that the Cole family wanted to avoid the topic of where she and Thomas would eventually settle because they had many misgivings about her living on the western frontier. Besides all the topics that were being avoided, Sarah could feel the tension in the air as they took turns glancing toward the stairs wondering when Rena would come down.

"As a special farewell treat, I've made a spice cake for dessert and if you'll give me a few minutes, I'll whip up some cream to put on top of it." Hannah excused herself from the table and went into the kitchen. Sarah followed, asking if she could help.

When they were in the kitchen Hannah embraced Sarah and said quickly before Emma might decide to join them, "Please write and let us know how you are, and be sure to let us know about the baby." Her words were a whisper in Sarah's ear.

Sarah kissed her on the cheek. "Aunt Hannah, I *will* write to you, I promise."

They all praised Hannah for the delicious cake and whipped cream. Dutifully, they cleaned their plates in honor of this farewell meal.

Hannah said, "We know you have to get up very early tomorrow and you need to get home for a good night's rest. Don't stay to help clean up because Emma and I can do it later."

Thomas said, "We want to thank all of you for everything. I want to thank you especially for making me feel welcome here, and I will remember you all with affection."

"Well said, Thomas." Isaac stood and everyone followed him by scooting back chairs and standing to leave the table.

Thomas said, "I'll go out and hitch Mac to the wagon and then we'll be leaving."

As soon as they heard the back door close, Rena entered the room. Other than some redness around her eyes, she was as beautiful as ever. She came to Sarah and embraced her. "I will miss you, Sarah, and I'm sorry you're leaving."

Sarah hugged her cousin. "I'll miss you, too."

Rena turned to her uncle and gave him a hug. "Goodbye, Uncle Tom."

Then each member of the Cole family took turns embracing Sarah and her father until there was not a dry eye in the room.

When Thomas came in, it was if the air suddenly filled

with electricity. All talking stopped and all breathing ceased as they watched Rena approach him. Her eyes locked with his and she extended her hand to him. "I wish you the best of everything, Thomas."

Thomas took her hand in his. "Thank you." That was all he said. He looked at Rena with such longing that it nearly broke Sarah's heart.

After what seemed an eternity, Thomas let go of Rena's hand.

Sarah felt compelled to bring this farewell to an end. She took her father's arm and the arm of her husband, saying, "We must leave now. Good night to all of you, and thank you for the lovely supper."

They walked out to the wagon and climbed up to the seat. The Cole family followed to see them off on this lovely warm night with its millions of stars in the sky.

"Have a nice trip to Ireland." Emma's voice called to them.

More voices called out to wish them a safe trip, but Rena's was not among them.

When they arrived home, Sarah took her father by the arm and stood patiently in the near darkness for Thomas to unhitch Mac. It struck her that this was the last time she would ever stand outside this barn and wait for Thomas to unhitch. It was such an ordinary thing that had happened so many times, but now it seemed very significant. She felt something cold and wet on her hand and looked down to see Rex wagging his tail.

"Rex, you naughty dog! You managed to get your rope untied and followed us home!"

Thomas came out of the barn carrying the brightly lit lantern. "Did I hear you talking to Rex?"

At the sound of his name, Rex came and sat down expectantly in front of Thomas.

"Rex, you are a rascal!" Thomas scratched around the dog's ears and patted his head.

"We'll just have to leave you tied to the wagon tomorrow morning. You and Mac can keep each other company while you wait for the Cole family to come and get you."

Thomas, Sarah, and her father walked up to the house and into the kitchen. Thomas lit another lantern for Sarah, and then he took Tom upstairs to put him to bed. Sarah's lantern sat on the table where it cast shadows of the past in this room that still held the presence of her mother. Sarah filled the teakettle for tomorrow morning's breakfast and checked in the pantry to see there were half a dozen eggs and half a loaf of bread left. Her eyes became blurred with tears as she looked at all the things her mother's hands had touched and used over the years. She picked up her mother's old apron that hung from a hook in the pantry and buried her face in its folds. When she heard Thomas coming down the stairs, she quickly wiped away her tears.

"Are you ready to go up to bed?" Thomas put his lantern on the table and extinguished the flame.

Sarah lit a candle, turned off her lantern, and they went upstairs to prepare for bed. In the dark room she lay next to Thomas, and pulled the quilt up to her chin. *This is the last night any member of the Keith family will sleep in this house.* She wiped her tears with the bed sheet and put her arm across Thomas's chest to feel secure again.

CHAPTER TWENTY FOUR

Will unhitched his horse, pushed the four-wheel carryall into its bay, and hung the harness on the wall. He led his horse out to pasture and turned it loose. Standing next to the closed gate, he pulled the letter from his pocket to read it again, still unable to believe all that his son had written. Once more, he read all five pages and scratched his graying head. What had gone wrong? Thomas's news was as incredible as purple milk coming from his cows. They had received a short letter from Thomas at the beginning of the year telling of Margaret's unexpected death, but since that letter they had heard nothing from him. And now this!

He folded the pages together and put them in his pocket. The family would not be seeing *this* letter from Thomas. He would have to share it with Anne and the two of them would need to discuss it before anything was said to anyone.

Anne, his dear wife of thirty years…she was a treasure among women and he still felt he had married the finest one in all Ireland. He loved her smile which broke easily into laughter, he loved her encouraging ways, and her devotion to him and the children remained strong through the years. Thomas's letter would bring her sorrow, and at the same time, he knew she would be glad he was coming home. They both thought they had said their final farewell to Thomas six years ago when he left Ireland for America.

That night, as they were in their bedroom preparing for bed, Will handed the letter to his wife. "This came today from Thomas. I think you'd better sit down and read it."

Alarmed, Anne looked at her husband. "Is he alright? He wasn't injured, was he?"

"No he seems to be in good health. Just read the letter and then we'll talk about it."

Anne sat on the edge of the bed and began reading.

Before she had come to the end of the first page she gasped, and after reading the second page, she groaned. "Oh Will! Whatever came over him to do such a thing?! And Sarah has only turned fifteen!"

"Read on, there's more to come."

By the time Anne had finished reading the letter, tears were streaming down her face.

"At least, our son is coming home and we will see him again." She took in an uneven breath and wiped her eyes.

Will removed his shirt and pants to hang them on the usual chair. "Not only is he bringing his pregnant wife and cousin home, he is bringing my brother, too. According to Thomas, my brother's mind has left him and he cannot speak. Whatever will we do with Tom and who will look after him?" He lifted the covers on his side of the bed and lay down.

"Don't worry about Tom. Among all of us, we'll be able to look after him. My concern is for Thomas and Sarah living in the wilderness on the western frontier. We've read many stories about the hardships the settlers suffer. They could even be attacked by Indians!" Anne continued to sit on her side of the bed while she wept again.

Will placed his hand on Anne's back and patted her in sympathy. It made him sad to see her in such distress. When her weeping subsided he asked, "What was the date they were supposed to sail from New York?"

Anne shuffled through the pages of Thomas's letter. "Here it is." She held it for Will to see. "He wrote they were due to sail from the harbor at New York on the twenty-fourth of June and their ship should arrive in Dublin by the seventh of July.

Will said, "Today is the fifth of July. They will be here in two or three days."

"We need to decide where they will sleep. I guess we can put Tom upstairs with William and James. William can share James's bed and Tom can have William's bed. But I have no idea where Thomas and Sarah will sleep."

Will suggested, "If we can find another large bed

somewhere, we can set it up in the front room downstairs and put a screen around it."

At one end of the large, rectangular front room was a long table where they sat to eat meals together. The door to the kitchen led off this end of the room, while at the other end of the room there was a door that led to the front hall and stairway. In between doors, on the center of the wall, there was a fireplace with two wing-back chairs and a small sofa facing the fire. There would be just enough room for a bed in the far corner that faced the hall entry.

Anne nodded, "I think it's the best we can do. What are you going to say to the children? I don't want the younger ones to know that Thomas and Sarah had to get married because she is expecting his child."

"We won't talk about the date of their wedding. But of course, James, and Sarah Lizzie, and Annie are adults and they will know without being told. Agnes and William are old enough to understand and I'm sure they will figure it out. Margery and Mary are too young to think about such things."

Anne nodded in agreement. "And there are Maggie and Fergus. We'll need to talk to them as soon as we can. Do you think you can arrange to pay them a visit soon?"

Maggie, who was three years older than Thomas, married Fergus Simpson last summer. They were expecting their first child in a few weeks, and Will and Anne were looking forward to being grandparents.

Anne continued, "Be sure to stop in at Cardiff House and talk to our son, Dr. Gilbert Keith." Anne spoke of her son's title with pride. "Gilbert will want to know, and he can be helpful when it's time for the baby to come."

Everyone who lived under the roof of Hill House was excited when they gathered around the dinner table and learned the news. They talked about the additional family members who would be crowding into the already filled household, and everyone wondered about Sarah, the young woman from America.

"Does Uncle Tom say anything at all?" Agnes asked.

Will explained to Agnes and the others, "He is no longer in his right mind. We'll all have to keep an eye on him or he will wander away and become lost. Thomas wrote that my brother stopped speaking right after his wife died last year. But I want you to know that until recently, my brother was a very intelligent man and he could speak as well or better than most people."

Sarah Lizzie asked, "Where will they sleep?"

Will patiently described the plans he and Anne had made the night before.

Young William groaned. "Why do I have to give my bed to Uncle Tom?"

His father said, "Have you forgotten when you four boys slept in that room every night? You shared a bed with Thomas, and Gilbert shared a bed with James. None of you are the worse for it."

Anne, directed a little speech to the two younger girls, Margery and Mary, but she meant it for all the children to hear. "Thomas and Sarah will have their bed screened off in that corner." She pointed to the far end of the room. "I want all of you to respect their privacy, just as if they were in an ordinary bedroom with a door that closed. Margery and Mary... that means you will not go into their screened area unless you are invited. Do you understand?"

Both girls nodded.

A bed was borrowed from a neighbor, and Will and his oldest son, James went to work building frames for a screen that hinged at one end. Anne and her oldest daughter, Sarah Lizzie, made curtains from old bed linens to fit inside the frames. When it was done it looked like a homemade screen cobbled together from odds and ends, which is exactly what it was.

Agnes looked at it after she and her mother made up the bed. "I'm glad I don't have to sleep with a husband behind a flimsy screen like this!"

Her mother reminded her, "We will all be upstairs in our own beds when Thomas and Sarah sleep here. They will have this whole room to themselves each night."

"Did Dad say that Sarah is only fifteen? I wonder why Thomas married someone so young."

Anne shook her head and decided to keep quiet about the reason for this hasty marriage. She placed her hands on her hips and surveyed the makeshift bedroom. "That bedside table is much too small to hold a pitcher and basin, and a candle, too. Maybe we can find a larger table somewhere soon. I'm going to look for a small rug, and they will need a chamber pot, too. Agnes, will you go and find your father and tell him to buy a chamber pot the next time he goes to town?"

Sarah was exhausted after three weeks of traveling. Her hair hung together in greasy clumps when she brushed it and her scalp itched all the time now. All she wanted was to sit in a tub of warm water and wash her head and body. Standing at basins to wash was alright most of the time, but now her whole body needed a good cleaning.

They rode on trains ever since they left Dublin this morning, and now they were just a few miles outside of Markethill. Sarah looked at her husband and said, "I know this is only Wednesday, but do you think I could take a bath when we come to your parent's home?"

Thomas smiled at her. "I will arrange for it myself."

"I will be very grateful." She looked up at her husband and said, "Tell me again the names and ages of your brothers and sisters."

Thomas started with James, the oldest who was twenty-nine years, and Sarah Lizzie, age twenty-six, both of them still unmarried. "My brother, Gilbert is a doctor in town and he's twenty-eight. He has some rooms over the surgery where he lives in Markethill, but he is a bachelor, too."

"I hope Sarah Lizzie is a good person because we share the same name."

"She's quiet, but good-natured. I'm sure you'll like her. Maggie is my next sister. She's twenty-four years of age, and last year she married Fergus Simpson. Mum wrote that Maggie is expecting her first baby this summer. Of the others still living at home, all of them are younger than I am. Annie is nineteen years and she's the quietest one in our family. She's so shy that she stays hidden out of sight most of the time. Annie likes to read and I understand she has collected quite a few books. Agnes is the bossy one and she's seventeen years old. My little brother, Willie, is fifteen years, which is not easy for me to imagine…he was so small when I left home. Then the two youngest are Margery and Mary. They are about ten and eight years."

"So, Maggie and Gilbert are the only ones who have left home besides you. That means your father and mother and seven brothers and sisters are still at home, and we make three more. I hope your parents have a big house."

"To tell the truth, I don't know where we will sleep, but they will find room for us."

Sarah was not happy to hear those words and she began to wonder if they might have to sleep in the barn or an outbuilding that had no heat in the winter. The closer they came to Markethill, the more Sarah dreaded it.

When they pulled into the station at Markethill, Thomas helped Sarah and Tom down from the train. Their trunks had been unloaded from the baggage car and Thomas told Sarah and Tom to stand guard over them while he walked up the hill on Main Street to the medical dispensary.

As he walked, Thomas looked about the town and realized that very little had changed since he left six years ago. Some of the shops had new paint on the doors but Markethill was still the same small village it had been. Thomas climbed the three steps to the wooden door which was framed on either side by tall columns with a large fan-shaped window over the top. A brass plate on the door was inscribed, 'Cardiff House'. He used the brass knocker, which was in the shape of a lion's head, and rapped three times.

A gray-haired woman wearing a servant's apron opened the door and peered out.

"May I help you?" She looked at Thomas as if she were

not sure whether she knew him. "The doctor's hours closed at six o'clock."

"I'm not here to see the doctor...I mean I'm here to see my brother, Gilbert Keith...Doctor Gilbert Keith. I'm Thomas Keith, recently arrived from America."

Her eyebrows went up at least an inch and, smiling, she said, "Come in Mr. Keith."

Thomas removed his hat and entered the front hall. He stood waiting while the servant woman rushed away to fetch Dr. Keith.

Gilbert strode into the entry hall and exclaimed, "Thomas! It's good to see you!" He grasped his brother's hand and shook it warmly. Gilbert was as tall as Thomas, and though his nose had a slight upturn at the end, it was obvious they were brothers. He looked his brother over and slapped him on the back. "You were just a boy the last time I saw you. And now you are a man with a wife, and you're soon to be a father!"

Thomas was relieved to know they had received his letter and the whole family knew about Sarah and the expected child. He said, "It's good to see you, Gilbert."

"Come upstairs to my rooms and I'll ask Mrs. Begley to prepare us some tea."

"No, thanks, I need to get back to Sarah and her father. It has been a long day and they are waiting at the station, watching over our trunks. I was really hoping you might be able to take us out to the farm."

"Give me a minute and I'll talk to Mrs. Begley's husband, Jack. I think we'll need his help."

When Gilbert returned he introduced his brother to Jack Begley and said to Thomas, "Doctor Pringle and I share a four-wheeled carriage, and I can take the three of you out there now. I'll bring your luggage tomorrow. Will that be alright?"

"Yes, of course. I can't thank you enough."

The two young men, along with the older man, exited through the back to a garden. Just beyond, they came to a storage bay for the carriage, and two horse stalls. Gilbert pulled the carriage out from its bay and grabbed the harness off the wall. With Jack's help, he hitched up the two matched black horses, and the three men climbed into the carriage.

"These are good-looking horses, and a fine rig." Thomas said.

"I'm afraid I can't take any credit. They belong to Dr. Pringle, but he has allowed me to use them for personal as well as medical purposes," Gilbert said.

"Do you have certain days when you see patients?"

"Yes, I am on duty every Tuesday, Thursday, and Saturday. Dr. Pringle has the other three days. The dispensary is closed on Sunday."

"Do you and Dr. Pringle share the living quarters upstairs?"

"Yes, since he and his wife are alone, they are happy with just a few of the rooms, and I have three of the smaller rooms to myself. So far, it has been a congenial arrangement."

"Dr. Pringle must be more than sixty years old by now. Does he ever talk of retiring?

"Yes, but he says that he wants to continue as long as he has good health. Right now, he seems to be strong enough."

"Did he and his wife ever have any children?"

"I know of only a daughter, and she died of a fever before she was twenty years old."

They pulled to a stop in front of the train station. The three men jumped down and Gilbert was introduced to Sarah and her father.

"I am happy to meet you, Sarah." He shook her hand briefly, and nodded at Tom saying, "Welcome back to Ireland." Tom merely stared at him without responding.

"It will take a little while for the trip to Clooney so shall we start?" Gilbert helped Sarah into the carriage while Tom climbed in and sat down.

Sarah looked at Gilbert and asked, "Don't you have room for our trunks? I really want to take my trunk with me."

"I told Thomas that I would bring your luggage out there tomorrow, or he can come and get them with Dad's wagon in the morning. Jack, here, is going to stay with your trunks until I return and then he and I will load them into the carriage and take them to Cardiff House."

Sarah turned to Thomas and whispered in his ear, "You said I could bathe tonight, and the only clean clothes I have are in my trunk!"

Thomas spoke into Sarah's ear, "You can wash out your underthings and they will be dry by morning."

"But, Thomas, I've been wearing this traveling suit for so many days, I can't stand to put it on again, especially right after I have bathed."

Husband and wife exchanged more whispered comments while the others waited.

Thomas touched his older brother on the shoulder and said, "Will you give us a few minutes so Sarah can open her trunk and remove some clean clothes?"

They climbed down from the carriage and went to join Jack who stood guard over the three trunks. Sarah insisted that the four men surround her with their backs to her while she opened her trunk and tried to find something clean to wear. At last, she had found the items she wanted, and with Thomas's help, closed the lid of the trunk. She turned to Jack and said, "Thank you for watching over them for us."

With the clean, folded clothing tucked into her already overloaded personal bag, Sarah handed it to Gilbert while Thomas helped her climb up to her seat. Finally, they were headed out of town toward their final destination.

William saw them first. He waved and called out, "Hallo". Then he turned and ran into the house to tell the others. "They're here! Thomas and the Americans are here!"

Soon everyone was gathered in the cobblestone yard to greet the travelers from far away. As soon as Thomas's feet touched the ground, his mother grabbed him and gave him a hug. She held him closely for a few seconds and released him to say, "You are a grown man! When you left here six years ago you were a thin boy and now you are a handsome man with a mustache." She smiled with tears in her eyes and touched the thick brown hair growing over his upper lip.

His father came to Thomas and shook his hand while embracing him with his other arm. "You are a sight for sore eyes. It's good to have you home, son."

All the others crowded around to ask if he remembered them.

Thomas looked at each one and began with James. "James, I'd know you anywhere."

James grinned at his younger brother and shook his hand warmly. "I can't say the same about you. You have changed from a boy to a man in the years since you left home."

Thomas looked at Sarah Lizzie, his diminutive older sister. He put his hands around her waist and lifted her off her feet. "Sarah Lizzie, I think you have shrunk since I left."

Sarah Lizzie laughed. "Put me down, Thomas. You are the one who has grown into a giant of a man."

Thomas searched through the crowd. "Where's my quiet sister, Annie?" The others made way for Thomas to step toward the shy young woman whose hand hid her smile.

"Annie, I hear you have your own library. May I borrow a book sometime?"

Annie ducked her head and said, "Of course, you may Thomas. Welcome home."

"And here's my bossy little sister, Agnes! I expected you to stick out your tongue at me."

"I'm not so little anymore, Thomas. And, though you might not believe it, I *do* know how to act like a lady." She gave him a big smile and quickly hugged him.

Thomas looked at his younger brother and said, "Let me think. I don't remember anyone in our family who looked like this. What happened to Willie, my scrawny little brother who slept with me and who managed to kick me every night?"

William grinned and shook Thomas's hand. "I'm called William now. Welcome home, big brother."

Margery and Mary stood together taking in all that was happening. Mary didn't remember Thomas at all, and Margery had a vague recollection of him. Margery spoke up and said,

"Do you remember me, Thomas?"

"Give me a minute." Thomas paused and pretended to think. "You must be Margery! Am I right?"

Margery gave him a big grin and said, "You are right. Welcome home."

Eight-year-old Mary was not about to be left out and she said very loudly, "You don't know me, do you?"

Thomas said, "Of course I remember Mary, my youngest sister. I used to carry you around on my shoulders, like this." He turned her around, lifted her up, and ducked his head to place her legs around his neck. He marched about the yard while Mary laughed uproariously from her tall perch atop his shoulders. Everyone joined in the laughter.

Thomas put Mary back on the ground, and looked up to the carriage to see his wife, his father-in-law, and his older brother waiting and watching. He said, "I want you to meet my wife, Sarah." He helped her down from the carriage while all eyes looked at the young woman who wore a stylish deep-red traveling suit and a nice hat.

Sarah made her best attempt to smile. Rather timidly she said, "I'm pleased to meet all of you."

Margery and Mary crept forward to stare at Sarah. Will, Anne, James, and Sarah Lizzie came one at a time to shake her hand and welcome her while Annie, Agnes, and William hung back and looked on. Their mother motioned for them to come forward and greet their cousin who was also their American sister-in-law.

Thomas continued, "And here is Sarah's father, Tom Keith, our father's brother."

Thomas reached to give a hand to Tom as he climbed down. Tom did not look at anyone, but kept his eyes lowered to the ground.

Will came and took hold of Tom's right hand, "Welcome back to Ireland, Tom. I'm your brother, Will." Though Tom looked at his brother, there was no sign of recognition.

"And this is Dr. Gilbert Keith of Cardiff House,"

Thomas announced as if they didn't know Gilbert. Everyone laughed again.

Gilbert sat in the driver's seat of the carriage. "I need go back to the station to help Jack with your trunks. Do you want to wait until I can return them tomorrow after office hours, or do you want to come and get them yourselves?"

Will said, "We'll come to Cardiff House and get them before noon tomorrow."

His mother called out as Dr. Keith drove away, "Be sure to come for dinner after church on Sunday. Maggie and Fergus will be here, too."

They all filed into the kitchen with its dark gray slate floor and huge black cook stove. Hams hung from the ceiling over a chopping block and a heavy work table stood in the center of the room. Pots and pans hung from hooks on each side of the stove. This was a room where large meals were prepared.

Anne looked at Thomas. "When did you eat last? Are you hungry?"

"We ate a light meal at about four o'clock when we stopped to change trains in Newry. Thomas looked at his wife and said, "You must be feeling hungry. I could eat something myself."

Sarah nodded and asked, "Do you mind if I remove my hat?"

Anne said, "Come with me." She led them into the front room where they saw the long dining table. "Thomas will you take Sarah to the far end of the room and show her your bedroom?" She laughed and said, "You'll have to pretend there are solid walls but James and your father made the frame for the screen and they placed hooks to hang your hats and clothing on the frame."

"Sarah Lizzie and Annie, will you set three places at the table while I slice some bread and ham?" Anne went to the kitchen to begin the preparation. Sarah Lizzie and Annie headed in the opposite direction to the scullery where plates and silverware were kept, and where eggs, butter, flour, salt, and sugar were stored.

Thomas and Sarah inspected their bedroom with its pretend walls. Sarah hung her hat from one of the hooks. She whispered into Thomas's ear, "This is worse than I expected. We have no privacy at all!"

Sarah, Tom, and Thomas sat at the long table. Anne brought them bread, butter, sliced ham, and cool milk which made a satisfying meal before bedtime. The others, who had eaten earlier, gathered around the table to visit with them while the remaining light from a long summer day came through the window behind them.

"How was the trip across the big pond?" Will inquired. "Did any of you suffer sea sickness?"

Thomas answered the questions and did all the talking because it was obvious that Sarah was tired. Her shoulders drooped and her whole body sagged from exhaustion. He said, "Tom and I had no problems with sea sickness but Sarah was troubled with it for a few days."

Thomas said, "Sarah is hoping for a bath tonight before she retires. The bathing facilities were nearly always in use on board the ship. Unless she wanted to bathe sometime after midnight, it was impossible to find the women's bathing room vacant."

His mother said, "You know where the tub is and where we keep the soap. I'll get a clean towel for Sarah, and you can set up the bath for her after we've all gone to bed."

The two little girls began to yawn, and soon Mary fell asleep leaning against Agnes.

The clock on the mantle began to strike the hour of ten o'clock and Will stood up from the table.

"James and I need to make a final check on everything outside before bedtime. Sarah and Thomas, and Tom, it's good to have you here with us. I'll see you in the morning."

Anne hurried the younger children off to bed. She and the older girls began to clear the table and make the kitchen ready for morning's breakfast. Sarah went to their 'bedroom' to find her bag with the clean clothing, while Thomas took her father outside to the privy, and then upstairs to put him into

William's bed.

Sarah was inhibited and withdrawn while they took turns bathing in the kitchen. She kept looking toward the doors as if she expected an intruder. Thomas poured clean rinse water over her hair after she washed it, then Sarah twisted her hair tightly to remove the water. She climbed out of the tub and dried herself off while Thomas bathed his own body. It was half-past eleven when they climbed into bed behind the screen. Thomas curled around her backside, his hand cupping her breast.

Sarah yawned and said, "Goodnight, Dearest." Almost immediately she was sound asleep.

CHAPTER TWENTY-FIVE

Thomas felt someone shaking his shoulder. He was in such a deep sleep that it took him a few moments to remember where he was.

"Thomas, we can't find Tom. Will you get up and help us look for him?" His father's voice was very quiet so that Sarah would not wake up.

Thomas stood and began to pull on his clothes. He whispered, "Is he not in the house?"

Will waited until they were in the hallway before he said, "We've searched upstairs and he isn't there. Do you think he might have gone outside?"

"He could have gone anywhere. We've found him in the most unlikely places before this. I took him out to the privy before I put him in bed last night. Let's look there first."

"I've already been out there and I didn't see Tom."

"Let's begin looking in all the buildings outside. Can James and William help us?"

"They are both outside with lanterns looking for him right now. It will be light soon and that will help us in our search."

Thomas said, "Sometimes he will start walking and keep on going. I think I'll follow the road downhill from here." He took one of the lighted lanterns from his father and left through the seldom-used main entrance. With his lantern held high, he headed east while his father walked the road toward Markethill. They could hear one another calling out in the darkness, "Tom! Tom Keith."

Soon it began to rain and Thomas remembered the time they found his uncle shivering in the cold November weather at home. 'At home...' He had lived in Ohio for so long it had become home to him, and now here he was at his Irish home, looking for his uncle again. Thomas wore only his shoes, shirt, and trousers because he left the house in such a hurry. Without any protection from the rain his teeth began to chatter and his body shivered. He decided to go back and see if anyone had found Tom.

Thomas entered through the kitchen door and saw that his mother and sisters were busy preparing for a big breakfast. His mother stood at the cook stove and when she turned to see him standing there with dripping wet clothes, she said, "Thomas, use that towel and dry yourself. Come over here close to the stove where you can warm up."

Thomas reached for a dry towel hanging from one of the lines that hung across one end of the kitchen. It was the towel he and Sarah had used last night. He wrapped it around himself and stood by the heat of the big cook stove.

"Has Tom been found yet?" Thomas reached to wipe off water that streamed down his face from his wet hair. His teeth chattered and his body trembled.

"Yes." His mother laughed. "He was right here all the time. Sarah found him asleep in one of the chairs in front of the fireplace."

The girls joined their mother in giggles and laughter. Thomas was too miserable to laugh. He managed to make a crooked smile as they enjoyed the humor.

"Has Dad come back yet? I hope the rain didn't drench him, too," Thomas said.

His mother said, "As soon as Sarah found her father, she came and told us. Agnes ran down the road after your Dad and he came back before he was completely drenched. He helped Tom get dressed and they both went out with the boys to do the milking."

Thomas sneezed three times, and wiped his nose on a corner of the towel.

His mother said, "I'm afraid you're going to be sick." She pulled him closer to the stove and began to unbutton his shirt. "Sarah Lizzie, will you go upstairs and see if you can find a clean shirt that will fit Thomas?" When she had unbuttoned his shirt she stooped to untie his shoes. "Take off those wet shoes, and I'll put your feet in a basin of warm water." It had been so many years since she had 'mothered' her third son Anne was enjoying fussing over him almost as much as he enjoyed her motherly attention.

"Annie, go to the linen cupboard and bring a large, clean towel. This one is too wet to soak up any more water." With the dry towel that Annie gave her she reached up to dry Thomas's hair. When his hair was no longer dripping she said, "Here, Thomas. Take this towel and wrap it around yourself so you can remove those wet trousers."

Thomas sat on a kitchen chair with his feet in a tub of warm water, wearing James's shirt and a towel wrapped around his middle. His own shirt and trousers hung from the line nearest the stove, and his shoes were placed on the floor next to the stove.

Sarah came into the kitchen wearing a simple clean dress, her hair brushed and tied back with a ribbon, the same as she wore it when she was a school girl. She looked at her husband in surprise. "What is wrong with you, Thomas?"

Anne spoke up first. "He was drenched in the rain and we're warming him up and trying to dry his wet clothes and shoes. I'm afraid he will be sick."

Thomas had another sneezing attack. His nose was dripping and he needed a handkerchief. Agnes pulled a handkerchief from her apron pocket and handed it to her brother.

"Thanks, Agnes." He wiped his nose and smiled, thinking this was the little sister he was so eager to leave behind six years ago. She grinned back at him as if knowing his thoughts.

Sarah stood there taking all this in.

Anne said, "Sarah, I hope you slept well. I apologize for the lack of privacy you have in your sleeping area. As you can see, we are still a large family and space is limited. I'm making some hot tea for Thomas to drink. Would you like some, too?"

Sarah smiled at her mother-in-law. "Yes, thank you, I would like a cup of tea."

A worried expression darkened her face. "Does anyone know where my father is?"

Thomas said, "He's alright, Sarah. Dad helped him put his clothes on, and took him outside to the milking barn. Maybe your father will remember how to milk cows again."

Sarah smiled at her husband. "Daddy hasn't milked a cow since you came to live with us six years ago."

"Tonight we're going to place a bell on the door knob where your father sleeps." Thomas sneezed again and wiped his nose on Agnes's handkerchief. "If he tries to leave the room, James and William will hear the bell and they can put him back in bed."

"I don't understand why he got out of bed to wander around in the first place." Sarah looked young and innocent as she accepted the cup of tea from her mother-in-law. "When we put him to bed at home, he always stayed there until morning when Thomas went to help him dress."

Anne said, "He knows he is not at home and it may be difficult for him to sleep soundly in a strange room with two others."

Sunday morning Sarah rose from bed and dressed herself quickly before the whirlwind of activity began. Her navy dress, the one she wore at her wedding, was too tight around her middle now and she was afraid the buttons might pop off. However, it was clean and something proper to wear to church. She would need to stand up straight and hold in her stomach as much as possible.

The lack of privacy was wearing on her nerves and she resented the fact that the two little girls, Mary and Margery always played at the end of the room where their 'bedroom' was located. It seemed to her they were forever peeking around the frame that enclosed the space belonging to her and Thomas, and then they would run away giggling.

Even though Thomas had coughed much of the night, he woke early and went out to help with the milking. Sarah went into the kitchen where her mother-in-law was standing at the stove.

Sarah still did not know what to call her mother-in-law so she said simply, "Good morning."

"Good morning, Sarah. I've a pot of tea ready to pour and this pot on the stove is of full of porridge. On Sunday mornings we each help ourselves to a bowl of porridge and a cup of tea and take it to the table to eat whenever we are ready. Here, take this bowl and come help yourself."

Sarah noticed that her father sat on a wooden straight-backed chair while he ate bread and butter and sipped tea in one corner of the kitchen. He seemed perfectly content to sit there and watch while he ate. Sarah Lizzie and Annie were busy peeling carrots and potatoes for Sunday dinner. They both looked up from their work and said, almost in unison, "Good morning, Sarah."

Sarah replied, "Good morning." She took her bowl of porridge and cup of tea into the front room where she sat at the table on one of the long benches against the window wall. She shivered and wished she wore her coat. At home it would be much warmer than this in the month of July. She turned to look out the window and saw that it was raining again.

Before she had finished eating her breakfast, the men came in from milking and joined her at the table. Each had a steaming bowl of porridge and a cup of hot tea. They ate hungrily and without much conversation. Shortly after that, Agnes herded the two little girls into the kitchen and the three of them emerged with bowls of porridge and cups of hot tea.

Soon Sarah Lizzie came through the door from the kitchen carrying a basin full of hot soapy water which she set down on the end of the table. "Be sure to place your empty bowls and cups in here before you leave the table."

Sarah was amazed at the efficient way Sunday breakfast was served to this big family. She took her own empty bowl, spoon, and cup to the basin and submerged them in the hot water. She went to their bedroom and found her comb and brush to arrange her hair up on top of her head so that she would not appear to be a school girl when they attended church later in the morning.

The women and girls rode to church in the four-wheeled carriage pulled by two horses, and driven by Sarah Lizzie. Fortunately, the carriage was enclosed to keep out most of the rain. Thomas and the four other males in the family raised umbrellas over their heads as they rode in the four-wheeled carry-all wagon. This was the same wagon that carried the milk cans, butter and cream to town three times per week.

Sarah Lizzie stopped the carriage next to several others in the church yard. Sarah waited to step down with her warm wool coat wrapped tightly around her. Thomas hurried to her side, helped her descend from the carriage, and held the umbrella over her head while he offered her his arm and directed her to the entrance of the white plaster-walled church. The family filed into two pews near the back and sat down. The service was about to begin because a man wearing wire rimmed spectacles and a long black robe stood and went to the pulpit.

Sarah looked about the sanctuary and thought the Presbyterian Church here was vastly different from the one at home, but the order of worship seemed to be similar. The minister, Thomas said his name was Reverend Mitchell, was not at all like their beloved Reverend Hardesty. This minister spoke in a calm quiet voice and seemed to be teaching them a lesson rather than preaching a sermon.

Sarah's mind began to wander during the sermon. Should she have worn her hat? Not many girls her age wore hats but she considered her status as a wife and mother-to-be, and wondered if she was attired appropriately. She felt something inside her body moving. Was that the baby? Then she knew it was the baby because she had felt movement just the other day when they traveled by train from Dublin. With the constant motion of the train she couldn't be sure, but now she had no doubt.

Sarah pulled on Thomas's sleeve. When he leaned his head toward hers she whispered, "I feel the baby moving."

Thomas raised his brows and smiled at her. He took her hand and held it throughout the remainder of the service.

After the church service ended, they came home to prepare for the big Sunday meal where the whole family would be in attendance. Margery and Mary had been assigned to set the plates and utensils on the long table. Hearing carriage wheels rattle on the cobblestones outside, the two young sisters looked through the rain-spattered window.

They shouted in unison, "Maggie and Fergus are here!"

Thomas and Gilbert left the fireside to go out and greet them, and to help Fergus unhitch his horse.

Maggie nearly screamed with joy when she saw Thomas. "Come and help me down, Little Brother. I can't believe it's really you standing there!"

Smiling, Thomas reached up to help his very pregnant sister down from the carriage. When her feet were on the ground she embraced him to her large belly. Maggie's laughter brightened the whole area in spite of the gray day with its drizzling rain.

"My! Haven't we changed? Look at you... a handsome gentleman with a fine mustache." She tweaked the ends of his mustache with both hands. "And look at me... I'm almost ready to explode with this baby growing inside me." Both of her hands patted the belly that held her child. Maggie pulled Thomas to her for another hug and they laughed together.

Thomas thought his sister was even more beautiful now that when he last saw her. He liked everything about her face: her captivating smile and even teeth, a perfectly placed nose, lively blue eyes framed by long brown lashes, cheeks that became like rosy apples when she laughed, and how Maggie loved to laugh!

Thomas said, "When we go inside, I want you to meet Sarah, my wife. She felt our baby moving this morning while we were in church. Ours will be born next January, but yours will come very soon I think."

Maggie laughed again. "I'm ready for this baby to come today!"

Gilbert said, "You two go inside. I'll help Fergus unhitch his horse."

"Thanks, Gilbert." Thomas stopped and looked at his brother-in-law. "I'm sorry. I completely forgot to say anything to you, Fergus. I remember seeing you back in the days when we went to the Friday sales at Markethill. Welcome to our family."

Fergus, a handsome man with a head of dark, wavy hair and black mustache, walked over to Thomas and shook his hand. His bright blue eyes creased at the corners when he smiled. "Thank you. I can't say that I remember you, Thomas, but at first glance, I would know you as a member of the Keith family. Take Maggie in out of this damp weather and I'll come in soon."

Inside the warm kitchen, Thomas was amazed at all the activity going on while his mother directed everything. When she and his sisters caught sight of Maggie they stopped their work and came to her, asking how she felt, was the baby moving around much , and did she want to sit down?

"I feel enormous, the baby is very active; I think he's already a champion at road bowling, and yes, I want to sit down."

His mother said, "Thomas, go with Maggie into the front room and sit by the fire. Maggie, you'll want to meet your new sister-in-law."

They went into the front room where Maggie fell into one of the upholstered wing-back chairs near the fire. Sarah sat on the small sofa and Thomas sat beside her.

"Sarah, I want you to meet my sister, Maggie. Maggie this is Sarah."

Sarah closed the Jane Austen novel she had borrowed from Annie, and looked up to smile at yet another sister-in-law.

Maggie said, "I'm glad to meet you, Sarah. Thomas tells me you are feeling the baby move now. I can remember how happy we were when I first felt our baby move."

Sarah looked at Maggie's huge belly and said, "Will the baby be coming soon?"

Maggie laughed. "He can't come soon enough! Yes, he is due before the month is out."

"How does it feel to be carrying around all that extra

weight? I mean, it must very uncomfortable." Sarah stared at Maggie's enormous belly.

"Yes, it's very uncomfortable!" Maggie patted her unborn child and smiled at Sarah's frank observation. "You will find that as the baby grows, you become adjusted to the extra weight. I think the last few weeks must be the worst because my back aches most of the time now." Maggie's smile became soft and tender. "But I think about the sweet babe I'll be holding in my arms soon and I know it will be worth the pain."

Thomas looked at his favorite sister with warmth and affection. He turned to see Sarah fingering the edges of the book while she stared into the glowing turf fire.

"You seem to be lost in thought," Thomas said to his wife.

Sarah looked up and turned toward Maggie. "I've never been near anyone who was this close to giving birth." She laughed and said, "I mean I've never been around a woman who was about to give birth. We had lots of animals on the farm."

Maggie understood and laughed with Sarah. "I know what you mean. Sometimes I feel like a pioneer myself because I'm the first one of my sisters to have a baby. Fortunately, I have some cousins and other relatives who have been in this situation recently and they have been very helpful to me." She reached to touch Sarah's hand. "Please come to me with anything on your mind and we'll have a nice chat."

Sarah nodded. "Thank you, I will."

The mouth-watering aromas coming from the kitchen soon had the whole family gathered together in the large room that served as dining, sitting, and bedroom. Sarah Lizzie came from the kitchen with two large bowls of boiled carrots and potatoes mixed together. She placed one bowl at each end of the table. Annie brought in two bowls of gravy and put them next to the bowls of root vegetables. Agnes brought in two bowls filled with cooked cabbage, and the matriarch of the family came in with a large platter of sliced roast beef and placed it near the head of the table where Will sat. Margery and Mary followed their mother, each holding plates full of sliced bread and butter.   Sounds of appreciation came from the family members who stood watching the parade of food.

Anne announced, "Everyone, please sit at the table now. Dinner is ready."

All fifteen of them sat shoulder to shoulder at both sides of the long table.   His father, who sat at the far end of the table, smiled as he looked around at his large family and said, "Let's bow our heads for the blessing."   Will cleared his throat, before praying.   "We thank thee, Lord, for this whole family gathered together around our table today.   We ask thy blessings upon us as we partake of the food provided by thy hand.   Accept our humble thanks, we pray in Jesus' name.   Amen."

When Will said the 'Amen', they began to pass the bowls around the table, filling their plates with hot food.   Sarah Lizzie came around with a large pot of tea and poured some in each cup.   The sounds of silver against china, the pleasing sounds of talking and laughter, and the sight of all these dear faces filled Thomas with such happiness he thought he would not be able to contain himself.   This was a moment he would like to capture and keep forever.

CHAPTER TWENTY-SIX

Sarah thought her husband was entirely too happy as he worked with his father and brothers on the farm. She envied the easy camaraderie that existed among them. They talked among themselves about the farm, the animals, and methods that worked better than others. They listened intently while Thomas described the farm in Ohio and how Tom had worked to breed the best horses in the area. She heard her father-in-law boast that his brother, Tom, was a master at breeding and training horses. Her husband's brothers and father even tried to convince Thomas to stay at home where he could use his skill with horses here in Ireland; besides the dairying, they would be known for their fine horses. Sarah held her breath but began to breathe easily when she heard her husband say he wanted to return to the States and establish his own farm.

Sarah listened as her father-in-law spoke to her husband.

"Thomas, as an Entered Apprentice in the Freemasons, you will have to memorize the answers to many questions and commit several pages to memory. Do you want me to be your coach or shall we ask James to do it?"

"I think you should help me as we make the deliveries into town and back. I hope the memory work will come as easily as it did when I was child."

Will said, "You shouldn't have a problem, but I'm hoping you can advance to the third degree before you leave Ireland."

Thomas said, "That's a lofty goal, but I'll try."

Sarah was discontent, feeling more and more like an outsider. Though she offered to help in the kitchen, Anne informed her daughter-in-law that she was their guest and didn't need to work. Sarah was not burdened with the care of her father because he seemed to be enjoying all the attention he received from the many residents in this household who looked after him and catered to his needs. His weeping spells had nearly ceased, and for that, she was most grateful.

Sarah finished reading the last page of *Pride and Prejudice* and closed the book with regrets that the story had come to an end. Never before had she the leisure to read a complete novel and she wondered how Annie found time to read. Sarah wished she could have Annie to herself for a while to discuss this interesting story but Annie was busy constantly with household chores.

There were two hired servants who came and helped with the churning of the butter and its preparation for market. One day, when it wasn't raining, Thomas took Sarah outside to show it to her and explain how it worked. Sarah had never seen a butter churn like this one. This very large churn was operated by a horse that circled it to turn the paddles inside which made the butter. The hired servants filled the cavernous churn with fresh cream and later they unloaded the butter. They washed the butter, added some salt, and pressed it into bricks which they wrapped in waxed paper. Thomas went with his father three times a week to deliver the fresh butter, cans of milk, and jugs of cream to the bakeries, grocers, hotels and to some of the residents in Markethill. Sarah wished she could go with them but there was just enough room on the seat for Thomas and his father. Milk, butter, and cream filled the rest of the wagon.

Sarah was unhappy that she and Thomas were separated from one another most of the daylight hours. Her days in Ireland were filled with ennui, and as she dwelt on her boredom she became more dissatisfied. If it were not for Annie's book collection, which included Jane Austen's absorbing novels, Sarah thought her life would be intolerable. She gazed out the windows at the nearly constant rain and longed for just one bright and warm summer day in Ohio. It seemed to be forever cold and damp here in Ireland, and she never felt truly warm while she sat reading in the front room. Her Irish relatives used words and expressions that she did not always understand and there were times when Sarah had no idea what they were saying as they spoke among themselves with their strong Irish accents and colloquialisms. She told herself once again that she did not belong here.

Just ten days after she met Maggie, Sarah learned from her sisters-in-law that Maggie had gone into labor and the baby was about to be born. Sarah grew apprehensive and worried that mother and baby might not survive. Because she and Maggie were newlyweds and expectant mothers, Sarah felt closer to her than anyone else in her husband's family. And Maggie's offer to be her confidante and counselor touched Sarah's heart.

Immediately after the noonday meal, her mother-in-law and Sarah Lizzie packed a bag and left in the carriage to go to the home of Maggie and Fergus which was about four miles away. Though Gilbert had been told, and they expected him to come to Maggie's bedside, Anne wanted to be there for the birth of her daughter's first child. Sarah Lizzie, who always worked alongside her mother, was needed, too.

Annie and Agnes were left in charge of the kitchen with responsibilities for the food preparation, serving, and clean- up after all the meals. Tea and breakfast were simple routines that Anne had already planned out for the girls to prepare. However, they were entirely on their own for the following day's noonday dinner.

Sarah walked into the kitchen to ask if they would like her help.

Agnes, who was two years older than Sarah, said, "What do you want to do?"

Sarah understood her to say, 'What *can* you do?' which made Sarah feel very young and inadequate. She stumbled over the words, "I... can make b-bread... and I can peel potatoes, and...I know how to...wash dirty dishes."

Agnes handed her a knife and said, "Here, you can chop this head of cabbage for a cold salad."

Sarah took the knife and began to work while Annie and Agnes hurried to prepare the remainder of the meal and to make sure that Margery and Mary set the table properly. With their combined effort, the girls soon had all the food on the table for the noon meal.

When everyone was seated Will announced, "Tom and I rode over to the Simpson's and learned that Maggie gave birth to a healthy baby boy early this morning." His face broke into a wide smile. "Your mother and I are grandparents now, and you are all aunts and uncles."

He was inundated by a barrage of exclamations, comments, and questions.

Margery said, "What's the baby's name?"

Agnes said, "He must have been a very large baby because Maggie was huge."

Thomas asked, "How is Maggie feeling?"

"When is Mum coming home?" Mary wanted to know.

Will laughed out loud. "First, let's ask the blessing." He prayed the usual prayer of thanksgiving and then asked God to bless this new baby, and thanked Him for the safe birth.

After the prayer, Will began to answer their questions. "It was a long labor but Maggie looked bright and healthy this morning. The wee one is all red and wrinkled the same as any newborn, but he can make himself heard!" Will grinned. "I'm sure his cry can be heard from any place on their farm. Maggie said she and Fergus had agreed to name him George after his grandfather on the Simpson's side."

Agnes mused, "Wee Georgie Simpson. When will be able to see him?"

Will said, "Your mother will be staying with them for a week, and after she comes home we'll learn how the baby is, and we'll know when we can see him."

"Is Sarah Lizzie going to stay there all that time, too?" Margery's voice was heard above the others.

Will said, "No, Sarah Lizzie will most likely come home tomorrow."

Agnes passed the platter of roast pork to her father. "Here, Dad, have some pork whilst 'tis warm." Everyone began to fill plates with food and much of the conversation stopped as they ate.

Sarah was allowed to help with the clean-up after the meal, and Agnes handed her a towel for drying the dishes. Sarah dried a pile of silverware, which was put away by the two young girls. She picked up a plate to dry it but handed it back to Agnes. "This one needs to be washed again."

With a petulant look on her face, Agnes inspected the plate. "That tiny bit of grease could be wiped away by your dish towel, but I will wash it again if it pleases you." She wiped the soapy rag over the plate, dipped it in the rinse water, and handed it to Sarah. "Does that look clean enough for you?"

Stiffly, Sarah said, "Yes, thank you."

When all the pots and pans had been washed and dried, Sarah's dish towel was very damp so she placed it over one of the drying lines and left the kitchen. She heard Annie call out, "Thank you for your help, Sarah."

After everyone had gone to bed that night, Sarah lay beside Thomas in the darkness and released a huge sigh. "I don't think I can be polite to your sister, Agnes, much longer."

Thomas said, "Why? What has Agnes done to offend you?"

"What hasn't she done? Whenever she says something to me she's trying to make me look stupid. She's bossy and rude all the time."

She could hear Thomas laughing quietly.

"What is so funny?" Sarah demanded.

"She's been that way all her life and I doubt if she will ever change. She doesn't mean to be rude. She simply thinks she knows better than anyone else how things are done."

"Thomas, do we have to stay here until after our baby is born? Couldn't we sail back to the States sometime in the next few weeks?"

"No, Sarah. I want our baby to be born here where we have family around us. I promise you will be glad for their help when the time comes. Besides, Gilbert has recently completed his medical training and he knows how to deliver babies safely so that mother and child have the best chance of surviving."

Sarah sighed again. She rolled over with her back to

Thomas and pondered her troubles in silence. Before she dropped off to sleep she promised herself she would try harder to be patient with Agnes.

When Sarah Lizzie returned home the next morning, all the brothers and sisters seemed to breathe more easily. If their own mother was not available, Sarah Lizzie was second-best, and a vast improvement over Agnes who had a way of irritating everyone with her imperiousness. Sarah Lizzie promptly put Sarah to work in the kitchen, and when the next laundry day came around Sarah's help was appreciated. She began to feel she was a member of the household even if her patience was strained by Agnes's overbearing manners and the prying curiosity of Margery and Mary who peeked into her bedroom almost every day. She hoped that soon she would grow used to all of them and be able to understand their Irish way of speaking.

"Put on your coat, Sarah. Dad said that you and I should go to fetch Mum from Maggie's and Fergus's house." Thomas reached to pull her up from the chair where Sarah sat reading *Sense and Sensibility.*

Sarah smiled at her husband and closed the book. "Can I have a few minutes to comb my hair and put it up? I look like a school girl when I wear it hanging down like this."

Thomas feigned a frown and pretended to be impatient. "Only a *few* minutes."

It was a 'soft' morning, as the Irish called this wet, drizzling weather. Thomas helped Sarah into the carriage and the two of them pulled away from the family farm as the horses trotted down a narrow lane heading south. The sound of the horses' hooves, the distant bleating of lambs, and the occasional cock crowing were pleasing sounds to Sarah's ears as they passed one small farm after another. She looked around the countryside and began to admire the green beauty of the land and the neat white-washed farm houses with thatched roofs. As they met other wagons and carts on the road, everyone called out 'Tis a lovely morning'. Sarah linked her arm through Thomas's and thought how good it was to have her husband to herself.

Maggie and Fergus lived in a three room cottage not far from his parents' larger home. Sarah gripped Thomas's arm as they walked up the path to the front door of the small white house with its slate roof.

Thomas called out, "Is anyone at home?"
He pushed on the latch and the door opened to let them into a dimly lit room filled with furniture that had been recently painted a pale green color. They saw Maggie sitting in a chair before the fireplace holding the baby in her arms.

She looked up with a wide smile on her face. "Come in Sarah and Thomas. Come and see your nephew, George Fergus Simpson." She lifted him up and handed him to Sarah. "Hold the back of his head with your hand, Sarah. Isn't he a precious wee one?"

Sarah held this tiny bundle and wondered how it could someday grow up to be a man. He was like the doll Thomas had given her years ago except that this priceless doll was alive and making sucking movements with his pink mouth. Instead of golden hair, George had a smooth cap of dark, soft hair covering the top of his head. She admired his button nose and perfectly shaped miniature ears. His eyes were closed in peaceful slumber and trust.

"Oh, Maggie, you have a perfect little baby boy!" Sarah's eyes filled with tears because she was overcome with emotion. She looked to see Thomas and her mother-in-law hovering near, admiring this small miracle with her. It was if they were under some sort of spell that held them silent in wonder and amazement.

Maggie broke the spell. "He looks peaceful now, but you should hear him yell when he's hungry, or feeling out of sorts because his nappie needs to be changed." Maggie squeezed her eyes almost closed while she laughed. "I don't think you'd be calling him 'perfect' then."

Anne remembered that Thomas and Sarah had just arrived and still wore their coats. "Give me the baby while you remove your coats and hang them on the hooks by the door." She gathered her grandson into her arms. "As soon as Fergus comes in from the field, we'll sit down and have dinner."

It wasn't long before the five of them were seated together enjoying a hot meal of cabbage and potatoes, roasted chicken, and warm fresh bread with butter. And just as Maggie had predicted, baby George wanted his share of attention so he began to cry loudly. Maggie left the table to pick him up from his cradle and nurse him in her chair by the fireside.

Fergus smiled and said, "He has no chance to be a normal baby when his mother jumps up and runs to him each time he makes a squeak."

Maggie grinned and replied to her husband, "You know that if I don't pick him up, you will be right there walking the floor with him in your arms."

The corners of Fergus' eyes crinkled with a loving smile toward his attractive wife. It was obvious these two were devoted to one another and to their baby.

Sarah smiled knowingly at Thomas as he winked at her.

When they finished eating, Sarah helped her mother-in-law with the dishes, and she swept the floor. While Anne removed clean, dry nappies from a line in the kitchen and folded them she encouraged Sarah to sit next to Maggie for a visit.

Fergus took Thomas outside to show him the beginning stage of construction for their new house, while the two young wives remained by the fire to talk about babies and domestic matters.

Maggie told Sarah about the birth and how the labor was exhausting, but after her water broke the baby came soon enough. Dr. Gilbert was with her and gave her confidence that everything would be alright. "I can't tell you how reassuring it is to have a brother like Gilbert who has such great knowledge," Maggie said.

Sarah wished that she and Thomas could stay with Maggie and Fergus for a few days. There were many things she would like to discuss with Maggie and she wanted to know more about caring for an infant. But when they took her mother-in-law home this afternoon, the time to share with Maggie would be over.

Maggie tore her gaze away from the sleeping babe in her arms and looked at Sarah. "Tell me. How are you feeling and is the baby becoming more active?"

Sarah smiled. "He wants to move around when I want to go to sleep at night. Did George do that to you, too?"

Maggie laughed. "He thought it was playtime when I went to bed at night. I still have sore ribs where he kicked me."

Sarah said, "My clothes don't fit me anymore either." She showed Maggie how the top two buttons of her skirt were unbuttoned. "I need to leave everything unbuttoned now."

"I want you to have some of my clothes. I let them out or added panels to them and I think they would fit you. We are close to the same height." Maggie turned in her chair to speak to her mother. "Mum, can you find some of my things that Sarah can borrow?"

Anne went into Maggie's and Fergus's bedroom and returned a few minutes later with a folded bundle of clothes. "I found two dresses and a skirt and blouse which might be useful to Sarah. We'll take them home with us."

Sarah spoke with gratefulness. "Thank you very much. I wish there was something I could do for you, Maggie."

"You came all the way from America to meet Thomas's family. I think that is thanks enough. I only wish you could stay and always be a part of our large clan."

At that moment, Sarah almost wished she could stay in Ireland just to have Maggie as her friend.

When they arrived back at Hill House, Sarah carried the bundle of clothes loaned to her by Maggie. She followed her mother-in-law into the kitchen while Thomas unhitched the horses and put away the carriage. Sarah Lizzie greeted them with a warm smile.

Anne placed her arm around Sarah Lizzie's small waist and kissed her cheek. "'Tis good to be home again. Thank you for taking care of the family whilst I was away."

"I'm afraid Margery and Mary were not on their best behavior this afternoon. They came to me in tears saying they had broken a brooch that belongs to Sarah."

Anne asked, "Can it be repaired?"

"I don't know. I haven't seen it because they told me just before you arrived."

Sarah said, "I'll go and look". She left the kitchen immediately and went through the large front room into their makeshift bedroom.

The brooch that had belonged to her mother lay on the floor where it had been stepped on and broken beyond repair. Not only was the brooch broken but when she looked at the small table where her hand mirror lay next to her comb and brush, she viewed with dismay a large crack across the center of the mirror. The two girls had been playing with Sarah's only hat and it lay on the bed with one of the feathers torn loose. Heart - broken, she sat on the bed and wept.

Thomas came in and found Sarah weeping. "Mum told me that Margery and Mary broke your brooch. Do you think it can be repaired?"

Sarah opened her hand, and without saying a word, she revealed the crushed brooch. As she continued to weep she showed him her mirror and her hat.

Thomas sat next to her with his arms around Sarah. She sobbed into his chest.

"Take me away from here, please, Thomas."

"We have no place to go."

"Could we move in with Maggie and Fergus?"

"Their house is small and we would be a great inconvenience to them now that they have the baby to care for."

"Would it cost too much to stay in a hotel in town?"

"Dearest, all our savings would vanish if we stayed in a hotel for even a few weeks. Our baby is not due to be born for many weeks. This is only the end of July."

"I don't like living here and I don't think I can bear it much longer." Sarah turned away from Thomas to lay across the bed where she sobbed into the pillow.

He rubbed her arms and back in gentle motions, wishing he could make things better for Sarah.

CHAPTER TWENTY-SEVEN

Margery and Mary were not allowed to join the family for tea that evening. They had to stay in their bedroom and go to bed early. Their mother sent Agnes upstairs with a slice of dry bread and a cup of milk for each of the girls and that was all they were allowed to have. Nor did Sarah want to come to the table for tea because her eyes were red and swollen and her face was blotched from crying. She asked Thomas to give them her apologies while she rested on their bed.

Sarah lay just behind the screen listening but there was very little conversation during the evening meal. Finally, she heard her father-in-law say, "Mother, tell us about our new grandchild."

Anne went on about his sweet face with its small nose and rounded cheeks. To her, he was the most beautiful baby to be born in this century. "Maggie is gaining back her strength and with Fergus's mother coming to help her for the next few days, I think they will all be just fine."

"When can we see the baby?" Agnes asked.

"The baby will be one month old on the twenty-second day of August and Maggie thought they might be able to come for Sunday dinner near the end of August."

Sarah regretted that her mother-in-law ordered Margery and Mary to come and ask her forgiveness the very next morning. She did not feel like forgiving them at all. The two girls stood just outside the entrance to Thomas's and Sarah's bedroom and looked downcast, unable to look at Sarah's eyes.

Margery cleared her throat. "We are very sorry we broke your brooch, Sarah."

Mary quickly added, "Will you forgive us?"

Sarah was not letting them off that easily. "That brooch

was the only piece of jewelry I had from my mother who died last year. What else did you break besides the brooch?"

The two girls looked very frightened because they had not told anyone about the broken mirror or the feather torn from Sarah's hat. They began to cry and tell Sarah how sorry they were about the other things.

"Admit to me what those other things were." Sarah demanded.

Mary spoke and cried at the same time. "I broke your mirror...I'm sorry."

Margery confessed, "When I took your hat off my head the feather came off. I wish we never went in your bedroom." She wiped tears from her face and looked down at her feet.

Sarah said, "I wish you never went into our bedroom, also. The mirror you broke was given to me by my aunt and uncle when I was nine years old. And the feather you tore off came from the only nice hat I've ever owned." Sarah crossed her arms and looked as menacing as she could. "I hope you two are ashamed of yourselves."

"Oh yes, we are," they said in unison.

Sarah said, "I forgive you but I will never forget what you have taken from me. Now go away and don't come in our bedroom ever again."

Margery and Mary ran from Sarah as fast as they could into the kitchen. She saw very little of them for several days afterward.

The second Sunday of August Sarah woke to see that Thomas had already left their bed. No doubt he had gone to help with the milking before they went to church. She stood to remove her nightgown and noticed blood spots on the back of the gown and on the bed sheet. Alarmed by the blood, and feeling certain it was not a good sign, she was paralyzed by fear. She wanted to keep away this hideous threat to her baby so Sarah lay back on the bed and pulled the covers up to her chin. She wished Thomas would return. Sarah pretended to be asleep and did not answer when Sarah Lizzie called to her saying that the porridge was ready to eat.

After a while, she heard the men come in from milking. She lay still and listened to them stirring milk into their porridge and their tea cups.

She heard Agnes say to Thomas, "I think you'd better go and see how your wife is this morning. She hasn't shown her face and she didn't answer when Sarah Lizzie called her."

Sarah heard her husband get up from the table and walk toward their bedroom. He came in and sat on the edge of the bed placing the palm of his hand over her forehead.

"Are you not feeling well, Sarah?"

She did not want to voice her fears to all the family sitting at the table behind the screen so without speaking, she threw back the covers and showed him her blood-spotted gown and bed sheet. Then she quickly covered Thomas's mouth with her hand and shook her head so he would not announce what he saw. She pulled him down to her and whispered in his ear, "Thomas, I'm afraid something is wrong with the baby."

Thomas's face became the road map to Worry. He looked into his wife's eyes and saw the fear that matched his own. He whispered, "Have you felt the baby moving today?"

Sarah pulled him even closer to her. "Yes, the baby moved this morning. That was what woke me up."

"Would you mind if we talk to Mum about this? She's had ten babies and she knows much more than we do.

Sarah nodded. "I'm worried. Would you ask her to come in here alone?"

Thomas immediately went into the kitchen where his mother was already preparing the roast for Sunday dinner. When he returned he leaned down to Sarah and spoke softly. "Mum will come and see you when everyone has left the table."

Anne patted the hand of her daughter-in-law. "How much have you bled, Sarah?"

Sarah pulled back the blankets and showed Anne the blood-spotted gown and sheets. "This is a bad sign, isn't it?" Sarah was nearly in tears.

Her mother-in-law looked at the blood spots for a few

moments. "These spots all appear to have been there for a while. I don't see any fresh, wet blood. I think you may have bled during the night and then the bleeding stopped."

"Do you think I will lose the baby?" Sarah wiped tears from her eyes.

Anne caressed Sarah's face with her work-worn hand. "Don't worry, Sarah. Spotting like yours does not necessarily mean anything bad will happen. But you *did* work hard yesterday helping Sarah Lizzie and the girls with all those wash tubs full of dirty clothing and bed sheets. And, you stood on your feet and ironed for most of the afternoon. I want you to stay right here in bed today. Thomas will stay home from church to watch over you. I'll have him bring in a tray with some hot tea and porridge for you right away." She leaned down and kissed Sarah's cheek, then motioned to Thomas, who hovered over them. "Thomas, come into the kitchen and help me set up a tray for Sarah."

Throughout the quiet morning Sarah dozed and Thomas sat on a chair at her bedside. The silent house seemed to bring a sense of calmness and peace. Sarah opened her eyes and looked at Thomas. He reached for her hand and smiled at her. "Are you feeling better, Sarah?"

"I'm still worried, aren't you?"

"Mum said they would ask Gilbert to come home with them after church. He will examine you and we'll soon know more." Thomas touched her face with his hand. "I prayed while you were sleeping that God will be merciful and spare our unborn baby."

Sarah's reply was heartfelt. "Thank you for your prayers."

It was shortly after one o'clock when Sarah and Thomas heard the family trooping into the kitchen and Anne's voice warning them to stay out of the front room. Dr. Gilbert Keith had his doctor's bag with him and he walked directly to Sarah's bed. He looked at the blood on the sheet and her gown, and he listened through a stethoscope which he placed on her abdomen. His hands palpated her abdomen, and then the young doctor

stood upright and spoke to Sarah, Thomas, and his mother. "The baby is making all the normal sounds and everything seems to be fine. As Mum said earlier, I think you worked a little too long and hard yesterday, Sarah. To be safe, I want you to stay in bed for the next four weeks. You can get up to eat at the table and to take care of your personal needs but nothing more."

Anne smiled down at her daughter-law. "Don't worry, Sarah. We'll take good care of you."

Sarah looked at her brother-in-law. "Do you mean I have to remain lying down for the next four weeks?"

"Yes, Sarah. When there is a threat that the baby may abort or come much too early, the best medicine is rest. That means lying flat in bed for the next four weeks."

Propped up on one elbow and then the other, Sarah spent many hours reading another one of Annie's Jane Austen books. This helped to keep her boredom to a tolerable level, but the best remedy to her ennui was Thomas's presence. He began to come and sit with her for a while after their noon meal. They enjoyed this time by themselves which passed all too quickly.

They laughed together over Rex and how he had followed them home the last night they stayed in the Ohio house. Thomas said, "I wonder how many times they had to go and get Rex before he stayed at the Cole's farm?"

Sarah said, "I hope he's decided to be their dog now. He was so smart and good with all the farm animals. I was surprised that your family does not have a dog like Rex. They have a lot of sheep and I would think a herd dog would be helpful,"

"They have old Toby, but he stays with the sheep and never comes up to the house. William takes food out to him every night. When you are able to walk about again, I'll take you out and show you all the animals here."

"Do you think it will ever stop raining long enough for that to happen?" Sarah glanced at the nearest window and saw the glass pane streaked with rain water. She looked at Thomas and smiled to reassure him that she was not feeling depressed.

Sarah spoke again of another dear pet. "I often think about Topsy and I wonder if he's happy with Emma."

"If Emma is still attracted to him as much as she was the day you brought him to their house, I'm sure he is a happy dog."

"They never kept an animal in their house before so I worry that Aunt Hannah and Uncle Isaac will turn him out to stay with Rex."

"Even if he has to stay in the barn, he will be alright with Rex to protect him."

Sarah said, "I miss Belle, too. I hope the people who bought her are treating her well."

Thomas tried to put her mind to rest. "I guess I never told you because we were busy preparing to leave. The man who made the highest bid for Belle said that he was buying her for his children so they could learn to ride. He had a small son and a nine-year-old daughter. Weren't you nine years old when your Daddy bought Belle for you?"

Sarah smiled broadly. "Yes, and you taught me how to care for her. Those were happy days."

Thomas said, "You know, it would be a good thing for you to write to your Uncle Isaac and Aunt Hannah. They care about you very much, and would enjoy receiving a letter from you."

"When I'm able to leave this bed I'll try to do that. I promised Aunt Hannah I would write."

Later that week, as Thomas sat on the bed where Sarah reclined, he held her hand and said, "We are in the middle of harvest and Dad could use my help. Would you be very upset if I went directly out to work with the family, at least while there is so much work?"

Sarah felt rejected and deflated. "How do I answer that question? Should I be the dutiful wife and tell you to please your father? I want you to stay here and visit with me for just a while. They can surely allow you to have one hour a day alone with your wife."

"But Sarah, the only way to pay my parents for our food and lodging is the work I can do to help them on the farm."

Sarah wanted to weep and cry out against the unfairness. Instead she decided that she was going to be a mother and must begin to act like a grown woman as Maggie would. She looked at her husband and spoke in a mature voice. "You must do what you think is right, Thomas. I will try my best to be happy with your decision."

She endured a whole week of endless daytime hours alone in the bed. Then one afternoon Thomas walked in and sat down on the bed beside her. He smiled and took her hand in his.

"What brings you in the house at this hour?" Sarah inspected Thomas's face.

"Dad said I must come in early and keep you company. The whole family has noticed how sad you are and they all insisted that I come to sit with you."

"Is it that easy to see through me?"

Thomas smiled. "You are an open book."

She pulled him down to kiss him. "Oh my dearest, how I love you."

Just then they heard Thomas's two youngest sisters come through the kitchen door to set the table for tea. They were laughing about something that caused prolonged giggling. Finally, Margery said in a subdued voice, "I almost forgot. Mum told us to be quiet and let Sarah rest."

Thomas and Sarah listened as the two girls lowered their voices and went about their work retrieving plates and silverware from the scullery and placing them on the table.

Margery announced quietly, "Now, the table is all set. Mary, go and close the door to the scullery."

Mary must have pushed it too hard because the door slammed shut with a loud bang. Thomas and Sarah heard the girls stifling their laughter. Next, they heard Margery say in an almost perfect imitation of Sarah's American voice, "I hope you are ashamed of yourself."

The hilarity of the two caused their brother to smile as he listened behind the screen. Sarah did not smile. Her face grew hot with anger.

When the two girls left the room Thomas said, "Margery gave a good imitation of you, Sarah. She has a good ear."

Sarah was not feeling appreciative of Margery's talent.

"She's a *naughty* girl! She knew I would hear it and she wanted to get even with me for scolding them when they broke my things."

"Oh, now I see. You said those words to them. Well, I think it will be best if you remain quiet and not talk to the girls about it. If they do something like this again, I want you to tell me and I'll speak to them." Thomas lay down beside his wife and stroked her back and kissed her until she forgot about her anger with Margery and Mary. Soon, Thomas needed to leave and help with the evening milking. He kissed her again and left.

This was the day Maggie and Fergus were coming and Sarah was excited because she wanted to hold baby George again, and she was eager to talk with Maggie. Maggie's voice could be heard as she entered the house talking to her family. Sarah was delighted that her favorite sister-in-law came directly to her first.

"How is the expectant mother?" Maggie sat on the edge of the bed and held Sarah's hand.

"I'm so happy to see you, Maggie. Gilbert says I can get out of bed in seven more days and I can hardly wait." Sarah's smile was genuine.

"You haven't had any more spotting since that first day?"

"No, I haven't." Sarah lowered her voice and spoke confidentially. "Thomas told me he prayed for our baby to be spared and I'm sure God heard his prayer."

Maggie squeezed Sarah's hand and smiled as her eyes moistened. "How I wish you could stay here and your wee one would grow up knowing his cousin, George."

"I would like that, too. But Thomas wants us to return to the States and find a place where we can have our own farm. I want whatever he wants."

"Thomas is fortunate to have you as his wife."

The family members came into the dining area and began to sit at the table as they talked and chatted, excited to see the new baby. From behind the screen Maggie and Sarah could hear Will talking about his handsome grandson and knew he must be holding the baby in his arms.

Maggie smiled. "Can I help you get up and dressed, Sarah? Gilbert said you are allowed to come to the table for meals."

"Thank you, Maggie, but I'm already dressed." Sarah threw back the top blanket that covered her and sat up to put on her shoes. "You can see that I'm wearing one of the dresses you loaned me. Go on ahead and sit with the family. I'll be there as soon as I put on my shoes and straighten myself."

It was such a pleasant afternoon that Sarah hated to see it nearing an end. After dinner, Gilbert gave her permission to sit in a chair and hold the baby for a while. George had grown and was looking about, focusing on things that caught his eyes. Sarah loved the way his tiny fingers wrapped around her finger. All eyes in the room were watching and admiring this amazing miracle of creation. When George began to fuss and cry, Maggie took him into Sarah's and Thomas's 'bedroom' and changed his nappie. She unbuttoned her blouse and nursed him until he fell asleep. Sarah had come with Maggie and sat next to her on the bed. The expectant young mother observed how Maggie held him and how she turned the baby over on her shoulder to burp him after he had nursed.

Maggie said, "Sarah, you need to be lying down and resting on your bed. George and I will leave now so you can lie down." She stood with the sleeping infant in her arms.

"I wish you didn't have to go away." Sarah lay down and looked up at Maggie.

"I know, but everyone else in the family wants to hold him." Maggie gave her a beautiful smile that compensated Sarah for their absence. "We'll come back to say 'good-bye' right before we leave."

CHAPTER TWENTY-EIGHT

Weeks crept by and the days were growing shorter. On a cold, dark morning in early November Thomas and his father traveled into Markethill with another wagonload of milk, butter, and cream. Margery and Mary followed behind the light of the wagon's lanterns as they rode to school on the back of Apollo, one of the older, reliable horses on the farm. They stopped at the school building where the girls dismounted with their books and lunch pails. Thomas tied Apollo to a hitching rail which was protected on three sides by walls and a sturdy roof to provide shelter from rain and snow. The girls ran into the school building shouting, "Good-bye, Thomas. 'Bye, Dad."

Thomas extinguished the flames in the lanterns because there was enough natural light to see the road now. He climbed onto the wagon to sit beside his father, and tucked his gloved hands under his arms for warmth. Their first stop was the James Harrison establishment which was a grocery store with the Post Office at the front of the building. The horses pulled the wagon to the entrance where father and son unloaded two cans of milk and a dozen bricks of butter wrapped in waxed paper.

Mr. Harrison, who wore a large white apron over his clothing, stepped outside and looked up at the gray looming sky. "Think it will rain this morning?

Thomas hoisted the returned empty cans into the wagon. "'Tis cold enough to snow!"

"Aye, ye're right about that." Mr. Harrison waved them on their way.

After six more stops around the town they headed for home with only empty milk cans and jugs rattling behind them in the wagon.

Will pulled his collar up around his ears. "You've made it into the second degree of Freemasons and I'm proud of you,

Son. Are you ready to begin working on the Master's degree?"

Thomas sat in silence for a few moments. He knew his father and his two older brothers were eager for him to reach the level of Master before he left Ireland.

"Where Sarah and I are going I doubt if there will be another Freemason for many miles around. I'm beginning to wonder if 'tis worthwhile to memorize those many pages and then leave for a place where I'll never use it."

"No matter where you are, if ever you need a friend, another Mason is one person you can depend on for help."

Conversation stopped for a while until his father spoke again. "What do you know about this place where you expect to get free land?"

"I only know what I've read in the newspapers. The danger from Indians is past because most of them live on reservations, or the warriors in the tribes have been killed off to the point where they can no longer make war against the white man. I hope you will explain that to Mother because I know she worries about us being attacked by Indians."

"Yes, that was one of her worries, and to be truthful, it was mine, too. But that part of the world seems to be far removed from civilization. Do you have any idea how far from a railroad you might be?"

"The railroads are all over the country by now, and Kansas has trains going to all the major parts of the state. I plan to find land located near a rail station."

"Your mother and I are concerned that Sarah will not be able to adjust to the harsh life you two might have on the frontier. Do you think she will be alright?"

"Sarah has been sheltered all her life, and her parents indulged her because she was their only child. But she is strong and healthy and Sarah has told me many times that she does not want to return to Norwich. She's willing to try for a homestead in Kansas."

Will looked at his son and asked. "Just how much land does your Uncle Tom own and what do you think it would bring if you sold it? Would it sell for enough to buy a farm in Ohio some distance away from Norwich?"

Thomas decided it was time to tell Dad all he knew about his uncle's situation. "When Tom became so bewildered and confused in the months before Aunt Margaret died, she often talked to me about the farm and her other property. She said that, altogether, she owned almost 800 acres. It was an inheritance from her pioneer family, the Huntlys, and it was all recorded in her name at the county court house. She and Tom lived on 270 acres outside the town of Norwich where the house, the large barn, and out-buildings were located, and that was the land Tom farmed. Most of the other acreage was near the town of Rich Hill where a tenant leased the cleared land for grain crops and paid her forty percent of his profits."

His dad let a small whistle escape from his lips. "Tom never told me he married a rich woman."

Thomas smiled and related to his father a little more information about Aunt Margaret. "She was very wise about running the farm and, because it was all in her name, I think she made the major decisions, so I would imagine Tom was not eager to tell you about that. Also, she was a huge woman who may have weighed as much as twelve or thirteen stones. She probably was not that large when Tom married her but, even then, I would guess she was not a handsome or attractive woman." Thomas stopped speaking long enough to tip his cap at a passing neighbor while his father called out the usual greetings. Thomas continued, "If Aunt Margaret had been a man she would have been respected as one of the wealthiest farmers in the county."

"I don't see why you and Sarah can't sell off some of that land and use the money to buy a farm of your own in Ohio several miles away from Norwich."

"Last January, Isaac Cole went with me and Tom and Sarah into Zanesville where we had the counsel of a respected attorney, a Mr. Stanley. He told us that by law, all Margaret's property belongs to Tom now, and Sarah has no right to claim it until her father dies. Both Isaac and I were worried because Tom is not able to care for himself, and he certainly couldn't manage the farm and all the other holdings. Mr. Stanley arranged it so Isaac and I would have joint power of attorney over all Tom owns. That meant Isaac and I would make all the decisions about the property and its management. But when Sarah and I decided to leave Ohio, I wrote to Mr. Stanley and asked him to remove my name so that now, Isaac has sole power of attorney over Tom's property."

Will released another low whistle. "You may have put Sarah's inheritance in great jeopardy."

"I trust Isaac to do the right thing. He promised to send you one hundred twenty to one hundred fifty dollars per year for Tom's keep, and I have no doubt you will be receiving it. In the meantime, all the income from the tenant near Rich Hill will be deposited into an account in Sarah's name. Mr. Stanley is overseeing that account."

"I'll be telling your mother what you've told me. She will be reassured to know that Sarah can draw on that account someday, and you have the means to escape to civilization if it is necessary."

Thomas smiled at that. "I'm counting on making a success of my homestead. Many people have become prosperous through homesteading and I intend to be one of them."

"I also hope you are one of the prosperous ones." His dad reached behind Thomas to give his son a pat on the back. "You and Gilbert have bright futures ahead of you, and James will inherit the farm here at Clooney. My only worry is William. He will have to struggle to afford a home and family of his own. It would make me very happy to know that all four of my sons were established with proper incomes and homes for their families."

"Perhaps you can send William to America. He and I could work together to make a success of his homestead and mine."

Will laughed out loud. "You want half the Keith family to become Americans?" He looked at his American son and said, "William is only fifteen. When he turns twenty-one he can make that decision on his own."

Thomas reminded his father, "You and Mum let me go at age fifteen."

"Only because you were so determined to go, and you had an uncle in Ohio who would take you in."

"If William wants to leave Ireland, he has a brother who will take him in."

"Believe me, *I* will not be the one to bring up the subject of William leaving home. He is a tremendous help on the farm and we would miss him as much as we have missed you. And, please don't give him any ideas about leaving. Losing another son would break your mother's heart."

The horses pulled the carry-all wagon through the gate and the wheels clattered across the cobblestone yard. By now cold rain was coming down and the two men worked quickly to cover themselves with rain gear. Father and son unhitched the team and Thomas turned the two horses out to pasture. They unloaded the empty cans and jugs which needed to be washed and sterilized with boiling water before they could be re-filled with fresh milk and cream. James came and joined Thomas to help with that task while their father rolled the wagon into its bay.

As Thomas scrubbed the insides of the cans and jugs with a long handled brush, his brother poured fresh water and coal to the hot water boiler which stood against one wall of the milking barn. When it reached a very hot temperature the boiling water was poured into each scrubbed container and rinsed thoroughly.

James, who was eight years older than Thomas, never had much to say to his younger brother before Thomas left Ireland. Since Thomas's return, James had shown interest in the farm in Ohio and how things were done there.

James said, "You told us that Uncle Tom sold off half the sheep about a year after you arrived in Ohio. Did you keep the rest for your own use?"

Thomas nodded. "Aunt Margaret knew countless ways to cook mutton and make it taste delicious. She also made a soft, tasty cheese with the cows' milk. She was a good cook and I only wish she had lived long enough to teach Sarah."

"How old was Margaret when she died?"

"She was fifty-five years old. When Sarah was born, Margaret was forty-one years, so Sarah was raised by parents who were old enough to be her grandparents."

"Are you suggesting that Sarah was a wee bit over-indulged?" James smiled at his brother.

Thomas returned the smile but said nothing.

James said, "Are you certain she will be able to cope with the problems of living in the Wild West?"

"She's told me many times that she is ready to try. We won't know until we live there."

When all the cans and jugs were scrubbed, rinsed, and turned upside down to drain the brothers went inside the house for their noon-day meal. By now the rain had become wet snow.

Around the table that day, his father and older brother talked to Thomas and encouraged him to work toward the third degree of Freemasonry.

"Would you like for me to help you, Thomas?" James said. "It hasn't been that long since I memorized all that work for myself."

"I think it might be a good idea." Thomas nodded at James as he cut another piece of meat.

That night the men sat near the fireplace while Anne and the older girls worked in the kitchen to clean up after tea and prepare for tomorrow's meals. Sarah, who was large with the growing baby, had been appointed to supervise the two school girls with their lessons. She sat with Margery and Mary at one end of the long table where a glass oil lamp illuminated their work. While the students prepared for tomorrow's lessons, William sat nearby for the benefit of the light as he read the latest issue of the *Horseman's Manual*.

The turf fire glowed and cast a gentle light upon the men seated in front of it. James said, "Dad, why don't you let me go with Thomas the next few weeks to make the deliveries in town?

I can coach him on his memorization while we travel to and from town."

Will leaned forward from his wing-back chair and looked up from the fire. "That's a good idea." He looked at James and then at Thomas. "Thomas knows all the stops we've been making each day, and it will give you two brothers some time together."

Sarah's voice became loud as she found it necessary to speak firmly to her charges. "Mary and Margery you must pay attention to your lessons. You don't need to listen to the men."

The girls returned to their work and the men resumed their talk.

A few minutes later, the talking around the fire ceased again. All eyes were on Mary who had thrown her lead pencil down on the table. They heard her explode in anger. "You are not my teacher and I don't have to do it again just because you say so."

Anne appeared from the kitchen and quietly asked Sarah if she needed help.

"I told Mary to write the spelling words three more times because she doesn't know them yet, but she became angry and threw her pencil."

Anne gave her youngest child a stern look of warning.

Mary reached for her pencil and began writing. As soon as her mother returned to the kitchen, Mary glanced at Margery and then at Sarah. Quickly, she stuck out her tongue at Sarah, and with a smug look on her face, continued to write her spelling words. Of the other adults in the room, only Thomas saw his little sister's impudence and, once again, he felt sorry for his wife. Almost every night at bedtime she told him of abuse she had endured from Agnes, or Mary, or Margery, and Sarah never ceased to complain of their lack of privacy. For her sake, he wished they had another place to live.

Dr. Gilbert Keith had just arrived at the farm for Sunday dinner. Thomas left the house to help him unhitch Dr. Pringle's horses, giving the two brothers time for a brief personal chat.

Gilbert said, "Tell me, Thomas, how is Sarah feeling these days? Does she complain of back aches? Do you notice any swelling around her ankles?"

"Her ankles appear the same as always, and because she rests a lot, she doesn't complain about pains in her back. To tell the truth, Sarah's only complaints are about our living conditions."

"You don't have any privacy; that is obvious."

"Yes, that is Sarah's main complaint. And Agnes is...well, you know Agnes. Sarah is always complaining that she makes her look stupid and inadequate. And then the two young girls are a nuisance and a constant thorn in her side."

"I've been thinking about your situation and I may be able to offer you another place to live if you don't mind moving your bed and belongings to one of my upstairs rooms. I've already talked with Dr. Pringle about this and he is in agreement."

For a few moments Thomas became silent in thought. He said, "Are you sure you want to give up one of your three rooms to us? That may be a great inconvenience to you."

"I would not have mentioned it if I wasn't certain. Besides, it will be temporary because you have always maintained that you want to return to the States as soon as the baby is old enough to travel. Have you changed your mind about returning?"

"No, I haven't changed my mind. But where would we take our meals if we moved in with you?"

"Mrs. Begley cooks for all of us and we eat together in the large dining room which is part of the doctor's quarters."

"Could we pay Dr. Pringle for our meals? I would not want to accept his food and the service of Mrs. Begley without paying something."

"I'll talk to him and let you know his thoughts on the matter."

Thomas's brow creased with worry lines. "How can Sarah and I move away from here and not hurt the feelings of Dad and Mum?"

264

Gayle Bookless Davis

"You will be moving in with me because I want to keep Sarah close by where I can monitor her condition. Remember, she threatened to abort earlier."

Thomas was pleased because his brother's suggestion was valid. "Sarah and I will be most grateful to you. Tell Dr. Pringle that we can afford to pay him ten pounds per month. I hope that will be enough."

Three weeks later on the third day of December, Thomas and Sarah settled into a room of their own at Cardiff House. Sarah's brothers-in-law had been very helpful to move their belongings and the bed from the farm into town. And her parents-in-law had understood the need for her to be near Dr. Keith.

Sarah began to smile and talk more freely than she had in months. Mrs. Begley, and Mrs. Pringle made over Sarah and pampered her as if she were royalty. All Sarah's favorite dishes were served during the first week and Mrs. Begley seemed to be in competition with Mrs. Pringle for Sarah's attention and approval.

As she sat in front of the fire with Mrs. Pringle, Sarah learned about the old woman's only daughter who had died when she was nineteen years old, and how Mrs. Pringle and her husband had mourned for years afterward. Sarah understood this sadness and explained to Mrs. Pringle how her mother's death last year continued to cause her heart to ache. When Mrs. Pringle inquired about Sarah's life in Ohio, Sarah reminisced over her happiest experiences on the farm and times with her cousin, Emma.

Mrs. Pringle's white cloud of hair framed pale blue eyes set in a face that must have been very attractive in her youth. She said, "My dear, you are a breath of fresh air! Your lovely young face and your sweet voice are bringing life to this place. And you will be giving birth to a precious baby soon. Are you hoping for a boy or a girl?"

"At first, I was hoping for a girl, but since I've seen and held George Simpson, Maggie's little boy, I'm thinking how nice it would be if I had a boy."

Mrs. Begley had grandchildren of her own but they lived miles away in another town so she seldom saw them. She was thrilled that Sarah was going to give birth in this house, and she voiced her hope that Sarah would allow her to help with the newborn's care.

Mrs. Begley said, "Sarah, do you have clothes and nappies for the baby?"

"I have a few things that Thomas's mother gave to me."

Mrs. Begley wanted to know if Sarah knew how to knit, and when she learned Sarah lacked that skill, she immediately offered to give lessons to the expectant mother.

"I have some soft yarn in a cream color. Let me show you how to make a simple knitted blanket to wrap around your wee one." The spritely servant hurried down the stairs and when she returned she handed the yarn to Sarah. "Feel how soft this wool is. Your babe will not be scratched by this at all."

Mrs. Begley supplied her with knitting needles and Sarah learned quickly. The new task was so enjoyable she began to understand why her mother always appeared to be calm and peaceful as she worked at her tatting and knitting. Many hours passed while Sarah knitted by the light of an oil lamp. She would rest her feet on a foot stool and sit by the fire enjoying the quietness while Thomas went with Gilbert to make house calls or he rode to the farm where he helped his father and brothers. Often, she was invited to join Mrs. Pringle who chatted pleasantly while Sarah knitted and offered her own comments. Sarah's contentment and sense of well-being brought all her complaints to an end. She was very happy to visit her husband's family when they rode with Gilbert out to the farm for Sunday dinners. But the best feeling of all came when she and Thomas went into their own room at bedtime and closed the door.

CHAPTER TWENTY-NINE

Sarah was thrilled to learn they would have a Christmas tree in the large dining room. Jack Begley, with Thomas's help, carried the tree in and placed it in a corner where it produced a wonderful fragrance.

Mrs. Pringle came in, her long dark skirt billowing out around her tiny body. "Oh, the tree smells wonderful! Did you cut it down on Lord and Lady Beckford's estate?"

Jack Begley bowed slightly. "Yes, Mam, we did."

She explained to Sarah and Thomas, "Lord and Lady Beckford have always been kind and generous to let us cut down a tree each year for Christmas. This one is bigger than most." She went to the tree and touched its branches. "Sarah would you help me and Mrs. Begley decorate the tree after Jack brings in the boxes of ornaments from the storage room?"

That whole delightful afternoon Sarah, Mrs. Pringle, and Mrs. Begley found one beautiful ornament after another and attached it to the branches of the tree. Sarah reached into one of the boxes and took the wrapping paper off a delicate glass tinsel ornament. "Oh, this one is my favorite! Look at the bright, shining colors." She had said the very same thing about many others.

The two older women laughed and Mrs. Pringle said, "Sarah, I think each one you unwrap is your favorite."

"I know." Sarah's face colored to a glowing pink. "Your ornaments are the most beautiful I have ever seen. Do you also put candles on your tree as we did at home in Ohio?"

"Of course, we place candles on our tree." She turned to Mrs. Begley. "Did you find the box with the candles and candle holders yet?"

Soon there stood a magnificent, decorated tree in the dining room, and the women admired it while Sarah clapped her hands in appreciation. She said, "I'm certain I have never seen a more beautiful tree, and I'm so happy we can enjoy it all this week before Christmas."

Mrs. Pringle said, "The reason we can keep it for several days is because Jack braced it upright in that tub of water. We must remember to add water each day or the tree will become dry and drop all its needles."

That night as Thomas and Sarah snuggled together in bed behind their closed door, they found ways to express their love for one another in spite of Sarah's swollen belly that came between them. She spoke into her husband's ear. "I'm so grateful to Gilbert for inviting us to stay here, and Dr. Pringle and his wife are generous to share their table and hospitality with us. They have made us feel welcome ...and Mr. and Mrs. Begley are very kind, too. I can't remember when I have been this happy."

Thomas lovingly stroked Sarah's body and rested his hand on her belly. "Our wee one is very active tonight. Does it hurt when he moves around like this?"

"No, I'm used to it. But sometimes he kicks me in the ribs and that smarts."

Thomas gently patted her belly as if he were trying to calm the baby. "If our baby is a boy, I would like to name him Gilbert. Would you agree?"

"Oh, yes! If we have a boy I would be glad to name him Gilbert in honor of your brother."

"We have a grandfather, Gilbert Keith, who died before you and I were born. Our child would be named for two notable people in our family."

"What if our baby is a girl?" Sarah ran her fingers through the hair on Thomas's chest. "What will we name her?"

"I don't know. Do you have any ideas?"

Sarah said, "I would like to name her after my mother. Mama's middle name was Lorinda and I've always liked the sound of it."

"Gilbert or Lorinda. Those are both good names." Thomas continued to pat her belly.

Sarah began to sniffle and soon she was weeping softly.

"You told me just now how happy you are. Why are you crying?"

Sarah wiped her eyes and nose on the bed sheet. "I was thinking about Mama and how much I miss her. I wish she could be with me when I have this baby."

"I'll be right here with you and so will Gilbert. I won't leave your side for one minute."

"Oh, I *do* love you, Thomas, my dear husband." Sarah kissed his mouth and her grief was forgotten when he returned her kisses.

The next day brightly wrapped packages began to appear under the tree and in its branches. Sarah mentioned this to her husband and said, "Can we afford to buy some small presents for the Begleys and Dr. Pringle and his wife?"

"They would have to be very small indeed. We need to buy gifts for all the members of my family, too."

Sarah had not been out of the house in many days and she was eager to shop in the stores. "I haven't been in any of the shops in Markethill since we came here. Do you think I could go with you to look for gifts?"

"It has been freezing and the walkways are covered with ice. I don't think it would be safe… you could slip and fall so easily."

"I would hold onto your arm and we could walk slow. Please, Thomas. I would dearly love to help you buy the gifts."

"Let's wait and see if the weather warms up."

In the morning the sun came out, there was a soft breeze, and the temperature rose, melting the ice. Sarah held tightly to her husband as they walked down Main Street together, stopping in each little shop to see what was available. After two hours, Sarah was extremely tired, cold, and ready to return to the fireside. They made no purchases but now they knew what the stores offered and how much it might cost to buy a gift for everyone.

The following day Thomas was sent to purchase all the

things he and Sarah had listed on a paper. The women in the family were to receive combs and hair clasps, and the men would be given fine handkerchiefs. The two younger sisters would each receive a miniature doll that fit inside a cradle-shaped box. Thomas purchased a small silver-plated spoon for George, and Sarah had decided they could buy two petite boxes of fancy chocolates for the Pringles and the Begleys; each box held six pieces of chocolate. And of course, their list included wrapping paper and ribbon. All those things added up to slightly more than twelve pounds but neither Thomas nor Sarah regretted the expense.

When Thomas returned with all the packages, he was radiating good cheer, and his face was ruddy from the cold. He placed the purchases on their bed and looked at his wife. "I bought them, can you wrap them?" A captivating grin on his face caused Sarah to hurry to her husband and plant a kiss on his mouth.

"It would be my pleasure." Her smile brightened the dimly lit bedroom. "Will you bring a lamp in here so I can see what I'm doing?"

She spent the rest of day wrapping the many gifts, and when the last one was done, Sarah hid most of them under the bed. She took the two boxes of chocolates which she wrapped in red paper tied with white ribbon, and placed them under the tree when she and Thomas went into the dining room for tea.

That evening at the table everyone remarked over the growing number of gifts under the tree. Mrs. Pringle looked at her husband and spoke. "We have an announcement to make and an invitation to extend." She nodded toward the doctor.

Doctor Joseph Pringle picked up his cloth napkin and wiped his white mustache, cleared his throat, and glanced at his wife. His dark brown eyes seemed to twinkle in merriment. "Yes, my dear, we do indeed. All of you are invited to celebrate Christmas with us tomorrow on Christmas Eve. After a special dinner, which my wife and Mrs. Begley have been planning, we will light the candles on the tree and open the gifts." He looked at Mrs. Begley and said, "My wife tells me you are going to make your delicious Christmas cake again this year. We are all in for a treat!"

Mrs. Begley bowed her head in embarrassment while Gilbert applauded the announcement. He said, "We are in for a *delicious* treat, and I accept your invitation."

"We also accept your kind invitation." Thomas spoke for himself and Sarah.

Sarah smiled and looked at their hosts. "Yes, we accept your invitation and we thank you very much."

Sarah sat in front of the small turf fire at the farmhouse in Clooney. She was holding baby George who sat upright on her knees while Maggie looked on and smiled in adoration of her son. The other females in the family brought in heaping bowls and platters of food and placed them on the long table for the Christmas feast. The room was festive with evergreen branches gracing the mantle above the fireplace, and a decorated tree stood in the corner where Sarah and Thomas had slept.

"He has grown so much since I last saw him! He must weigh more than a stone's weight by now." Sarah kissed his chubby cheek and lifted baby George up toward his mother.

Maggie took her precious infant and held him close. "He is a big boy for sure. He reaches for everything and especially likes my hair." She pulled a handful of her hair from George's clenched fist.

Maggie looked at the lovely gold broach pinned to the dress she had loaned to Sarah. "Did you receive that beautiful broach for Christmas?"

Sarah beamed with pride. "Yes, Thomas gave it to me last night when we were opening gifts at Cardiff House."

"If he chose it himself, I must say that my little brother has very good taste."

"Yes, he bought it in town, and I was certainly surprised...I didn't have anything to give him. He asked the clerk to wrap the box in special gold foil with a white satin ribbon. It was so pretty I almost hated to open it."

"The single blue stone in the middle is exquisite with the

gold filigree surrounding it. And it looks so lovely on my dress."
Maggie laughed out loud. "Now if you forget to remove it when
you return my dress, I won't be heart-broken."

Sarah joined her laughter and said, "You needn't worry
that I will forget."

Anne called them to come to the table. It wasn't really
necessary because the men were standing nearby just waiting for
the invitation. After Will asked the blessing over their meal, he
said, "This may be our last Christmas with Thomas and Sarah,
and they must choose their pieces of turkey first." He passed the
platter of carved turkey meat to his daughter-in-law. The serving
of all the other food proceeded in the same way, with Thomas
and Sarah filling their plates first because they were honored
guests.

Anne said, "We hear you had Christmas Eve dinner with
Dr. Pringle and his wife yesterday. Did they also serve turkey?"

Sarah said, "Yes, they had turkey and ham. Mrs. Begley
is a good cook and she served her famous Christmas cake for
dessert. Mrs. Pringle insisted that Mr. and Mrs. Begley sit down
at the table and join us for dessert."

"We've heard about that cake from Gilbert." Agnes
passed the bowl of gravy to her right. "I doubt if it's any better
than the one that Mum makes."

"Sarah, did they have a Christmas tree?" Margery spoke
before she stuffed a huge piece of turkey in her mouth.

"Yes, it was a lovely tree that Mr. Begley cut down on
Lord and Lady Beckford's estate. Mrs. Pringle has some
ornaments that are the most beautiful I've ever seen."

Mary spoke up. "Margery and I made the paper
ornaments on our tree this year."

Politely, Sarah said, "They are very nice."

After dinner, the women and girls cleared the table and
Sarah Lizzie brought in a fresh pot of hot tea. Then Anne came
through the door with a large cake held in front of her.

"Here is my version of a Christmas cake. It may not
rival Mrs. Begley's but I've never seen it refused by any member
of our family." She set it down and began to slice through it to

serve the cake on special china plates used only for holidays. The first piece went to Sarah and the second went to Thomas. When all fifteen pieces were served the room was filled with the sounds of 'Mmm-mmm'. The dried fruits and chopped nuts mixed with spices and other ingredients made a moist and tasty dessert.

Will, said, "You've outdone yourself this time, my dear. The cake is delicious!"

When the cake had disappeared into stomachs that were very full, Anne said, "Gilbert told me he wants to leave by three o'clock. They want to return to Cardiff House before dark and he does not want to hurry and cause too much bouncing for Sarah." She handed the empty cake plate to Sarah Lizzie who took it to the kitchen, while Annie and Agnes carried away all the empty dessert plates and the tea cups. "Let's move our chairs around the tree so we can open gifts before they have to leave. The girls and I will clean up later."

When all were gathered around the tree the master of the house said, "First, we must light the candles on the tree." Will nodded toward his two children who were in their 'teen' years. "Young William and Agnes should have the honors this year."

Margery was upset. "When is it going to be my turn to light the candles?"

While William and Agnes performed their honored task, her father said to Margery, "When you are twelve years old you can light the candles."

Margery groaned. "I'll have to wait for two more Christmases!"

Mary wailed, "I'll never be old enough to light the candles!"

Everyone laughed at the youngest child's remark while she hid her face behind her hands.

Anne consoled her two little daughters by suggesting they deliver the presents that were placed under the tree. She reminded everyone, "Remember to open one gift when it is your turn."

Margery and Mary read the names on each gift and

scurried around feeling very important while they handed out the brightly wrapped packages.

Sarah was pleased to see that Margery and Mary were delighted over the miniature dolls, and all the women seemed to be very pleased with the combs and hair clasps. The gifts that Sarah received were practical items for the baby with a few exceptions. She held in her hands a small box from Margery and Mary. When she opened it she found a delicate brooch made of silver with small deep red garnets mounted in a circle.

"Thank you Margery and Mary. This is beautiful and when I wear it I will remember you."

The two girls smiled shyly at Sarah's words of praise.

Too soon the three o'clock hour arrived and it was time for Sarah, Thomas, and Gilbert to leave. The two young men hitched the horses to the carriage, and when they came back inside they said their farewells. The gifts they had received were bundled into a large handbag that Anne loaned them, and she handed it over to Thomas. The family gathered around the departing trio to give hugs and handshakes.

Maggie grabbed Sarah and embraced her. "Maybe you will be a mother the next time I see you."

Sarah said, "I hope you are right. I'm ready to hold this baby in my arms instead of my belly."

Anne looked out the window. "It appears to be dry at the moment. Maybe the rain will hold off until you arrive at Cardiff House."

The whole family followed them out into the yard to see them off. The matched blacks pulled the enclosed carriage through the gate and out onto the lane while the sounds of farewells echoed in the cold, dimness of the afternoon.

Sarah sat as close to Thomas as she could. "It was a lovely day, wasn't it?"

Thomas placed his arm around her. "Yes, it was. Our baby received some useful clothing and blankets, and what did you think of Margery's and Mary's gift?"

"Oh Thomas, I'm sorry for treating them so badly. They are just curious little girls and I could have been much more forgiving when they broke my things last summer. The brooch they gave me is almost as lovely as the one from you." Sarah smiled up at her husband.

Gilbert turned around and called to them from the driver's seat. "It looks to be raining hard up ahead."

Soon the rain pounded down and the visibility was poor. Suddenly, out of the drenching downpour a horse and buggy appeared in front of them. The driver had lost the reins and he was waving his arms and shouting. Gilbert pulled his team sharply to the left to avoid a collision. Before Thomas and Sarah knew what was happening their carriage had gone into the ditch and tipped over on its side. Sarah screamed as she fell heavily onto Thomas's body.

Gilbert had been thrown clear of the carriage. Sarah looked up to see him stumbling toward them through the downpour of rain. Then she looked at her husband to see that his bleeding head was covered by the stream of water flowing swiftly through the overturned carriage. He was unconscious and drowning. Sarah sat dazed, looking first at Thomas and then at Gilbert.

Gilbert crouched down and reached for Thomas trying to pull him up out of the water. He shouted, "Sarah, are you able to move away from Thomas? I need to be where I can lift him."

Sarah attempted to raise herself up but the rapid flow of water threw her off balance and she fell onto Thomas. "Oh, help me, Gilbert. I'm making things worse for Thomas."

"Here, Sarah. Take hold of my hands and step out as far as you can to clear the water."

With Sarah safely on the bank, Gilbert reached again for his brother and managed to place both of his hands under Thomas's arms. Using all his strength he pulled Thomas's limp body up and out of the water-filled carriage onto the grassy bank. Immediately, Gilbert placed Thomas on his stomach with his head to the side, and began to press downward on Thomas's rib cage to force the water out of his lungs.

Gilbert shouted over the noise of the pounding rain, "Sarah, come around on this side and press down on the grass near his nose and mouth."

Sarah moved as quickly as she could.

Gilbert said, "That's right, keep the grass away from his face. Try to kneel over him to keep the rain off his face." Gilbert reached inside Thomas's mouth to see if there was anything obstructing his airway, and continued the rhythmic pressing as he watched Thomas closely for any sign of breathing.

Sarah knelt over her husband and prayed for him to take a breath of life-giving air.

It seemed an eternity went by before Thomas began to cough and choke. Gilbert spoke to his brother, "That's it, Thomas. Keep on coughing up the water." He did not stop, but continued to press against his brother's ribs.

After a few minutes of coughing and spitting, Thomas turned over and sat upright. He began to breathe more normally. He looked around and motioned to his brother to come near. In a voice that was barely audible, Thomas said, "Gilbert, get to that horse before he drowns."

One of the horses was lying on his side in the ditch trying to keep his head above the rising water. The other animal had broken free and stood nearby.

"First let me check the gash on the side of your head, Thomas. I need to stop the bleeding." Gilbert pulled his brother's wet hair aside to look at the cut. "The bleeding has slowed but not yet stopped. Sarah I need to cut away a strip from your underskirt to bandage Thomas's wound." Gilbert held his pocket knife in his hand and began to cut and tear a long strip from Sarah's undergarment. He wrapped it three times around Thomas's head and tied it securely.

The young doctor stood and went to the helpless creature in the ditch. He saw that he needed to release the animal from the harness before it could move away from the swift water. With a great deal of maneuvering and effort, he was able to cut the horse free. The black animal stood and shook his head and his whole body before joining his team mate. The four-legged creatures stood together staring at the rain-soaked people as if wondering what other surprises might be waiting for them.

Thomas stood slowly and walked to his brother. His voice was raspy and soft. "Gilbert." Thomas moved closer to be heard above the downpour. "We can't let them get away. You head for the one on the right and I'll take the one on the left."

"No, I want you to stay with Sarah. Those blacks know me and my voice. All I have to do is catch one of them and the other one will follow."

Sarah held her clenched hands to her face and Thomas stood motionless as they watched Gilbert walk slowly toward the pair. He spoke to them and one of the animals stepped toward him.

Gilbert returned, his hands holding tightly to both horses' halters. He said, "Thomas, can you hold onto them while I remove the reins from the rig? I intend to use them as leads so I can get them home. I'm hoping you and Sarah will be able to walk with me back to Cardiff House."

Thomas moved between the horses and held their halters. "I can walk, but Sarah, can *you* walk that distance? I think we must be at least a mile away from Markethill."

Sarah pushed wet hair from her face. "I'm not going to stay here in the rain by myself!"

Gilbert said, "Sarah, I would put you on the back of one of these horses but they are not used to riders and I don't know how they would react. I'm afraid they've had enough excitement for one day."

"You're right. I think it would be safer for me to walk."

Soon, Gilbert returned from the overturned carriage with leather lines which he tied to each horse's halter.

Thomas went to the carriage to gather up the bag his mother had loaned them. When he showed it to them they were all amazed it had stayed closed and the wet gifts were still inside.

"I found an umbrella inside a leather pocket of the carriage." Thomas opened it and handed it to Sarah. "It's a bit late for this, but it will keep more rain from drenching you."

The three slogged toward Markethill while the rain continued to pound down. Gilbert held the leads of the two blacks who followed behind, Thomas carried the handbag full of wet gifts, and Sarah held the umbrella over her head.

Sarah fell behind and called out, "Wait for me, will you? I can't walk as fast as you."

The brothers stopped and allowed Sarah to catch up. Thomas took her arm and said, "Do you want to stop walking for a few minutes to rest?"

Sarah braced one hand under her large belly and gasped, "Yes, please." As they stood still to rest, they all began to shiver so much they could barely speak.

Gilbert's worry was evident. "We can't remain here...it's too dangerous."

The two men walked on either side of Sarah holding her steady with their arms. Soon darkness descended and they feared that others on the road would not see them. Because it was pitch black, they had to guess where the road was. The rain had slowed to a drizzle, but the temperature was dropping and the trio suffered from the extreme cold.

Gilbert shouted, "Look ahead... do you see the lights of Markethill? We'll be home in a few minutes."

Sarah was too tired and cold to say anything. She thought only that she must place one foot in front of the other...one foot in front of the other.

CHAPTER THIRTY

Will rushed into the house to find Anne. He saw Sarah Lizzie at the stove in the kitchen and said, "Where is your mother?"

"I think she went upstairs. Is something wrong?"

Will did not take time to answer but ran up the stairs to find his wife.

Anne looked surprised. "Are you alright, Will?"

"Mr. McHenry stopped by just now and said he saw Dr. Pringle's carriage overturned, and lying on its side in the ditch about a mile away. He said no one was near it and the horses had been cut loose."

Anne's face turned white. "What could have happened, Will? Our children might be injured!"

"I'm going right now to find out. Do you want to come with me?"

"Yes! While I get my hat and coat, will you go downstairs and explain to Sarah Lizzie?"

"I will. It will take me a few minutes to get the horses hitched to the carriage. Meet me outside." Will ran down the stairs to find his oldest daughter.

Sarah Lizzie gasped when she heard the news. "Go quickly, Dad, and tell Mother not to worry about anything. We'll take care of everything here at home. But be sure to get word to us as soon as you can."

By now, most of the family had heard the news that something bad may have happened to Gilbert, Thomas, and Sarah. They all gathered in the yard to see their parents off.

The winter sun came out from behind the clouds and the new snow reflected its gleaming whiteness. The snow was not deep and their carriage rolled easily along the road as they searched for the scene of the accident. When they came to Dr.

Pringle's overturned carriage they stopped. Will climbed down from his carriage to look around and make an assessment of the situation. He became alarmed when he saw blood inside the doctor's carriage, but decided he would not tell Anne about it.

"It looks like they may have cut the horses loose and led them on foot to Markethill." Will sat next to Anne and urged his horses on.

Anne held gloved hands together near her mouth. "I pray they have not been hurt."

At last they rolled into town and turned onto Main Street. They went to knock on the door of Cardiff House where they waited and waited, but no one came to the door. Once more, Will hammered the lions head door-knocker hard against the heavy timbered door. Mrs. Pringle opened it and recognized them.

"Do come in Mr. and Mrs. Keith."

Before Anne crossed the threshold she began asking questions. "We saw your overturned carriage and want to know if our children are injured. Is Sarah alright?"

"Let me get Dr. Keith, your son, and he will explain everything. This being Boxing Day, our servants have gone to visit their children. I will tell him you're here."

Gilbert appeared and his mother immediately reached to embrace him. When she released him from her arms she inspected a swollen bruise on the left side of his face. "You've been hurt! Tell us what happened."

Gilbert shook his father's hand and tried to look cheerful. "Follow me upstairs where we can visit, and I'll tell you all about it."

Will and Anne were upset to see that their son limped up the stairs. They looked at one another, preparing themselves for the worst of news about Thomas and Sarah.

He led them into a dimly lit room where there were two upholstered chairs and a sofa placed around a coal burning heat stove. Sarah reclined on the sofa and Thomas sat in a chair. His head was bandaged and his face was cut and bruised in several places. Sarah quickly sat upright when they entered the room.

"Here, let me take your hats and coats." Gilbert placed their things on a hook. "Find a chair and make yourselves comfortable."

Anne went to Thomas and leaned over his chair. "Thomas, you've been hurt, too! Are you able to walk?"

Thomas smiled at his mother and held her hands in his. Slowly he stood and demonstrated his ability to walk as he stepped toward Will and took hold of his father's hand to shake it.

Thomas explained, "When the carriage tipped over we all were bruised and banged up. I got a cut on the side of my head." He pointed to the place where his head was cut open. "We had to walk to Markethill last night in the rain and Dr. Pringle sewed me back together. We need a few days to heal but we'll be fine soon." Carefully, Thomas sat down in his chair.

Anne touched Thomas's wounded head and groaned. "You poor dear."

She looked at Sarah and went to sit next to her on the sofa. "My dear child, how are you?"

"I have some bruises on my upper limbs but I'm alright because I fell onto Thomas and his body protected mine. He nearly drowned last night."

Thomas gave her a warning look as if she had betrayed a secret between them. To his parents he said, "We were not going to tell you about that because Gilbert saved me from drowning."

Will was tired of the evasions and half-truths. He said, "Gilbert, since you are the oldest, I want you to tell us everything that happened after you left us yesterday afternoon."

Gilbert did as his father requested. He told them about the heavy downpour of rain, the buggy that came toward them out of nowhere and how they avoided the collision by heading for the ditch. As he described the details, his mother shuddered and gripped her hands together.

When the whole story had been told, Anne said, "To think we came so close to losing you, Thomas. We are very grateful to you, Gilbert, for saving his life. And Sarah, you must have a guardian angel watching over you. I'm surprised you did not go into labor after all that has happened."

Gilbert said, "We were worried about her, but Dr. Pringle and I examined her and the baby seems to be healthy. It's fortunate that Sarah is young and strong."

Will said, "What did Dr. Pringle have to say about the wreck of his carriage? I'm assuming his horses survived."

"Dr. Pringle could not have been more sympathetic or understanding. He said it could have happened to anyone in that situation and he's happy we all survived, and his horses will recover from their injuries." Gilbert stood, poured a shovel full of coal into the heat stove, and opened the damper slightly.

Will said, "Dr. Pringle is a good man."

Anne echoed her husband, "Yes, he is a very good man."

Gilbert offered his parents a cup of tea. "Mrs. Begley and her husband left to visit some of their grown children and won't return until tomorrow. But I can go downstairs and heat up a pot of tea."

Will shook his head. "No, we must leave for home soon...all the family made us promise to bring back news about you as soon as possible."

Anne said, "I wish we had our wits about us and gathered up some of yesterday's food to bring to you. Did Mrs. Begley leave food in the kitchen that you can prepare for your meals? You know how important regular meals are."

"Mrs. Pringle has told us not to worry about it. She will see that we are all fed," Gilbert said. "And by tomorrow evening Mr. and Mrs. Begley will return."

Anne embraced Sarah and each of her sons before she put on her coat and hat. "When will we see you again?"

Gilbert answered for the three of them. "I think it will be better for Sarah if she stays right here until the baby comes. You may come by for short visits before you go home from church on Sundays."

Will said, "Tomorrow is Sunday. You can count on a visit from all of us." He guided his wife to the door. "Stay right where you are; we can see ourselves out. Give our regards to Dr.

and Mrs. Pringle."

Anne settled herself in the carriage and Will urged the horses forward. They had not gone far when Anne began weeping. Will said nothing because he knew how difficult it had been for her to hold back her tears in the presence of her sons and daughter-in-law. He put his arm around his wife and pulled her close to him. Silently, he gave thanks to God for protecting his family.

Sarah reclined on the sofa Sunday morning as she listened to Thomas read several chapters from the book of Psalms, her favorite book of the Bible. Gilbert had gone to church, and when the worship service was over, the family from Clooney was expected to stop in for a visit. Sarah heard voices downstairs and interrupted her husband. "Thomas, I think they are here."

Sarah watched as Thomas closed the Bible and took it to their bedroom. The book was bound in black leather and the edges of the pages were gilded in gold...a beautiful gift from his parents on Christmas Day. But now the Bible looked battered and abused because it was soaked in rain water when they had the accident. Thomas tried to dry it out but it was a distorted image of its former beauty.

The door flew open and Gilbert led his family inside. Sarah sat up immediately. Not only did Sarah's mother-in-law and father-in-law come in, but also James, Sarah Lizzie, Annie, and her own father. The small room was very crowded. Gilbert invited the ladies to sit down on the upholstered furniture while his father, James, and Tom sat on three wooden straight-backed chairs around the perimeter of the room. Gilbert remained standing while Thomas sat in the same chair he had occupied all morning.

James spoke first. "We had to see for ourselves that you are alright. It was a miracle that all of you survived." The others agreed with James.

Sarah Lizzie said, "We worried about Thomas the whole time he was in America, but he came home to nearly lose his life." They all nodded in agreement with her statement.

Annie sat next to Sarah and spoke to her in a quiet voice. "Sarah, we are so happy that you and the baby are going to be alright."

"Thank you Annie. And I want to thank you again for lending me your Jane Austen books. When I was in confinement they helped me to pass the many hours."

Sarah stood and went to her father to embrace him. Tom sat still but did not return her embrace. His face and eyes were blank as Sarah said, "Daddy, it's good to see you."

Anne said, "It's time for the four of you to go downstairs and get the others." She explained that they had decided to take turns coming upstairs to see their injured family members.

The three residents of Cardiff House said farewells as they embraced and shook hands with those who were leaving. Soon they welcomed the younger members of the family who trooped up the stairs. Agnes, William, Margery, and Mary came in to stare at Thomas who was still wearing a bandage on his head and had many cuts and bruises on his face.

Mary exclaimed, "Thomas, you look like you were in a fight!"

Everyone in the room roared with laughter.

Thomas said, "You're right, Mary. We were in a fight to save our lives. We were all banged up and bruised when the carriage tipped over, and then we had to walk home through the rain and darkness. Believe me, it was not a picnic!"

William said, "How are you feeling, Thomas? Your head looks to be sore."

Thomas grinned. "This is one time when looks are *not* deceiving. I have headaches that last for a long time and I almost feel sick to my stomach. But both of the doctors here tell me it will pass with time."

As if she were compelled to say it Agnes announced, "Last year we heard about a family who was in an accident. The carriage tipped over and everyone was injured, and the mother and her unborn child died. That was over in County Tyrone."

Agnes's remark made everyone uncomfortable and they

all remained silent for a few seconds.

Margery looked at Sarah and said, "How are you feeling? Were you hurt bad?"

Sarah was surprised that the ten-year-old cared enough to ask. She said, "I have bruises on my upper limbs but I was not injured nearly as bad as Thomas. When the carriage tipped over I fell on top of him so his body protected mine. But he was hurt the most because of it."

Thomas smiled to reassure them. "We need a few days to heal and we'll all be fine."

Anne said, "We need to leave and let you rest." She and Will stood to usher their family out the door. She hugged Sarah and embraced her sons. "We'll stop by next Sunday if we may."

Gilbert said, "Of course, we want any of you to stop by here when you come to town."

Sarah's heart was warmed by their concern. "Please come to see us whenever you can."

The following Saturday evening Sarah said good-night to Dr. and Mrs. Pringle in the dining room and returned with Thomas and Gilbert to their quarters. The three were nearly healed from their injuries and Thomas's headaches were greatly diminished. They were in the habit of playing a few games of Parcheesi before they all retired to bed each evening. The board game was a Christmas gift to Thomas and Sarah from Gilbert.

Sarah said, "Are we playing Parcheesi tonight?"

Thomas said, "I'm willing."

Gilbert placed the three wooden chairs around a small table. "I really don't want to spend any more time studying and reading medical journals. Let's play a few games."

Sarah sat down at the table to arrange the board. She gasped and sat very still, waiting for the pain to stop.

Gilbert saw this and said, "Are you feeling pain Sarah?"

"Yes, but it didn't last long. I feel fine now."

"You may be going into labor. The baby is due to come any time now."

Thomas looked worried. "Maybe you'd rather go to

bed, Sarah."

"The game will keep my mind busy. I'd rather stay here and play Parcheesi."

Gilbert looked at his brother. "Sarah's right. It will be better if she keeps her mind on the game."

The three played one game and then another while they laughed and joked about their strategies for winning. Sarah experienced pain a few more times but each one was brief. She was enjoying herself because she had just won the last game. Then a very hard and long-lasting contraction gripped her in fear while she leaned forward and sat motionless. Her husband and brother-in-law watched her closely. By ten o'clock Sarah's contractions were coming every five or six minutes.

Gilbert said, "I'm going down stairs to inform Mrs. Begley that Sarah is in labor." When he came back into the room he carried a lamp and a bottle filled with dark liquid. To Sarah's question regarding the contents of the bottle, Gilbert replied, "This is carbolic acid. It prevents sepsis." He took the lamp and the bottle to Thomas's and Sarah's bedroom and when he returned he said, "Mrs. Begley will be up soon. Shall we start another game?"

The three began to play once more. However, Sarah's contractions were becoming more frequent and intense. Finally she said, "I'm tired. Do you mind if I go to bed now?"

Gilbert said, "You can recline on the sofa, Sarah. Mrs. Begley will come soon to make up your bed."

"I made the bed this morning. Why is she coming to make it now?" Sarah said.

Gilbert explained, "She will be bringing clean sheets which we keep downstairs in the surgery. Under the sheets she will place a waterproof covering to protect the bed. And she will bring clean towels."

Thomas said, "Will I be able to help in any way?"

"You are going to stay right beside me the whole time. I want you to learn the safest way to help Sarah through this childbirth. You will need to know everything I can teach you because you are apt to be entirely on your own when you go to

Kansas." Gilbert spoke not only as a brother, but as a skilled and knowledgeable physician.

Mrs. Begley pulled back the heavy draperies at the window and light flooded the room where Sarah lay. She saw the smiling servant standing at the foot of the bed and Sarah said, "I had a baby boy, didn't I?"

"Yes, and he is the sweetest wee thing. Let me bring him to you."

Mrs. Begley placed Sarah's baby beside her on the bed. Sarah looked intently at his red and wrinkled face. She said to Mrs. Begley who hovered over them, "His name is Gilbert."

The older woman's face became one huge smile. "I know that will please the doctor. He and your husband are just finishing their breakfast and they will be in here soon. Can I bring you something to eat?"

Sarah said, "Yes, I feel tired and hungry. Giving birth is hard work, isn't it?"

"'Tis indeed. I'll bring up some food right away. Would you like a soft boiled egg and some buttered bread?"

Sarah nodded, keeping her eyes only on her tiny son. "Yes, thank you, Mrs. Begley."

When Thomas and Gilbert entered the room Sarah was propped up on one elbow admiring her sleeping infant. The young doctor came to her side and asked how she was feeling.

"I'm very tired." Sarah sighed and pulled loose strands of hair away from her face.

"That's to be expected. You were in labor for almost ten hours, and that is less than many mothers when they give birth to their first child."

"I remember screaming out a few times. I hope I didn't wake everyone in the house."

Gilbert said, "You needn't worry. Mothers giving birth are expected to make noise. You did a fine job of pushing when you were told."

"What time was it when he was born?" Sarah said.

"It was half past seven on the third day of January. He

287

is now three hours old. Thomas tells me you have decided to name him Gilbert."

Sarah smiled at her brother-in-law. "I hope that pleases you. We think it's only proper to give him your name because you have been so kind to us, and you saved his father's life."

Mrs. Begley entered the room with a breakfast tray and brought it directly to Sarah. "Here, let me put him back in the cradle while you sit up to eat." She put the tray down on the foot of the bed and gently lifted the baby to place him in a wooden cradle that had belonged to the Pringle's little daughter many years ago.

"I'll hold him while Sarah eats her breakfast." Thomas reached for his son. Almost immediately baby Gilbert began to cry. Thomas held the baby close and jiggled him in his arms as he walked back and forth across the room hoping to quiet his son.

Gilbert said, "Don't worry. All babies are supposed to cry a certain amount every day; it strengthens their lungs. When Sarah finishes eating her breakfast, she can put him to her breast."

Sarah felt strange revealing her breasts to a room filled with three onlookers. However, Mrs. Begley, who was very experienced in motherhood, showed Sarah how to hold her infant and how to offer the nipple of her breast to his mouth. Baby Gilbert caught on to the nipple with his pink mouth and suckled as if he knew exactly what he was doing. Everyone smiled in approval.

Sarah looked on in amazement. This tiny creature, her little son was receiving nourishment from her body! She was in love with her newborn. Reverend Hardesty was right when he told them this baby would bless them because he was a gift from God. She looked up to see Thomas gazing at her and the baby. He smiled at her in a way that told her she was his beloved, the mother of his child. For several minutes Sarah experienced a peaceful bliss as she watched her baby nurse.

Mrs. Begley said, "I think I hear someone rapping on the front door. I must leave you now."

When she left the room, Gilbert looked at his pocket watch. "Church service has ended and it must be our family coming to visit."

Sarah's face revealed annoyance and apprehension. "Oh, heavens! I must look a fright. Do you think they could come back another time to see us?"

Thomas sat next to her on the bed. "My parents will want to see their new grandson. They will expect you to look tired...you gave birth just a few hours ago."

Gilbert reassured her. "We'll let only Mum and Dad come in the room this time. Next Sunday, if the whole family wants to see the baby, we'll allow them to come up briefly. I'm going down now to explain to them."

Will and Anne followed Gilbert into the room where Sarah and the baby lay. They came to stand over the bed and look down at the newest member of the family.

Anne's voice was almost a whisper, "He's beautiful. What are you naming him?"

Sarah said, "His name is Gilbert, in honor of his Uncle Gilbert."

Will said, "My father was named Gilbert, also. This wee one is joining a distinguished line of Gilbert Keiths."

Dr. Keith said, "He was born at half past seven this morning so he is less than six hours old. And his mother needs rest so I suggest we go into the next room where we can sit down and visit."

Anne said, "No, we need to take the family home and feed them their dinner." She reached down to pat Sarah's arm. "You have a perfect wee baby boy. Thank you for allowing us to see him even though you must be exhausted." She turned to leave, and Will nodded, smiling at Sarah just before he followed his wife out the door.

Sarah was sound asleep in less time than it took for her husband and brother-in-law to follow their parents downstairs where they greeted the rest of the family.

CHAPTER THIRTY-ONE

The days multiplied into weeks and before it seemed possible Baby Gilbert was one month old. Mrs. Begley said he was a good baby because he ate, slept, and filled his nappies regularly. Thomas and Sarah wished he didn't need to strengthen his lungs quite so often, especially in the middle of the night. But they could see that he was developing and growing so they gave thanks to God for their healthy son.

Mrs. Pringle and Mrs. Begley took turns holding the baby as often as possible. The whole household became centered on the infant's every new development, and because he was such a good baby, crying only when he needed to have his nappies changed or needed nourishment, they doted on him as if they were his grandparents.

"Look, he's smiling at me." Mrs. Pringle held wee Gilbert in her arms.

"I don't think so. My infants did that, too," Mrs. Begley said. "At this age it's a grimace from gas pains but it looks as if he is smiling."

Mrs. Pringle pursed her lips in doubt as she continued to admire the baby in her arms.

Thomas went with his brother, Gilbert, and Dr. Pringle to a lodge meeting of Freemasons at the Orange Hall down the street. Thomas had just attained his Master's degree, and he felt like celebrating. After the formal meeting, the men left the large room and went into a smaller adjoining room where they visited and exchanged the local news. Thomas noticed that only those who lived in town came to the lodge this night. He was told that those living in the surrounding communities were called 'fair weather members' because they drove into town for lodge meetings during the summer months when the hours of daylight lasted fourteen to sixteen hours.

Some of the men lit up pipes and others smoked cigars or cigarettes. Thomas and his brother were among several who did not smoke. The brothers regarded it as an unnecessary expense and a possible health hazard.

Dr. Keith explained to some men standing nearby that this was the last time they would be seeing Thomas at a lodge meeting because he and his family were leaving for America soon. When they learned Thomas would be a homesteader on the western frontier, many were interested and had questions for him.

The Worshipful Master of the lodge, a white -haired Mr. Kirkpatrick, said to Thomas, "Remember to contact us if you want to form a lodge in your new township. We can send all the materials you will need."

"Thank you. My first priority will be to build a house for us. They live in sod houses out on the Kansas prairie because there are very few trees."

"Just how do you build a house of sod?" A tall, thin man asked the question.

Thomas said, "I don't know for sure, but I think it would be similar to the way we cut the turf. Most likely they cut large squares of sod and stack them to make walls. They need to import lumber to build a roof."

A man not much older than Thomas asked, "Do you think you'll be having troubles with the Native Americans…you call them Indians?"

"No, according to everything I've read in the newspapers, most of the Indians are settled in reservations, and the others roam peaceably."

A Mr. Graham removed his pipe from his mouth. "It takes a young, strong man such as yourself to take on this challenge of life in the wilderness. I hope you have an equally strong wife."

This brought some laughter and many who called out, "Aye," in agreement.

Thomas grinned. "She's recently given birth to our son

and in a few years he will be my helper on the farm. My wife is as eager as I am to try out this 'challenge', as you call it."

Mr. Kirkpatrick stepped forward and extended his hand saying, "Thomas, we wish you all the best and may God bless you."

Others repeated the words. "Aye, may God bless you." Many of the men shook his hand.

Thomas came into their bedroom where Sarah was nursing the baby. "I bought our train tickets and made our reservations on the ship sailing from Dublin to New York. We're sailing the first day of March."

"How did you make the reservations for the ship?" Sarah looked surprised.

"There is a telegraph office at the train station and I paid them to send the message. They have the sailing schedules as well as the train schedules." Thomas removed a paper from his pocket and looked at it. "We are taking the morning train from Markethill to Dublin on Sunday the last day of February. We'll spend the night in Dublin and our ship sails early the next morning."

Sarah drew in a sharp breath. "Oh, that is very soon!" She looked down at her son. "Maggie hasn't even seen our baby yet."

"I saw Dad and William in town today when they were making deliveries. Dad said we are invited to come and eat dinner with them on Sunday. I think they have asked Maggie and Fergus to come, too. They knew we didn't want to bring the baby out in the weather when he was less than a month old, but by Sunday he will be five weeks old."

Sarah bit her lip in thought. "I think I will have enough time to get Maggie's clothes mended, washed, and ironed before Sunday."

Thomas gave her a puzzled look.

Sarah said, "You know, the clothes she loaned me when I was so large with the baby."

Sunday morning they went with Dr. Keith to church. It had been many weeks since they attended church, and now Sarah realized how much she missed it. She sat close to Thomas with the baby in her arms. She was happy for many reasons: their little son was healthy and growing, Thomas was her husband, and they were headed back to America soon. And she was glad to be wearing her own clothes again, to feel like a normal person who was able to bend down and button her shoes. The baby slept in her arms throughout the service and made not one small noise.

That afternoon after dinner at the farmhouse in Clooney, the family enjoyed taking turns holding Baby Gilbert and his cousin, George. Maggie and Sarah sat together on the sofa watching everyone take delight in the two babies.

Maggie grinned at Sarah. "You would think we had given birth to a couple of young princes. The family is so taken up with these babies they might as well be royalty."

Sarah laughed. "They are little princes to us, don't you agree?"

"Aye, George is the prince at our house. When he cries we jump and run to him." Just then, George began to cry in the arms of his Aunt Margery. "Here, bring him to me, Margery, and I'll take care of him."

George was nearly seven months old and when he was held he wanted to stiffen his legs trying to stand. He stood upright on his mother's lap, smiling and making noises as if answering those who talked to him. He drooled and made bubbles constantly; Anne thought he may be getting ready to cut a tooth. Sarah could hardly believe her baby would be that large in just a few more months.

Thomas, Gilbert, and Fergus came in through the kitchen door and stamped the snow off their feet onto some old rags before they entered the big front room. "The snow is beginning to fall again. We need to leave," Gilbert announced to the family.

Fergus said to Maggie, "The horses are hitched and

we're ready to go."

The two young mothers put hats on their babies and bundled them up. They donned their own winter wraps and left the house amid many quick hugs and farewells. With the babies in their arms, they hurried to their sleighs.

"Take care of that darling wee boy," Maggie called to Sarah.

"I will and you take care of sweet George."

Both sleighs held family members who were covered in wool tartan blankets. Gilbert drove the team of blacks through the gate and up to the main road. There they turned to the right while Fergus directed his team to the left. They all shouted out a final farewell and hurried off in opposite directions through the falling snow.

Thomas held the wool blanket over his and Sarah's heads to protect themselves and the baby from the elements. Gilbert drove the team as quickly as the horses could pull the sleigh through the snow. At last they pulled into the yard near the stables at Cardiff House.

Gilbert said to his brother, "Take Sarah and the baby up to the house. I can manage the horses and sleigh…and here comes Jack to help me."

Inside Gilbert's quarters, Thomas took the crying baby from Sarah while she removed her coat and gloves. She sat on the sofa and opened the front of her dress. Thomas handed Baby Gilbert to her, and immediately their infant became quiet as he nursed at his mother's breast.

Thomas removed his own coat and watched them briefly, almost envious of the bond between mother and child. He shivered and realized how cold the room was. He reached for the short- handled shovel and began to pour coal from the large bucket into the stove. Soon the fire was hot and the room felt more comfortable.

Sarah said, "I wonder if we saw your family for the last time today. Three Sundays from today we leave on the train for Dublin."

Thomas said, "Surely we'll spend another Sunday afternoon with them before we leave."

As it turned out, his wife's intuition was right. Winter storms blew in one after the other and it was not safe to venture out with the baby. His family at Clooney did not even come into town to attend church. A few days before Thomas and his small family were to leave Markethill the weather calmed, the temperatures rose above freezing during the day, and the snow drifts began to disappear.

The last night of their stay at Cardiff House was filled with many emotions. They all gathered round the table for tea and much talk about what the future may hold for the departing young family. They lingered over the light meal, reluctant to end their last evening together.

Mrs. Pringle was near tears. "Sarah, I hate to see you go. You have been like a daughter to me and I will miss our chats by the fire. And we all will miss your precious wee babe."

"I will miss you, too. But I promise to write letters to you if you will answer them." Sarah looked sorrowful.

The elderly woman took Sarah's hand in hers. "Oh my dear child, I would be happy to answer your letters. Please write to me when you are settled in Kansas."

Thomas watched as Mrs. Pringle laid her napkin down, stood and walked over to the large upholstered chair where Baby Gilbert lay near the fire. She lifted the infant into her arms and sat down to hold him. Sarah left the table to sit across from her in a wing-backed chair as they admired the baby together.

While Mrs. Begley cleared the dishes away to take them downstairs, Dr. Pringle, Gilbert and Thomas sat at the table talking about the change in the weather, and how this would be helpful to the travelers tomorrow. When the servant woman returned, she went to Sarah and asked to hold the baby one more time. Thomas smiled to himself, thinking of all the attention and useful gifts their son received from these kind and generous people.

While the women talked among themselves around the fire, the men remained seated at the table. Thomas put his hand in his pocket and removed thirty pounds he had placed there earlier. He said quietly to Dr. Pringle, "This is not nearly enough to pay you for everything but I hope you will take it." He extended the notes to the older man.

The white-haired man looked at Thomas's offering. "My boy, you are going to need every pound of that and more to start a farm out in Kansas. Please keep it."

"But I feel responsible for the wreck of your carriage, and we do appreciate having the private bedroom here in your lovely home, and the meals have been delicious. These thirty pounds will not begin to cover all that we owe you."

"The carriage will be repaired in another week or so. You are not responsible in any way for that accident. And look at the joy Sarah and the baby have brought to our home. Mrs. Pringle has not been this happy in many years. Please keep your money and consider yourselves our guests."

Thomas was overcome with emotion and blinked away the moisture from his eyes. He shook the doctor's hand and managed to say in a hoarse voice, "Thank you, Sir."

Before they retired to bed, Thomas and Sarah asked Mrs. Begley to prepare them a simple meal of hot porridge for breakfast the next morning. They wanted to eat sparingly to avoid any problems as they traveled to Dublin.

In the morning Gilbert and Jack loaded Thomas's and Sarah's trunks into the sleigh for the short trip to the train station. The two men carried the heavy trunks inside where they would be placed on the baggage car. When they returned, Gilbert took Sarah, Thomas, and the baby to the station. As they walked into the small waiting room, the clouds parted and the brilliant sun came out with the promise of good weather. They stood with Gilbert watching the clock on the wall while sunlight streamed through the tall windows.

Thomas spoke the obvious, "Our train should be here in fifteen minutes."

Gilbert began to laugh and said, "Look who came to see you off."

Through the door came the whole family from the farm

at Clooney. Margery and Mary ran toward them shouting, "We came to say good-bye."

When the family gathered close to Thomas and Sarah, they began talking all at once. It was a time of much joy and much sorrow, and tears were close to the surface. They kissed the baby's rounded cheeks, tugged at Thomas and hugged him repeatedly, and Sarah was embraced by each of her sisters-in-law. Then Thomas's mother and father embraced them both.

Thomas saw Gilbert standing near Tom to make sure his uncle did not wander away while the family was occupied saying their farewells. Thomas went to him, put his arm around his brother, and shook his right hand warmly.

"Gilbert, how can we ever thank you? You shared your living quarters with us and never once complained. And I learned so much from you I might hang out my shingle and call myself a doctor when I get to Kansas."

Gilbert smiled. "Don't even think of it!" He slapped Thomas on the back in a brotherly fashion.

With the baby in her arms, Sarah stood next to Gilbert and looked up at him. "We are grateful to you. You brought this beautiful baby into the world and you have been so very kind to us. I want to thank you from the bottom of my heart."

Gilbert reached to give her and the baby a gentle hug. "Take care of yourself, Sarah, and take care of that wee lad, my namesake."

Thomas took the right hand of his father-in-law and shook it. "Tom, we are leaving now. We want to say goodbye and wish you well."

Sarah quickly handed the baby to Thomas and put her arms around her father. "Good-bye, Daddy. May God bless you."

Tom's stiff pose and blank expression troubled Sarah. Thomas could see that she was close to tears as she turned away from her father and stood close to him and the baby.

Before anyone was ready, the train rolled into the station. More hasty hugs were given and promises to write were said, then Sarah boarded the train holding Baby Gilbert in her arms. Thomas followed behind them carrying their personal bag filled with nappies for the baby. They found seats next to a window where they could see the family standing on the platform waving at them.

Tears were streaming down his mother's face and his father had his arm about her. Thomas waved to his parents as the train began to move. Sarah held the baby up to the window so they could see him. Thomas saw through his own blurred vision that almost everyone on the platform was wiping tears from their eyes and trying to smile as they waved.

When his family was no longer visible, Thomas sat back to look at his wife and child.

Sarah smiled and said, "Just think. In two weeks we will be back in America!"

Thomas was unable to speak. He merely placed his hand over Sarah's knee as she held their son in her arms. He was amazed that his wife's thoughts had already left Ireland. She was eager to leave these loving people behind and return to America. But to be fair, he remembered Sarah had already said good-bye to both of her parents, her aunt and uncle, her cousins, friends, and her comfortable home in Ohio. He and Baby Gilbert were her family now and her home would be a house made of sod.

Thomas looked down at Sarah's young, innocent face, her eyes filled with love for him. He wrapped his arms about his wife and child, leaned into her ear and said, "Sarah, I love you."

Roger Davis
1189 N Thompson Ave
Nipomo, CA 93444